Bearotica

Bearotica

Hot, Hairy, Heavy Fiction

EDITED BY RON SURESHA

los angeles | new york

MANUFACTURED IN THE UNITED STATES OF AMERICA.

THIS TRADE PAPERBACK ORIGINAL IS PUBLISHED BY
ALYSON PUBLICATIONS,
P.O. BOX 4371, LOS ANGELES, CALIFORNIA 90078-4371.
DISTRIBUTION IN THE UNITED KINGDOM BY
TURNAROUND PUBLISHER SERVICES LTD.,
UNIT 3, OLYMPIA TRADING ESTATE, COBURG ROAD, WOOD GREEN,
LONDON N22 6TZ ENGLAND.

FIRST EDITION: APRIL 2002

02 03 04 05 06 **a** 10 9 8 7 6 5 4 3 2

ISBN 1-55583-577-5

COVER PHOTOGRAPHY BY BODY IMAGE PRODUCTIONS.

A portion of the author's proceeds from sales of this book will be given to Brown Bear Resources, based in northwest Montana. Since 1989, BBR has worked proactively to give humans an understanding and a respect for grizzlies as an indicator of the health of other species as well as the ecosystem in which we all live. BBR is a resource and research nonprofit corporation endorsed by federal, state, and tribal agencies. BBR uses a variety of educational and resource mediums, including: educational trunks, "Be Bear Aware" presentations, a nonprofit gift store, a quarterly newsletter, the Adopt-a-Grizzly program, and a Web site. Readers are encouraged to contribute further. More information is available at http://www.brownbear.org.

Contents

Introduction

Bearotica is almost as hard to define as the term *bear,* as now in use among gay men around the world. If, as conventional wisdom holds, "clothes make the man," do jeans, a plaid flannel shirt, a gimme cap, and work boots make the bear? Some mysterious combination of traditionally mature masculine physical attributes—facial hair, hirsuteness, girth, brawn, and even baldness or graying—somehow factor into the basic American bear sexual image. Layered over, or perhaps embedded beneath these superficial characteristics, is something unique and different from mainstream gay sexuality. But what?

Some would claim that softer, teddy bear qualities of bearmen distinguish their sexual relationships. After all, the name of one of the first sexual venues for these men, and one of the more enduring images of the subculture, has been the Bear Hug. In contrast, others would claim that bears' uncommonly masculine adult strength, their fully developed sexual power, is a defining characteristic.

Maybe bearsex can be both soft and hard, playful and commanding, cuddly and crushingly potent.

This collection of all previously unpublished "bearotic" fiction gathers a zoo-ful of varying styles, settings, subjects, characters, and author backgrounds. Like the bear subculture itself, there is something stimulating for everyone: literary and smutty, romantic and hard-core, rustic and citified, historical and postmodern. Collected here is a jungle orgy of grizzlies and musclebears, daddybears and cubs, chubs and otters, bikerbears and bearlovers, "straight" bears and gorillas and lions and wolves and bulls, oh my!

Although I sought diversity to represent the spectrum of bears, I regretfully received no submissions by or about bears of color of a quality sufficient to include in this anthology. However, I'm pleased to include the work of contributors from all over the United States and from the United Kingdom, Germany, Denmark, and Australia. One can't necessarily tell from their pen names or writing, but several outstanding stories by women are also included.

While acknowledging the fine fiction published in magazines such as *American Bear* and *Bear,* I must explain that I was looking for stories that were more than "genre fiction" that tweaked more than one's furry gonads, although there's plenty of hot, hairy, heavy homosex in these pages. I also sought well-crafted tales that display depth of heart and understanding and humor—essential qualities that have endeared to me the sexy creatures we call bears.

Many thanks to: Richard Labonté, Tim Martin at *American Bear,* Darrell and Daniel at *Handjobs,* Jack Fritscher and Mark Hemry at Palm Drive, Susie Bright, Tristan Taormino, Mike Ramsey and Chris Griffith at Resources for Bears, Forrest at BearPress, Eric "Bucky" Chappell, Jim Fauntleroy, Steve Dyer, Scott LaGreca, Les Wright, Bearoticabook.com Webmaster Jeff Schaumeyer, David Keepnews, Mapbear and Lustybear and Beargrrl, and especially Michael with his Bone-ometer™. Thanks too to Scott Brassart at Alyson, who approached me with the idea of editing this anthology, and the rest of the Alyson staff, who ably assisted in bringing the book to print.

Honey
DAVID BERGMAN

As the summer began, Matt spent the mornings on the deck of his parents' house, checking his E-mail on the laptop and drinking a couple of cups of coffee before he would pull out a book and begin to study for his bar exams. He'd stretch out with his books to review *Evidence,* his yellow highlighter in his hand, and hope to study. It wasn't easy. After three years of nonstop cramming, he was bored with the law. All he wanted was to feel the ever more intense sun pour down on him, turning his shaggy legs a deep brown dusted with gold. He wanted to feel a river of sweat run down to the runnels of his stomach from the high plains of his chest, to bake the dough between his legs until it was a hard loaf ready for eating.

But what made the studying even harder were the two guys—Steve and Joe—who had bought the house beside his parents. In their late 30s or early 40s, they conveyed the confidence and power of mature men—not the boyish uncertainty of Matt's ex-lover, whom he had left that last semester of law school. He was sick of boys who didn't know what they wanted to do with their lives or in bed, and he saw in his neighbors—as they worked in their yard or sat around laughing with their friends—men who had purpose in their lives as well as a deep capacity for pleasure. He could see them now behind the glass doors that led to their kitchen, half dressed at breakfast. Joe was dark, Italian, his squat body thick with muscle; Steve was taller and thinner—but no less hairy—and his bristled legs were balanced by his full beard. Steve had the grace of a runner, and Matt had seen him early in the morning jogging through the empty streets, his powerful legs launching his body forward. Matt tried to figure out which of them he desired more, but he couldn't tell. They entered his dreams together and alone almost every night.

He tried to get to know them, but they seemed remote. He'd smile and wave to them from the deck if they went into the backyard, and they'd call hello back to him, but that was all. Matt understood. It was a conservative neighborhood, and the last thing they needed was a reputation for ogling college kids home for the summer, although Matt wasn't a kid anymore. Once Joe had brought over a letter for Matt that had been wrongly delivered to their address. Matt had invited him inside, but Joe declined. "I'm filthy," he had explained. "We've been working in the house."

"I've noticed," Matt replied. "The place was going downhill ever since Mr. Reynolds died and Mrs. Reynolds had to take care of it herself."

"Yup, there's a lot to do to put it back in shape, and of course, Steve and I want to make some changes."

"I guess you would," Matt answered, smiling, his dick lurching beneath his pants. But Joe didn't seem to notice.

"I'd better go clean up. We're going out tonight." Smiling, Joe ambled off, the rounded cheeks of his ass tight against the jeans. The sight of where the pants rode down, exposing a trail of hair rising from his ass cheeks, had been so exquisite that Matt jerked off twice in quick succession thinking about that one image.

In the midst of reading again about hearsay exceptions, Matt decided that the project of the summer was not passing the bar but luring one, or preferably both, of his neighbors into bed. As the days went on he began wearing tiny shorts, then a Speedo. He started to work out outside. But nothing seemed to move Steve and Joe from the polite but distant attitude they had adopted.

One weekend, Matt's parents decided to visit their aunt in the mountains. "Good," he told them, "that will give me more time to study contracts."

"All this studying can't be good for you," his father said. "You need a bit of fun."

"Don't worry about me, Dad. I'll have fun once I pass the bar."

With his parents out of the house, Matt had one more idea of how to break the ice. He asked himself: What is the one thing bears cannot resist? And the answer was simple—honey. He'd lure them with honey. He decided to go all out. At a gourmet shop, he found a whole shelf of different sorts of honey. There was honey from Maine, honey from the desert, honey from France and Australia. Some were a warm brown, others reddish. One bottle from Peruvian bees raised in a field of chrysanthemums was nearly yellow. There was lavender honey from Spain and yellow star thistle honey made, as the bottle said, "from a vibrant Northern California wildflower." Matt bought all of them.

On Saturday morning as Steve and Joe carried out a ladder in order to scrape the peeling paint on the eaves of the house, Matt brought out his collection of honey and began slathering it on a thin piece of toast. He watched as the honey, which clung to his knife, absorbed the morning light and glowed, suspended like a small sun.

"Hey there," Steve called out to him.

"Hi," Matt answered, trying to hide the excitement in his voice and in his gym shorts. Not that he wanted to be subtle—he just didn't want to appear too naïve.

"Nice breakfast you got there," Steve said, holding on to the ladder, on whose rungs his long, muscular legs looked particularly graceful.

"Honey on toast is my favorite."

"Forget the toast. Joe and I sometimes eat it straight from the jar."

"Come over and try some with me. This jar is from New Mexico, made by bees who only gather pollen from desert plants. It has a really pungent flavor."

"Let me just tell Joe where I'm going." He stepped down from the ladder and into the house and was out in a minute. Reaching for the crossbar of the fence that separated the backyards, he hoisted himself in one graceful action over the fence. Matt was astonished by the ease of Steve's movements. In a second Steve was on the deck, his hand stretched out. "Hi. I'm Steve. I don't think we've really been introduced."

"I guess not. I'm Matt."

"I know. We got a letter that was sent to you. Joe brought it over. Wow! Look at all this honey!" And Steve began lifting jar after jar, reading the labels. His green eyes squinted slightly in the sun. Matt took them in and the slightly crooked nose between them. "You must be a honey fanatic," Steve said.

"No, not really, I just like to taste different things."

"I bet you do." And for the first time, Matt got the sense that his own desires had been communicated to the hairy hunk beside him.

"Gourmet honey? Did I hear right?" Joe was standing just below the deck. Matt could see the little circle where his hair was thinning, but what attracted him more were the thick arms drizzled with fur.

"That's right—honeys from around the world."

"Let me get some more toast," Matt said, "and we can have a feeding frenzy."

"Sounds good to me," Joe answered.

In a short while, the three were sitting around the table on Matt's deck. Several jars had been opened. As Matt was explaining what he was doing home that summer, a large globule of honey dripped from his knife and landed in his belly button. "What a mess I'm making!" he exclaimed.

"No harm done," replied Joe, and he stuck his finger into Matt's belly button. "Tastes better that way."

"Yeah," said Steve, "I always liked sloppy seconds." Then he put his own finger in the hole and wiggled it around to get every drop. "We like it when it fills those unexpected nooks and crannies."

"Well, where else should I drip it?" Matt asked provocatively.

"Joe and I have been thinking for a while that we'd like to roll your whole body in honey and lick it off."

"That sounds a bit sticky. How about if I just drip a little here?" And he pulled down his gym shorts to reveal his hard, thick prick and heaped a teaspoon of honey on it.

"I think it would need to be cleaned off," replied Joe, who knelt down and put the dripping prick in his mouth.

Steve stood, dipped his fingers in one of the honey pots, and then began to play with Matt's tits, which immediately became hard at the sweet assault. Then Steve bent down and began to suck the nipple, playing with it as though it were a brown berry that needed plucking with his teeth. Matt moaned at the dual action. He reached out to stroke the mass that had formed in Steve's jeans. It was enormous, and when he finally loosened it from the denim, he gasped with delight—for it was not only long, and would have been longer if it didn't veer to the right, but wonderfully thick, a torpedo gone astray. Matt reached for one of the jars and then, pulling Steve's cock down, shoved the shaft into the jar. Steve's yowl of pain turned into a sigh of pleasure as the young man swallowed his arching menace.

Steve sat back on the table to give Matt full access to his cock. He could see the young man was swallowing hard to make room for his dick and the sweet jelly that surrounded it.

Joe pulled the chair out from beneath Matt so that Matt crouched over as he serviced Steve. Matt's wonderful fuzzy blond ass bubbled up. "Now I've got something I really want to taste," Joe said, and he poured honey down Matt's crack and licked it off. Matt felt the bristles of Joe's beard moving between the hard cheeks, and then the hot tongue entering his hole. For a second he didn't know what was sweeter—the taste of the cock in his mouth or the feel of tongue in his ass. And then it occurred to him: There was something more than a tongue he wanted up there—he wanted that honeycomb of a cock; he wanted Joe's stinger in him.

But Joe had gotten the idea long before Matt had, and he had come prepared. After lubricating the young man with even more honey—a big squirt from the plastic-bear container straight into the hole—and dribbling more on his condom, Joe pressed his cock against Matt's ass. It was tight, all right. It had been weeks since anything had gone up it, and never anything quite so thick. For Joe's cock—which wasn't long at all—had a head like a child's fist. But the honey eased it in like sap in a maple. The hydraulics were just right. Matt was pistoned, his arms holding tight to the table to steady him.

Steve raised his legs, wrapped them around Matt's shoulders, and leaned back on the table. Matt lifted his legs still further back, those wonderful runner's legs, long, elegant, and forceful. Steve's hole rose up like a winking eye. "Here," he said, and handed Matt the plastic-bear bottle that Joe had used on his ass. One good squeeze and his crack was glistening. Those pursed lips of his ass opened, hungry for honey. If the anus had a tongue, Matt thought, it would have licked those moistened chops.

Matt's cock had never been so hard, what with the pounding he was getting from behind and the incredible sight of Steve's ass waiting before him. Joe reached in front, and with his sticky hands he carefully unrolled a rubber over Matt's cock. "Give it to me," Steve growled, and with Joe pushing behind, Matt entered Steve with a quick thrust. It was delicious in there. Warm, juicy, a hive of nerve endings. Matt felt his whole body buzzing. He wasn't going to last too long, not after having waited so many weeks to meet them. He let out a great "Arrgh!" of ecstasy, pumping his own creamy honey into the man in front of him, who, without touching himself, shot his own load against Matt's chest. It wasn't long until Joe let loose a hot stream too, and then they fell into a sticky lump on the deck floor, virtually stuck to one another with sweat, cum, and honey.

There they would have lain all day, except the flies and the mosquitoes got wind of it.

"We'd better go in and get cleaned off," Matt said.

"Well, we'd better go in at least. But bring the honey," Steve replied. "There are a few things I haven't tasted yet, and I've got a big appetite." Matt knew that this wasn't a case of Steve's eyes being bigger than his stomach, or even another part of his anatomy.

Luckily, honey is easy to get out of sheets, although it's hard to explain to mothers how it gets there, especially when the honey glues hairs of all different colors and textures.

That summer, honey flew from the shelves of the supermarkets nearby. Local grocers looked through the pages of the food magazines to see if they had missed some new cooking trend. But they couldn't find any. It was just some marketing aberration, they decided, or maybe, as one clerk joked, bears had moved into the neighborhood.

Fuckcub and Bruce
Thom Wolf

I woke up on Sunday morning with a bad head and a sore asshole. I couldn't even open my eyes at first. I reached across the bed, hunting for the guy I had brought home from the club. My fingers slithered across an empty space. He was gone. Bastard! He must have crept out while I was unconscious.

Then the telephone started to ring.

Shit!

I forced my eyes open. It took a moment for my vision to focus on the bedside clock. It was 11:30. The phone continued ringing. My headache was getting worse. I grabbed the receiver just so the noise would stop.

"Yeah," I grumbled.

"Good morning, Fuckcub. Another Sunday morning hangover?"

It was Bruce. I immediately perked up at the sound of his big gravelly voice.

"It's nothing I'm not used to." I grabbed the packet of cigarettes from beside the phone, stuck one between my dry lips, and lit it with the lighter Bruce had given me on my last birthday (along with a thick leather cockstrap). I inhaled and then coughed.

"I saw this movie the other night," Bruce said. "It was a Spanish film, subtitled. A woman shoved a handkerchief up her lover's ass."

I already had an early-morning hard-on. The sound of Bruce's voice caused it to throb. "Why did she do that?"

"It turned the guy on. She tugged it out when he blew his wad. How about it?"

I laughed. "Bruce, I can think of better things to stick up my ass than a handkerchief."

"I was hoping you would say that. I've got a big hard boner throbbing in my lap right now and nowhere to stick it."

"Where's Dean?"

"He's not here. He won't be back until tomorrow night."

Bruce only called me when Dean was out of town. "So you want me to just drop everything and come running over?"

"Uh-huh."

I sucked in more smoke. "I'll be there in an hour."

I hung up and swung my legs out of bed. I felt a sudden rush to my head when I tried to stand. I steadied myself against the pine wardrobe and waited for the dizzy spell to pass, sucking on the cigarette for support. After a moment my head cleared. I flung back the curtains and opened the window on a gray drizzly day. The bedroom stank of smoke, sweat, and stale spunk. There was a used condom on the floor beside the bed; it had fallen just short of the wastebasket. Apart from my aching asshole, it was the only remaining evidence that I had not been alone last night.

I picked up the used sheath and balled it up in tissue. I wandered down to the kitchen, naked, guided by the hard lance of my cock. I threw the spunk-heavy rubber into the trash and grabbed a bottle of water from the fridge. My thirst was almost unquenchable; I downed the bottle of water in one long gulp.

My cock jerked, the wet head smacking against my belly. I slid my hand over the long shaft, curling my palm over the cut head. I was a complete mug when it came to Bruce. He used my ass like a public convenience when there was nothing else around. But I was crazy about the bastard. I would drop anything for a few hours alone with him: tongue-bathing his balls, riding high on his big cock. He knew I would too.

I went up to the bathroom and winced at the sight of my reflection in the full-length mirror. I felt like shit and I looked even worse. The consequence of a hard night of sex, drugs, and booze was all too evident in my face. I'm only 28, but in the cruel light of day, I looked a good 10 years older. My stubble was starting to look scruffy too. What was it now? Four days' growth? My deep-blue eyes were ringed with even deeper black circles.

Fuck!

There was nothing I could do about the black rings—sleep was the only cure for those—but the rest of my appearance I could deal with. I got into the shower and turned the jets up to full power. I washed my hair first; although it was cut short, it still stank with the sweat and smoke of the club the night before. I squeezed a glob of shampoo into my bushy pubes and lathered up my stomach and chest hair too.

After five minutes in the shower I had cleansed my body from head to toe, taking extra care with my cock and balls and especially my sore asshole. The hair around my hole was matted with lube. After rinsing out my nipple and navel rings, I started to feel half human.

After stepping out of the shower and drying myself off, I decided not to bother shaving. I had a heavy growth but what the fuck—Bruce liked that kind of thing. I gave my teeth a good scrub to get the taste of booze and cum off my breath.

Bruce and I had been fucking around on and off for about three years. We were introduced at a party by a mutual friend. We got it on together that very first night along with Bruce's long-term lover, Dean. The two of them had been an item for about six years. After that first threesome, Bruce and I stayed in touch. It wasn't long before we started fucking around. Dean knew all about us, though I hadn't screwed around with him again after that first time.

Bruce and Dean had the very model of a "daddy/boy" relationship. Bruce is 42 and two inches over 6 feet tall, with a big, brawny frame and a dominating personality. Dean is 10 years younger, with a stocky, buff body and a pretty, boyish face. He's a handsome little fucker, and I'd be lying if I said I wasn't jealous of him. He's got the perkiest little ass I've ever seen. All tight and hairy. It's the tastiest ass I've ever eaten out.

But it was always Bruce that got me horny, with his big tattooed shoulders and mountainous pecs. Bruce has a body of pure muscle, with a tight pelt of dark blond hair that goes from his neck all the way down to his toes. I love cuddling up against his big body. He's got a heavy eight-inch cock and a virility that I have never seen equaled, even in much younger men. When he gets that big cock going he doesn't stop; even after two or three orgasms he can still keep that fat baby hard and ready for more.

My ass is capable of taking a good pounding, and I have had cocks even bigger than Bruce's in there, but none quite so satisfying. With that fat monster in my ass and my face pressed against his hairy chest I'm in seventh-fucking-heaven.

My own cock is a more modest 6½ inches, but I have a very nice set of low-hanging balls. Once I was dried off, I hooked a black leather strap around the base of my cock and under my balls. I fastened it tight. My whole package jutted forward from my body. My piss lips were dripping. My excitement for Bruce had already banished my hangover.

Bruce was a simple guy with simple tastes. He liked cock, he liked ass, and he liked to put his cock in my ass. There was no need to dress up in leather or fetish gear for a fuck session with Bruce. I stepped into a faded old jock and hitched it up over my dripping basket. The washed-out cotton stretched over the hard curve of my cock, my pubes curled over the waistband. After that, all I had to do was pull on a pair of jeans, a T-shirt, and a pair of sneakers. I was ready.

Bruce always had poppers, but I grabbed a bottle from my bedside cabinet before leaving. I also had a present for him: a big fat Cuban cigar that I'd been saving especially for my favorite daddy.

My guts were already churning with excitement. It had been about six weeks since the last time I had seen him. Not that I had been lacking in the sex department in all that time. Bruce was only one of several guys who serviced my hole on a regular basis, and there was always plenty of casual trade around when I wanted it. On the whole, though, I preferred to fuck around with guys that I knew well. Casual sex could be pretty damn hot, but it is even more exciting giving up your butt to a guy who knows *exactly* how to work it and just what it takes to get you off.

Bruce was the leader of my little gang of daddies. Though I loved each of my masculine men in quite different and unique ways, Bruce was by far my favorite. It wasn't just sex either, though he was the best. He was the only man that I was interested in further. I wanted to get past the sex and have a deeper, more meaningful relationship with him. Little chance of that with Dean around. Despite my many talents, I just couldn't compete with that handsome little fucker.

The drive from my three-bedroom house in the suburbs to the hillside cottage that Bruce shared with Dean was a short one. In good traffic, it was less than 20 minutes. As I steered my car down the long road to their drive, my excitable heart started to beat even faster.

I was so fucking horny. You would think that I hadn't had my rocks off in months, let alone less than six hours ago.

It was absolutely pissing down rain when I parked up behind Bruce's huge Range Rover. My breath quickened as I pelted through the rain and climbed the steps to the wooden porch. The front door was open. Kylie Minogue's sublime *Light Years* album was blasting inside. I had bought it for Bruce as a present on my last vacation to England.

It was a decent-size cottage. I shook myself off in the hallway and walked through the open door into the living room. Bruce was stretched out on the couch, flipping through the pages of some European skin mag. A pair of tight blue trunks caressed his trim hips. His steely blue eyes glanced up from the magazine as I entered.

My cock leapt at the sight of him. Bruce is one good-looking bastard—handsome in a roughish, lived-in fashion. His body is big and lean with long, sweeping curves of bulky muscle. His skin, beneath its pelt of dark blond hair, is baked brown by working outside so much. His blond crew cut is heavily peppered with gray, and the deep lines of maturity that are etched around the corners of his eyes and mouth only enhance his masculine beauty. He used to have a thick mustache but recently ditched that in favor of permanent, very sexy stubble.

I sat on the arm of the couch and kissed his bare feet, slavering my tongue over his long toes.

"I didn't expect you so soon," he said.

I wriggled my tongue between the toes, tasting his salty sweat. "I couldn't wait. It's been too long."

"Do you want a beer?"

"No," I said. "There's only one kind of refreshment I need."

"Then I won't deny you any longer."

Bruce stuck his thumbs in the front of his shorts and hitched them down. His long, veiny cock slapped back against his belly. I dragged his shorts the rest of the way down his thick, hairy limbs and tossed them aside. Then I kissed a slow trail up from his toes, over his ankles, calves, knees, toward his groin. I rose lazily over his taut thighs, the thick blond hair rasping beneath my tongue, moving from the outside in. After weeks of waiting for this exact moment, I was delaying it even further. I traced the line of his inner thigh until I finally reached the bulging sac that hung down low between his legs.

Bruce has a thick seam that runs from the tip of his cock all the way down the shaft, over his balls, and into the dark cleft of his ass. I ran the tip of my tongue over the seam of his balls, feeling his heavy nuts hanging down on either side of my tongue. I slavered all over the loose, fleshy purse, licking and nipping him gently. I sucked a big ball into my mouth, rolling it over my tongue, swirling round it. I spat it out and sucked in the other one. I had long ago realized that there was no way I could fit both of his big plums inside my mouth at once. I had to satisfy myself with one juicy nut at a time.

A loose hair tickled the back of my throat.

I followed the seam of skin higher, skirting along the underside of his heavy cock. The organ throbbed against my tongue. Bruce groaned softly as I reached the more sensitive skin near the top. The shaft leapt.

"Go on," he said in his deep, gravelly tone. "Suck me off."

I pressed my lips against the large, skinless head. A long stream of precum was already drooling from the tip. I stuck my tongue into the tiny piss slit and devoured the salty juice.

Bruce's cock is long and pale, and the bare head is a deep shade of pink, the same cast as the skin of his balls. I swirled my tongue around the blunt tip, coating him in a sticky mix of my saliva and his own juice. The pink head glistened like a crown jewel.

"Come on, Fuckcub." He always called me that. "You know what I like."

I did know what he liked. Bruce liked me to deep-throat his cock. He claimed that not many men were ever able to take him all the way down to the root. Apparently, even Dean had trouble accommodating his lover. For me it wasn't a problem. I can swallow any man, whatever size, all the way down to his nuts.

I opened my mouth over the fleshy pink crown, took a deep breath, and then swallowed the entire shaft of Bruce's cock. His blunt head slid right to the back of my throat. His hairy nut sac pressed against my chin, and I stuffed my nose into his bushy pubic nest. The thick blond curls were damp with sweat. I inhaled his savory scent, sucking air past the monstrous obstruction in my throat.

Bruce let out a deep, chesty groan to show how happy he was with my achievement. His big shovelhands were on the back of my head, and he shoved my face deeper into his groin.

"Go on, Fuckcub, choke on that big fat fucker!" He humped upward, forcing his cock deeper into my throat.

My jaw ached. I dug my fingers into the hard flesh of his thighs, but he would not loosen his hold on the back of my head. I knew now that he wouldn't let me go until he had what he wanted. It was the one thing I was capable of giving that no other guy could.

I worked the muscles in my throat, tightening the already constricted passage around his thick tool. He grunted, groaned, jerked his hips. I swallowed, milking his cock with my tender throat. He thickened. I knew he couldn't last against the tightness and friction of my gullet.

His cock jerked violently against the delicate walls.

"Oh yeah, here it comes, Fuckcub. *Here it comes!*"

He locked his hands fast around the back of my head and pushed my face down even deeper. I felt the warm jet pulse against the lining of my throat as he filled me with spurt after spurt of potent spunk. I swallowed instinctively, his warmth flooding my stomach. My jaw ached as it stretched further around his increasingly thick cock.

When he was done he slumped back into the couch and slowly released his grip on the back of my head. I eased up carefully, withdrawing his cock from the deep recesses of my throat. His cock still drooled spunk across my tongue as he pulled away. He was still hard. I knew he would be. That wonderful piece of meat would be good for another orgasm or two before softening like other men.

"Are you horny, Fuckcub?" He sat back, his wet dick leaning against his hairy belly, matting his fur, a satisfied grin on his broad lips.

"I'm always horny for you," I said, swallowing painfully. "I want your cock."

Bruce laughed. "Don't you get enough?"

"Not like this," I said, wrapping my fist around the soaking rod. I squeezed a big drop of cum up from his tube and gobbled it up.

I stood and dragged my tight white T-shirt over my head. This is where I knew I had the edge on Dean. My main rival for Bruce might have had a prettier face, but I had by far the better body. Dean is stocky, with thick, compact muscle and huge, hard tits.

I'm much longer and leaner; my torso is cut with smooth, graceful lines of muscle. A thick mat of hair runs down over my chest and stomach. I ran a slow hand up over my flat belly and brushed my palm lightly against my nipple piercing.

Bruce smiled. "Take it all off."

He watched me strip down to the old jockstrap. I threw my jeans over the back of a chair. Bruce's cool eyes looked me slowly up and down.

"So who were you with last night?" he asked.

I shrugged. "Just some guy I met at the club."

"You didn't get his name?"

"I don't remember it."

Bruce caressed his hard cock. "What was he like?"

"Nice," I said. "He was big. Good-looking. Pierced cock."

Bruce gripped his cock at the root, squeezing. "Was his cock as nice as this?"

I shook my head. "No way. No cock is as nice as that."

"Turn around, Fuckcub. It's been awhile since I had a good look at that ass of yours."

I turned slowly. Very few guys outside of porno movies manage to look good in a jock. I didn't have anything to worry about. My ass looked just great within the open frame of the worn cotton straps. The cheeks of my ass are taut and round, and there's a nice nest of dark hair in the tight crack.

I leaned forward, allowing the tight orbs to part naturally, savoring the cool kiss of air against my hot ring.

"Still like what you see?" I asked breathlessly.

"Very much, Fuckcub. Very much. Get down on your hands and knees and give me a good look at that fucked-out ring of yours."

I sank to the floor, leaning over onto my hands and thrusting my ass back, pressing it open. Bruce pressed his bare foot into my crack, sliding his toes up and down the sweat-slick cleft. I moaned. I knew what he was going to do next and I couldn't wait.

He pressed his blunt big toe against the resistance of my wrinkled bud and shoved inward. My ass lips were lubed up with sweat, and he slipped straight into me. I pushed back against him. I loved the way his toe felt inside me, probing my tight ass chute like a fat little cock. Bruce was the only guy who had ever done this to me, and I loved it. Most guys were more than happy to finger-fuck my ass ring, but the divine sensation of having a big, squat toe inside me was unique to my sessions with Bruce.

He twisted his foot slowly, rotating all the way around inside me.

Oh, wow! That really got my juices going.

He wriggled his toe.

"You surprise me, Fuckcub. Your hole is nice and tight. I expected it to be pretty loose and fucked out after the night you've just had. You did get your ass fucked, didn't you?"

"Oh yeah," I gasped. "He fucked me all over the house."

Bruce forced it deeper. "Then I've got good news for you, Fuckcub. You're about to get your ass fucked a whole lot more."

"Oh yes, please."

He gave it one complete rotation. "Then you know what to do, don't you?"

Bruce withdrew his toe, and the lips of my ass sucked shut. I turned over and lay down on my back, flat on the floor. I lifted my hips and slipped off the jockstrap. I rolled back down, naked but for the black leather strap fastened tight around my cock.

Bruce swung his legs over the side of the couch and perched on the edge, watching me. I knew exactly what he wanted me to do.

I curled my fist around the shaft of my dick and started to jerk, dragging my hand steadily back and forth. I slipped my other hand down between my legs and tugged at my tight ball sac. My big pink head was throbbing. Bruce leaned forward intently, knowing that this wouldn't last long.

With a deep grunt, my stomach muscles tightened and my cock blew a massive white wad over my hard abs. It blasted again and again in long ropes that stretched from my navel to my nipples.

"That's the stuff, Fuckcub," Bruce said with a grin. "That's what I wanted to see."

The white heat of my balls dribbled down over my pale skin.

Bruce dropped down onto the floor. He ran his hand along my chest and stomach and scooped up as much of the stuff as he could. There was plenty of it to go around. I always managed to come up with the goods when Bruce was around.

He rubbed my cum between his hands, dividing it into each palm. He smeared one handful of ball juice over his rock-hard cock and pressed the other into the crack of my ass. His fingers slipped into my tiny ring, stuffing my own cum into my deep canal.

It was warm on his fingers. He pushed my spunk in deep, loosening up the tight passage. I looked into his steely eyes; they glinted, mirroring the hard hunger in my own. He had three fingers inside me. He rotated his hand slowly, opening me up. I spread my thighs wider and bore down hard against his hand.

"You really are hungry for it today, Fuckcub," he said with a deep laugh.

"Yes Sir," I gasped.

Bruce withdrew and lifted my hips up into his lap. He passed me a bottle of poppers. I clutched the little brown bottle in the palm of my hand. He pressed his spunk-coated cock down under my ass. I felt the blunt head slip between my cheeks and press against my ass ring. I trembled with anticipation. This was it. Not long left to wait.

He held his cock at the root and guided it into position. I felt the pressure against my hole. He pushed. The wide head pressed against the tiny ring. My asshole took the strain and began to widen. I breathed deeply, willing myself to open further. I unscrewed the lid from the bottle of poppers and inhaled through each nostril. They took effect on my head first. And then my ass. The last remnant of tension disappeared, and my tiny ring opened up.

The blunt head popped through the narrow lips. He was in.

He gripped my hips and pushed in deeper. I felt his wide length slide along the sensitive walls of my ass, filling me entirely. I pushed against him, taking him deeper, until the ample sac of his balls pressed against my butt.

He was still for a moment, giving my body time to adjust to the intrusion.

I opened the bottle of poppers again and held it up under each of his nostrils. He breathed in deeply.

Then we started to fuck. Slowly at first, he moved easily back and forth inside me. My insides seemed to shift with each inward stroke. I wrapped my legs around his waist, drawing him closer to me. I opened my mouth and kissed him. It was passionate. His tongue fucked out my mouth like his cock fucked out my ass: strong, steady, and deep.

It quickly intensified. He pulled out, and I rolled over onto my hands and knees. He entered me again, fucking me hard from behind. I bore the brunt of his weight as he pounded his cock deep into my bowels. It was incredible. We were both worked up into a hell of a sweat. My sight was blurred as the heavy perspiration on my brow trickled down into my eyes. His thick fingers dug into my waist as he held me rooted on his dick.

We sniffed the poppers and changed position again. I stood, bent over the back of the couch as he rode me from behind. I held onto the couch for support—my knees were already going weak. My cock was slapping back and forth against my stomach with the rhythmic frenzy of our fucking.

Bruce slapped my ass.

"Ready to come again, Fuckcub?"

"Uh-huh." My mind was way past trying to form words.

Bruce's thrusts became more frenzied. It was shorter, sharper. He was just about there. I stroked my own cock. *Jesus, the sensitivity.*

Bruce roared in my ear. I felt his dick lengthen and thicken in my ass. It pulsated. My bowels were flooded by wave after wave of white-hot cum. It washed deep into me.

My own cum shot high. It sailed through the air, almost in slow motion, before landing in long streaks across the back of the couch.

Later that night, around 9 o'clock, we lay beneath the covers of Bruce's big double bed, smoking the fat cigar I had brought for him. We'd been fucking all day. His cock had finally gone soft, and my ass was tired and fuck-worn. I lay on my back, propped up on two huge pillows, and watched the dense clouds of cigar smoke drifting up to the ceiling.

My balls were sore too. After emptying them of six loads of spunk in less than 24 hours, it was little wonder.

Bruce rested an ashtray between the mountainous peaks of his chest and puffed contentedly on the cigar.

We were casually talking when the telephone rang. Bruce handed me the ashtray and the cigar and reached over to answer it. If we were at my place, I would have just let it ring.

I knew before Bruce even started talking that it was Dean. I lay there quietly for over 10 minutes while Bruce chatted to his lover on the phone. As he spoke, his hand slid under the covers and gently stroked the sensitive flesh of my inner thigh. At no point in the conversation did Bruce mention my name. He even said something to Dean about just lazing about all day and doing nothing.

Finally, after telling Dean he loved him, Bruce hung up. He rolled back over and draped his thick arm across my stomach and rested his head against my chest. His stubble grazed my skin.

"That was Dean," he said.

"I gathered. Why didn't you tell him I was here?"

He shrugged. "I thought it best not to."

"Why?"

"Dean doesn't approve of our arrangement."

"Why not? I thought you two were cool with each other playing around with other guys."

He took the cigar out of my fingers and drew on it slowly. He exhaled with a thoughtful sigh. "We *are* cool with it. I know for a fact that Dean will have fucked his brains out all weekend. It does-n't bother me."

"So why does this bother him?"

"It's not the fucking around that bothers him. I could have fucked 10 different men this weekend and he wouldn't mind. It's the fucking around with *you* that Dean doesn't like."

It only occurred to me at the moment. My God, Dean was *jealous* of me! I had thought all along that Dean just didn't like me. I would never have believed that Dean, *Dean* of all people, would be so insecure about himself to ever be jealous of a guy like me. He had everything: looks, money, a great body, heaps of confidence. And he had Bruce. It was quite ironic, considering that I had been jealous of him for so long.

We fucked again after that. My body and my ass were exhaust-ed with sex, but after such a revelation, I had to have Bruce again. I wanted him inside me. I wanted to feel him deep in there and know that a small part of him truly loved me. He had to love me— there was no other reason for him to go on seeing me when his lover disapproved of me so vehemently.

My ass was dripping with his spunk, and once I coaxed his dick back to life, it slipped back into me effortlessly. He had been pounding my body mercilessly all day, but this time he took it easy. He moved inside me with an unhurried contentment. I wrapped my arms and legs around him and held him even closer. I lifted my ass gently from the bed to take him deeper into me.

After what seemed like an age, we eventually came. After squirting load after load all afternoon, my ejaculation was less impressive this final time. My cock twitched and dribbled a few drops over my belly. But despite the apparent lack of spunk with this orgasm, the sensations were no less vivid than all the others were. It seemed to last forever.

Bruce moved on top of me, smearing my warm cum between our two bellies. His body trembled, and I felt his gentle release inside me. He groaned softly.

I left around midnight. Dean was due back early in the morning, so there was no point in me staying the night. I didn't want to cause any trouble for Bruce. I knew that I would never be able to force a break between him and Dean, and that if it came down to a choice between the two of us, I wouldn't stand a chance.

It was enough to know that a very small part of him belonged to me.

There was a message on my answering machine when I got home. It was Bruce.

"Hi, Fuckcub." It was good to hear his voice in the lonely darkness of my bedroom. "I was just ringing to say good night. Thanks for coming over today. I wish you could have stayed the night—it would be nice to wake up around 3 and feel you in bed beside me. I'll call you sometime next week. Dean is going away again soon for a whole weekend. I'll let you know when. Good night then, Fuckcub."

Just before he hung up Bruce said, "I can still feel your ass on my cock. I guess it's used to spending time inside you now."

I smiled. After all that I'd been through, those last few words of his managed to get my sore cock stirring again.

I blew a kiss toward the answering machine.

"Good night, Daddy," I said before collapsing on top of the bed.

I was fucking exhausted.

The Hired Hand

SKIP BRUSHABER

The sound of the gravel under the tires is familiar, even though it has been over 20 years since Ben has driven up the long driveway. When he turns the corner and the house comes into view, he stops the car. The old house looks basically the same, but the years of disregard have begun to show. The flower gardens that his mother had cultivated are gone, and the lawn that he always kept neatly trimmed is overgrown. The house, obviously unpainted since he left, stands gray and peeling in the afternoon light.

He pulls the car into the dooryard and takes in the condition of the fields and pastures. Most of the fence is down and the posts lean like aging sentinels against the onslaught of the years of neglect. He recalls how it once was, then the wind catches a sagging door, slamming it against the side of the barn, which jars him back to the present.

Ben is tempted to go find a motel in town to escape the confrontation with the past. Wanting to be in more familiar surroundings, he wishes he could have caught a flight right after the funeral. Giving in to curiosity and exhaustion, Ben struggles to get out of the compact rental car and stretches, running a large hand through his salt-and-pepper beard. He loosens his tie, takes his bag out of the backseat, and walks toward the back door of the house.

The kitchen is silent and dirty. The place does not look like it has been cleaned since his mother died 20 years before. Ben thinks for sure that he smells wood smoke and walks toward the enormous wood cookstove. He touches his hand to the top, and it feels warm. No one has lived in the house since his father went into the hospital over a month before. If this was the city instead of rural Maine, Ben would suspect some homeless person was living in the family homestead.

Ben stumbles out to the woodshed and returns with an ax handle he finds. He walks cautiously from room to room, holding the handle, just in case. The entire house is blanketed by a layer of dust. He opens the door to his old room, and everything looks just about the way it did the day he left, the day of his mother's funeral. Now he is here, the day of his father's funeral. It is the same event, but different emotions.

Ben strips out of his dress clothes and grabs his jeans out of his bag. He turns and catches his reflection in the mirror of his old dresser. It is strange seeing a mature man looking back from the same mirror he checked himself out in so many years before. Running his hands through the mat of thick chest hair, Ben finds himself getting aroused. He is in the room where he first learned to bring himself to orgasm, and it brings his dick to full attention. Recalling those days as a boy, Ben drops his shorts and lies on the bed naked. He turns on his stomach and grinds his hard dick into the old mattress. He comes quickly without touching himself, just like he did as a boy, and the extent of his orgasm sends shudders through his massive body.

Ben awakens in old familiar surroundings as the setting sun casts golden shadows across the old furniture. He knows where he is, but he has to remember why he is there. He is recalling the day's events when he hears sounds coming from downstairs. For a split second he is a boy again, listening to his mother make dinner on the old wood cookstove. Snapping out of it, Ben realizes his intruder is back and he jumps off the bed. He slides into his jeans, grabs the ax handle, and proceeds slowly down the stairs.

In the fading light, he can see an old Chevy truck parked beside his rental car through the living room window. His heart beats heavily in his chest as he pads barefoot toward the kitchen.

As he rounds the corner, Ben catches sight of a figure bending over the wood stove, stirring something. He raises the ax handle and is about to speak when the figure turns toward him.

"Howdy, Ben. I was just making us some dinner." The voice comes deep from the massive chest. "What was you intendin' on doin' with that piece of wood in your hand?"

Ben squints toward the figure and drops the handle to his side. The voice sounds familiar, but he can't make out who it is. The guy is big and rugged, but his smile eases the tension.

"Who are you and what are you doing here?" Ben finally chokes out.

"It's been a long time," the man says, advancing toward Ben and extending his hand. "I'm Sonny."

"Holy shit, Sonny. How are you?" he says, grasping the huge, rough hand.

"Fine. Jesus, you're all grown up. You weren't as big and hairy the last time I saw you. How long's it been?"

"My Mom died over 20 years ago, and I left the day of the funeral. Let me go finish getting dressed and we'll catch up," Ben says, turning to go back upstairs.

"Don't do it on my account. I made us some dinner."

Ben sits on his bed, pulling on his socks, his mind a whirl of questions, to say nothing of the aching in his groin. The encounter with his past has been overwhelming, and now Sonny, the object of most of his adolescent sexual fantasies, is downstairs cooking him dinner. The years have been good to Sonny, as Ben figures he must be close to 50 and he looks to be in fine shape. The lines on his face from the constant exposure to the weather only give his handsome face more character. Ben thinks about how many times he still recalls Sonny and remembers how he used to spy on him when he was a kid. Ben stands and feels a little light-headed as he rearranges his dick in his jeans.

He goes back down to the kitchen, and the smell of chili and corn bread greets him. Sonny is busy putting the grub on the table. Ben watches him for a moment. He is still as heavily muscled as he was years ago, with the addition of a little bit of a gut, which only adds to his masculinity. He has lost most of his hair and keeps the rest buzzed short. His beard is well-trimmed, with traces of white interspersed with the copper.

"Come on, have a seat," Sonny says, flashing that grin that still can melt the hardest heart of any man. "I hope you don't mind me making myself at home."

"God, no. I don't mind. Where you been all these years and when did you come back?" Ben asks, sitting down.

"I worked for your pa a few more years after you left. Then he started selling off the stock and letting the place go. I stayed as long as I could, and then there wasn't anything left to do. So I left and traveled around the country. I even went up to Alaska and worked on the pipeline. How about you?"

"I went to Boston and put myself through school. I worked in the corporate world for a while, but it wasn't me. Now I'm a teacher. I love kids and it's a natural job for me, but I'm getting burned out on that too. I've been thinking about doing something else, maybe getting out of the city. How long have you been here?"

"I was passing through on my way back from Portland. I thought maybe I could find a fishing job, but fishing's dead. So I stopped by to see the old place, and your pa was already in the hospital. I went to see him a couple of times, but he didn't know me.

"So, I decided to bunk here for a spell 'cause the place was empty. I hope you don't mind," Sonny says, searching Ben's eyes.

"Hell no, stay as long as you want. I'm meeting with a realtor tomorrow to put the place on the market. You can stay until it sells. By the way, how'd you know it was me?"

"Thanks, Ben, for letting me stay. I was at the funeral. I sat in the back, but I figured out who you were real quick."

The two sit quietly and enjoy their meal. Occasionally one catches the other staring, and they just smile. Sonny gets up to clear the table, but Ben places a hand on his broad chest and gently pushes him back down.

"Let me do that. You cooked. Want some coffee? Do we have any coffee?"

"Up in the cupboard. Let me stoke up the fire," Sonny says.

"Not too much—it's pretty hot in here already."

"Yeah, I know what you mean. I'm gonna shed a layer, if you don't mind," Sonny says, unbuttoning his flannel shirt. "I always dress too warm for being in the house."

Ben busies himself, washing the dishes and cleaning up. He is almost afraid to turn around as he hears Sonny's work boots hit the floor. He feels Sonny behind, reaching around for a couple of coffee mugs. The younger man can feel the warmth emanating from the other and the musky smell of his body. Ben could swear that Sonny intentionally brushes against him as he finds the mugs. It makes his throat dry and his heart beat faster as he washes out the sink.

"Come on over and get your coffee. I think that sink is clean enough."

Ben turns and walks toward the table, where Sonny sits clad only in his long johns. The top couple of buttons are undone, and a mass of coppery chest hair spills out. Ben can plainly see the outline of the prominent nipples straining against the white cotton. He is sure he can make out the outline of Sonny's dick down one side of his long underwear. He quickly averts his gaze, falls into the chair across from Sonny, and looks down at his coffee.

"How do you take it?" Sonny asks.

"What?"

"Your coffee. Do you want anything in it?"

"No, I take it straight up."

"Ben, are you OK?"

"Just tired. It's been a long day."

"Yeah, man. I'm real sorry about your pa," Sonny says, putting his hand on top of Ben's.

"Thanks. We never got along, though."

"He was a tough man, but I think he had a good heart. He sure fathered a handsome son," Sonny says, grasping Ben's hand.

Ben lets out a sigh and looks deeply into the eyes of Sonny, who reaches across the table for his other hand. He clasps both of Ben's hands firmly and smiles.

"I have to tell you something," Ben says.

"Go ahead," Sonny says, getting up and walking around behind Ben. He stands behind him and begins to firmly knead Ben's broad shoulders.

"Man, that feels wonderful. What I wanted to tell you is that you were my fantasy growing up. I used to beat off all the time thinking about you. I used to spy on you, especially when you were working with your shirt off. One time I even watched you beat off in the hayloft."

"I know, kid, but this is all new for me. I knew you liked looking at me, and I used to give you every opportunity," Sonny says, running his strong hands down Ben's chest and squeezing his large, hairy pecs.

"But why didn't you ever do anything?"

"Because you were a boy and I wasn't into boys, but now you're a man. One hell of a man. Stand up, let's get some of those clothes off. It's getting hotter and hotter in here."

Ben stands and turns to face Sonny, who pulls him into a firm embrace. They find each other's mouths and explore with their tongues, all the while grinding their hips into each other. They break apart for a moment, and Sonny pulls Ben's shirt over his head. His lips immediately go for Ben's nipples as the younger man fumbles with the buttons of Sonny's long johns. Ben struggles to move the cotton over Sonny's hairy shoulders and finally drops to his knees to pull them down over his massive thighs.

Below the waist, Sonny's body is pink, compared to the

bronze of his upper body, but is covered by the same reddish-brown hair. Sonny's firm dick rests on Ben's forehead as Ben buries his face in the older man's hairy balls. Sonny's large pink dick hardens even more and slides against Ben's broad forehead. They slip to the kitchen floor in unison, and Sonny struggles to loosen the button fly of Ben's jeans before he grabs his fat, firm cock with both hands; they slide down into position, facing each other's crotches. They both behold their prizes briefly before taking each other's dicks in their mouths. Working hot mouths down the length of their dicks, the two men are like two giant pistons working in unison. Ben works hard to take all of Sonny's hot pink dick as Sonny buries his nose in the dark mass of Ben's pubic bush. They groan like rutting bears as they reach their peak. Ben grabs Sonny's powerful ass cheeks as he pumps his cum all over Sonny's hairy chest. Ben works harder on Sonny's dick, which spurts a massive load, filling Ben's throat. They stay locked in the embrace as they try to catch their breath, and finally Sonny moves up to lie next to Ben.

"Jeez, that was the best," he says, smelling his own cum in Ben's breath.

"Yeah, I'm still seeing stars," Ben says, pulling Sonny close, "and I think there's more where that came from."

They find their way up to Ben's old room and crawl into the bed that is way too small for men their size. Cuddled in each other's arms, the two men fall into a deep sleep.

Sonny wakes before sunrise, the same as every day. He looks down at the sleeping bear whose head rests on his chest. Ben stirs, as Sonny rubs his hand over his muscled back, and looks up with sleep-filled eyes.

"I thought it was all a dream. How'd we ever sleep in this tiny bed?"

"I had the best night's sleep I've had in a long time," Sonny says, kissing the top of Ben's head. "You wanna get up or do you wanna play?"

Ben doesn't answer, but reaches down and grabs his buddy's dick, which is already hard as a rock. Sonny groans and opens his legs.

"Is this for me, or do you have to piss?" Ben asks, squeezing harder.

"I got up and pissed a little while ago. That's all yours, baby."

Ben slides down and examines his coveted prize closely. He follows the veins with his fingertips and traces the area just below the head. His touch sends a shudder through Sonny's entire body. Ben takes Sonny's cock in his mouth and looks up at him at the same time. They keep eye contact while Ben moves his mouth expertly over Sonny's dick. The tension builds, and Sonny lets out a yell as he comes in hot torrents. Ben slides up, kisses him, and their beards feel electric as they rub against each other. Sonny tongues Ben's ear, and they writhe as much as the small space will allow, finally falling on the floor together, which does nothing to break the spell.

"I want you to fuck me. Do you have any condoms?" Sonny says.

"In the side pocket of my bag. There's lube there too," Ben says, watching Sonny's massive form rise with his dick swinging majestically.

Sonny returns, kneels between Ben's legs, takes his dick firmly in hand, and rolls the condom on. He then lubes the younger man's dick and his own hairy ass.

Sonny squats over Ben and slides the dick in his hand inside himself. The rhythmic movement begins slowly and builds as Ben reaches up to fondle both of Sonny's large nipples, which protrude through the mass of chest hair. Their eyes remain locked in an intense gaze as Sonny moves his hips more rapidly.

"I'm close," Ben says with teeth clenched.

"Let it rip, baby," Sonny says, clamping his ass muscles.

Ben lets out an animal cry as he comes inside his buddy's ass.

Sonny in turn shoots a load all over Ben's hairy belly and chest. They both grin broadly as they try to catch their breath. Finally, Sonny falls across Ben's chest, and they kiss with tongues intertwined. They are brought out of their afterglow by the sound of tires on gravel coming up the driveway.

"Shit, what time is it? That's probably the realtor coming to list the property," Ben says, struggling to get up.

The realtor's car pulls out of the driveway, and Ben walks all through the house calling Sonny's name, but there is no answer. He goes out through the woodshed to the barn. He looks all through the first level of the barn.

"Hey. Up here," comes a familiar voice from the hayloft.

Ben slowly climbs the ladder, and the years seem to slip backward. As his head clears the floor level, he sees Sonny lying in the hay naked in the filtered sunlight.

He is stroking his hard cock; Ben remains frozen on the ladder.

"Come on, guy. You're a man now, you can join me."

Ben grins broadly and climbs up the rest of the way. He rips off his shirt, kicks off his boots, and pulls off his jeans as he walks toward Sonny, who hasn't missed a beat. Ben falls down in the hay next to his buddy. Sonny reaches for him and pulls him close.

"We need to talk first," Ben says.

"Ok," Sonny says, releasing his grip.

"What are your plans?"

"I'll stay here until the place sells. It will probably sell fast. Why?"

"Would you think about settling down and helping me run the place?"

"Ben, what the hell are you saying?"

"I told the realtor no—that for now I'm not going to sell the place. I'd like to get it up and running again. With your help, that is," Ben says tentatively.

"I don't know, farming's a tough business. A lot of work for little return," Sonny says. "But with you as part of the bargain, how can I say no?"

The two big men pull into a bear hug, and their laughter booms over the big loft.

Blade

JAY NEAL

My friend Paul was waving his hand in front of my face. "I said: Don't you think maybe he's a little too young for you?"

"What? Why? Who's too young?" We had just finished a taxing afternoon of shopping, and we were sitting in the food court, enjoying our much deserved refreshment. Paul had been saying something characteristically clever when I glanced toward a rowdy group of high school kids walking past the escalator. Unexpectedly, time stopped, silence arrived, and then I saw him. Or he saw me. Actually, we looked simultaneously. Looked a lot, apparently.

"That rather fierce-looking young thing over there that you were staring at as he entertained his barely pubescent friends with his adolescent antics."

"I was not staring and I don't have any idea what you're talking about." Of course I did, but I wasn't going to give Paul that kind of ammunition. But it had been a long, long time since my heart rate actually responded to the sight of another man. Boy. Young man. Whatever.

"Oh, please. You're too old, too fat, and have too little hair on your head and too much on the rest of you to be making come-hither eyes at some young thing who's barely legal. Although he does look far from inexperienced."

"I was not making eyes. I was simply looking distractedly in that direction and I hardly even noticed him and I'm only 45 and besides, body hair is almost fashionable and he started it anyway."

At least, I thought he did. I was pretty sure he did. Not that it really mattered anyway. I was starting to feel a little flushed.

"Quite aside from his advanced state of youth, I don't think he's really your type, do you? I'm sure you noticed his tattoos, and you remember what my mother said about men who wear tattoos. Personally, I've always thought that barbed wire around the arm looked a little creepy. He's probably into heavy-duty S/M and you know you're just too vanilla for that. I don't really like his hair cut that short, either. Do you think maybe he's a neo-Nazi skinhead white supremacist?"

"No, I think he's just some kid who wants to shock his parents by looking like everyone else his age." His skin was so tanned that his tattoos almost glowed. I could count three. There was the barbed wire around his left bicep, one above his left ankle, and one on his neck at the top of his spine. No, make that four: There was another one I couldn't make out just below his left collarbone.

"Well, all these kids look alike to me with their short, post–Gen X hair and requisite Vandykes. Frankly, I've never been able to figure out how they keep those baggy jeans from sliding past their butts and onto the ground. Aren't his legs a little short? I think long legs are sexier myself. And you know, he really shouldn't wear athletic shirts since he's a little on the fleshy side. Maybe he just hasn't lost his puppy fat yet and would firm up if he went to a gym."

I liked the way the ribbed T-shirt curved so intimately over his chest and outlined the soft bulges of his torso. I was a bit disappointed that his long shorts were so baggy and hid what had to be husky legs to match the rest of him. But they did emphasize his admittedly voluptuous ass. His youthful beard and short, dark hair punctuated his face and made it poetry.

"I think he's cute." I didn't realize I said that aloud until it was too late.

"Cute! Whatever. He may be cute, but he certainly doesn't display even a modicum of good taste. I mean, that T-shirt leaves little to the imagination, doesn't it? Did you notice how you could see his nipples?"

Oh, yes, I'd noticed.

"And, as I'm sure you remember, in our day we didn't even wear earrings in public, let alone publicly flaunt a pierced nipple."

But it wasn't the nipple ring, or the tattoos, or even his tanned skin that kept me awake most of that night. It was his glance, that intensity in his eyes. I kicked myself to keep from obsessing over some street-smart kid who was probably barely 19 years old, but I didn't kick hard enough. Every time I closed my eyes all I saw was him, looking at me. But why?

Finally, around 4 o'clock in the morning, I reached the stunning conclusion that he definitely was looking at me and I definitely was looking at him and none of it made any sense but if I didn't see him again and find out what was going on I would be very frustrated and probably never get to sleep ever again. Ever. I actually did get a little sleep after that.

The next morning I felt pretty ragged—and more than a little restless about the whole situation. I couldn't quite picture myself with this cub on my arm, going about my usual social life. What if he escorted me to Susan's wedding that spring? Would they point at me and whisper about the cradle-robber? I could just imagine the scandal if we decided to dance. Shit, would we even know the same dances? And my mother's 70th birthday was coming up in a few months. No doubt she would be happy to see me dating someone 50 years younger than she is.

Looking at myself in the mirror that morning didn't cheer me up. I didn't remember when my hair had gotten so gray, and when did all those white patches show up in my beard? I tried but couldn't seem to find a way to trim my beard so that it didn't look too wild. And I didn't have any clothes to wear that would cover all the lumps in my body. I looked like an old fart.

At work I kept forgetting the things I was supposed to be doing. It was another walk outside of reality. There was one point where I saw him again—for about the hundredth time—only this time he walked toward me, almost close enough for me to see the tattoo below his collarbone, and he started to say something. That was the time I left the customer on hold for 17 minutes.

I don't know when I decided to go back to the mall, but the thought had obviously been at the back of my mind since I woke up. That moment, his eyes, the look—all kept playing over and over in my mind. If I didn't go back, I knew that I'd never see him again, and that clearly was the wrong path to choose.

What I would do when I got there, I didn't know. I had to drive there, go in, see him again, and something would happen. Maybe I could talk to him this time. But what would I say? "Nice weather we're having," or "Hey, those are really cool sneakers." They're not even called sneakers anymore, so that would make me sound real cool. Nobody says "cool" anymore either.

Could I date someone with a barbed-wire tattoo? I couldn't even remember how to date. Whatever. We had to be together. That much was clear.

When I parked at the mall I really started feeling self-conscious. I was yet another old bear making a fool of himself over a cute young cub. It took over half an hour, but finally I convinced myself that nobody except me would know. To everyone else in there, I'd look like all the other husbands sitting on a bench watching the people go by, waiting for their wives to finish.

Inside, I went back to the food court and found an empty bench to sit at. From there I could survey a large space, including the spot where he had been the day before when it happened. Whatever it was. If it was magic, then by working the same spell over again, by going there and sitting in that same spot, maybe it would work again.

It worked. Without warning, surely by magic, he appeared at the other end of my bench. Being careful not to look in my direction. Trying to look casual. He sat on the edge of the bench, chin in hands and elbows on knees. But his right foot tapping with nervous energy undercut the look.

He sat silently, staring straight ahead of him, pointedly ignoring my stare. Clearly, for whatever reasons of his own, we were going to pretend to be strangers sharing the bench. We would be exchanging information like spies might do, afraid of surveillance. So I looked away and stared into the distance in front of me.

Finally he broke his belligerent silence. "So, like, are you a dirty old man or something?"

"Are you a dirty young man or something?"

Irony was definitely the wrong approach, but I didn't know what I was going to say to get my point across. I didn't even know what my point was. Certainly I don't usually...what? Usually, I don't even notice someone his age.

I started, "I don't usually—"

"Hey man, I don't neither, OK?"

His foot stopped twitching, but he seemed more tense than before. However, despite his refusing to look at me, it was clear that whatever it was that aroused the strong emotions between us was reasserting itself.

"My name's Jack."

"Blade."

Blade! I hoped my face didn't reveal my terror at the thought of being stabbed in a dark alley somewhere. I tried to stay calm.

"So, what would your father say if he knew you were picking up old men in the mall?"

"Fuck that shit. I don't have a dad. And my mom's dead, OK?"

I felt worse than an adolescent trying to make his first date. I still wasn't sure what I wanted out of this conversation, but this wasn't it. The whole situation was obviously way beyond my experience. Blade must live a harder life than I might even imagine. What to say? Oh, sorry about your mom and dad, must be rough. I'm sure that patronizing tone would make just the right impression on him. He'd probably heard it all before anyway.

He was starting to look restless. Maybe his young friends were coming within range, giving off radar signals that I couldn't detect but he could. No doubt it would mean social death for him to be caught talking to me.

It was getting on my nerves. Not being able to say the right thing, not knowing what I was doing, feeling way too far into the deep end and forgetting how to swim. "You know, I didn't choose for this to happen."

"Neither did I." Abruptly he turned and looked unblinking into my eyes. His sapphire-blue eyes held that same burning look and seized my gaze for several seconds.

"You are so fucking hot," he said to me. Just like that. And then he was gone. Like magic again. I realized I'd been holding my breath, so I exhaled.

The sudden feeling of loss was surprising. I felt like I'd really missed a chance for something important, something valuable. It's not like I'd invested that much in this kid: We'd seen each other twice, spoken for all of two or three minutes. But there was something there, I was sure of it, and it had just withered.

I must have looked a pretty sight sitting on that bench, not knowing how or why to move, feeling the emotional knot in my chest and an increasing threat of tears in my eyes. Thinking all the time that there was nothing there to ruin, I still kept wondering where I had fucked it up. I'm sure I could have stayed like that all evening if the young mother and her baby hadn't intruded on my grief by sitting on the bench.

I left the mall, walking out into early-evening sunlight that surprised me by being there. I started walking toward my car when I saw that my long shadow had been joined by another. Every curve in its shape looked so familiar that I didn't need to see the tattoos to know who it was. Suddenly the air itself became lighter and easier to breathe.

Although I knew the answer, I felt the rhetorical need to ask: "And just what do you think you're doing now?"

"Going home with you. That's what you want, isn't it?"

We reached the car. "Yes. No. I mean, sure, but not like this. Well, I mean, not like this could be, but it isn't..."

He stopped with his hand reaching to open the door. "Fuck, man, what is your problem?"

My verbal paralysis was returning. "Middle-aged neuroses."

He accompanied an exasperated sigh with rolling of the eyes, but he opened the car door. "Well, I want to. Let's get the fuck outta here."

Obviously, we'd have to smooth out a few wrinkles before I could take him to meet my mother. I have never felt more distant from a younger generation than I did right then, driving home with this fascinating and adorable cub in my car. I felt like I didn't have anything in common with someone too young to remember Reagan, who wouldn't know who Judy Garland was. For him, the Vietnam War was as much forgotten history as the Civil War. He might remember his first CD; I could remember the first CD. I didn't know what we would find to talk about, presuming that he even wanted conversation.

"Let's grab a burger, I'm starving." OK, so his thoughts were moving along different lines right then.

We stopped. I'll admit that stopping felt like an intrusion, delaying our arrival home so that I could discover what was going to happen. But it also was a relief that I didn't have to face that quite so soon. We ordered, we sat. I nibbled my fried chicken nuggets and watched while Blade devoured three quarters of a pound of fast-food hamburger. I was fascinated looking at his hands with their tanned, stubby fingers and the delicate patch of hair just below his wrists. I tried not to stare, only to find my eyes drifting toward the outline of his nipple ring, where his shirt pulled tight across his chest, idly thinking how I could flick it up and down with my tongue.

That would never do! Already I was convinced that other people in the place were staring, trying to figure out why my son didn't look more like me, wondering what sort of loose woman my wife might be. Tsk, tsk, so sad. But I could surely forget all their sympathy if they noticed my tongue wiggling while I thought obsessively about my presumed son's nipple piercing.

Blade finished eating. "Let's blow."

It was an indication of my edginess that at first I imagined he was proposing that we have sex right there, an idea I found more tantalizing than shocking. It was easy to fall into a daydream that had us kissing across the booth then tearing off bits of each other's clothing and making out right there on the table. Now I'd admitted it: I wanted to have sex with Blade, a young cub less than half my age.

Back in the car, to ease the tension—my tension, at least—I turned on the radio.

"Do you like jazz?"

"Don't really know, but I like Ryce."

I hate to admit that I actually giggled a bit. "Jazz isn't a food. It's a type of music, actually."

"I knew that. Ryce is a music group, actually."

Shit. It surprised me that Blade hadn't demanded that I stop the car so he could get out. But, sneaking a peek at his face, I saw that he was smiling a bit, all the while studiously looking out the window and pretending indifference.

This was even more confusing. I couldn't imagine how I might be making a favorable impression nor why it was so important to me. It wasn't just because I hadn't taken anyone home (hadn't had sex, in fact) for longer than I cared to admit. My biggest fear was coming true: I was beginning to care more about Blade than I had realized. In fact, I hadn't realized that I was even thinking relationship. Great! Even more to worry about.

I was so tense by then that I hadn't even noticed we'd arrived home. We must have been stopped in the driveway long enough for Blade to wonder what was wrong with me. His voice jerked me back into awesome reality.

"Let it go and chill some, man," he said. Then he opened the car door and got out, acting like nothing out of the ordinary was happening. Not that it was. Well, of course I felt that it was out of the ordinary, but I kept wishing that I could stop feeling that it was out of the ordinary.

I opened the door. We walked into the front hall, where Blade dropped his backpack, looked around, and said, "Nice place."

"Thanks. I've lived here since I moved to town about 16 years ago." Gosh, almost before he was born! Everything I said seemed to be a reminder of my age or his.

"Why don't you sit down," I said, gesturing toward the couch, "while I get us something to drink. What would you like?"

"Scotch."

That stopped me in my tracks. I would have been hard-pressed to think of something he might have said that could have surprised me more. It must have shown.

"Single malt, if you have it," he added.

From the kitchen I called out, "Why not put on some music?"

I thought he was joking when he called back, "Aren't you afraid that I'll steal your stuff?"

"No, should I be?"

"Most of the dudes I end up with are uptight closet cases who think I'm a punk thief. So they fuck me, give me 20 dollars, and get me gone as fast as they can."

I was finding this new information rather disturbing, so when I returned with our scotch, it took me a moment to realize what music he'd put on.

"Ella Fitzgerald?" So there. He'd done it: He'd made me smile. He reached for his scotch and raised his eyebrow at a spot on the couch next to him. I may be an uptight old fart, but I still know an invitation when I see one, so I sat next to him, reclining insouciantly into the corner.

"That's appalling. Why in the world should anyone think that? I'm no closet case, but if I'm a bit uptight, it's just because you're—"

"Because I'm a street-smart, no-good punk hustler."

I clamped my hand over his mouth and looked directly into his daring eyes.

"Because you're someone I could fall in love with very easily."

That got his attention. I was delighted to see his eyes open wide with surprise. I kept my hand over his mouth.

"Since we first looked at each other yesterday I've thought of nothing else but you, how I want to be with you, see you, feel you near me, know everything there is to know about you. Yes, I want to have sex with you too, but I can't think of anything I'd prefer right now to having you sitting here with me. What's gnawing at me inside, the hurdle I can't seem to get past in this idyllic picture, is the fact that I'm more than twice as old as you, and I don't know what to do about that."

Having said more than I probably should have, I let my hand drop from his mouth. He seemed to study me with some curiosity before he said, "I like older men."

"There's more to it than that. It can't be that easy."

He set his drink down. Without hesitation he reached over and began unbuttoning my shirt, which startled me and pleased me both. With my shirtfront open and the tails pulled out of my trousers, he ran his hand across my chest, spreading his fingers through the embarrassingly gray hair that grew there.

"Man, just let it go," he said. "Don't get hung up about our ages."

Blade slowly slid his hand around my ribs, embracing my belly, then laid his head against my chest. I put my arm around him, stroking his short, bristly hair before settling with my hand resting on the side of his neck. He closed his eyes. Soon his breathing slowed, and he slept.

What a day it had been. Barely 24 hours before, I had been the old Jack, shopping with my friend Paul. And now, having been a bundle of nerves all day, I was suddenly feeling like a new, transformed Jack. How in the world had I gotten from that old Jack to this new one, lounging on my couch with this adorable man lying asleep on my chest? I fell asleep myself, holding Blade in my arms, listening to him breathe.

I opened my eyes to find Blade opening my trousers. Already he had unbuttoned the waist, and now he was sliding the zipper gently down, intent on silence. He slid his hand through the fly in my boxer shorts. His hand lingered a moment, then he lifted my dick and balls through the opening in my shorts and lowered his head to meet them. Holding my balls loosely in his hand, he took my dick completely into his mouth and held it there. We both felt it getting stiffer.

Blade no doubt realized that I was awake. I lay there for several minutes, simply looking at the shape of his head resting on my hip, feeling my dick swell in his mouth. I moved my hand to feel him, the bristles of his hair, the shape of his ear. I felt his pulse when I rested my hand on his neck.

"You don't have to do this, Blade."

He slid his lips slowly up the shaft of my dick, kissing the tip as he let it fall from his mouth. He turned his head so that he could look at me, mesmerize me again with his eyes. "I know. I want to." He watched me until I blinked. His mouth took on the same hint of a smile that I smiled, and the matter was settled.

Blade pushed himself up onto his knees at the end of the couch and started tugging at the cuffs of my trousers. I raised my hips and slid trousers and shorts down to my knees. Rather quickly, if somewhat inelegantly, my clothes were lying on the floor, and Blade snuggled between my legs, wiggling his ass in the air, and wriggling his arms under my thighs, preparing to enjoy himself.

I might never understand the life that Blade had led so far, but right then I was quite willing to be grateful for at least some of his experiences. He licked my balls, moving in ever-widening circles to lick the insides of my thighs. That, combined with the sensation of his beard scratching against my skin, caused my skin to ripple.

It was unbearable ecstasy, relieved only when Blade finally pulled my dick into his mouth. By comparison, the way he moved his mouth up and down my dick was almost soothing. Almost. To be honest, I had no idea what sleight of hand, mouth, and tongue was producing the magic that I was enjoying, but it was compelling.

My dick was not pleased when I reached down and moved Blade's head away from it. "You have to stop, or I'll come."

"What's wrong with that?"

"Not yet. That's all. I want more than this."

He squatted again at the end of the couch so that I could stand. I felt remarkably at ease standing naked in front of Blade, my dick still hard, harder than it had ever been. I was unconcerned by his frank appraisal of my middle-aged body, able finally to accept his obvious desire.

I reached out for his hand. "Let's go upstairs."

Blade followed me to the stairs. We had nearly reached the top when I felt him stroke my ass, heard him say, almost in a whisper, "Stop. Please."

I halted, three steps from the landing. Blade began massaging my ass cheeks. His attention seemed focused on the patterns he could make in the fur covering my ass.

His stroking grew firmer. He pushed gently, suggesting with his hands that I rest my knees on the step, my arms on the landing. As he stroked, my ass cheeks pulled and relaxed. My asshole trembled at its exposure, certain of what came next. Still, I gasped to feel the warm, wet touch of Blade's tongue. His tongue, accompanied by the scratch of his beard, moved from my balls, across my asshole, and up my ass crack; persistent, slow strokes—over and over.

He paused in his licking and I relaxed a bit, again too near orgasm, only to feel his tongue press firmly against my asshole, trying to force it open. His tongue pulled back slightly, then pressed in again. I was too close, much too close. I had to stop now.

Reluctantly, I reached behind me and moved Blade's head back so that I could turn and sit on the step. I held his head in my hands, saw the longing in his face. "Almost."

We stumbled up the remaining steps and into the bedroom. I stood looking at him, finally up close, holding him by his shoulders, wanting him as much as he wanted me. I couldn't believe my good fortune, but felt immeasurably happy.

I dropped my hands slowly down his chest; my fingers traced the ridges in his T-shirt. When I reached his waist I began peeling the shirt up and away from his skin, watching tiny hairs spring back as I exposed his flesh inch by inch. Blade raised his arms, revealing thick patches of hair.

Next, I unbuttoned his jeans and they dropped to the floor. I dropped next, getting down on my knees to untangle his legs. As I helped him step out of his jeans the head of his dick poked through the fly in his boxer shorts. Our attention was not arrested for long. I yanked his shorts to the floor, admiring his dick as it sprang back up to his belly after such brusque treatment. It deserved better.

Grabbing Blade's ass with both hands, I pulled him toward me and buried my face in his crotch, compulsively licking his balls and his dick as though he were my first ever. This time Blade had to call a halt.

"Man, you really don't have to do that!"

I stopped and smiled at him. "I know, but I want to."

He grinned back at me. I stood, taking his hands in mine. I pulled him toward me and we fell, laughing, onto the bed. Our mouths met and we kissed, tongues dancing with passion. We kissed, and kissed more, one long kiss, endless kissing, until we had to stop, panting for breath.

Blade, lying on top of me, pulled his head away from mine. I saw the tattoo below his collarbone. This time I could make out that it was a small bear fetish. I stretched my neck up and licked it tenderly. Blade's head fell back down next to mine.

I turned my lips to his ear. "I want you to fuck me."

He didn't expect that. His body tensed and he jerked his head up to look at me, scrutinizing my face with those cool-blue, sapphire eyes. To be honest, it wasn't what I had expected either, but right then I wanted nothing more than to feel Blade's dick shoved up my asshole. He must have seen that too. His suspicions evaporated and he nodded his assent.

He sat back on my belly, legs straddling my body. I tore open a condom package and unrolled the thing down his dick. I squeezed on some lube and stroked his dick a couple of times.

Blade moved back between my legs, lifting them to his shoulders. I reached around and guided his dick to my asshole. He pushed, I grunted, and we both closed our eyes. Here, at last,

Blade demonstrated a lack of experience, but that didn't stop either of us from screaming with pleasure as his dick forced its way into me. What his fucking lacked in technique he more than made up for with vigor. Natural talent soon prevailed, and his fucking settled into its own rhythm.

I had been so close to shooting twice already that it didn't take long to bring me back to the edge. Blade's thrusts soon slowed, became jerky, and he started panting. I was about to grab my own dick to finish off when Blade arched his back, pressing his dick even deeper into me. I was transfixed by the near-death look of ecstasy on his face and the animal sounds that escaped his body, and shot my enormous load onto my belly without even touching myself. Blade's body jerked, I shot. He jerked, I shot some more.

Finally, we were both spent and he collapsed onto me, our sweat squeaking as our bodies heaved. I reached my arms around him, holding on tight, as tight as I could.

Blade's mouth was next to my ear. When his breathing had slowed some, he whispered to me: "Man, can I crash here tonight?"

I hugged him tighter still. "You don't have a place?"

"I'd rather stay here."

I'd deal with my mother later. Right then all that mattered was having Blade in my arms. "Yes, of course, please. Tonight. Tomorrow. The next night, the one after that..."

He covered my mouth with his hand, then lifted his head and looked at me. Eyes still sapphire-blue. "Man, you don't have to do that."

I returned his look. He pulled away his hand.

"I know, but I want to!"

We laughed, and laughed, and then laughed some more.

Four Times in Room 230

Daniel M. Jaffe

I glimpse you in the maze, rounding a corner, your hairy chest disappearing behind a black wall, your ponytail. A beard?

I hear you from around the corner, from behind the wall, your voice soft and firm, telling another man to turn around. I eavesdrop for moans.

Others walk by me, muscular men, lean men, who size me up in the shadows of Chicago's baths, who notice the hair coating my chest, my pudgy waist; they sashay quickly past.

I hear a sigh from around the corner. You or the other? I reach beneath my white towel, excitement growing at men's sounds. I think to steal a glance around the corner, but you might want privacy in this public space; some do; I don't wish to annoy because, even though another occupies your maze-lair now, later the chance could be mine.

Whether or not we actually meet, I decide, you will be the memory I leave with tonight, the grizzly wraith I'll conjure when, later at the hotel, I telephone my lover back in Boston, when I make him playfully envious of my night's harmless romp.

From behind your corner steps a man, tall and hairless and thin. Oh. Is that what you want—smooth and lanky? I haven't a chance.

Then you emerge, tall and thick, hair covering your full chest, your solid belly, brown hair tangling down somewhere behind the towel. And yes, a beard, yes.

You walk, notice me, stop. You stop still. Stock-still, two arm

lengths away. Your eyes, I see your eyes seeing mine and you stand
there still. Maybe? Maybe I should...? Or maybe you'll slap my
hand away, mock with a laugh?

Hell, I'll take the chance.

I step forward, reach out, graze the back of my knuckles
against your chest, and...you move toward me. I splay out my
hands, fill each with hairy flesh, your nipples hard against my
palms, your hair entwining my fingers, and you reach out to me,
stroke my upper arms, reach around me, pull me close, bend your
head down to nuzzle the hair swirling on my left shoulder.

Your Fuller Brush beard against my shoulder, my left, then my
right. "Turn around," you whisper, and I, usually resistant to command, obey without question. You reach your arms, your hands
around me; my nipples between your thick fingertips. Ahh.
Gentle nuzzling, beard against back of neck, tongue in my right
ear, my left, and someone else, some unknown hand reaches out in
the darkness to grab at my hard-on meant for you, he squeezes—
did you know? Your arms around me, your thick arms, your arms
pulling me close, you pressing against me, all of you against me,
around me. A whispered invitation to your room.

I disengage from the anonymous groping hand to follow you,
watching as you lumber just a bit side to side and stomp, your feet
thumping against the indoor-outdoor carpeting, your calf muscles
flexing, your butt now tightening, now releasing beneath the
white towel, fine damp hair filming your back, light brown hair to
match the ponytail half matted with sweat.

A cold, late December night, but Room 230 is warm.

Inside, towels off, I reach up to embrace you. You look down
at me. Your thick mustache against mine, your wet lips covered in
soft bristle, your tongue reaching to soothe.

You want to know—do I like massage? Is oil OK?

For you, this Yogi Bear with blue eyes and gentle touch, I lie
face down, my eyes blinded by pillow. So unlike me, usually wary
and guarded and closed, to lie on my belly for a stranger, to lie vulnerable, unable to see an approach from behind.

You kneel over me, straddle me, your heavy cock and balls brush my ass, I hear the rub of your hands together warming the oil. You begin with my shoulders. Ahh. Gentle and firm, strong, deep, ahh. Shoulders and back and butt, your fingertips along my butt, gently inside and—oh oh oh, tongue replacing fingers, beard against my ass, tongue deep, oh oh oh—then your hands on my thighs, on calves, on feet. You lift my feet one at a time, take charge of my feet as if to assure yourself I won't run away, you fill your mouth with my feet, toe by toe, your tongue in between, your beard, the bristles.

Violin tremors. Chocolate ice cream chills.

Your mouth between my toes then up my calves, your tongue, again my butt—oh, God—and up, your tongue along my spine, your beard, you take my arms between your hands, my thin, hairy arms between your thick fingers and you...do something...some rubbing or squeezing or kneading, I can't even tell, but my fingertips feel ready to ejaculate blood.

"Are you relaxed?"

I moan.

You roll me onto my side then. I open my eyes to see you lie down facing me on the narrow cot. I want to feel all of you, your body, I nuzzle your eyes and your beard and taste your massage-oil lips, your tongue with the flavor of my butt, and I clutch your face, probe my tongue deep into your mouth so deep it drags out half my chest, I fill you with me and you squeak, a little river-otter squeak of delight, your blue eyes squeezed shut at the force of my tongue against yours, my hands filled with your beard, me shifting us both so I lie on top of you, rubbing hairy chest against chest, kissing you, not pulling away, not letting you pull away, breathing your breath, filling your lungs with mine, your arms around me, your hands grabbing my ass, our cocks against each other and you, you whimpering sweet surrender and trumpeting conquest: "Fuck me."

A moment of preparation—me kneeling, sliding it on, lifting your heavy legs to my shoulders—slipping in. I tell myself I should focus on the tingles, the sensations of your hands on my chest, my cock inside you, but it's your face that fills my mind, your beautiful face, your hair, your beard, your chest, your eyes again squeezing shut, your head snapping right and left, your moans, your groans loud now from the gut, your growls, you not caring who in other rooms, in the hall, on upper floors might hear your howls and roars, and we are two bears rutting a winter summons and challenge to spring.

Your sounds wane to whispers, I slow, your eyes open and you tell me I'm the most this in the world, the best that, and again I gently pound my belly against the backs of your thighs, filling you as deeply as I can, slowly now. I thrust. Your eyes shut. Again the moans. And again the roars, and you gasp, motion me to stop. You've come twice, without even touching yourself.

Your thighs down, I lie on top of you, satisfied that you're satisfied; you look away and say the most romantic phrase I've ever heard: that if you stare into my eyes, you will come yet again.

We shift so I'm on my back, you're on your side, your head resting on my chest, your hand playing with my gray hairs among the brown, and I hear that same joy-whimper as before; I hug you closer.

"I'd fall asleep on your chest," you say, "but I'd lose my heart." This is a statement, but also perhaps a question, a tentative request for permission.

I so want you to fall asleep against my chest, to lose your heart to me, but I've no right, holding, as I do, the heart of another, back home, who holds my own. What is this need to forage and hunt when the larder is full?

So we talk. You of your home in Seattle, me of home in Boston, his home and mine. You whimper again, perhaps in residual joy, perhaps in regret. I'm sorry and I'm glad.

You're a cellist, you explain, come here to Chicago to audition for the symphony the day after next; I'm here for a conference of literature professors, will leave town tomorrow. A chance encounter. You say: if your relationship ever ends, not that I hope it will, but if...

Sweet sweet sweet.

What is this capacity to share so with a stranger, to feel tenderness toward a furry wanderer amid shadows? To meet and within minutes to trust, to place ourselves in each others' hands, to trust our bodies, our eyes, to trust the perimeters of our hearts?

We kiss again, you make me hard. You caress my balls as we kiss and I suck in your tongue, vacuum your mouth while your finger enters my ass, index finger or thumb or both or more. Inside me, I feel you inside me. I pump my cock with my hand, and instead of the usual quick surge to Everest, I rise slowly to foothills, then higher amid brambles, your fingers inside me, your hand, maybe your arm, your shoulder, your head climbing in while I rise to a ledge, hear moans, my moans, feel your ponytail tease the tip of my cock, and my back arches for you to crawl up inside me, pound me, fill me up and up and up until peak after peak after peak.

I'm in a swirl of darkness, feel only the heaving of my chest, then you pull out your hand, I hear you stroke, you come onto me.

I gasp, breathe deep, sit up, sit up straight, try to clear my head. I stare into your blinking eyes, pull your head down to my lap, the back of your head on my lap, your face looking up at mine, your lips, I graze your bearded lips, our eyes lock, you whisper "I see your heart behind your eyes," you reach down to yourself and...a fourth time.

You are amazed at your fourth time. I am amazed at your fourth time. To come four times, you are not bear but lion. To be able to inspire such vigor, I feel myself lion as well.

More whispers and caresses, nipple tweaks and hugs, sincere declarations of how special and what a fantasy. Completely sincere. Sighs. Exchange of addresses on matchbooks.

A final kiss. Final for now, we say, knowing it's likely final for always.

I leave Room 230, shower and dress, bundle up, leave the bathhouse, take a taxi through the windy cold to my hotel.

I could have invited you to the hotel with me, could have

tempted you to count beyond four, could have tried for a record of my own. But if I had, if I had made you risk losing your heart, if I had risked losing my own, if I had lost it, how could I then telephone my lover, as I'm now about to do, and make him smile at an honest, lusty tale?

Overland Jim
TREVOR J. CALLAHAN JR.

May 24, 1847—somewhere in Kansas

Today I became a man.

To be more precise, today is my 18th birthday. Eighteen years ago today I was born into this world, a helpless babe struggling in Mama's arms. Now I am a man.

Yet I do not feel like a man. I still feel like the same boy that I was when we left Massachusetts two months ago. I suppose the long journey has already hardened me some. I have noticed I am no longer all "skin and bones," as the boys back home used to tease me. All the walking and lifting and labor has made me stronger. I've grown too, almost a full inch. My blond hair is longer and fuller, though I've yet to experience the first down of hair on my face. But Papa always told me that when I turned 18 I would be a man, and since today is that day, it must be so.

Papa did not wish me a happy birthday today. Little Susan did, the first time I think my sister has ever said anything kind to me, as did Mama, who gave me some extra stew when Papa was not looking. She also gave me this little journal, so that I should be able to write down my experiences and impressions of this journey, so that I will always be able to recollect it. I am unsure as to why I'd wish to remember this journey; it has been long and hard, and many are the nights I wish we had never left Massachusetts for California. I remember only two months ago we were all so excited at the prospect of the frontier, of finding our fortunes out West. The overland journey had seemed long then, the Oregon

Trail so rugged and mysterious, but I never imagined the toll it would take. Already we've lost two horses, and we've yet to reach the mountains. And we are the lucky ones. Many families have lost children; many wives lost their husbands to diphtheria or influenza. I am glad that so far we have all survived.

June 1, 1847—leaving Kansas

As we approach the mountains, Papa has been searching for a hand for hire to aid in the crossing. A minister and his wife, who supped with us yesterday, recommended a man named Overland Jim. They said that he has made the crossing a dozen times and each time arrived safely on the other side. I have been so tired lately, with all the extra chores, and the work has made Papa more stern and cross than I have ever seen him, so I hope we find this Overland Jim when we get to Colorado.

June 11, 1847—Pike, Colorado

In all my 18 years I have never seen a man as large as Overland Jim. He's a veritable Hercules! He's a head taller than Papa, which must make him six feet and a half. He has legs like wagon wheels, arms like tree limbs, and a chest like a giant barrel full of spiced wine. His clothes are stretched taut over his whole body, he's so big! He has a full head of wild, dark hair and a thick, full beard. His forearms are likewise covered in dark fleece. I wonder if the rest of him is as well? I think that is a sight I would like to see.

Today, as Overland Jim and I loaded supplies into the wagon, I was amazed at how much he could carry. I struggle to lift more than one sack of flour; he carried four with ease! I watched as his muscles bulged with each load, his back getting sweatier in the afternoon sun. Overland Jim caught me staring at him, and I mumbled an apology, but he only gave me a broad smile and clapped me manfully on my back. "Don't worry there, Matthew," he said. "I reckon you've just never seen a real live mountain man before."

"No, sir," I replied truthfully.

Overland Jim laughed—a long, loud peal. "Well, son," he said,

"I reckon you'll see more before this trip is through!" And before leaving, he smiled at me again and did something I thought very odd. He patted me on my arse, three short slaps, and then a quick squeeze. I have never seen anyone do this before! Perhaps it is some queer local custom, something the mountain men do to express their respect for one another. I shall have to remember to do it back to Overland Jim the next time he pats me there.

June 13, 1847—somewhere in Colorado

Today we reached the base of the mountains. From here on out, our journey becomes much more difficult.

Still, I have faith that Overland Jim will get us across these hills. Things have seemed so much better since he arrived. He and I often talk, and yesterday, when he patted me on my arse again, I patted him back. I said I hoped it was the right thing to do, and Overland Jim smiled and assured me it was indeed.

Last night I had the strangest dream about him. Overland Jim and I were struggling to climb a massive oak tree together. The sun was beating down on us and we were quite sweaty, but in a mad frenzy we strained towards the top of the tree, grunting in exertion all the way. When we reached the top, Overland Jim held me so I would not fall. I looked down, expecting to be dizzy, but I was not. It was rather quite exhilarating. The base of the tree was wrapped in thick thistle bushes, and I remember two large rocks to one side. I was afraid I would fall into the rocks, but Overland Jim held me fast in his arms, and I was safe the whole time.

When I awoke, I was panting and sweaty, as if still climbing the tree in my dream. When I caught my breath, I noticed a peculiar wetness in my drawers. It seemed as if I had wet myself, but the smell was not that of piss. Still, I stole off, rather embarrassed, and cleaned myself before morning.

June 15, 1847—somewhere in Colorado

Today a marvelous thing happened. We stopped for two days near a large, clear lake. Papa scouted on ahead, though Overland

Jim told him it wasn't necessary. The rest of us bathed quickly and made preparations for Papa's return.

Overland Jim, though, had not returned from the lake, so Mama sent me to fetch him. I rounded a corner, looking for the mountain man, when a wondrous sight befell my eyes. There was Overland Jim, stretched out between two large boulders, naked as the day he was born! His entire body was covered with fleecy dark hair, and he seemed to be drying himself after his bath. But what was even more amazing than Overland Jim's naked form was what he held in his hands! I could not tell what it was at first. It seemed almost a foot long, large and rather monstrous, like one of those python snakes I once studied at school. But it was attached to Overland Jim, and he held it firmly in his fist, moving his big paw up and down over it. I heard Overland Jim moaning too, as if in great pleasure. Suddenly I realized that this was his organ, large and engorged, and that Overland Jim was gratifying himself! I had never seen such a thing in my life! Stunned, I could only stare as the mountain man moved his fist in a blur over his large organ. Overland Jim's cries caught the wind, ringing in my ears as great repeated shouts of "Oh! Oh! Oh!" as his hand continued its motion. Suddenly he stopped, and while he let out a loud, guttural sound, I watched as Overland Jim's organ shot forth massive amounts of a creamy white liquid. The liquid coated Overland Jim's hairy chest and belly, and by the time his organ finished spurting forth, a large amount of it covered the man. Panting now, Overland Jim lay where he was, seeming to enjoy some more what he had just done.

I wanted to avert my eyes from this scene, but I could not. I knew such things were sinful, but as I turned to go, I realized with a start that my own organ had grown rather stiff as well! This had happened before, and I had always willed it away, but this time it seemed not to work. I could not go back to Mama and Susan like this! And I found myself with an overwhelming urge to touch it. Finally, I slid my hand into my breeches and eased my organ out. I thought perhaps the cold of the air would make it small again, but the cool breeze on my warm flesh felt like heaven. I squeezed it, trying to bring it back down, once, twice—and then jumped with a start when I saw my own flesh spurting forth the same seed that had come out of Overland Jim's organ! I watched helpless as three streams shot out of my organ and onto the ground in front of me. The rest of the seed spilled all over my hand. Curious, I smelled it. It smelled like my breeches did after one of my dreams! Even more curious, I brought the liquid closer to my face. Sticking out my tongue, I tasted it. It did not taste bad: agreeably warm, salty, and slimy, but somehow, I liked it. I licked my hand clean and then washed it in the lake again for good measure.

I felt for sure when I returned to camp Overland Jim would be there. He was not, and I told Mama I could not find him. He appeared only moments after me, explaining that he had been tracking game. He gave me an odd smile, though, and I shuddered to think that perhaps he knows I watched him spill his seed.

June 18, 1847—somewhere in Colorado

Today one of the wagon wheels cracked, and we lost a whole day replacing it. I had been driving. At first I considered this responsibility a relief; I had been mostly walking since we got to Missouri and we had to pick up extra supplies, and the chance to lead the team seemed a dream come true. But I found I could not take my eyes off of Overland Jim's rugged form, and I did not see the large hole in the road.

Papa was furious. Ever since we started this journey he has been angrier than normal, but this time I had gone too far. "You stupid bastard!" he yelled at me time and again as he struck my face repeatedly. I reckon I deserved it for what I did. I didn't cry, though, didn't even flinch. I just stood and took my punishment like a man.

I noticed when Papa was striking me that Overland Jim got the most curious look on his face. His entire countenance clouded over, and for a minute he looked sore struck with rage. I was afraid he was mad at me too, but later on, he patted me on the arse and told me I was a good boy. I was too sore and I forgot to pat him back, but I did smile at him, and somehow, it all made me feel better.

June 19, 1847—somewhere in Colorado

Papa was not nearly as angry today as he has been this journey. He only struck me once and did not hit Mama or Susan at all.

Papa was always choleric, even back in Massachusetts. We never really struggled there, but Papa was always scrabbling for money, and this journey has been even harder than he anticipated. I guess he has reason to be angry. I pray that when we arrive in California life will be good and Papa will be happy with all of us.

I had another dream last night about Overland Jim. He was lying on his back again, asleep near the water's edge, naked as a newborn babe. Only his organ was bigger than I had ever imagined, bigger than even in real life! In my dream I crept silently over to him, like an Indian in the brush, until I was close enough to touch him. I reached for his organ and squeezed it, hard, many times, until finally his seed burst forth again. I saw the milky whiteness shoot out of his organ and spray all over my face, warm streams of liquid coating my skin. Several of them landed in my mouth, and I swallowed them, though when I awoke, I could not remember how they tasted.

I did wake to find that I had soiled myself again. I went to the river's edge and cleansed myself, but found that my own organ was firm as iron. I grabbed it, just like I had Overland Jim's in my dream, but it only took a few short strokes before my own seed spilled into my hand. Without pause I swallowed it all down, enjoying the warmth of this new treat. Then I cleansed up and went back to the camp. Daylight had been breaking, and Papa struck me once for skulking off before first light. "It is too dangerous near the water!" he shouted. "There are many wild animals about!" Overland Jim spoke up for me. "The boy will be fine," he said, but Papa disagreed. I hurried away to complete my chores, but Overland Jim and Papa did not speak the rest of the day.

June 21, 1847—somewhere in Colorado

Today I truly am a man.

Last night I beheld wonders. My dreams all came true, and more—all thanks to Overland Jim.

It was near midnight when I awoke to the sound of crashing in the brush near the camp. Overland Jim was gone. I am not sure what compelled me to follow him—perhaps some portent of my own dreams. But follow him I did, watching as he walked into the wood, stopping by a mossy knoll underneath a large oak tree.

I crept to his side, keeping an eye on him at all times. I was sure he did not know I was there. I watched as he removed his organ from his breeches. He held it in his hands, but he did not squeeze or caress it. Soon, I saw a steady stream of his piss flow out. More and more it flowed, and I was in awe at a man whose bladder can hold so much water! I must have gasped, for Overland Jim turned and saw me. He grinned at me. "Did ya come out to take a piss too, Matthew?" he said to me. I stood and nodded. "Well, get over here, boy, and join me." I walked over to Overland Jim. By now, the liquid had stopped flowing from his organ, but still he held it in his hands. "Take it out, boy, let's see what you've got." I pulled apart my breeches and took out my organ. To my embarrassment, it was as rigid as a tree limb. Overland Jim looked down on it and laughed. "Well, that's gonna make it hard to piss now, ain't it?" I strained, trying to will the liquid out of me, but nothing came. "There, there, boy," Overland Jim said, taking two steps, one back and one to the side, so that he was behind me. "Do not hurt yourself." He reached his massive arms around my waist. With one paw he removed my hand from my organ; with the other, he grabbed onto it himself. I could feel his oversized organ growing against my backside. "Just let it flow," he whispered. He reached up and licked his fingers, moistening them. He placed the fingers on the tip of my organ, tickling me. His other hand reached under my boy's sack and massaged me down there. His own organ was now rigid against my back. I wiggled in his grasp, but secretly, I was in awe and ecstasy. "There it goes," he whispered in my ear as my organ released a small amount of yellow liquid. Overland Jim held me tightly while I continued pissing. When I was done, he shook my organ a few times, but did not let it go. Instead, he continued squeezing it in his hands. "How's that feel, boy?" he asked. "Very good, sir," I replied, the first words I had spoken since following him into the woods. One hand he placed firmly on my chest, the other still caressing my tingling, rigid organ. Within seconds, I was moaning and writhing in his grasp, and then, almost against my will, I spilled my seed all over his hand and the cold forest floor.

"There," Overland Jim said when I was done, "that wasn't so bad, was it?" His beard tickled my ear, his lips were so close to my skin. "No, sir," I said again. "Now," he said, still whispering, "how would you like to help Overland Jim do the same thing?" I nodded my head. "I would like that very much, sir," I replied.

Overland Jim whirled me around in his arms, holding me close to him. "Good boy," he said. "I'm gonna show you some things tonight, Matthew, gonna make you a man." I only nodded, my eyes glued to the massive organ pushing straight up against Overland Jim's belly. "What do you want me to do?" I finally asked faintly, a part of me very scared indeed, but a larger part of me remaining very, very excited.

"First, let's take off these clothes," Overland Jim suggested. I slid out of my nightshirt, Overland Jim's rough, callused hands massaging the smooth flesh of my chest. "So smooth, such a beautiful boy," he whispered. I bent to remove my boots, but Overland Jim negated this. "There are sharp rocks on this land. Better leave them on." I did, removing my breeches and underclothes without taking off my boots.

I stood naked in the woods in only my boots, the cold wind slapping me gently on my bare arse, with Overland Jim's large hands roaming all over my body, touching my shoulders, my flat stomach, roaming over my backside seemingly 100 times. I lost myself in his touch, as if I now only existed in the part he was paying special favor toward, as if I became my shoulders or chest, where he pinched my pink nipples savagely, or my arse, or even my boyish, tight sack, puckered close against me in the cool night air. Then he wrapped his massive arms around me, holding me closer to him than ever before. "Yes indeed, boy," he said to me, "you are perfect in every way."

It was his turn to disrobe now, and he took off his nightshirt. So close to his hairy chest, I reached my arms out to touch it. Encouraged by this, Overland Jim pulled me towards him again, my hands roving freely all over his large chest and belly. The hair was both soft and harsh, tickly to my touch, and I reveled in it. "Do you like me touching you?" I asked Overland Jim. He smiled at me. "Very much indeed" was his reply.

His massive organ, straining and firm, still jutted from his pants, and now we took those off. Overland Jim wore no under-clothes, so we stood, the two of us clad in our tough leather boots, naked, man to boy, in the vast dark wilderness. I touched every inch of Overland Jim's body, just as he had done to me, hoping he derived as much pleasure from it as I had. I ran my hands through his thick mane of dark hair, and through his equally thick black beard, then over his broad shoulders, straining to reach his height, and then again with the chest, resting my head against it for sev-eral minutes, listening to the strong beating of his heart, and then his belly, and his thick strong legs, and finally, on my knees in front of him, I clutched with two hands his massive man sack. Unlike my tight boy's balls, Overland Jim's were large and warm, covered with dark hair. Moving in closer, I inhaled deeply, smelling them. Their scent was not unpleasant, but sweaty and musky, an appro-priately manly smell. Holding his sack, I looked up at this moun-tain man; our eyes locked, and giving me the smallest of nods, he encouraged me to continue my exploration.

I reached out with two hands and wrapped my fists around his massive organ. Overland Jim groaned as I touched it; clearly, he derived as much pleasure from me touching him as I did when he touched me. I squeezed it once, then twice, several times in fact, and finally began to caress it as he had only minutes ago shown me. Overland Jim threw his head back, moaning much louder now, and encouraged by these sounds, I increased the speed of my movements. "Oh, Matthew, boy, that's fine work," he said to me. "Thank you, sir," I replied, intent on my desire to please him. I caressed his organ even faster. "You know, my boy," he said between grunts, "there's another way of doing this."

"There is?" I said surprised, letting his organ go.

Overland Jim grinned at me. "You can also caress me with your mouth," he said.

I was puzzled, yet intrigued. "How do I do that, sir?"

Overland Jim's smile grew even wider. "Would you like to try it then, boy?" he asked. I nodded. "OK, do what I tell you, and it'll be fine. You need to get a taste for it first. Just move on in and give the head of my meat a little lick. Yeah, just like that. Do it again, do it a few more times. Do you like that, Matthew? Does that taste good, boy?"

I nodded eagerly. "Oh, yes, sir," I replied truthfully. It tasted wonderful, tasting just as I imagined it would, musky and sweaty and manly, just like his smell.

"Good," Overland Jim continued. "Now lick it up some more, up and down this time, up and down this part, yeah, that's the shaft, lick it like a piece of candy—oh, that's good there, yeah, that's real nice, yeah. See that? See that drop of white? Lick that off. Go ahead. Yeah. Tastes good, doesn't it? I thought you'd like it. Keep licking the shaft. Good, good boy. Now go lower, down to my sack, yes, that's it, lick it good, open your mouth really wide, and suck some of that sack in, yeah just like that—oh! Not so hard now, yeah, like that, mmm, that feels very nice, Matthew, very nice indeed, you're making Overland Jim feel very good. Keep licking it, yeah, now come back to the shaft, lick a little more—yes, there's more white stuff, go ahead, taste it. Now, don't be afraid, all I want you to do now is put the head of my organ into your mouth. Just like that. Yeah, that's a good boy, does that taste good too, Matthew?"

I nodded up and down, that thick head filling my entire

mouth. Never had I experienced such ecstasy before, such won-drous amazement! Overland Jim was delicious, every inch of him better than the last, and this was certainly the best of all.

"Good, now lower yourself just a bit, swallow a little more of my meat, yeah, that's a good boy. We call this sucking the meat. Yeah, that's right, suck on it like a candy stick, boy, good, oh yeah, you're doing a very good job, Matthew, like you've been waiting to do this all your life, such a good boy. Now a little more—careful, not too much, there's a lot of meat down there. Now slowly go back, raise your head off the shaft, good, now back down, there you go, you got the hang of it now, oh, boy, do you ever, yes, Matthew, that feels really good, very good indeed. Now reach up with both your hands, both of them, squeeze my sack, a little harder than that, yes, that's it, oh yeah, yesss, good, now tug on them, harder, keep sucking me boy, oh yeah, keep sucking my meat, that's it, that's a good job, oh Matthew, you're making me feel so good boy, oh, you don't even know how good that feels, God, Matthew, I—I'm going to spill my load, Matthew, I'm going to spill, Matthew, I'm warning you boy, it's going to come out any second now, I—oh! Oh! Matthew!"

I wanted to taste Overland Jim so bad that I swallowed every last drop of his seed, guzzling it down my throat the second it shot from his organ. There was a mess of it, much more than had ever come out of my organ, and Overland Jim's seed tasted different than mine, but better somehow, more mature, and I sucked and sucked on his meat, just like he taught me, until I tasted no more seed shooting out of him. "There, there, boy," Overland Jim said, pulling me off of his organ. "Let it rest a second now." He dropped to his own knees in front of me, wrapping his arms around me again, one hand resting on my arse, the other on the back of my head, placing it on his brawny shoulder.

"I was very surprised you swallowed all that seed," he said to me. "Had you been planning on that all along?"

I nodded my head against his hairy chest. "Ever since that day I saw you spill your seed by the lake."

Overland Jim smiled. "You little rascal," he said to me. "I thought you were watching."

I cringed. "Are you mad at me, sir?" I asked in a quiet voice.

Overland Jim took my face in his strong, strong hands and peered deeply into my eyes. "Listen to me, boy," he said in a serious voice. "I could never be mad at you, understand? You are a good boy, a very fine boy. What you and I just did, I wouldn't do with just any boy, understand? I only do that with special lads, lads like yourself. Do you understand me?"

I nodded.

"Good," he said.

And then he did something I never expected.

He kissed me.

I had seen other people kiss before, Mama and Papa, or my grandparents. But never had I seen or felt a kiss infused with such emotion as the kiss I received at that moment kneeling in the woods from Overland Jim. His lips met mine, his beard tickling my face and chin, and for a moment, everything was soft and warm and gentle, but then passion overcame Overland Jim, and his lips parted mine, his tongue pushing its way into my mouth. I had heard of this—this was how the French kissed—but had never known of anyone who did it. But I liked it, I liked his warm, wet tongue in my mouth, so much like his organ had been moments before, and when he took his tongue back, I pushed mine into his. Overland Jim seemed to like this, and locking his arms around me, we kissed like this for many minutes.

My own hard organ, though, was pushing right into Overland Jim's belly. I loved how that felt, his hairy belly scratching the head of my sensitive shaft, but Overland Jim finally pushed us apart. "You want me to show you what it's like when another man has your meat in his mouth?" he asked me. I nodded, dumbfounded, and with a smile, Overland Jim bent double and swallowed my entire organ whole.

I gasped with a pleasure and an ecstasy I had never felt before! My organ felt warm and wet in Overland Jim's mouth, tingling with sensations far greater than anything I could have ever achieved on my own! Instinctively I leaned back, and Overland Jim swallowed even more of my meat, one of his brawny hands savagely squeezing my boyish sack. I watched as his thick black hair bobbed up and down in my lap. Finally, I couldn't take it any longer. "Oh, sir!" I shouted as I felt my seed spill forth from my organ and into Overland Jim's mouth.

When he was done milking my shaft, Overland Jim stood, pulling me up with him. "Normally," he said, "I don't swallow another man's seed. But since you were brave enough to take all mine, I figured it was the least I could do."

"Thank you, sir," I said, and impulsively, I hugged his naked form close to me.

Overland Jim sighed happily as he wrapped his large arms around me yet again. "Maybe we should get some sleep, boy," he said. I moved to break towards camp, but Overland Jim restrained me. "Why don't we sleep right here, on the moss. It's soft enough, and this way, I don't have to let you go right away." That sounded like heaven to me, so I agreed, and soon I was fast asleep in Overland Jim's strong, safe arms.

I awoke an hour later to something stout sticking me in the backside.

Overland Jim's arms were still wrapped around me, one hand combing my blond hair, the other wrapped gently around my face. It was his engorged meat I felt poking me in the rear. "There's something else I want to show you, boy," he whispered in my ear. "If you're up for it."

If my straining organ meant anything, I certainly was.

"Good," Overland Jim continued. "I want to try fucking you. Do you know what that is?"

I shook my head no.

In response, Overland Jim took his index finger, slid it into his mouth, and, with a small sucking sound, wet it. Then he took the finger and placed it between my legs. "Fucking," he said, "is this," and with one swift, sure motion, his thick finger found my hole and pushed in. "Uhhh," I moaned, surprised at the intense feeling, the small prick of pain and the faint tingling of pleasure inside of me. "Except, of course, I would put my meat in there."

I eyed his large organ warily. "You want to put that in me?" I asked, incredulous.

Overland Jim nodded. His finger was still up my arse, and he moved it around a bit. Now that I had adjusted to its presence, it felt very good up there, full and satisfying. "I do, Matthew," he said, "very much so. I want to show you how two men love each other. Do you want me to show you that? Do you want me to show you how I love you?"

I felt tears suddenly blink my eyes, and, as the ecstasy in my arse grew, I knew what I wanted. "Yes, sir," I whispered.

"Yes what, boy?"

I sighed softly. "I want you to show me how you love me, sir."

Overland Jim smiled at me, holding me closely to him. "Then I will, boy." He kept his finger up my arse while sliding onto his back. "I want you to get me real wet, boy, suck my meat like you did before, only get it real wet, yeah, good, oh that's good, spit on it, yeah, lots of spit, we need to get it really slick for your arse." I licked and spit all up and down his shaft, making sure it was really wet for when it was to pierce my hole.

"Turn around," Overland Jim said, "no, not that way, yeah, with your backside in my face. Good. I'll need to loosen ya up a bit." As I continued to suck Overland Jim's organ, I felt his finger slide out of me, felt two of his fingers pry my arse cheeks apart, and felt something warm and wet slide into my hole.

"Oh, sir," I said, dropping Overland Jim's organ as I gasped in utter amazement. I could tell from the scratching and tickling of his beard that he had put his tongue up my arse. "Oh, sir, that...that's amazing," I stammered.

After several minutes of this, Overland Jim alternating licking and spitting in my arse with sticking one or two or three of his fingers up there, I remembered his hard organ, and I started licking it again, getting him real slick for when he was to penetrate me.

We continued this for several more minutes, our grunts and moans and gasps filling the chilled night air until, finally, Overland Jim slid his two fingers out of my arse, smacked my backside hard one time, and told me to turn around once again.

He placed me on my back and loomed over me. I must confess, I was sorely afraid when he placed my ankles, still clad in my leather boots, onto his shoulders. But Overland Jim looked deep into my eyes. "Don't be afraid, boy," he told me. "Remember, this is how men love each other."

I nodded. "Yes, sir."

Overland Jim placed the head of his monstrous organ against my hole. "I won't lie," he said. "This is going to hurt at first. But just relax, and stick with me. It'll begin to feel real good real soon. I promise." I nodded, and inching forward slightly, Overland Jim placed the head of his organ into my arsehole.

I gasped when I felt that monstrous piece of meat tearing me apart! It was as if I was being impaled! I tensed and wriggled underneath Overland Jim's immense weight. "Relax, relax, boy," he soothed me, stroking my hair with his hand, bracing himself against the mossy forest floor, and peering intently into my eyes. I calmed slowly, and eventually the pain subsided, a feeling of fullness overtaking my arse.

This continued for what felt like hours, the thrusting of his organ into me, his gentle calming, the feeling of fullness now supplemented by warmth and satisfaction. Finally, when I thought I could not take another inch of him, I felt his large man sack brush against my legs. "You did it, you did it, boy!" he said excitedly. "You took it all in! Good boy! Good job, Matthew!" I grinned at him. "Thank you, sir!" I said, excited too.

Overland Jim held me in this position for 10 minutes, never growing soft, letting my arse adjust to his girth. Then, slowly, he pushed in and out. "Ugh!" I cried, a sound of pleasure, not pain. Again. "Ugh! Ugh! Ugh!" He thrust his organ into me harder and faster. "Oh Matthew, this is how men love, boy, this is how men love!" he panted to me. "Yes, sir!" I shouted, wanting for some reason to yell as loud as I possibly could into the empty night air.

"God, boy, this feels...amazing. Your arse is so tight, so unbelievably tight. You look so beautiful beneath me. Oh yes, this is how men love, I'm sure of that," Overland Jim said as his thrusting continued to grow deeper and harder. My own organ sputtered to life and soon became rock-hard as Overland Jim thrust his meat into me again and again.

Suddenly I felt an amazing sensation and realized, almost too late, that I was about to spill my seed. "Oh, oh, ohhh!" I moaned as another load of white liquid sputtered forth from my shaft, catching Overland Jim square on his hairy chest before dribbling back down onto my smooth body. "Oh yes, boy!" he yelled. I felt my arse contract and expand against his meat as I spilled my seed, and soon Overland Jim was shouting, "Me too, boy, me too, I'm gonna spill my seed up your arse!" With one last loud "Ugh!" Overland Jim spurted his load deep inside me. I could feel his organ pulsing in my arse, could feel it getting wetter and slicker as he pumped his seed inside me. "Oh yes, that's it, boy, that's it, Matthew, yes!" Overland Jim moaned as the last drops of his spill flowed from the head of his mighty organ.

Finally, both of us panting and sweaty, he pulled out of me, a delicious feeling, one that left my arse hot and wet. Overland Jim kissed me once again, and once more wrapped me up in his arms. "Did you like that, boy?" he asked me. "Oh, yes sir!" I replied eagerly. "Can we do that again?"

Overland Jim laughed. "Not today, for sure, but tonight, and tomorrow night, and every night if you like. There's lots more I can show you too. But come along now. We'd best get cleaned up and back to camp. It's almost daybreak."

When we returned to camp, it was impossible to act as if nothing had happened. This is why I had to write it all down as I did. And while I hope this little journal keeps my secret, today, to me, is clearly the day I became a man.

June 23, 1874—approaching Wyoming

This is my week for the most extraordinary events.

Besides what has been happening between me and Overland Jim, another extraordinary event occurred between me and Papa.

It started on our afternoon ride. The shadows were falling, and a recent windstorm had blown lots of brush across the trail. Consequently, I did not see the hole in the road before it was too late.

Fortunately, no damage was done, but Papa was very angry. "You stupid fool!" he shouted, striking me across the face. Normally, when Papa hits me, I feel all afraid and timid. Today, though, I felt angry, and did something I never thought I would do. Standing up to my full height, as soon as he struck me I struck him back, square across the jaw.

Papa was so amazed that all the anger left him. Mama looked terrified, but he left me alone without another word. For a moment, I thought I had done something terribly wrong. One is supposed to honor one's father and mother. But when I saw Overland Jim smile at me, I knew I had done the right thing.

June 26, 1847—entering Wyoming

Clearly, this is the best time of my life.

Papa has not touched me since our confrontation the other day. I think perhaps he is afraid of me. How strange for me to have feared him all these years! Last night I told Overland Jim that I think Papa truly is a coward. Overland Jim agreed, and then he kissed me, and told me I was his beautiful boy forever.

Last night he also showed me something new. He had me lie on my side, and he entered me from behind, hoisting my boot-clad leg into the air. I liked this; it felt rougher than when I lie on my back. Yet without a doubt, my favorite is when he lies on his back and I ride him, like a cowboy rides a bull. Why, Overland Jim is built like a bull, thick and dark and fleecy, and I like the idea of being a cowboy. I think Overland Jim likes this best too; his shouts are loudest when he spills his seed up my arse in this position.

July 4, 1847—approaching Idaho

I have a secret to share.

Last night, after we fucked, when Overland Jim was holding me in his arms, he said to me, "I've shown you how men love, boy. Now you've got to tell me—do you love me?"

I had been waiting for him to ask me this question. "Yes, sir," I replied happily.

Overland Jim smiled and kissed me. "And, after we get your folks and sister over those mountains, would you like to come back with me, be my boy, and live with me in these woods forever?"

I smiled and snuggled happily into his arms. "Yes, sir," I said again. And then I kissed him, kissed his lips and his chest and belly and, finally, I took his organ into my mouth again, and didn't stop kissing him until I tasted his seed in my mouth one more time for the evening.

October 3, 1847—Northern California

It has been a long time since I have written in this little journal of mine. I had nearly forgotten it while starting my new life over.

I had come to California with my parents to seek my fortune. Instead, I found Overland Jim. I shall live with him forever, sleep in his arms at night, and make love to him whenever he wants. We will be as married man and woman, and be happy together.

I left Mama and Papa at Barstow. Mama cried, and Papa said very little. I told them I was a man now, and that it was time for me to seek my own fortunes on my own in this world. I shall never see them again. That life is behind me now; my new one has begun. I am ready to accept whatever the good Lord provides, and as long as I have Overland Jim, I shall be more than content. I suppose now that I am a man, I have no need of this little journal. I doubt I shall ever write in it again.

MWAHC

JEFFREY LOCKETT

My heart was supposed to be in intensive care but my dick straightened out another fold in my jeans. Amazed I could ever be interested in sex again, I brushed my finger across my crotch— just checking, you understand. Big mistake—the rebel dick became ramrod hard. Hopefully, nobody in the bar would notice.

I should have just picked up a bottle of vodka from the liquor store, taken it back to my guest house, and got blind drunk alone. But I should have done a lot of things differently: never flown over to New York; never given my boyfriend a second chance; never looked at that mountain of man in the corner of the bar.

Half an hour earlier, my now-ex had taken me to a restaurant so pretentious it only served one thing: filet steak with a green salad. As our food arrived, he launched into a long speech about why our relationship would never work. I stood up and marched straight out—leaving behind my untouched dinner, my self-respect, and my dreams of eternal love. Alcohol would perhaps temporarily fill the void, and the neighborhood gay bar was the nearest place.

I'd hardly started my first beer when I spotted a big bulky man with a shock of black hair and a full bristly beard. Probably Greek or maybe Italian ancestry—except they normally don't grow that big. I jumped down from the top of the bar's bunkhouse-type seating and ordered another drink; at least I'd have something interesting to look at while I drank myself senseless. He was too busy talking to friends to realize he had a fan, and I rather enjoyed the opportunity to stare. Perhaps it was the way he threw back his head and laughed at his mate's jokes, his legs confidently splayed three feet apart, but he seemed to take up twice as much space as everybody else. Or maybe his chest really was a mile wide!

Back on my perch with a second beer, I watched enviously as he slapped another friend's back to emphasize a point in his story. Instead of cataloguing my misery, I began to imagine how damn good his hairy arm would feel draped across my shoulders. It was as effective as having a hundred volts pulsed through my body—no wonder my cock had risen from the dead!

Having never kissed a man with a beard before, I moved on to fantasizing about the sensations: soft and downy or like being scratched by 20-grit sandpaper? My crotch was telling me that either would be wonderful! In my daydream, I'd just shot a load over that springy beard and, with an evil grin, he stuck out his tongue to lap it up—when he broke away from his friends and strolled over in my direction. The hot summer evening and crowded bar had produced a dark sweat stain across the center of his white T-shirt. Closer up, I could easily make out the pattern of his mat of hair through the fabric. We didn't have men like that back home in London. I prayed to myself: *Please let him be coming over to talk to me!* I took a big swallow of beer.

The closer that Mountain Man lumbered, the faster my blood pumped. I shifted on the bench to try and ease my throbbing erection. Even in a smoke-filled New York bar, he radiated an open-air animal musk—maybe those natural mammal pheromones had overwhelmed my pain at being dumped. Like an Olympic athlete on the starting blocks, I tensed, ready for his opening line. Except he stopped two steps away to chat up a man slightly to my right!

My whole body sagged dejectedly as I looked over my competition. Judging from his clothes, he was most probably an office worker with no time to return home and change. Initially, I was fed up, but what the hell, I was there to get shitfaced, and anyway, there was something encouraging about Mountain Man finding a skinny little office worker attractive. I'd always thought mountain men stuck to their own kind. He was laughing and trying to draw out Mr. Nine-to-Five. In fact, he reminded me of an overgrown puppy leaping around and chewing ankles. But the harder he tried, the less progress he made. My spirits rallied slightly; perhaps everything wasn't lost.

My Mountain Man had noticed me witnessing his fruitless chat-up, so I gave him a wink and hoped it might cheer him up. He smiled ruefully back, made his apologies to Mr. Nine-to-Five, and went back to his friends. By now the bar had become quite crowded, but I managed to make some space on the top bunk and signaled that he should join me. Rather than a wake for a dead relationship, this was promising to be quite a night. Mountain Man brought over two beers and handed them up to me. Although earlier I had awkwardly clambered onto the bunkhouse seating, he swung up next to me as if he'd spent his whole life leaping across scaffolding. He shoved a hairy paw in my face: "Tommy."

His square triceps and biceps were covered with thick black hair that stretched down over the back of his hands, with dark clumps hanging to his fingers.

"Jeffrey," I replied, trying to match his firm handshake. I loved the way his muscles tensed as we shook. My eyes followed the line of hair back up his arm to the beginnings of a black furry pit. I had never before buried my face in a man's armpit, but suddenly I had an overwhelming craving.

We exchanged pleasantries. I told him I was a journalist from England and he talked about his life as a carpenter. We had another beer, and he shyly asked if I'd like to come home. You bet! But I liked the way he didn't take my conquest for granted. He took me firmly by the hand and led me out of the bar.

Tommy's flat, on West 26th, was just a stroll away. I let myself fall a couple of paces behind so I could study the way his shorts showed off his tree-trunk legs. The way he walked drove me crazy; it was more a rolling swagger. I wanted to be trapped between those hairy thighs and squeezed to death. At the door to his apartment block, Tommy gathered me into his arms and planted a wet sloppy kiss. Such a hairy embrace felt strange, but good. Tougher, more masculine than I had imagined, purer even—as if by shaving other men were cutting themselves off from their basic essence. His kiss lasted long after he'd slotted his key in the lock. Wiping my mouth on the back of my hand, I could still feel the traces of where his beard had rubbed across my lips, tenderizing them.

Tommy's one-room apartment was simple and uncomplicated. From under the dining table, he produced a bedroll and unfurled it. "Make yourself at home," he commanded.

"I'll just go and have a wash," I suggested. It had been a long and muggy evening.

"No need," he said emphatically. Being a well-brought-up, middle-class Englishman who preferred to brush his teeth before kissing somebody, I was a little embarrassed. But Tommy gave me a look that accepted no arguments. "I'll get you a beer," he changed the subject, so I took my shoes off and settled down on the bedroll.

As he came over with a frosted bottle, Tommy started peeling his clothes off and throwing them casually about.

By the time he reached me, he was just wearing his white Jockey briefs. My position on the floor was the perfect place to worship this colossus of a man: 6 foot 3 with a forest of hair stretching across his broad chest. In the center sprung one or two gray hairs, enough to make it interesting, and I could barely make out two dark nipples. He was so furry that the torrent of hair was not even interrupted under his pecs but flowed down to his shorts. He reminded me of the initials I used to idly write on my school notebook: I.W.L.T.R.D.W.A.M.W.A.H.C. This stood for a desire I was not brave enough to publicly declare: I Would Love to Rub Dicks With a Man With a Hairy Chest. Looking at Tommy, I knew I was about to make up for lost time!

"Do you like what you see?" he asked. "Afraid I haven't been going to the gym recently, so I've put on a few pounds."

He was right, but the hint of a beer belly only added to his beefiness. Hell, there were even more inches of hairy flesh to explore!

"Looks good to me, very good," I murmured. In fact, not realizing how gorgeous he was only added to Tommy's appeal.

"Why don't you strip off too?" he suggested. "But keep your underwear on."

I was soon standing in only my briefs, which (I'm ashamed to confess) were covered in cartoon characters—Wile E. Coyote chasing Road Runner!

I wanted to finally bury my face in his hairy chest and get a chance to spit out those hairs one by one, but he was too quick for me. He chucked off his shorts and dropped to his knees, his nose exploring my crotch.

"The smells and tastes of a man's body turn me on just as much as the sight and feel," he explained, coming up for air. No wonder Tommy had been keen to keep me out of the bathroom. I could tell his tour of my briefs was certainly turning him on, because poking out of his bush was a short thick cock dripping a long trail of precum. It looked about five inches long but twice as thick as average. I wanted to pull that dick down and watch it slap back against his belly, spraying man juice in every direction. However, with his arms solidly round my waist, I had no choice but to submit to his nose and tongue tracing the outline of my uncut cock through the soggy fabric of my shorts.

His journey continued up to my pits, where he launched a full-out assault. It felt so good I wanted to break away—up to that moment, I'd never believed in the concept of too much pleasure!

"I'd say you showered about five hours ago," said Tommy. God, this man was a male-aroma aficionado. "Pity you used soap," he continued. Ashamed of covering up my natural scents, I vowed never to use soap again. "At least you don't use aftershave, the curse of gay life."

I perked up at the backhanded compliment and decided it was time to take a taste test myself. A pungent aroma filled my nostrils as I headed for his damp pit. With trembling hands, I parted the hair and sunk my tongue into his sweaty patch. Overwhelmed by a wave of raw nectar, I felt like the floor had dropped beneath me. Thank goodness he was holding onto me.

"Where's the loo?" I asked.

"I'll come with you, if that's OK," Tommy said very politely. I shrugged and he led the way.

While I stood in front of the porcelain, Tommy knelt down on the bathroom floor.

"Can I watch?" he asked.

I thought it a bit strange, but what harm was there in letting him stay? Although hesitant at first, a good strong stream of piss was soon hurtling into the toilet.

"Looks good." Tommy was obviously mesmerized. "Do you mind if I hold it for you?" I shook my head, and his paw gently encircled my cock. The flow hardly slowed as my cock swelled again. From his rapt expression, I guessed Tommy wanted to run his hand through my golden waterfall. Perhaps he sensed the idea would freak me out, so he was prepared to settle for watching.

When my bladder was finally empty, I didn't get a chance to shake the last drops from my foreskin as he immediately leaned forward and started sucking my cock. The sensation of his tongue running under the hood and capturing every lingering taste was so incredible that I started thrusting my dick way down his throat. My pubic hair entangled with his beard, I drew back so the tip rested on the end of his tongue before I thrust back home again. Bloody Hell. We were both so worked up, I was in danger of coming while he risked having a hole drilled in his throat.

I stepped back, but Tommy used the opportunity to slip his tongue under my cock helmet. I wanted to scream obscenities as his rough tongue pounded my ultrasensitive skin. Instead I begged for mercy, but it only made him hungrier. I had no choice but to grab two handfuls of furry face and pull him off my shaft. Two sad almond eyes stared up from the cool bathroom floor.

"OK. You want it, you've got it," I growled, and rammed eight hard inches back down his throat—bucking like a wild animal. It was incredible how much mouth-fuck abuse he could take. Finally, from somewhere deep in his stomach, Tommy begin to spasm and choke. I pulled out my slobber-covered pole and watched the slime fall onto his chest. I stroked the juice against the grain of his hair until it dried hard. We took a break.

Back in the other room, Tommy put a pillow on the bedroll and placed me over it so that my ass was sticking up. His hands started gently stroking my backside.

"You have a lovely hairy ass," he told me, and gently tweaked at a couple of strands around my hole. He grazed up: "What a great collection of hairs in the small of your back." Other men had noticed them with surprise because I'm not particularly hairy, but he was the first guy to give them a good lapping over.

"You know what I'd really, really like?" he broke off for a second. "To eat out that ass."

"Be my guest," I said. Even extremely horny Englishmen are still invariably polite.

"There's a nasty bout of stomach parasites doing the rounds here," he wet his finger and fondled my ass chute entrance, "but then, you're not from around here." He considered his dilemma for half a second and dived in between my legs.

My butt had been licked before, which was quite pleasant, but really it just a couple of swirls and that was that. So I was not prepared for the pure electricity that shot through my body as Fuzzy Chops rubbed his beard into nerve endings never visited before. I moaned with pleasure as Tommy grabbed me round the waist and flattened my ass against his beard. He must have known his tongue was a dangerous weapon, because he backed off and started nibbling on the hairy globes of my ass cheeks instead. I wondered how sexy they would look covered with his teeth marks. Slowly he worked back toward my crack, and the closer he strayed, the more I wanted to wriggle out of his viselike hairy grip.

"Now, this time I want you to really spread your cheeks, and most important, push back as if you were taking a dump," Tommy instructed. I was the prisoner of a butt-hole gourmet. So I followed the command, and his tongue shot even further up my chute.

I have never felt so secure or safe as I did at that moment—or, indeed, more special. Every inch of my body, even the hidden ones, were adored by his man: Smells, piss, spit were all wonderful treasures to him. Except I was greedy and wanted him deeper still. His tongue felt like a big throbbing dick but with twice the sex pleasure. His paws constantly strained to pull my cheeks wider, his tongue rotating round in my butt hole—probing, pushing, relaxing. I moaned long and hard as a shiver of pure pleasure rocketed up my spine. Tommy pulled back a fraction and I fought to reclaim his fuck weapon, but I needn't have worried: He was just marshaling his troops for the final ass assault.

My throbbing dick was demanding a piece of the action. I reached down and started to jerk off, but he pulled my hand away. When I started bucking against the bed, he slapped my buttocks. I was stranded right at the edge of an orgasm, threatening to explode somewhere deep inside.

Finally, Tommy let me up again and planted a big wet kiss on my other lips. His beard tasted of my ass juices—another new experience—and the wiry hair smelled all musty. I longed to return the favor and lick out his crack, but mindful of his warning about parasites, I pulled him down on top of me.

Finally his stubby dick was rubbing against mine. It felt good, but I knew something better. I twisted him over and took control, bucking my chest against his infinitely hairier chest, pulling back to concentrate on the pleasures of tickling my chest against the very ends of his rug, diving down to bite on his sensitive nipples.

Our dicks fought each other, and the friction from his black mat spun my brain into a blur. The veins along my shaft began to pulsate—there really could be no more holding back. I grabbed him closer and buried my face in his beard, scratching every inch of my smooth face with his rough brush, which threw me over the edge. My screams were muffled as I pumped wave after wave of hot cum all over our bodies.

Tommy kissed me so tenderly, I thought I was going to cry. He reached over for his T-shirt and wiped the spunk off our bodies. After a quick sniff, he used the soaked garment to lube up his dick. With only 10 strokes of his rock-hard cock, white cream erupted into the T-shirt, matching my healthy deposit.

Slowly, our breathing resumed a more normal pace as we lay in each other's arms. Back on planet Earth, Tommy held his shirt to my nose. For the first time, I truly used all five senses for sex. Inhaling deeply, I smelled salty sweat from a steamy night in Manhattan, the hint of cigarette and cigar smoke from the bar, and the delicate aroma of life itself: spunk. We took turns breathing in his used and abused T-shirt until it was time for me to leave.

In memory of a mind-blowing night, and to guard against the demons of being dumped, I decided to wear those same cartoon shorts for the flight back to England—and for the next three days. Finally, I mailed them to Tommy, making certain the parcel was well-sealed so as not to shock the postman. Although after all that time on my body, they could have almost flown back to America on their own.

A week later I received this reply:

I could not have been more pleased to get those beautiful-smelling pants of yours, except of course to see the contents in the flesh. How did you manage to get that big dick and balls and butt all into those little pants? You should have seen me on the subway to work, sniffing the various smells of your pants, acting like there was a bottle of poppers hidden in them. In my head and cock it was a real tour of your crotch and ass: the pungent, musky smell of your crotch, the tangy, nutty smell of your piss, and the camembert-like smell of your asshole! God, I could almost taste all of them—and oh God, how I would have liked that!
Your very admiring and loving friend,
Tommy

Of course, he extended an open invitation to return to Manhattan. I thought it was too soon to get involved again, but sent another pair of soiled shorts—he liked those too! Pretty soon it became a habit: Instead of throwing my underwear in the laundry basket I dispatched them off to the States.

A month later, I was down to just one pair of multicolored pants—a birthday present from an aunt. So I set off on a shopping expedition for more supplies. After hours trying to decide what underwear would turn Tommy on, I decided, What the hell! Sometimes you have to take risks. I marched out of the shop and into a travel agency.

Tommy and I had a great holiday together. Now, even 15 years later, we still exchange Christmas "presents," except these days, it's a two-way trade. Tommy opened a whole new arena for me, which has grown bigger and bigger, until it could be more accurately described as a theme park!

Playtime!

JOHN MCFARLAND

Others could laugh, but David was a believer. It all started way back with his book of Bible stories, chock-full of humpy, bearded men dressed in easy-off burlap. *Hercules Unchained* only confirmed that there was every reason to believe. And now in the age of lasers, he saw it big as life almost everywhere he looked. Especially on the dance floor. First there would be this certain blinding flash of light, and then everything that came next was adventure. David never doubted for a second that it was always going to be this way. He had that kind of faith.

And so, late on a Friday night in April, when the paths of two laser beams crossed to draw him and the tall burly man together on the dance floor, he knew what to watch for. There was that special shower of light, and without a second's hesitation, he stepped right up into the dance for adventure.

The music pulsed through them and drove them. They danced as if this were their last chance, as if everything they treasured might be outlawed in the morning. They danced on and on in a contest of muscle and heat until David at last cried uncle and had to take a break.

He pointed to the bench on the sidelines and headed for it. When the man plunked down beside him, David had just enough breath left to say, "You sure can dance."

The man nodded and leaned back. His arm pressed against David's sweat-slick, heaving side. "I'm Rob," he said.

Once David identified himself too, Rob had other questions

he wanted answered. Lots of them. The stream continued until they both had sworn on all that was sacred that they observed the rules of the road scrupulously—never, ever risking the worst, courting disaster, or tempting fate. Almost as an afterthought, Rob asked if David was partial to fantasies.

"Sure, sure, the works," David said. This early on, there was no need to close the door on any possibility. After all, David knew firsthand that some people's idea of a fantasy was to share a Dr. Pepper with a stranger who had just fucked them in handcuffs. Plus, he liked the looks of Rob's wild beard with beads of sweat glistening in it.

Rob didn't seize that moment to go into whatever details, which would have to come later. He jumped up from the bench, announced "Playtime!" and led the way outside.

That he had no idea of what was coming next was one of the great joys of David's life. His hunger for experience was gigantic, his eye was bigger than his fine, solid belly. Those who hadn't read their Bible stories carefully or watched every last Hercules movie sometimes traveled the world over in search of mystery and adventure. David found those things right around the next corner. The men, their trips, the sexy sweet secrets in their pants and apartments.

Once inside Rob's apartment, David still didn't have much of an idea of what he had wandered into. There wasn't a single light on and Rob hustled him through the living room to a room the size of a closet off the dining room. There, in total darkness and pushed close together, they tore each other's clothes off. Every adventure should have one reassuringly familiar element, and this was it.

When they were naked, Rob crouched down and rooted around for what seemed like forever. David felt hot breath rustle the hair on his legs. At long last, strong fingers found his foot and dug under his toes. Rob lifted David's right leg and slid something very soft and smooth over his foot and rolled it up his calf. While Rob was slipping its twin on David's left leg, David reached down and his fingertips touched suede with a fringe around the top of boots. It was a start, a fantastic one.

After getting the footgear on, Rob worked David up to a fever pitch. Whoever dreamed up hands and the tongue deserves an award—and should know that in the dark the mouth can seem like a velvet furnace. For his part, though, David had only enough time to roam once, quickly, across the grand rolling expanse of Rob's furred chest before being launched back out into the larger world of the apartment.

Padding along in fringed boots, his throbbing dick pointing the way west, David saw himself as a fearless Indian scout. He turned around to let Rob know that his eyes were finally adjusting to the darkness, but he didn't say a word. He was as quiet as the Plains on Sunday once he'd gotten a gander at Rob's porno-size hog flying aloft.

Rob streaked by and charged to a couch in the living room. He flung himself down on the couch and was reaching over its back to grab for something.

"Now we're cooking," David thought as he brought up the rear.

A few pinpoint spotlights set into the ceiling popped on, and Rob lifted up a 10-gallon Stetson with a long feather in its band. He put on the hat and motioned David over and up onto the back of the couch. Breathing easier now and with the conviction of a veteran scout, David climbed up onto the spot Rob indicated. A mysterious beam of light shone directly down on his cock. It took all of David's acrobatic talent to hold his pose. He didn't want to fall at least until after he got what was coming to him next.

Rob took the feather out of the headband. He ran it over David's balls. It traveled back and forth between his buns (called furry-luscious more than once), down the shaft of his cock to the head with its opening now glistening.

"Morning dew," Rob breathed low, "morning dew."

"Oh, God," moaned David. Balance was everything. To maintain it, he recited to himself, "The quality of sex is not strained, it droppeth as the gentle rain from heaven upon the place beneath." It worked like a charm for a while.

Before David lost his balance, Rob motioned him down from his perch and sat him on the couch. Rob knelt in front, easing off one boot. Slowly, slowly, and in total silence, he showed how he wanted David to move the boot, to graze his skin with the suede fringe. Barely, and moving like a soft breeze.

David had to suppress all thoughts of a Dr. Pepper in the maybe-future to stay tuned in to the moment. The military had trained him to follow orders with no questions asked. It came in handy now. He applied the fringe as directed.

Rob thrashed about on the couch, groaning with pleasure, growing even larger. One of the spotlights caught Rob's tight pink rosette shining out of a thicket of hair, although the room was almost dark.

Though it was strange that certain items grabbed more than their share of the spotlight, David didn't have much time to think about it before he heard a terrible racket coming from outside in the hallway. First the sound of a door being slammed off its hinges, then a crash against the wall, a scream, and what sounded like a gunshot.

Waiting for the next report, David increased his stranglehold on the boot and stopped the fringe job. Rob was so intent on the scene that he didn't seem to notice the noise outside. He was still pleading for David to get back to business when something hurtled against the apartment door.

The door gave way, and in flew a woman. Swearing and sobbing, she fumbled to lock the door behind her.

We're all going to die, David thought. *The world was my oyster, now I'll be buried in shells.*

The woman stumbled into the living room. David froze, naked except for the boots, one clutched in his hand, one still on his left foot. Rob sprawled on the couch with his eyes closed. Light shone on his glistening rosy butt hole and the dick that just wouldn't quit.

Time is elastic. What we know has wings slows to a crawl. What takes time is gone in a flash. Time is a river. Time devours all things. So much packed into so little time. Time stands still.

The intruder wore a lemon-yellow miniskirt, a matching blouse, beige-patterned hose, and impossibly high heels. Her long straight blond hair swung from side to side as she tried to run in those impossible shoes.

A scream came from deep in the mass of swinging blond hair. She came to a halt. She stared straight at the couch. David wondered if she was torn between retracing her steps to take her chances ducking more hot lead outside or collapsing to the floor in hysterics to wait for a fate worse than death, whatever that could be. David was wrong twice. Instead she rushed the couch.

David was so caught up in the spectacle of her running, wobbling on those shoes, that only very late in the game did he realize that the woman, now very close to Rob, was working her way out of her panty hose.

Oh, God! he thought. *She sees that dick and can't help herself, poor thing.*

Knowing the supreme trashiness of the world, David didn't doubt what he saw before him. He simply moved the boot to cover himself. Rob hadn't budged. His face was jammed against the back of the couch and he couldn't see what was about to settle on him.

As the panty hose was worked down to mid thigh and the miniskirt hiked up, David had tried so hard not to laugh that his grip loosened and he dropped the boot. Right there in front of him was the third hard-on in the darkened room. It was glistening too as shafts of light bounced off the pale-yellow, almost transparent, greased condom that sheathed it. *A brave man makes a short sword long,* David thought.

Without further ado, the newcomer caressed Rob's thighs

slowly and then slipped his dick into the shining and inviting accommodations.

"Ah!" sighed Rob. His eyes stayed closed. When meat is in, anger is out.

"Contain yourself," David told himself. "Keep calm." And so, when he felt the hand on his leg pulling him up onto the couch, he followed the leader.

Rob moved David directly over him. He drew David down so that he was crouching just above his face. Rob ran his tongue all over David's balls. He brushed the feather up and down his legs. He tickled his asshole to within an inch of heaven. Inside, outside, oh, oh-oh, oh! In front of him, David watched the wheaten hair slapping back and forth, back and forth, against the padded shoulders of the blouse. From time to time the hair covered and completely hid the massive dick that Rob pumped and pulled furiously.

"You're hot, so fucking hot," Rob whispered in between mouthfuls.

This is the fantasy then—David was sure. A good wife makes a good husband, whatever. There won't be any Dr. Peppers passed around in this crowd.

David bent forward to find the lips buried under the mass of swinging hair. He grabbed the back of the couch with his right hand. He used his left one to work half of Rob's impressive hog. Sure, sure, the works. The first dish pleases all. And the full feast is fantastic.

As the three of them approached the key moment, the grunts, moans, and panting kept escalating until two flying loads described their vigorous arcs across the room. The third's booty stayed entirely in its trusty yellow wrapper. That was unrolled last, only after the newcomer had pulled off the yellow miniskirt, its matching blouse, and blond wig.

"Very nice. Very, very nice," said Rob, entangled with David on the couch as the third man, leaving his getup in a pile on the floor, dove between them.

"What do you think, big boy?" the man grilled David, as he slapped his ass rapid-fire. "Would you recommend that yellow number to just about everybody you know and love?"

Not to leave him in the dark any longer, Rob said to David, "Ted likes to see how his latest designs go over. With a man's man. It's harder and harder to get really objective reactions in his business."

"In terms of, you know, style, impact, ease of movement, and...fuckwearability," this Ted person rattled on. He pinched Rob's tits. Rob slapped his hand, hard.

"Lots of impact," David said, managing to slip his two cents into the antic routine the two were doing.

"I can vouch for the last one," Rob offered, rolling onto his side. "Ease of movement not bad either." Rob lifted a heavily muscled leg over David and Ted and drew them closer to him.

"That leaves style," David said.

"Goes without saying," Ted and Rob said together as the threesome rolled around the couch, this time with as much laughter as ass grabbing.

Nobody could quarrel with the fun. But when David spotted the telltale signs of a shift away from a woolly three-way adventure toward the conventions of coupledom, he beat his own retreat to the bathroom.

Standing at the toilet, he alternated between trying to control the wayward stream of piss and completely giving up on it. When he finished he looked up to see a framed photo of a bodybuilder whose name he could never remember. In this one, he was nude and hard, and not a hair had been shaved anywhere on his body. He looked so hot that he was solar. The sly lopsided grin and the foreskin pulled halfway back over the head of his cock didn't hurt one bit. David leaned forward to read the inscription on the photo: "For Ted and Rob, You sure can dance, XXX." But there was no way he could make out the scrawled signature.

"Join the crowd, buckaroo," David laughed.

On his way back from the bathroom, he stopped by the closet-size room to slip into his jeans and shirt. It was a sticky business, a trick's exit in these tattered times. When he carried his shoes and jacket into the living room Ted and Rob were pulling themselves together after the duo-treat-and-tangle he'd seen coming.

Trusting his instinct on when to head out, David put on his jacket and bent down to touch the nearest shoulder.

Rob rolled over. "You're not going!" he cried out.

"You should stay. Actually," Ted added.

"A man's gotta do..." David began. They all finished the line together and then laughed.

When it was clear that David intended to go, Ted at least moved on into the future. "Party tonight!" he winked. "If you'd come, it'd be great. New blood, we need new blood! Starts at 8."

"If we can get the cum stains off the couch by then," Rob chimed in.

"If we can get the cum stains off *you* by then," Ted corrected.

As the two of them tried to settle the argument by wrestling it out, David put on his socks and shoes and then headed for the door. "See you tonight," he called in farewell.

"Be there," they said before sinking from sight on the couch, an ocean getting into motion.

Downstairs, the front door of the building closed behind David, a final click. When one door shuts, another opens. He took a deep breath of the night air. He squared his shoulders. He stood completely still.

The streetlamp across the way cast a muted orange glow on the parked cars. A window slid open high above him. The quiet in the street at that hour was eerie. And then all of a sudden, without even a warning flicker, the street went dark for a minute before the lights flashed back on at once, more illumination than you can ever use after totally nothing.

A familiar sensation seized David, a thrilling spasm rippling up from the base of his spine straight to his skull, the can't-miss-it reminder of the possibilities. A spectacular flash of light, as big as all outdoors, and now the whole world was offering its next adventure. All David had to do was step right out into it. That night he was a believer, more than ever before. He took that step.

Teachin' Manners

Jim Mason

ADULT BOOKS says the red-and-black painted sign in the front window. This is an out-of-the way place—just a shack, really—across from an old gas station, a beer-only bar, and not much else. There's a gravel parking lot out back. Inside, old fuck magazines and dusty "marital aids" are in the front of the store, and there's a movie arcade with eight doored booths in a back room. About half of the films are of man sex.

"Gus" keeps the place so that he doesn't have to spend time with his shrew of a wife. He doesn't much care what goes on in the back arcade, as long as nothing gets broken. There's no other place like it in the county, so it gets its share of business.

My buddy Mike and I are standing just inside the arcade portion of the store, chatting. Gus knows us well enough by now that he tolerates us hanging around like that. We've jacked off and sucked off to all the films before, so we're there to see who comes in—maybe something nice, maybe not. Sometimes there's no one here of interest to us, but then other times the local ranchers and farmers and cowboys might show up just to get their rocks off. We've been this route before, and we always know we'll give each other a hand if it's a slow evening.

We're big-built guys, kind of like football players who have had a few too many beers over the years, hairy fuckers and bearded. Mike's beard and hair are still jet-black, but his hairline is receding some at the temples. I've got shorter hair and beard but a 'stache that hangs below my chin at the corners. I'm sportin' a bit of gray too. We can be damn intimidating if we need to be.

Mike escaped the knife and has a long foreskin he can stretch out a couple inches. I'm cut but have low-hanging, big bull balls. We're both probably a bit longer than average in what's swingin' between our legs, but who the hell's measurin'.

It's a warm enough night to be sweating some. Mike is wearing a denim jacket with the sleeves torn off and no shirt underneath, showing lots of chest, belly, and pit hair. He's also in his Wrangler jeans, black cowboy boots, and a ratty ball cap advertising Skoal. I've often told Mike that those jeans make his ol' butt look good enough to eat! I'm in my jeans as well as a tank top that's seen a lot of wear, showing a few holes that give a peek at my own fur from my chest spilling out over the top. Knees are ripped out in my jeans, and I'm wearing my brown muddy construction worker boots.

Then this thin kid in his early 20s comes in through the doorway, wearing new Levi's jeans, Nike sneakers, and a T-shirt from some music group we ain't heard of. He's not really our type, so we just nod to him and go back to shootin' the shit. But as he passes us he says, "Don't even think about it! I don't do hairy fat old men," and then he goes down about three booths, enters, and closes the door.

Mike and I look at each other, jaws drop, and we growl, "What the fuck was that?"

"That little shit-ass punk!" Mike spits, and continues just above a whisper, "Forties ain't old, you little fuck!"

I say, "Ya know, some grown-up oughta teach that boy some manners!"

Mike notes, "Well, he has to use the same door to go out that he came in by, and go through the parking lot where we're parked."

"Yeah," I say, "You feel like a lesson-teachin' grown-up tonight?"

"Right," responds Mike. 'Course, we're still not really sure what we're going to do. We exit the store, go to my pickup, and wait for the snotty kid to come back out. Business remains slow at the store, and we have only about 15 minutes to wait. We're standing by the cab of the pickup, having a smoke, when the kid comes out of the store. His sporty car's parked right next to my banged-up truck. "No luck tonight, kid?" I ask.

"Naw, just you old fuckers," he snipes.

"Mike, this boy needs to be taught some manners," I announce, as Mike moves in behind him and puts him in a firm bear hug.

"Hey! You assholes!" he yells, and he starts thrashing and kicking.

But good ol' Mike has a strong hold on him and hisses to the kid, "Hey, asswipe! You can make this difficult on yourself, or you can make it easy! Either way, shit's gonna happen!"

The kid whimpers some, then calms down but says, "I've got a friend coming by here soon to meet me."

"Then we'll watch for him and deal with him when he gets here," I say. "But first, kid, drop your pants." Mike loosens up his hold a bit so the kid can reach to undo his pants, but then the kid squirms hard and kicks, getting me on the shin. Mike is trying to grab hold again, and as I try to grab the kid's hands he latches onto my tank top and tears it straight down the fuckin' center! Then with another kick he knocks me off balance, and I find myself on my butt in the gravel lot. "Shit!" I yell, and then realize that in falling I've ripped the fuckin' seat out of my jeans!

By the time I'm back on my feet, Mike has the kid again. The three of us are sweaty, and I'm dirty, standing there pissed off in a ripped shirt with my hairy ass visible through the new hole in my pants! "So, you decided to make it difficult, eh, kid? That's your choice." I then bark at him, "Get outta your fuckin' pants!"

This time the kid obeys, unbuttoning his Levi's and awkwardly pushing them down as far as he can with Mike holding on to him. "Shorts too!" I command, and he pushes his Calvin Kleins down. Kid's got an average dick, probably a bit shriveled from fear, but I wasn't interested in his dick.

"Hang on to him, Mike," I say, as I reach for the kid's legs. I lift his legs up, remove his expensive Nikes, his socks, and pull his pants and shorts the rest of the way off. The shoes I toss in two different directions. The pants and shorts I throw toward a wire fence behind me, hoping they'd make it over the top. Instead, they land halfway across it.

"I don't think he's gonna run anywhere now," grins Mike, letting go of the kid, who's rubbing his arms.

"Naw," I say, "but the shirt's gotta go too. Off with it, kid!" He takes his shirt off and lays it over the back of the truck bed. He's got a decent build and doesn't look so bad naked, but he's bare-hair-chested. I guess he's shaved any man hair he might have.

"Well, Mike," I ask, "what ya want—backside?"

"You know it," Mike answers, and I hear the zipper of Mike's Wranglers being pulled down and his big cowboy belt buckle being opened.

"Then I'll take his mouth!" We soon have the kid on his hands and knees in the gravel between the kid's car and my truck. It didn't take long for Mike to shove his jeans to his knees, get his sleeveless jacket off, and get into position behind the kid. He spits on his hand a few times for lube, smears it around on his prick and the kid's asshole. I tear the rest of my shirt off and toss it through the open window of the truck cab. The kid's eyeing my dick as I stroke it, getting it hard and wet with precum. I have a hunch that he now wants this "hairy fat old man" dick. He can't see Mike's purple-headed prick that's about to split his ass. I just watch from up front as Mike aims and starts to push. I always enjoy seeing the pleasure grow on a man's face as he pushes forward, inch by inch. The kid gasps as he feels the cock head enter his butt hole. He doesn't yell out, but he's sure-as-shit sweatin'! With an "A-a-ahhh," Mike lets me know he's in, and he begins some slow pumping action.

"Naw," Mike says, "this ain't no virgin hole, but it feels fuckin' nice." I take the kid's T-shirt from the truck bed for something to kneel on and position myself in front of him. I rub my free-flowin' precum around the kid's face with my dick. He ain't fighting it now.

"OK, kid," I say, "here comes your first lesson in manners." I take his head in both hands and pull it down over my crotch, spearing his mouth with my hard peter. Mike and I hump and pump for about five minutes when we hear, "Hey! What the fuck you doin' with my friend?!"

The kid's buddy has arrived. He wasn't shittin' us. But we also hear, "What the fuck's it to ya, shithead?"

Behind this new kid stands a buddy of Mike's and mine—Dan. If Mike and I look intimidating, Dan looks plain scary! Dan's a big ol' fuckin' bear. His pickup's dirtier than mine. Dan's hair hangs halfway down his back and his beard's mid-chest length. A lot of men would be proud to have his back and butt hair on their chests. Now he's standing there shirtless, in all his hairy glory, wearing his shit-kickin', knee-high logger boots and Levi's jeans so old, most of the buttons have torn through the holes. His three-gauge nipple rings are barely visible through all that chest hair.

The new kid looks worried. Mike, Dan, and I look at each other and grin. The first kid is still rocking back on Mike's prick and forward on mine. Yeah, he's enjoying it. I know that three-against-two doesn't sound like much of a fair contest, especially when you consider we three bruisers are a lot bigger than the two kids before us, but we just didn't give a flying fuck about "fair" by that point.

Dan's got one big hairy paw clamped around the back of the new kid's neck and repeats, "I said, What the fuck's it to you what my buddies are doin'?"

The kid snaps back, "I know my friend Charlie wouldn't do that with guys like them."

"She-e-e-i-i-it," Dan spits, "and I suppose you were gonna take 'em on by yerself? Hah! What's yer name, kid?"

"Roger," he answers.

Dan continues, "Well, looks to me like my friends are just havin' some fun with your friend Charlie. Looks like they're just enjoyin' themselves and havin' a good time. Ain't that right, boys?"

Mike answers, "That's right! And we'd kinda like to pick up

again where Roger there interrupted us."

"Right!" I repeat. Then I address Charlie, who's still got a mouthful of cock, "Charlie? You like what we're all doin' here?" Charlie lets out a low, muffled moan. I look back at Dan and Roger and report, "Charlie here says that he very much likes having his throat filled with my hard peter and Mike's wanger up his ass."

Dan turns Roger's face around, so Roger is looking up into Dan's beard, and says, "I don't think Roger here is goin' to object any further, are you, Roger? In fact, I'd bet Roger would like to have me and him join you guys in the party. Bet his friend Charlie there would like that too."

I turn Charlie's face up enough from my crotch to meet his eyes and ask, "What you say, Charlie? Let's have Dan and Roger join us over here." Charlie tries to grin, I think, so I continue, "Yep, Dan! Charlie says he'd like that." Roger is so fuckin' scared, he can't talk, much less object by running.

"All right," calls Dan, "here we come! But let's get the fuck outta the damn gravel, and by the way," he adds, "you got any rope?" Dan has Roger by the back of the neck and the seat of the pants as they approach the spot where Mike and I have been teaching Charlie his manners. Mike and I pull out of Charlie, brief Dan on the situation and how it came about, and the three of us have a good laugh.

Mike and I hike our pants up a bit, and we decide the five of us would fit in the bed of my truck—barely. "Hell, I've had five guys fuckin' each other back there before," I mumble. I climb up first, then Mike pushes Charlie up to me. I hold him while Mike climbs in. "Don't catch your dick on anything," I warn. "Don't want you to lose that dangling foreskin of yours." I've got a mat and some old blankets on the truck bed, so we aren't going to get too banged up.

"Dan," Mike calls out, "you joinin' us or not?"

"Just a minute, I gotta skin mine first," Dan replies, referring to the still-clothed Roger. With that, Dan's hand moves from

Roger's neck to the top of his T-shirt and tears it downward, then pulls if off from around Roger's torso. I watch and note that this kid's not as hairless as Charlie. Also in his 20s probably, Roger sports some chest and belly fur and has enough shadow to indicate he could grow a beard, if he'd let his balls do their job. Dan pulls the knife from his pants pocket, slits the top of Roger's jeans, then with both hands splits the back. He moves to the front of Roger, slits the front of the jeans, and rips them open. "Now hold still," Dan warns, and he slices Roger's Jockeys off.

"OK!" Dan calls out to us, "Here comes the next one!" Dan hoists Roger's ass up to the truck bed wall and pushes him backward. Roger lands on top of Charlie, but with his feet in the air. Dan grabs and pulls off Roger's sneakers and socks. Last up into the truck is Dan.

Mike and I pull Charlie out from under Roger, and the three of us are just sitting and waiting to see what Dan has in mind. "Yep! Damn nice lookin' group for a party." Dan finally announces, standing up against the cab with Roger, naked at his feet. "You said you got some rope?" Dan repeats.

"Yeah, right in the center of that tire," I direct him.

"Roger, boy," he tells the kid, "you're in for a treat. Now turn around!" Roger turns his back to Dan, who pulls Roger's wrists together behind him and binds them.

I'm up near Dan and Roger, in case I need to assist, when I hear the unmistakable sound of butt fucking. Looking behind me, I see Mike has gotten impatient, has Charlie's ass in the air, and is slip-slidin' away. Makes my cock twitch in anticipation of getting Charlie's mouth back around my dick.

Dan finally has Roger trussed up by the wrists but leaves his ankles free, "just in case I want to spread 'em," Dan grins. Then he addresses Roger, "OK, boy! I'm gonna teach you a lesson 'bout interruptin' other folks' good times."

The sound of Mike fucking Charlie has really gotten to my nuts, so I decide to leave Dan and Roger for a while and go back to getting my cock sucked. Mike and Charlie are sweatin' like pigs!

Like Mike, I strip completely this time, get on my knees in front of Charlie's face, and plug in. Mike always likes to fuck doggystyle. He has Charlie by the waist, and it's hard to tell if Mike's thrusting his hips or if he's just moving Charlie's ass back and forth on his dick. Mike and I get back in sync pretty quickly. My heavy, low-hanging nuts *thwapp* against Charlie's chin and throat.

I look back over at Dan and Roger. Dan's knelt down in front of Roger and has Roger's face pressed into his wet armpit. That has to smell nice. Dan's twisting Roger's nipples with his other hand. I can't tell if Roger's still scared or what. He has one of those pained expressions on his face, like he's either having a great time or is so scared he could shit. I think his prick's longer than it was before, though.

Dan stands back up and starts to unbuckle his pants and haul his cock out. Dan and I have made it a few times before, so I know what to expect. Roger, however, doesn't. *Now* he looks scared enough to shit! Dan has the biggest, longest, thickest peter I have ever seen. He puts long-necked beer bottles to shame and has a foreskin longer than Mike's. His three-gauge PA completes the effect. Dan's had guys who claimed they wanted him to fuck them, but they changed their minds when they saw his meat! That just pisses Dan off, and they end up with stretched assholes or widened throats anyway.

Dan unlaces and tugs off his logger boots and sweat socks and sticks a smelly, hairy bare foot into Roger's face and commands, "Suck it, fucker!" Roger opens his mouth for a couple of toes.

"Hey! Wanna trade spots for a while?" Mike asks me.

"Sure," I answer. Mike pulls out of Charlie's ass, stands up with his hard dick a-bobbin' and slappin' against his furry belly, and walks over to where I am. I crawl around to Charlie's ass and get ready to pop in when I notice something about Charlie. His dick's as hard as a fuckin' rock and leakin' precum from piss slit to balls. "Hah! He's enjoyin' this more than he thought he would," I tell Mike, and point to Charlie's cock.

"Well, fuckin' A," Mike says, "guess that makes us pretty good teachers!"

Charlie seems a little resistant to taking into his mouth a prick that's just been up his funky ass, but Mike convinces him. He bops his dick against Charlie's face a few times.

Roger and Dan are still in foreplay, I see. Roger's propped up against the sidewall of the truck bed, and Dan's finally stripped all his own clothes off. Dan's prick is perched just above Roger's mouth. Again, I know Dan well enough to know what's next. With that meaty-ass foreskin peeled back, the golden stream is just beginning to flow from Dan's piss hole into Roger's open mouth. Dan then directs the piss over the whole of Roger's body—*It'll drain out the back of the truck,* I think to myself—then plunges his still streaming cock into Roger's mouth. Roger gags. Piss comes erupting back out of Roger's mouth, but finally his throat accepts the offer and begins to swallow.

Once inside Roger's mouth, Dan's dick begins to grow even more. He moves Roger's head so it's propped up on the back of the cab. Easier level to face-fuck him. Roger's eyes are really beginning to bug now, but I turn my attention back to fucking ass.

I can tell that Mike's getting close to coming. He's starting to wince, and his breaths are becoming shorter. I have to admit that my balls are beginning to tingle a bit themselves. Well, shit—we'd been going at these two guys for well over an hour. I see Dan turn around and shove his ass down onto Roger's face, ordering him to "lick it!" and "stick that fuckin' tongue up there!"

My attention's drawn back to Mike, who's making "Unh, unh!" guttural noises. Soon Mike's letting go with a string of "Oh, fuck! Shit! Fuck! Yeah! Yeah! God! Fu-u-uccckkk! Ssshhhe-e-i-i-it!" and a final "Awww fuck!" Mike's humping slows, his mouth hangs open, sweat has pooled under him, and I know he's blown his load into Charlie's mouth. A drool of cum leaks down Charlie's chin and onto the truck bed. Oh, my truck's going to get slimy tonight.

Seeing Mike shoot sends me over the falls. My balls draw up and start to ache. I get that glorious sensation in my groin that soon travels through the rest of my body and finally erupts! "Gawd! Yeah! Shit! Aww, yeah! Fuck!" I feel the globs of jizz fire off out my piss hole and up Charlie's innards as I slap the palms of my hands hard against his ass. I collapse on top of Charlie's back, sending him flat against the mats on the truck bed. Damn! That felt good!

When I finally get the strength to lift myself off Charlie, I see naked Mike sitting and having a smoke, grinning at me. I return his grin, and Charlie gets up and squats next to Mike. Charlie's still got Mike's cum spread all over his face, and some of my cum has leaked out his hole and down one thigh.

The three of us turn toward Dan and Roger. Dan's just got a stoned look on his face as he continues to get a butt hole wash from Roger. Dan seems to wake up from the haze, points toward us and says, "Hey, looks like your kid's got a boner." Charlie's still throwin' a rod and his prick's turned a red-purple color from wanting release—kinda like he's worn a cock ring too long.

Mike quips, "Hey! Tough shit! Part of this lesson in manners is that you don't get what you want by insulting your elders!"

"Well, you know," I say, "Maybe Charlie's learned his lesson here, and for a reward he should get to drain his balls." Then I suggest, "Dan, let Charlie come over there and help you out with Roger."

Dan waves Charlie on over. Dan lifts his butt off Roger's face, turns him over to release his wrists, then puts his backside down on the mat. He tells Charlie, "Fuck 'im, kid!" Roger is hardly in a position to protest his friend pokin' his ass, and Charlie's cock isn't protesting about doing it!

Charlie hoists Roger's legs into the air, sucks on a couple of fingers, and slides 'em into Roger's unprepared ass. I have the idea they've done this before. Dan sits himself down astride Roger's chest and plants Roger's mouth securely over his peter, as Charlie rams his dick home up Roger's butt. Charlie's been needing release for a long time, and it doesn't take long before he fires his kid load into Roger. Dan's getting close to coming himself. His eyes are glazed, then shut. He grimaces and grunts, then begins to fuckin' yell. Shit! I'll bet ol' Gus can hear this from inside the damn store.

Dan bangs down Roger's throat once, then a second time, then he explodes. Dan's body shakes with tremors from the force of spunk released from his big fuckin' nuts! He tosses his head back as he yells, sending sweat flying from his face and hair all over the rest of us and my truck cab. Roger can't swallow those thick wads of jizz fast enough, so cum spews from his mouth, down Dan's veiny dick, and into his crotch hairs.

Dan pulls Roger's mouth off his wanger but then rubs Roger's face around his spunk-soaked pubic bush and balls, finally wiping his dick on the kid's face, using it as a cum rag. Dan then sits with his hairy back against the truck cab, relights a half-smoked cigar, and gives Mike and me one of those just-cum, exhausted-but-fuckin'-satisfied grins. "Shit!" he says. "I need a fuckin' beer."

Last chore for the night? Dump the kids. Hell, Roger's clothes are cut up, and Charlie's are tossed in all directions and lost. Don't know where in shit their car keys might have disappeared to.

We use some more rope and have Roger and Charlie in the truck bed, trussed up by the wrists and ankles and joined back-to-back. Something about that rope gives Roger's prick a boner, but we decide to ignore it. If he wants to get his balls off, he can discuss it with Charlie later.

Dan pulls his pants and boots back on, and Mike gets back into his clothes. My pants and shirt are ripped, so I just say fuck it and get behind the wheel bare-butt naked, with Mike and Dan filling up the cab.

Going on for a few miles, we finally stop near a soybean field and get out. The night's warm, so no one's going to freeze his balls. We get the kids out of the back, untie their ankles but keep 'em still tied back-to-back, and set 'em down on their asses by the road. If they want to go anywhere, they can still walk.

For the final lesson, Mike, Dan, and I hose down them down with hot, pent-up whiz from our bladders. There's some protest, but the last thing they hear from these three hairy fat old guys is a hearty "Yee-hah!" as we leave them tied, naked, cum-filled, and piss-wet in the dust raised by my truck.

Bernard and the Energy Circle
LANCE GAP

I wrapped my arms around Bernard's neck to prepare for the daily humiliation. His thick muscles bulged beneath my wrists as he pulled me to my feet. In two careful steps he twisted sideways and dropped me into the potty-chair. Always discreet, he stepped outside the door of my small bedroom until I'd finished my business. Chemo is a bitch.

Sitting, waiting for my bowels to work, I thought about Bernard. He was the type of man I'd fucked when I was alive: barrel-chested, bearded, hairy as my cat. I'd been that big before cancer chewed me up. Now I envied those muscles inside his tie-dyed T-shirts, and that round, tight belly. Desire pricked me when I looped my hands around his furry neck.

Unfortunately, Bernard was almost 30 years younger. And probably straight. And our relationship was purely professional. So sex was out of the question. Even so, we formed a bond when he became my home health care attendant a month ago. We joked together and shared stories about fishing the Northwest. He did the *River Runs Through It* bit better than I did, spending his summers as a guide near Henry's Fork in Idaho. Me, I was lucky if I got out four or five times each season. During radiation I'd promised myself that, if I survived, I'd spend a lot more time with my rod in hand.

I liked Bernard. Not just because he washed my back and tucked me in. Bernard was my type, down to his scent. When he helped me in and out of the shower, I caught that slightly stale blend of Old Spice, garlic, and pot.

My young helper smelled like my first Daddy, the man who molded me. He was one of the gang who played poker with my father. This was up in Oregon timber country. Pop worked at the mill. Most of his buddies were scrawny little weasels who tossed back a bump and a brew or five after work. But one was a big man who fit the lumberjack image. Cord was tall and muscled with bright blue eyes and a heavy thatch of wavy dark blond hair. A handsome and well-trimmed beard framed an almost continuous smile. When he walked into our tiny kitchen, he looked like a giant.

Then he'd settle his ass onto an aluminum chair, pop open a beer, and settle into the game, one thumb hooked around a red suspender, the other pressed against his cards.

As a child, I sat on the kitchen counter, sipping a cola, watching the men play. Sometimes I watched Pop's hand, sometimes Cord's. As I grew up, I started hanging out with friends on Friday nights, and the men at the card table vanished from my thoughts. It wasn't until I was a freshman at Boise State College that I noticed them again. Boise was seven hours away. I didn't make it back home until Thanksgiving vacation.

Friday after the big meal, I was getting ready to go out with my high school friends when the doorbell rang. I answered it and saw Reedy Sims, one of the card players. Skinny, bowlegged, mouth bulging with a big wad of chew, Reedy had been a rodeo star in his youth. Before he got to his third beer, you could see, wince by wince, what walking now cost him.

"Hey, it's the college boy!" said Reedy. "What's the big word *du jour*?" he asked, laughing, poking a sharp tongue through the hole where his left incisor used to be. He stepped in, carrying a six-pack. Cord followed him up the walk.

The big man stomped snow onto the welcome mat. Flakes glittered on his thick blond beard. Blue eyes flashed above glowing, rosy cheeks.

"So, you've been away to school?" said Cord. Taking his brown leather gloves off, he jerked on the zipper beneath his neck. It didn't budge. He bent his head, trying to see where or how it was sticking. The zipper remained hidden just below his beard.

"Oh, shit. Not again," he said.

"What?" I replied, smiling because I could see that the zipper was caught on a fraying seam.

"It's this damn jacket," he said. "Mary says I should get a new one but I just can't, not for poker night. This is my lucky jacket. I don't suppose you could—"

" 'Course..." I replied, and played with the zipper, testing the material. I gave it a tug. My fingers slipped on the cold metal. I found it and tugged again. This time my hand slipped and rested for a moment against his chest. For a second I felt the great thud of his huge heart. A hot jolt surged directly from my hand to my cock. It rose against my pants without my permission.

My face turned fiery. I grabbed the zipper tightly and managed to jerk his jacket open to his belly. Then it caught again on the lining.

"I'll take it the rest of the way," he said, his big hands closing over mine, pushing the zipper down. When his jacket pulled open, he kept my hand dropping. He pushed it against the bulge in his own pants. The fire coating my skin filled my brain. My heart thundered as I stopped breathing. I looked into the bright blue eyes, in their nest of fine lines. They drilled into my dark ones, reaching the secret places I'd kept hidden from everyone, especially myself.

"After the game," he said, his voice so low only the dog and I heard it.

He took off his coat and moved toward the kitchen. The entire action occurred in the time it took for Reedy Sims and Pop to say howdy, open two beers, and put the rest in the fridge.

I put my own jacket on and went out. I barely felt the chill as I walked to a nearby coffee shop to chat with a couple of girls and a guy from my high school clique. But I kept thinking about Cord. What exactly would we do after the game? It was the late 1960s. I knew about queer folk and I'd seen one gay porn mag, but I wasn't really sure who I was. I wasn't one of the utterly beautiful ones who get invited to lose their virginity early. I was nerdy and gangly and utterly repressed. I liked girls and had kissed a few but never anything else, in spite of their occasional insistence.

So I sat with my friends, barely noting their conversation, my eyes shifting from my watch to the night sky and back again. The poker games usually ended around 1 in the morning. I wanted to go back just when it was letting out. At some point in my waiting, our little group went out to someone's car and passed a joint back and forth. At 12:30, restless, I said good night. I drove home slowly over the black ice.

When I got back to the house, only Pop and Cord were left. Pop was drunk. He was really happy and he pointed to me. "Look at him. College kid. Damn. Who'da thought a fucker like me coulda had a sharp kid. Damn. Proud of you, son." He grabbed me into a bear hug. I could smell the whiskey on his breath. I gently pushed him away. He smiled. "Think I better go ta bed. Lock up, Lance."

Pop pushed through the swinging door, his hand automatically flipping off the overhead light. A couple of moments later I heard his feet on the stairs.

Cord leaned against the kitchen sink, looking across at me. Moonlight poured across his handsome, bearded face. I wasn't sure what to do. Should I act like a young man in a queer porn magazine? Should I act like the son of an old friend? For a moment I simply stood there, looking at him. He swept his eyes up and down my body but did nothing more. He just stood there, arms across his chest, holding my eyes with a blazing blue gaze.

A switch clicked in my head. One minute I was busy worrying about all of life's rules, about straight rules, gay rules, the rules of the new world of college, the rules of the old world of the woods. The next moment there were no rules at all.

I walked around the table and moved in front of him, keeping my arms at my sides. We stood staring at each other. Then my hand slowly moved across to the front of his jeans. My knuckles moved up and down against his zipper. I felt the now-warm metal against them. I also felt the curve of the bulge within.

My eyes followed Cord's hands as they dropped to his belt buckle. He undid the brown leather, unzipped, and pushed his jeans and shorts toward his knees. Then he put his hands on my shoulders, pushing me down. I bent over, putting my hands on the sides of his big belly, kissing the shirt between his breasts. Then I slowly dropped to one knee, running the right side of my face down his belly toward his cock. As I reached the floor, I helped him out of his shoes, socks, shorts, and jeans. He kept his balance with one hand on my shoulder. I smelled the potato chips, beer, and piss.

Once his pants were off, Cord put one hand on the back of my head and the other on his heavy dick. He pushed my face toward something that looked like an entire kielbasa. I thought I'd be able to suck him, but the size of the cock daunted me. How could I put that in my mouth? What if I choked? How silly would that be? Finally I said, "I've never done this before."

His hands stopped. A bass chuckle rumbled in his big belly. He squatted and put a big hand between my legs. His heavy hand gently squeezed my thickened cock. The other hand carefully pushed me backward, until I was lying on the floor, half on and half off the rag rug. I shifted my body until I was completely on it. As I did, his hands moved over my pants. He tugged them over my hips. Reaching down, he pulled my shoes, shorts, and pants off. The hair on my legs pricked in the chill.

Then, without warning, I felt the most astonishing sensation. Something hot, soft, but incredibly strong had captured my throbbing cock. I looked down. Cord's thick head of wavy hair shimmered silver in the moonlight as he rode my cock with his mouth. He played it with his tongue and held my balls. I moaned and twisted around.

"Shhh," Cord whispered. His hands slid snakelike up my body. He shifted his position on the rug, now kneeling next to my head.

I could see the table legs behind his own thick timbers. I felt my cock curving over his tongue and down his throat. I felt wild. I hungered to be consumed by my own fire or have the flames put out by Cord.

He lifted a strong thigh and put it over my head. His heavy ball sac, thin skin holding two ripe plums, dangled over my eyes as his long cock bumped against my nose. It smelled musky and ripe. I instinctively guided him into place so that I could just suck the tip of his cock. He didn't force it further, though I could feel his legs tensing against my ears as the desire to thrust rippled through him. His mouth acted out the desire of his hips as he pushed himself harder and harder onto my dick. My cock replaced his own, his mouth became my mouth. Desire echoing desire, his mouth invited me to allow the urgency of his need.

I was breathing harder. Energy built inside of me in my root parts. I wanted to explode. Suddenly, his mouth was gone. There was nothing but air against my cock. I felt overwhelmed with desire for that mouth. Crazed, I wanted nothing more than release.

I stopped my gentle tonguing of his cock. I settled my hands on his mighty thighs, digging my fingers into the furred flesh. I thrust my mouth and throat onto his fat cock. I almost gagged, so I released myself. Then I tried again.

He grunted and dropped his mouth again onto my cock. Now I wanted to come and I wanted him to come. I wanted to swallow his spunk and feel him swallow mine. His legs started to wobble and pulse. Our hips were like pistons. His hand pressed my asshole and knew what I wanted. I thrust my hips back further, feeling the hunger of that hole. Then, my cock needy again, I pushed forward, shoving against the length of his throat.

His finger followed my thrusts. I felt it at the pucker of my ass. I clasped it with my butt cheeks and pulled forward. Then I pushed back and the finger slipped inside. At first, he merely responded to my thrusts. Than I felt him moving against me again, thrust for thrust as his hand worked my asshole. We were in a circle of energy as Cord swallowed my power and passed it back to me through his mouth and hand.

The circle went faster and faster, stirring our release. I saw the circle against my eyelids: white, yellow, enflamed. It rolled faster and faster, carrying me to its center. I let go. It sucked me deep into its vortex then spewed me back as I came, thrashing wildly against the older man. Even as I shot, I felt his hot liquid pulsing down my hungry throat. With the explosion, everything in my mind burnt clean and clear. All the boredom, the wandering, the strange spaces of lost time in front of television and homework, were irradiated and redeemed. As I started to deflate I felt free, at peace.

The cool air came sweeping back. In the quiet night, I could hear the sound of a street sander a few blocks away. It was pouring red volcanic dust over the icy roads to make them safe for the next day's shoppers. I tasted Cord's spunk. We pulled away from each other and lay for a moment on the moon-sprinkled floor. Snow-reflected light painted a gray glow on the ceiling. Cord sat up, rubbing the back of his neck.

"Huh," he grunted, pushing his head to the side. Then he stood, bent over to pick up his shorts and pants. He pulled them on, balancing against the sink. He sat down to put his shoes and socks on, humming. I pushed back against the cupboards and watched him. Finally I noticed the chill in my legs and got dressed. By the time I got to my boots, he was watching me. Our eyes met. I nodded, knowing that he needed reassurance that the whole scene was OK.

I returned to school a new person. I knew what life felt like and the fire was in my mouth and hands and belly. I saw everything differently and measured men with my eyes, remembering the powerful circle of energy running through the world. When summer came, I had a brief affair with Cord, silent and swift. But nothing we did ever matched that first moment.

Nevertheless, for 30 years I loved bearish men and even lived with one for 10. But then I was alone. Or I should say that before

I had the cancer, I was alone. For the past six months I've lived in my sister's flat. Bernard comes five days a week to help me bathe. Over the weekend, my nephew who works in the city hospital does the job.

Before the last horrible set of treatments, we thought I'd have to contact the folks at our local hospice. But something scared the beast and it has backed off. I may be able to bathe myself soon. But such freedom will come at a price. I'll lose Bernard.

When I finished with the potty-chair I wiped myself and tried to push to my feet without help. My arms got me standing but my wobbly legs wouldn't hold. Bernard heard me moving and stood at the door, shaking his heavy head and frowning. The tail of his snake tattoo wiggled under the taut sleeve of his shirt.

"Soon, soon," he said, smiling, and came over to move me again. Once he got me into the chair, he pushed me toward the bathroom.

"You know, I can roll this chair myself," I told him.

"I know," he replied. "But isn't it nice sometimes to just let go and let someone take care of you?"

"That's all I've done for six months," I said with a weak growl. "Let other people care for me. Hell, I'm 50 years old. I should be caring for others." I thought about my sister's kids, now in college, and about the students in my physics class. How could I be a mentor when I was so tired and broken?

Bernard was silent as he pushed me through the doorway into the blue-tiled room. He moved the chair next to the tub. I pulled off my pajama shirt. My skinny white chest gleamed in the bright light. I looked out the window at the neighbor's rosebush. Its bright yellow blossoms were shining in a light spring rain. It was one of those strange Northwest days when the sun played hide-and-seek with clouds, tossing improvident rainbows over the hills and spotlighting flowers.

"Do you want to go out after your shower today?" asked my nurse, following my eyes.

"Yes, yes, could we please, huh, huh? Could we? Huh? Huh?" I half joked, anxious as a child.

"OK, then. But first, the tub!"

He put my feet on the floor and stood. Once again, I put my arms around his thick neck. He wasn't supposed to lift with his neck, and I mentioned this to him the first day. He told me that some rules weren't made for a man "built like a bull." When he straightened, my body pressed against his as he calculated how much weight I could take on my own legs.

"You're just about there," he said, gauging my sturdiness. As he held me in those heavy round arms, I felt a mixture of comfort and arousal. That shocked me. I hadn't had more than a memory of sexuality for a year. Even so, that soft, swinging bell clapper between my thighs began to feel as though it might ring again.

"I can lift my legs, I think," I said. I raised a foot and stepped into the tub. I picked the other one up and put it beside the first. Both were firmly planted in front of the plastic bench. Bernard helped me down to the bench and handed me the shower hose. He turned on the water. I pointed the head away as it raced cold. Gradually the spray heated. I held the nozzle overhead and felt the cleansing warmth pour over me. For two weeks I'd been able to shower and soap myself. It was just getting in and out of the tub that was the problem. I laid the showerhead down in the tub and put shampoo on my hair, closing my eyes. The sharp, woody scent smelled so clean in this friendly blue room: nothing like the musty caged-animal smell of my bedroom.

Then, while my eyes were closed, I felt another pair of hands in the lather on my head. Then they were massaging my back.

"That feels good," I said, as Bernard's thick thumbs moved beside my shoulder blades. The body gel acted like massage oil, making my skin slick.

Then his healing hands brought forth a miracle. I felt blood moving south. My cock thickened. I got embarrassed at what he must see: a broken man with a sad little hard-on. I couldn't imagine how pathetic I must have seemed. I picked up the hose and rinsed my head and body, hoping to remove evidence of my inappropriate response to his professional touch. His hands disappeared as I once more felt the spray.

But the water did nothing to dampen my cock's enthusiasm. When I opened my eyes I was surprised to see something much more presentable than I'd imagined. My half-hard dick curved above my balls. Even as I glanced down, it twitched, rising higher. I realized that the energy rushing through my chest and mind wasn't simply pleasure at the beauty of the season.

"I'm sorry," I said, more bemused than embarrassed. I looked at his strong form, squatting beside the tub.

"For what?" he said, grinning behind his carefully trimmed beard.

"For this, um, response to your kindness." I said, one hand waving over the offending member.

"Oh, it's nothing I haven't seen or been before," he said. "You know, massage can sometimes create stiffness as well as mend it. I should be sorry. Would you like me to fix it?"

I couldn't believe I'd heard him correctly. Didn't he have a girlfriend? Wasn't he a professional? Did I actually care about the answer to either question? "Oh, yes, please," I said, grinning back at him.

He put some shower gel into his big hand and slid it around my cock. At first his hand was gentle as it moved up and down, pulling more blood into my rod, making it thicker and longer. My mind buzzed with desire. I held on to the sides of the bath chair and felt my biceps bulge. Then his hand left my cock.

"Do you mind if I join you?" he asked.

Without waiting for a reply, he pulled off his shirt. Curly brown hair covered his chest and belly. His nipples were thick and dark as blackberries among the hairs. He took off his boots and socks. Turning to look at me, he moved his hands to his belt.

I watched him hungrily and stroked the miracle in my hand. The dead could return, I thought. He loosened the wide leather belt and unbuttoned his jeans. He wore plain white shorts underneath. He reached in and adjusted his cock, making its fat head pop up over the elastic. He pushed his shorts and pants down past his fattened rod and huge set of balls, then stepped out of both and into the tub.

"May I turn the water back on?" he asked, adjusting the knobs on the hose. I nodded. He leaned past me toward the showerhead on the wall. As he did so, his dick bobbed under my nose. I stuck my tongue out, licking the tip and tasting his salty precum.

"No, no," he said, chuckling. Then I felt warm water falling over me from behind. Bernard pulled two washcloths off the rack behind him, dropped them next to my feet, and knelt on them.

"The shower is like the rain," he said. "Have you ever done it in the rain?"

"I'm an indoor guy," I said, as his hand moved over the one I had on my cock.

"I'm not," he said. "I love it outside. Day like today. Rain mixed with sun. A shining dark. The strangeness. The wet."

"It's very wet here," I said, my hand squeezing the thickheaded rod so close to my own.

As we stroked each other's cocks, joy of the return increased my desire. The pain in my body, the dullness from weeks of recovery, began to slip away. I felt nothing but the life thickening below.

Then Bernard moved closer, putting his cock against mine. "Use your hands to hold on," he said, helping himself to more shower gel. He put his hands around both of our cocks, mashing the hard meats together. I felt his heat along the length of mine. Mine was thick at the base and narrow at the head; his was the opposite, with a huge mushroom dome. He gripped them both with one big hand. It almost fit around both. He began working, sliding his meaty fist up and down.

I moaned in joy, aligned with his strength and power. His hard cock blessed me with his desire for an older, sicker man. Bernard saw the life in me and invited it into daylight. It rose up dancing. I pushed forward on the chair.

He accepted the invitation and slid a hand under my ass. I felt a finger at my asshole, first rubbing it with gel, washing it. And then it slid in. The probing finger sent an electric shock to the base of my skull. I rode one hand as the other worked our cocks. The build began. It suddenly stopped. Exhaustion and pain flooded me. It would be impossible for me to come. I stared across the infinite inch of space between us.

His face flamed behind the beard, with wild eyes and a huge toothy grin. Perhaps he saw the doubt in my face, for he leaned forward and put his mouth on mine. I held to the chair, the muscles in my arms and chest pressing against him. His tongue played and then probed, matching his hand movement as we sucked, creating a wild energy circulating between us. This energy became a circle, moving from our mouths down Bernard's body to his hands, into my asshole and cock, and back up my body to our mouths.

In that holy, miraculous circle, I revived again. The whirling pulse banished time while pouring me into my history. There was nothing but the wild energy of the movement within. Flashes pulsed around me, through me. White and yellow burst against my inner eyelids, and I came in a sound like rushing water. As I groaned, arms spasming, I felt him shudder. He pulled his hand out of me and grabbed the chair. I felt the heat of his jism on my belly before the water washed it away.

Then his arms were around me as he hugged me and growled in my ear, "Are you OK? I kinda lost myself."

"I'm great," I said. And I was. Lightened and clear. For the first time since the diagnosis I believed I'd have a life again.

Bernard got more bath gel and rubbed it over his fur, humming, making a mound of white between his thighs. Then he switched the water back to the hose and washed the foam off both of us.

"How are your arms?" he asked.

"Shaky but happy," I said.

"Good deal. Still want to go out?"

I looked out the window. I saw sparkling crystals falling in front of a pure blue sky. No clouds. No rainbows.

"Yeah," I said. "Yeah. I want to go out."

Custom-Made
JESS DAVIS

In general, I avoid the world of suit-and-tie people as much as possible. Tough to find a place that sells a decent size 50 anyway. Luckily, the boy cleans up great for that sort of thing, wears what I dress him in, and does the deals for me. One of the ways he earns his keep. Leaving me free to work and try to stay on schedule, not disappoint my long waiting list of nice ladies just creaming for a custom-built this or that by Jay Ducharme for their houses because all their nice friends have them.

This week I'm stuck: The boy is down to Boston visiting family, and some joker up from New York "just today" needs to tell me about the desk he needs for the house my buddy Rich is renovating for him. Rich says the guy has cash to burn—especially if I have to meet with him myself, you know I'm going to overcharge him for all the assorted inconveniences. I told him to come on out to my shop any time this afternoon so at least I don't have to kill the afternoon on it. Meanwhile, I'm sanding away by hand at a section of mahogany sideboard due to be finished Tuesday for a family just down the road. It's coming nice, the wood is gorgeous, and I'll only be a week behind schedule when it's done, so I'm happy enough about that, humming along with Muddy Waters on the stereo. Nice thing about this kind of work: People don't bitch at you too much if it's a little late—they're too busy trying to imagine how my two hands and a bunch of tools made whatever they've gotten themselves. I give 'em the line, third-generation Vermont craftsman raised to bend the wood to my will, but really it's just practice and time, and you can bend anything to your will. The boy's better proof of that than a sideboard, but I keep that to myself.

I hear Mr. New York's tires in my gravel, but I keep sanding, figuring he'll find me if he's bright enough to tie his own shoes without help. Whatever kind of car it is, it's throaty, sounds American. One point in his favor, anyway. The shop door bangs, and I look up ready to be annoyed, but keep quiet instead. This guy's not any kind of suit from the city I ever seen. Hell, he fills up the doorway, and not an inch of it sloppy at all. In a suit, yeah, probably tailored for him, since I don't think any of those weasel-ly Italian designers ever thought to dress a set of shoulders like that, and the brightest blue shirt I ever saw with a suit. Fuzzy, but neat about it, not but a half inch of hair on his head and on his face too—like mine. I hold out my hand and introduce myself; he shakes a good firm shake and tells me his name is Walt, with a look that says he's just as surprised to be pleased to meet me as I am him. I grab a rag to wipe the sweat off my face and sneak a look at his basket, which looks to be as meaty a snack as the rest of him. Amazing how a day can start to look up, just like that.

I offer Walt a beer, which he takes without any yammering about was it a microbrew from virgin malt harvested in a full moon, and lead him out onto the front porch. Strategic—the porch built by me, all the scrollwork done by me, and the chairs and glider are my designs too. I figure it couldn't hurt to surround him with my work. I settle in an oversize Adirondack-style chair, put my feet up, and say, "So, Rich says you need some special type of table for your office?"

"Yes," Walt says, loosening his tie, "I need a desk that's very sturdy, and adjustable in a few ways."

I gesture for him to go on, curious—what the hell does he want to put on this desk?

"I want it to have three sections, so that the ends can be fold-ed down, one at a time or together, so I could, uh, move it into a smaller place temporarily, and I also, uh, need the center section to have a removable top. I think maple would be nice, with, uh, brass hardware." I'm trying not to laugh now, because I know exactly what he wants—a goddamned bondage table! I have one almost exactly like the one he's describing down in my playroom. I keep quiet and play with him a minute—I want to see what exactly I have here.

"I can do what you want," I say, "but that's a hell of a funny design. What are you gonna need to do all that adjusting for?" He coughs, and his cock jumps a little in his suit pants. I'm loving life. I wait.

Finally he controls his cough and says, "Well, in my business, I, uh, have specialized equipment that, uh, which necessitates the use of certain configurations. Of the desk...you see..." He's starting to shift a little in his seat, and I'm giving him the look that my dyke friend calls the "appetite" look—am I hungry enough to have you for a snack? I make a mental note to call her, and get up from my chair.

I cross to right in front of him, way too far into his space, stand right between his legs and say, "Come inside—I have something a lot like what you're describing. You'll just tell me how yours needs to be different." Standing right over him, I can smell his sweat-and-soap smell, and I can see the dark fur on the backs of his hands. Hoping to see more, I lead him in though the front door, though the kitchen, and to the basement door. I nudge it open with the toe of my boot, flick the switch, and send him down first.

He's on the last step when he sees, and makes a strangled kind of whimper in his throat. Three steps later, I'm right behind him, holding both his elbows in my hands hard behind his back, saying in his ear, "See what you need here?" He nods, silently, and I walk him all the way in, keeping his back bowed and chest thrust forward until we get to the full-length mirror so I can take a good look. I yank at his tie, running it down, and pull it off over his head, cinching it back around his elbows. One hand holds it there while the other tugs his shirt out of his pants and then open—a chest covered in coal-black fur is underneath, with a pair of small, soft nipples barely peeking out. I muscle him over to my version of his "desk," slam his chest down onto one of the padded sections, and say "Take a close look" while I reach up for the cuffs that will lock around his wrists. I get my leg between his, pressing my thigh in a rhythm against his balls, laying most of my weight right down on him while I take my time locking him into the cuffs, trapping him between the padded leather and my sweaty self. Once he's locked with his arms stretched out long, I release the last section of the "desk" so he's bent right over it, ass shoved out to me, still in his city pants.

My dick is making a painful knot in my jeans, so I walk around to the front side of him and put my crotch right where he can see it, unbuttoning my jeans, unzipping my fly, and hauling out my length, which I let smack up against my belly. My precum is starting to flow, and a few drops splat right down in front of him on the bench. I grin. Spitting once in my hand, I lube it up a little bit, right in front of his face, then lean up to the bench and stick my dick in his furry, sweaty armpit. Nice and hot under there, and the hair feels great—I fuck back and forth along his skin for a minute or two, my hands squeezing and slapping at his ass through his pants, just feeling along his hide and checking things out. His pits are slick with his hot sweat and my precum—and he tries to tuck his elbows as close to his body as he can, giving me a little friction. I appreciate the gesture—I can feel my nuts drawing up already.

A couple minutes, though, he starts to feel the burn and tries to find a more comfortable position. Of course, the more comfy positions don't show his hot, hard muscles straining, and as a fellow who makes his living on form and the purity of lines, I think my taste should come first, right? Also, I'm not the one in chains right now. Not that I don't love his efforts—he manages to show himself off all the better and work up a nicer sweat. Then again, natural beauty can always be improved on.

Pulling away, I jam my big hands under him, unbuckle his belt and slide it out of his pants, double it, and crack it right in his ear to watch him jump. I grab hold of his suit pants at the seam and tear them right in half, leaning down to growl in his ear, "Mine now, buddy, you're mine, hot man, wandering in here so innocently to the spider's web. You like it? You like being chained down here, no one around to hear you? You do like it, don't you, you like being mine, moving your ass like a hot little club bunny, such a slut for me, you want me to fuck your hard ass, is that it? That's what I thought," I say when he strains up against the chains, hurting himself to rub his skin against my fur. "That's what I thought," I repeat. He wriggles some more, and I tear the rest of his pants away, until he's chained on my table wearing just a pair of white boxer briefs, a lot of sweat, a hard-on, and a grin. "There's an extra charge for this, you know," I say, rubbing the leather of his belt back and forth over his ass to make some friction.

"Just tell me what I owe," he rumbles, "take what you want, please, yeah, take me," and I smile at the invitation. My dick is starting to actually hurt, it's so hard, so I step back for a minute and rubber up, rolling on my trusty Trojan and stepping back up to the plate. I start rubbing my dick back and forth against his lips, standing just far enough back so that he can get his tongue on it. He tries to lasso it into his mouth, but I'm merciless, tormenting us both, until he's stretched to the length of the chain with his mouth open wide, whimpering, with the tip of my dick just barely grazing his lower lip. I take a step forward all at once and smack his ass with the belt at the same time hard, muffling his yelp with my dick shoved straight down his airway. He takes it pretty good, choking at first but letting me in as much as he can on the first stroke, working hard for me. His mouth is hot and feels so good, the base of my neck starts to tingle in that way when you just know it's going to be great. With my left hand, I grab his chin to help support his head and control how much of me he gets, and with my right, I use the belt on him. My long arms let me reach tight over his back and pepper his ass with hot licks from the tip of the doubled belt. I get into a rhythm, giving him a smack on each stroke in. I take each gasp of pain as an opportunity to get in a little further, fucking his mouth until the head of my dick rides right past the back of his throat.

It isn't long before my balls are boiling and my sac is trying to crawl back up into my belly, so I take my dick back out, the safe dripping, and walk around to really concentrate on smacking his ass. He yowls at being left empty, then he does it again when I lay the line of the belt right down along the white cotton, giving him the type of stripe he'll have for days. I want to see it, and since there's no one to stop me, I work his shorts down and off. They've got a huge wet spot on the front, so I stuff them in his mouth so he doesn't feel so empty. I'm a sensitive guy, what can I say? Sure enough, his flanks are reddening up nicely—he braces his feet back on the floor so he doesn't start to swing, then shifts, spreads his legs as far as they'll go, and today's special comes into view, already starting to open up. Stepping back from his invitation, I give him another unmerciful crack across the milky backs of his furry thighs, and follow it quickly with two more, enjoying the muffled noises from his stuffed mouth.

My cock is sending my brain do-or-die messages, so I grab the lube and squeeze, coating my dick thickly with goo and wiping the excess in his crack. Just the touch against his hole makes him sing a happy tune, so I take a minute to enjoy, rubbing my rough calluses hard on his red skin with my left and working one finger up his ass with my other hand, making him squirm away from the pain right onto my hand. Possibilities. I take my finger out and pry my dick down from my belly, touching the tip to his hole, and try again. Walt moves his ass like a dancing boy on stage and starts trying to back up onto my meat, wiggling and grunting like a pig. I slide in slowly, keeping the pace steady, until I'm standing still between his thighs, balls-to-balls at the edge of the platform. My hands reach under to grab his nipples, and I start to throw him a serious fuck, tugging on his tits to swing the table on its chains, fucking his whole body back and forth onto my dick as I stand still, while he flies like Superman. We pick up the pace, and my hips get into the action, grinding into him, short-shucking every few strokes to keep him off balance. It's great, my cock buried all the way into his slick guts, his sweaty, reddened body still straining to make sure I can touch and torture whatever I want. We both know this won't last too long, so I slide my hand right under and pull his prick down over the edge of the table. I jack it lazily with my slick hand, knowing that between his body and the table, he's made himself a little cock ring, and he won't come until I do.

I'm ready to shoot right up his ass, and it feels like the cum might burst right out his throat, I'm so ready. I shift my grip on his dick, shoving my fist into his belly to take the weight off his dick, and I squeeze it at the base, in rhythm with the fuck. He starts to really thrust his ass back at me, and I jam my cock in once, twice, and then the magic third time, giving his prick a good pump and letting his cum spray all over my hand while I fill the rubber up his hot ass with a growl of happiness. I flop forward, covering his torso with mine, my cock softening up his ass, and listen to his heartbeat for a minute, swaying him gently and breathing in his smell.

Pushing off his back, I take his underwear out of his mouth and unchain his arms, wrap one arm across his chest, and half carry him to the couch, where I sit down hard and pull him on top of me, rubbing the strain out of his arms and shoulders, chewing on his ears. We don't speak for a while but just lie there in our sweaty heap, breathing, cocks still jumping from time to time. After a while, I say, "So...is that the desk you need?"

He picks his head up, and smiles at me, and says, "I'm not sure, really—I might need to take a closer look."

Walt and I catch each other's eyes and dissolve into laughter. I throw an arm over his chest again, wiggle around into a comfortable snuggle, and say "Absolutely" into his ear. We drift off to sleep that way, naked and tangled up, the city boy and me.

Moving Day
Fred Towers

"Shit."

I turned from my hedging to see who belonged to the deep, growling voice. When I saw him, I froze. He had short, midnight-black hair, a chiseled jaw, and a tan covering his face and shirtless hairy body. All I wanted to do was grab him by his hair and pull him in for a kiss.

I followed my hard cock across the street to where he was standing.

"Need help?"

"Yeah. Thanks," he said, nodding toward the full truck. "A buddy of mine's supposed to be helping. He conned me into letting him ride my bike over. He's probably out joyriding."

"I'll help take boxes in. We'll string him up by his balls when he arrives."

He responded to my threat with a chuckle. "That would teach him," he said, picking up a box.

We had unpacked about half of the van when his buddy finally decided to arrive.

"Where the hell have you been?" my neighbor demanded.

"I stopped by a couple of places to try to round up some help," the buddy said, shrugging. "Looks like you've found help."

I turned to look at the man on the motorcycle when I heard him refer to me. He was short, stocky, and hairy. He was shirtless and wore cutoff jeans. His thighs bulged and threatened to rip his shorts. Also, his cock looked like it could break free at any time from the faded jeans.

Thinking of his bulge, I decided to lower the box I was holding to cover up my hard-on.

"I'm sorry. I didn't get your name. I'm Ron. This is Bill," Ron said, pointing to the man on the motorcycle.

"I'm Frank. Frank Hades."

"Shit. You put him to work and don't even know his name?" Bill asked, punching Ron in the arm.

"I'm really sorry. That was rude."

"Don't worry about it," I said.

While we continued to unpack the moving van, Bill flirted with me. He brushed against me every chance he had. I caught him staring at me several times. It frustrated me because I was more interested in Ron, but I certainly wouldn't turn Bill down for a fuck. I couldn't read whether Ron had any interest in me. He appeared to be deep in thought. I hate it when I can't read a man.

Since I am not much of a flirt, I smiled at Bill for his antics. I decided I needed to give Bill a chance. I had always gone for the quiet, reserved type like Ron and myself, and it never worked out.

"I want to lick the sweat off of your hairy back," Bill said, sneaking up behind me.

"Bill, could you behave for just once?" Ron said.

"He's fine. I can take care of myself."

"I bet a big bear like you can take very good care of yourself."

In response, I smiled at Bill. Out of the corner of my eye, I saw Ron shake his head.

"If I'm a good boy, can I give you a tongue bath?" asked Bill.

"I don't think you know how to be a good boy," I said.

Ron busied himself by organizing the boxes we had brought in. Seeing my gaze shift to Ron, Bill went out to the van to get more boxes.

"Is he always so flirtatious?"

"Yeah. That's Bill, Mr. Superflirt."

I laughed.

"What's so funny?" Bill asked, returning.

"You are," Ron said. "Give me that."

Bill handed Ron the box. Bill turned and looked at me with his right eyebrow raised. I could tell he wondered what had been said about him, but wasn't going to ask.

"When are we going to eat? I'm starving," he said instead.

"Do you only think with your dick and your stomach?"

"What's wrong with that?"

"I'm getting hungry too."

When I spoke, Ron turned to look at me. He glanced down at his watch. "I guess we've been working a long time. We should stop and take a break."

"Oh, I see. Mr. Bear gets hungry and it's time to eat. I get hungry and I'm just a food slut. I don't get any respect around here."

"You are a slut."

Bill looked at me and said, "See what I mean."

"Are you trying to tell me you are just misunderstood?"

"Precisely."

"Give me a break," Ron said, shaking his head. "Misunderstood, my ass."

"Your ass. Talk about slut," Bill said, fondling a handful of ass.

"Don't touch the merchandise," Ron said.

My dick jerked in response to all of the talk about ass. I imagined clutching Ron's hips and slamming my tool into him. In response, precum drizzled from the head of my cock.

"I think someone is getting worked up," Bill said, staring at the front of my shorts.

"Maybe I am."

"Just what the doctor ordered for dinner, a big slab of meat."

I grabbed my crotch. Bill covered my hand with his and looked into my eyes.

"Eat all you want," I offered.

"Don't mind if I do." Bill lowered himself onto his knees and gnawed at the front of my shorts.

"Do you two want me to watch or leave?" Ron asked, trying not to look.

"I'd rather you join in," I said.

He whipped his head around to look at me. I smiled to let him know I meant it.

"I'll get condoms. They're in a box in the bedroom," Ron said, walking down the hall as he spoke.

Bill unbuttoned my shorts to free my throbbing cock. He licked and nuzzled his face in the hair on my stomach. "You are so deliciously furry. I love a hairy man."

I ran my fingers through his coarse blond hair and moaned. "I know what you mean," I said, yanking on his back hair.

I captured him by the hair on his head and pulled him up to me. I bent down to kiss him and pressed my dick against his flat, muscular stomach. My little pouch of belly flattened against him. I cupped his ass in my hands and kissed him on the mouth. I pushed my tongue into his mouth like I wanted to push my cock down his throat.

As if he knew, Ron returned naked with the rubbers. Bill snatched one. He sucked the head of my cock into his mouth while he rolled the condom down my shaft.

"Greedy little brat," Ron said, still holding the box in his hands.

When I saw Ron's long, slim cock pointing to the ceiling, I said, "Come here."

While Ron walked toward me, I studied the black hair covering his body. It bushed around his nipples and tapered down to his cock. He stopped in front of me. Unlike Bill, Ron was my height. I felt his breath on my face. Since I had my left hand laced in Bill's hair, I wrapped my right arm around Ron's waist to pull him against me. His dick pressed against my hip. I kissed him and moved my tongue in his mouth to the demanding beat of Bill's sucking.

I felt my cock sink deeper down Bill's throat. Bill played with my balls as he fucked my dick with his mouth. His finger would occasionally slip back to tease my asshole.

Ron pulled away from the kiss and stepped behind me. He

wrapped his arms around my waist and traced my neck down to my shoulder with his tongue. He pulled at my back hair with his teeth, and then he bit my shoulder. I groaned. He pressed his cock between us. It followed the crack of my ass. I felt his juices on my lower back. He pumped his hips and ran his tool up and down between my cheeks. I felt my asshole expanding to receive him.

"I want you in me."

He reached down to caress my opening and slipped in a finger. When he realized one finger wasn't going to satisfy the hunger, he slipped in another. As he finger-fucked me, I felt myself on the edge.

"Oh, please, give me your cock. I have to have it." I couldn't believe that I was begging, but I was beyond caring.

I felt the head poking at my hole. He slipped the tip in and pulled it out. He slowly teased my hole several times. I felt like backing myself onto it, but I didn't want to fall out of Bill's mouth. I wanted both. Finally, he began to inch more in each time he entered me. When I was about to burst, he slammed his whole cock into me and came. I grunted and shot cum into the condom. Bill licked the latex like he wanted to eat it.

Continuing to lick, Bill forged a path up from my crotch. I leaned down to kiss him while Ron pulled himself out.

"I'll be back in a minute," Ron said, walking backward down the hall.

"Don't be gone too long," I said, following him with my eyes until Bill took back my attention.

"Nothing like a sweaty bear to turn me on," Bill said, running his fingers through my coarse chest hair. He pinched and sucked my nipples into his mouth. I cupped his chin in my hand and pulled him up for another kiss. I wrapped my hand around his cock and gripped his meat.

"Nice cock," I said, pulling away from the kiss. I lowered myself onto my knees to get a better look at his package. I pumped his growing cock with my hand. The tip turned red and the veins bulged. When I could not resist the urge to swallow his tool, I looked around the room for the rubbers.

"Looking for this?" Bill asked, holding a wrapper in his hand. I took it from him and ripped it open. I unrolled it over the tip and flicked my tongue over the tip of his cock. He moaned and tugged on my head with the fingers he wrapped in my hair. I knew he wanted to slam his cock down my throat, but I forced him to wait.

I teased his throbbing cock by trailing my tongue down his shaft. I licked his balls and sucked them into my mouth like candy. I massaged each nut with my tongue while I had it in my mouth.

"Oh, God," Bill said, yanking on my hair to pull me up. "Please, suck my cock. Oh, please."

I eased my mouth down his tool and licked around the shaft. I teased him with this motion until his breathing raced in and out of his body. When I knew he couldn't take it anymore, I gobbled his meat down my throat.

"Oh, God," he said, pumping into my mouth.

I repeatedly licked the rim of his head before I devoured his cock. On my descent, I scraped my teeth over the condom. He tried to guide me by my hair to his own insistent rhythm, but I refused to follow.

"You'll come when I'm ready to give it to you."

"Oh, man," he said, releasing his grip on my hair.

After I tortured him for a couple more minutes, I began to suck him at a demanding rhythm. Once I started this, he shot the condom full of his juice.

I wrapped my arms around his hips and nuzzled my face against his stomach. I followed the creases that defined his abdomen with my tongue. I worked up to a standing position, not taking my hands or my mouth off of his body. I was hugging him when I noticed Ron leaning against a wall, masturbating.

"Let me help with that," I said.

Bill handed me another condom while Ron crossed the room to me. I ripped it open. When he stopped in front of me, I slid the rubber over the head and down his pole. I gripped it and held onto it like a handle.

I kissed him, sucking his tongue into my mouth. I outlined his lips with my tongue before I bit his lower lip. I kissed all over his face and neck, feeling his stubble with my lips.

"I don't mean to interrupt..." Bill said and waited for us to respond to his voice.

"Where are you going?" Ron asked when he noticed Bill had dressed.

"Well, now that I've had an appetizer, I'm going out to hunt down my main course." Turning from the opened front door, he said, "Ron, I'll bring your bike back tomorrow. I'll come over to help finish the move because I'm sure you two won't get anything more done tonight." He stepped down onto the porch. "Have fun, lovebirds." Then he shut the door behind him.

"Damn it. He's done it again," Ron groaned.

"What do you mean?"

"He played matchmaker. He always sidetracks me when he flirts with a guy. All along, he's planning how to get the two of us together."

I laughed. "Are you saying we've been set up?"

"That's exactly what I'm saying."

"Well, if that's the case, he's damn good at it."

I pulled Ron in for a kiss to bring his thoughts back to his cock in my hand.

"Aren't you upset that he set us up?" he asked, pulling away from the kiss.

"I'm glad he did," I said, starting to kiss a trail down his body. I detoured from my path to suck on his nipples. Getting back on track, I continued to kiss him down his stomach. I licked the hair trailing from his belly button to his crotch.

I devoured his cock, sucking it down my throat. I squeezed and caressed his balls until I felt them spasm. When I knew he was close, I milked him dry with my mouth. When he came, I imagined it shooting down my throat. Instead, it shot into the pocket of the condom.

When I stood, he hugged and kissed me. I wrapped him up in my arms and said, "He's right. We're not going to get anything more done, except for this." I kissed him and said, "Not that I mind."

Berserker
GARETH MACKENZIE

A.D. 750, along the coast of Norway, the region of Rogaland.

His name was Thorkel, but the others called him Bjorn, the Bear. He led The Twelve, the berserkers, who once served a great chief in Jutland. They had grown bored of being kept on a short leash, like dogs. Only sent out to punish the occasional rebellious Jarl, never allowed to step beyond the bounds of their Chief's law.

They were berserkers, warriors who fought under the protection and guidance of the spirit of the Bear, and the One-Eyed Father, Odin. They wore no armor into battle, no mail shirts nor leather jerkins, only bearskins over their backs. They used their hands and teeth as much as their spears or axes. They were feared by all. They struck terror into the hearts of the bravest warriors when the spirit of the bear came on them, when they went berserk!

They had left Jutland. Bjorn confiscated a longship and forced the frightened sailors to carry them across the Vik, away from Jutland, away from the land of the Danes, to the rich land of the Norsemen. They landed in Jaeder district; good farmland, rich steadings, plenty for the taking. With no Lord or Chief over them, The Twelve were free to take what they wanted.

They plundered Jaeder, sending the farmers and herdsmen into hiding. They took food, so much food—fat, greasy meats, wheels of cheese, and beer. They harassed the wives and daughters of great landholders in Jaeder district. Then they fucked the young men. The warriors that they did not kill became their toys. When The Twelve moved on, they took much gold and silver, and the pride of many men.

It was no shame to be fucked and used by a man of high standing, a Lord or warrior. It was a great shame for a warrior to be used by another warrior. It destroyed his standing among his peers. It degraded him. Many men were left degraded and humiliated in Jaeder.

Now The Twelve were in Rogaland. They raided many farms and steadings of both the rich and the poor. They killed any man who stood against them. They raped and fucked anything that did not run and hide from them.

It had rained all night, but the berserkers were warm and dry. Eating mutton, salted fish, cloudberries, and cheeses in the hall of a prosperous landowner. They drank the sweet mead the housewife had hidden in the brewhouse, all the beer, even the fresh milk. They fucked the sons of the house before their father. Disgraced and degraded them, then sent them out into the cold, wet night. They fucked the father, each of The Twelve taking his turn. They slept by the hearth fire, full and satisfied.

In the morning they set out again for new plunder. Each of The Twelve wore a new gold chain or broach taken from the household's chest. They trudged through mud into the dense fir woods. They were split up by the thick forest and a growing fog. The Twelve were divided into twos and threes. They would meet later at the next large farmstead.

Bjorn found himself alone. He didn't give it a passing thought. He would find the others today or tonight, or the next day. They would take another steading and feast and fuck. They would be together again, The Twelve, fearless and feared.

Ulfr Fenrison stood at the door of his hall. He watched the sun settle on the top of the western mountains. It spread its red-gold rays across the valley. It had burnt away the mist and driven the rain beyond the mountains. The rain would return tonight. He could smell it. For now, weak sunlight sparkled on the wet, rich, green hay in his homefield. Beyond the field he could see his horses run in the pasture. His cattle were in the hills with his servants.

Ulfr saw the big man come out of the forest. He saw him climb over the fences and lumber across the fields like a bear. His keen eyesight saw that the man was much like a bear. Huge, broad shoulders, hairy and coarse. The man was dark-haired with a full beard. He wore a bearskin over his shoulders. His bare chest was like a second bearskin, brown-skinned with coarse black hair. He carried an ax.

Ulfr fingered the horn bound in silver that hung by the door. He could blow it and summon his people, his pack, but he was intrigued by this invader. So he waited. This could only be one of The Twelve berserkers who were robbing the countryside. Ulfr had heard of them. This evening could be interesting. The furthering of a cycle of revenge.

Bjorn watched the man at the steading under his thick, dark brows. The place looked deserted, but that could be a ruse. The hall might be filled with men-at-arms waiting with spear and knife. He hefted his broad ax in readiness as he approached the hall. He eyed the lone man carefully. He was tall, straight, and lean. His hair was golden-brown and hung down over his shoulders. He wore a leather vest, opened to show a wide chest covered in golden fur. He seemed unarmed, but Bjorn approached with care.

The golden man stepped back into the hall. Bjorn thought to himself that this was when the others, who were hidden, would rush out at him. He was wary, but ready for a fight and a good fuck. He charged the open door. He hardly noticed the carved wolves on the doorposts as he rushed past them. The spirit of the bear was coming on him. He began to growl.

Bjorn entered the hall with a shout. It was empty, except for the golden man. He stood across the hall with his arms crossed, a sneer on his face. Between them was a board laden with food: red meat, cheese, beer, and flatbread.

"You're not late for supper," the golden man laughed. "You needn't rush to the table."

"I'll eat *you*," growled Bjorn, "after I fuck you!"

Bjorn circled the table. He snatched a piece of rare beef, a bit of cheese, and ate them. He grabbed a horn and took a drink of beer. It was cool in his dry throat. He came around the table slowly, feeding his hunger. The golden man moved with him, keeping the table between them.

"Who is lord of this hall?" Bjorn demanded as he took a bite of bread. "And where are its folk?"

"I am lord of this hall, and the folk are mine to worry about, not yours," Ulfr snarled.

Bjorn was feeling more confident. There seemed to be no one else around, not that he wouldn't have fought 20 men when the spirit of the bear came on him, when he went berserk. Still he was alone, without The Twelve, and he was cautious.

"I will fuck you, piss on you, and burn this hall," Bjorn said, laughing as he drank more beer. "I am Bjorn, leader of The Twelve, and I will be your master."

The golden man picked up a horn and drank a toast to Bjorn. "To the bear who roars," he said, smiling. "The sun has not yet set, and you are already claiming the night as your victory."

"Who are you?" Bjorn roared, throwing a horn of beer across the table. "I want to know before I piss in your ass!"

"I am Ulfr Fenrison of the Ulfhednar, and this is *our* place, bearman!" Ulfr snapped back, then added with a laugh, "Watch your manners."

Bjorn growled low, but he made no sudden move. Werewolves,

the Ulfhednar, his ancient enemies! Here was a son of Fenris, the great wolf, the enemy of Odin. He could win a place for himself in the hall of dead heroes if he served his Lord and vanquished the hereditary enemies of his God.

Bjorn took the time to watch his adversary. The golden man was handsome, young, and lean. Muscle rippled in his arms, his neck, and shoulders. He would not be so easy to take. Now Bjorn truly missed The Twelve.

Bjorn studied the man. Ulfr had a long, drooping yellow mustache, no beard, and clear blue eyes. His jaw was square and clean. He dropped his vest to the floor and flexed his muscles. He body was tight and lean, no extra fat. His chest and forearms were covered in yellow hair. Golden-brown fur ran in a line down his muscled stomach and into his leather breeches. There was a bulge worthy of a warrior in the front of his breeches.

Bjorn noticed Ulfr carried no weapons. Axes and spears hung on the walls with shields bearing the device of wolves, wolf paw prints, and snapping jaws, but none was within close reach. Bjorn intended to keep it that way. His instincts warned him this man would not give in without a fight.

The berserker pulled his bearskin over his head. He growled to summon the bear spirit. He swung his ax one-handed and moved around the table. Ulfr waited for him. He stood his ground in front of the high seat, carved from a solid oak trunk.

Bjorn rushed at him, swinging his ax in a high arc. Ulfr waited until the ax began its descent, then he stepped to the side. The ax blade cut into the oaken chair and stuck fast and firm. As Bjorn struggled to pull it free, Ulfr sprang at him with a howl. The two beings fell back into the table, food and wooden trenchers scattered everywhere.

The berserker had lost his ax, but it didn't matter, his bear spirit was upon him and he could kill a man with his bare hands when he went berserk! Bjorn rose out of the debris like a great black shadow. He roared. When he did, Ulfr sprang at him again, this time not aiming for the berserker at all.

Ulfr grabbed the heavy, greasy bearskin and snatched it off of Bjorn. He ran to the far end of the hall and threw it into the rafters near his own wolfskin. It stuck there and hung beyond the reach of a man without a ladder. Bjorn cursed in his fury, but even as he roared he felt the berserker spirit, his Fylgja, leave him.

The two men circled each other three times. Then Ulfr lunged for Bjorn. He caught the bear around the waist, his face crushing into Bjorn's sweaty, rank chest hair. Bjorn stood solid as an oak. His own arms wrapped around Ulfr as he tried to crush him. Ulfr slipped free and leapt back from his opponent.

Bjorn rushed the wolf, but he hadn't counted on Ulfr's quickness. Ulfr dodged the bear, tripped him, and sent Bjorn sprawling across the dirt floor. Before Bjorn could react or roll over, Ulfr was on him. Ulfr threw himself across the bear's back. He banged Bjorn's head into the hard-packed dirt floor until the bear was nearly senseless.

Ulfr reached down and ripped open the back seam of Bjorn's leather trousers. He opened his own and his thick, hard cock sprang out. Ulfr's slippery, wet cock head pressed against Bjorn's ass. Bjorn realized what was about to happen and he fought to free himself.

Ulfr slipped both arms under Bjorn's thick upper arms to gain leverage. He grabbed Bjorn's hairy forearms and pinned them behind his head. Bjorn struggled, but could not move. Ulfr drove his cock into Bjorn's ass. The bear growled in pain and despair.

The wolf began to fuck his captive, driving his long rod into the virgin bearhole. Bjorn snarled and cursed. He thrashed about beneath Ulfr, but could not free himself.

Bjorn had felt the first pain, both physical and emotional, as his enemy's cock rammed into his hole. He struggled, but the spirit of the bear was gone from him. He felt the shaft of Ulfr's cock drive in and out of his hole. He tightened his muscles to try and stop the invasion, but that only excited Ulfr more. The wolf forced himself deeper, and Bjorn felt the hot pain searing his bowels.

Bjorn heard Ulfr howl in his ear as the wolf shot his seed into his hole. Bjorn's world, his position in it, crumbled around him. He remembered the men he had seen, warriors, who had to endure the jeers of others, despised and used by their fellows, because he or another member of The Twelve had used them.

Semen surged into his ass. Bjorn shook his body, gnashed his teeth, struggled against the strong arms that held him, the big cock that pinned him to the floor like a spear. He could change nothing. It had happened, was happening, and for all his rage he could do nothing. Ulfr howled in triumph as he shot the last of his load into Bjorn's hole. The bear was utterly defeated.

"Who fucks who?" Ulfr growled into Bjorn's ear. "You are my catamite, my hole. I have made you my bitch-dog."

The fuck continued. It didn't stop after Ulfr shot his load of hot, white wolf gravy. He increased his speed, his intensity. He pumped harder. His cum-slick cock sliding in and out of Bjorn's freshly raped ass made a sucking sound. His hairy chest rubbed against the coarse-haired back of Bjorn. His hips pounded into the other's ass. He pressed his lips against the bear's ear, first to taunt him, but then the rage began to change to lust, the lust to immense physical pleasure.

Ulfr's teeth nipped at Bjorn's ear. He licked and nuzzled Bjorn's neck. He pressed his hips into Bjorn's hairy ass, deep into the warm, virgin hole. His chest felt good against the hard, broad back of the bear. He began to relax his grip on Bjorn's arms.

Ulfr pounded Bjorn's ass, ripped open his clenched hole. Bjorn's body caught the rhythm and he found himself moving with the swollen meat in his anus. He struggled less, finding the feel of the other man on him, in him, more agreeable than he might have imagined.

In the rafters, high above the scene of rape and lust, the Fylgjur of the two shape-shifters battled with each other and the world they knew. Among the smoke-darkened beams, the Fylgja of the Bear fought with the Fylgja of the Wolf. Both spirits growled and roared, their voices heard in the ringing of the thunder, the crackle of the lightning. A new storm was coming. The rain began to fall.

Even the spirits found the smell of sex too powerful for their taboos. The Wolf fucked the Bear, or was it the Bear who fucked the Wolf? Spirit cocks spraying hot, white spirit cum. Spirit ass-holes sucked up spirit seed.

Ulfr released his hold on Bjorn. Why fight for what he had already taken? Bjorn ceased to struggle; he had nothing left to pro-tect. In the grip of passion they forgot who was the enemy, who was the loser, who the victor.

The golden man felt his lust rising again. He wanted more of this bear's ass. He didn't notice how his own hands had begun to caress the hairy body beneath him. His hands slipped down the heavy, muscled side of his victim. He didn't think how his lips brushed the thick bear neck. The movement of his pole in Bjorn's ass became slower, more deliberate, more pleasurable.

Bjorn rose up onto his elbows. He didn't struggle to escape; instead, he pushed his body back toward Ulfr's rod. He slowly got onto all fours. Ulfr knelt between Bjorn's legs and shoved his cock deep into the bear's round, firm ass. Bjorn grunted and flexed his ass muscles. He felt his flesh grip Ulfr's cock tighter. He liked the way it felt.

Slowly, the two fucking men made their way toward the bench that ran along the walls of the great hall. The bench was covered in elk and sheepskins. Bjorn crawled up to the bench with Ulfr still buried deep in his hole. He put his hands onto the edge of the bench and pulled himself up.

Ulfr reluctantly let his cock slip out of Bjorn. His hard, throb-bing meat was slick with cum and shit. It stood out from his body like a lance. He waited for Bjorn to lie down on his back, his legs in the air. Ulfr's penis drove back into Bjorn's anus as soon as the hole was presented to him.

"Ughh," Bjorn grunted when the cock was inserted again. "You have beaten me, now take it all from me, my hole, my man-hood, my own seed."

Ulfr held Bjorn's legs wide open as he began to plow the berserker again. He looked down and watched his wet cock move in and out of Bjorn's tight, hairy asshole. It slid easily now, there was no resistance. Bjorn was completely subjugated.

Ulfr clasped Bjorn's hairy thighs and pulled him further onto his dick. The sweaty, pungent man smell drifted up to his sensitive nose. He drank in the aroma of men and sex. It heightened his excitement.

Bjorn reached up with his big, hairy knuckled hands and grabbed Ulfr's hard pecs. He squeezed them, felt through the golden-blond fur and found two stiff nipples. He twisted them, pulled them, as he tried to draw Ulfr closer to him.

"Fuck me!" Bjorn shouted. "You won. Fuck me!"

Ulfr leaned down over the hairy bear. He ran his rough tongue over the black-haired body. He licked up the center of Bjorn's chest, between the two beefy pecs. He nuzzled the bear's neck.

Bjorn wrapped his legs around Ulfr's waist. He had fucked many men, but had never been fucked. He had always felt contempt for those men who enjoyed being fucked, who craved it. Now he realized the pleasure involved. He wanted more of this wolfman. He wanted the long cock deep in his ass, the semen in his hungry hole.

Bjorn tried to pull Ulfr closer. His hands slipped over Ulfr's shoulders. He felt the golden fur covering his back, the muscles beneath the fur. His hands moved down the other man's back, his side. Bjorn felt the lateral muscles moving under his hands. He growled with lust.

Ulfr pounded the bear ass before him. He rammed his rod deep into the dark, hairy hole. He had made many of his own pack into bitch-dogs for his pleasure. Men who were there to be fucked by other men, by warriors and men of power. He had always chosen weaker men. Now he was fucking a strong berserker. He had made this berserker warrior into his bitch-dog.

Ulfr stood erect. He shoved his piece deep into Bjorn. He increased his speed as his second load of seed began to surge deep in his balls and fight to burst out. Bjorn was squeezing Ulfr's cock with his ass. It was so tight. So tight and warm. Ulfr felt his senses tingle as his rod grew near to bursting.

Bjorn had his own cock in his hands. It had been hard and throbbing the whole time he lay face down on the dirt floor. It was stiff and bounced on his belly when he lay on his back for Ulfr. He jerked it with quick, powerful strokes. The throbbing in his ass and the throbbing of his own cock blended with the beating of his heart. It blended with the rumble of thunder.

Both men roared simultaneously as the thunder clapped. Their bodies jerked out of control as they shot their loads of spunk. Ulfr filled his enemy's ass with a second serving of cum. Bjorn's cock exploded in a stream of hot, lumpy cum like buttermilk. Above them, in the rafters, the Fylgjur shared their seed and their essences. The hall shook when lightning struck a nearby tree.

The fire had burnt low in the fire pit. The two men slept in each other's arms, their breathing quiet. Strong, masculine chest supported rough-haired head. Powerful legs thrown over hairy, thick thighs. Cock resting wilted against warm, hairy skin. The wolf and the bear slept entwined. Above them the Fylgjur of the Bear and the Wolf had become one spirit for a time. Above the roof the storm raged on.

In the morning the two men fucked again. Slower now, less urgent, but just as intense. One man had found a new pleasure in life, a pleasure denied him by the very code of war that made him a warrior. The other had won a victory, but maybe not. A small victory at best.

Bjorn ate pickled herring from a wooden trencher and drank beer. He sat across the fire pit and watched Ulfr. Yesterday they were enemies. Last night, what were they? And today? He saw no comrade this morning. Only an enemy, a victorious enemy, but victory over what?

Bjorn retrieved his bearskin and his ax. He left the hall quieter than he had entered it. The spirit of the bear followed him. He walked toward the woods in the fresh morning air. He had much to think on. He was not eager to leave.

They, The Twelve, would smell the sex on him. They would know he had not won this fight. Someone would challenge him. Maybe Finn. Finn was strong. Or maybe Thorstein. He had always wanted to lead. They would want to tear him apart, use him as he had used so many others, but he would not give in. Was he not Bjorn? Let them try and take his command. If they took his ass, it would be because he chose to give it to them.

Bjorn laughed. Give his ass to another man? The thought excited him. He could still remember the feeling of a man's cock in his hole. Finn had a huge cock. The image of Finn naked and hard made his cock throb in anticipation.

Ulfr watched until the berserk was gone. He had won a victory, or should have, but his enemy seemed hardly touched by shame. The bearman had left his hall in the morning light with his head held high, his pride intact. Ulfr had fucked him, degraded him, yet he seemed as strong as when he rushed into the hall the night before. He was still a worthy opponent, and Ulfr was not happy to see him go.

What about his own feelings? He had reveled in subduing the berserker, but he had enjoyed more the pure act of sex with this man. He had fucked him more than once, and with some feeling of affection. Even now, his cock ached to feel the tight, warm, furry ass wrapped snugly around it. Even now, his arms missed the feel of the big, burly body in them.

Ulfr shook his head to clear it of thoughts. He fetched his own skin, his wolfskin. He placed it over his head and ran half-naked from the hall. He sprinted toward the wood edge. He would follow the bear, at a distance, just for a while. Maybe they would fuck again.

Tonight he would meet his pack and they would sing his victory song to the moon. Howl his triumph over the berserker to the great Wolf, Fenris. Yes, tonight, after he followed the bear just a little way, followed his bitch-dog. Tonight he would meet the pack, or maybe tomorrow night, when the moon would be nearer to full. There was no hurry. For now, he would follow the berserker.

Glossary:

Berserker: A Norse warrior who fought in battle often dressed only in a bearskin. The spirit of the bear helped him to fight fiercely and without concern for himself. Some believed they actually became bears. Berserkers were often dedicated to Odin.

Bjorn: Bear, or bearlike.

Fenris: Sometimes called Fenrir. A giant wolf who was destined to destroy the world. The Norse gods bound him with magic chains. It was prophesied that Fenris would break these chains and kill Odin in a battle that would bring about the end of the world.

Fylgja/Fylgjur: Protective spirit(s) which could guard and guide a warrior, and give him supernatural strength.

Ulfhednar: Literally, *wolfskins.* Similar to the berserks, these warriors wore wolfskins into battle and fought under the guidance of the wolf spirit. Also translated as *werewolves.*

Ulfr: Wolf.

Lurch

BEN ENSYDE

I had never placed a personal ad before, but was going through a dry spell ever since Mayor Giuliani started cracking down on anything gay, *anything* sexual, basically anything I might like here in New York City. Fuckin' Nazi! Forty-second Street had begun to look like a bad carnival to me. Personally, contrary to my buttoned-up button-down art director exterior, I really missed the hookers in all their gritty splendor. I've always had a soft spot for big-haired, big-hearted whores, in a platonic sense *of course;* and a very non-platonic hard spot for any hairy-chested hustler barely poured into a pair of black jeans about three sizes too small!

I often fantasized about rough trade and their taboo lives, but rarely acted. In short, my eyes were bigger than my stomach, or more appropriately, my appetite far surpassed my bravado. When it came to raunchy sex, I had the imagination of a gay Walter Mitty but the courage of Don Knotts in *The Ghost and Mr. Chicken.*

What really gets my pecker to stand and salute is the sight of a big, tough jock or a big, butch biker. The kind of hulking, hairy, out-of-control man I would never have the wherewithal or follow-through to actually seek out and "do" but had had wet dreams of ever since puberty. From the time my own hirsute carpet started to wall-to-wall my chest, I'd fantasize about theirs, as bigger, broader, thicker, ranker.

The first time that my fantasy turned into a reality was in high school, and the experience marked me for life. I was water boy for the football team. I had stayed really late cleaning up the locker room one night after a game and was showering before heading home, not wanting to get my new Mustang dirty. Brian Ramos, a star jock, had stayed late too, following a nasty fight with his girlfriend. I steered clear of him for the most part. But now, he was in the shower too. He was a big building of a guy with a huge forehead. Brian made King Kong look like Fay Wray. He was almost 20, having flunked out three times. And he was the hairiest fucker I had ever seen!

I couldn't help but sneak an occasional peek. His chest looked like one of those gorilla costumes you'd rent for Halloween, all rippled and defined with a shitload of dark black hair. I guess I had a thing for hair even then! I interjected my sneak peeks with thoughts of my Aunt Phyllis's bad teeth, coming at me for her annual Christmas kiss, to keep my cock in check. The last thing I needed was for Brian to catch me gawking at him with a boner. But it didn't seem to matter; he figured it out nonetheless.

As he soaped up his face, he bumped into me "accidentally" and immediately started with the macho bravado. "Hey, watch it faggot," he barked. "I'll bet you did that on purpose, you fuckin' little pansy." He backed me into the corner against the cool white tiles, forced me to my knees, and plunged his dick past my lips in one swift, intentional thrust. "Who cares if that bitch dumped me? Who needs her? I can always find some Momma's boy to suck my dick." With the steam lifting off the shower floor, all I could see was a mass of wet black pubes and a rock-hard prick coming at me, his towering torso completely disappearing above me into the mist.

Apparently it was something he thought about a lot too, because he came quick and then jerked my head back forcing me to swallow. He proceeded to wash my mouth out with soap, and said worse would happen if I ever told anyone. I never did until now, but I was always half tempted to provoke him again just to find out what "worse" would be. Still, the Don Knotts half of me kept me in line, and my fear won out.

As an adult, I frequently spied on a group of bikers across the street from my apartment overlooking the West Side Highway with a pair of liberated opera glasses. My idea of heaven was getting gang-banged by a bunch of hairy Hells Angels who looked the hybrid offspring of Bob Hoskins and ZZ Top. Guys with faces like pug dogs and bodies covered in thick, dense tufts of dark hair almost like werewolves. Guys as mean and hairy as Brian Ramos!

I used to stand in my window fantasizing about the strong man smells that must permeate in the clefts of their shaggy ass cracks soaked in sweat from that constant rubbin' against leather and hot machinery. I'd listen to those guys from my window barking depraved insults and foul slurs at one another and imagined they were talking directly to me. I've shot so many times on my windowsill, imagining their ripe ball sacs dropping into my mouth like a baby bird at feeding time, that the paint has actually stripped away from the ledge.

Sometimes I'd walk by their just-parked bikes, and drag my fingers through the sweat marks on their warm leather seats, then lick the moisture from my fingers. One day, having reached my saturation point with fantasy, at the peak of my sexual frustration, I thought, What the hell, go for it! And even though I had only fantasized about actually owning a bike myself, I submitted this personal ad to a smutty biker rag whose pages I often cemented together when my "neighbors" were away on road trips:

Get off your hog and on to your pig!

After a road trip, spread that big, hairy ass of yours across this warm mouth and magic tongue. Ease back, Big Guy, and let this clean-cut, sexy, professional bear bottom suck your ass in long, hot sessions. Let me lap off every drop of your sweat, the rancid smell of your leather pants after a long haul, and your high-petroleum pheromones on overdrive. Then stand up, turn around, and hose me down with a hot beer piss.

Now I'm good-n-ready for some biker bangin'! Grease your pig, plug it in, and start porkin'! Make me squeal! Pound your hot jizz deep into my bear cave. I'm built to satisfy. You be big, bearded, tattooed, and grizzly, and you can ride this warm "seat" all the way to hell and back.

Oh yeah, and if you want, I can suck forever! I've got a lot of stamina—as long as your kickstand's up, my throat's ready. C'mon fucker, take the rightful ownership of my mouth and ass that your cock commands and deserves.

Yours, The Porkchop

A couple weeks later I came home from work as usual, loosened my tie at the door, fumbled with my keys, and let myself in. I went straight to my mailbox, as I did every night, hoping for the first letter prompted by my ad. Curiously, there were still no responses to my out-and-out request for debauchery. I worried that potential tricks could somehow see through my hollow words and know that I was really a white-bread novice with an overactive imagination. However, this particular night, there was a yellow sticky on my mailbox requesting that I see the super, written in an almost unintelligible script. I assumed he wanted to finally fix my leaky faucet or something like that.

When I got to his apartment, tucked away in the bowels of the basement of my building in Hell's Kitchen, I found that I was altogether wrong. I rang the buzzer, and he answered back in his usual Brooklynese dese-and-dose bass to come on in. This guy's voice was deeper than my unused hole! He sounded like a New Yawk version of Lurch on the *Addams Family,* saying "You rang?" in a register so deep and so slow that it almost sounded like a Bronx cheer sliding out.

I had always referred to him as "Lurch" behind his back. We had never really gotten along. I hesitated for a minute, but then pushed back the big black metal door, half expecting to see Pugsley, Wednesday, Gomez, and Morticia. Lurch was definitely an ugly son of a bitch with a disposition to match, who could easily pass for the missing link. If you dressed those wax figures from the Museum of Natural History dioramas in stained Guinea T's, you'd swear they were Lurch at a family outing. His forehead was somewhat broad, and it looked as if his skin was too small for the giant cranium it stretched over, with one protruding eyebrow that ran above his features like a misplaced Pancho Villa mustache.

If he weren't so damn mean, he might not be quite so ugly, but his bitterness only acted as a magnet bringing his many physical and emotional flaws to the surface. My friends from work, a swank Chelsea gay-run ad agency, had often speculated what his inner sanctum might actually look like. We had even conceived an office computer screen saver depicting his imagined rat trap, with La-Z-Boy recliners patched with electrical tape and other remnants of dreadful taste. The saver depicted him with King Kong's face and "Lurch in Hell" written across the bottom in a Gothic script. For now, I was entering my personal hell.

There he sat, in a dirty plaid easy chair with electrical tape on the worn armrests, in his atypical KMart sweat suit and enough gold chains around his neck that he looked like a big, fat, Cro-Magnon Mark Spitz. His arms hung from his chair like a gorilla's, his knuckles scraping the fiesta shag carpeting of his garage-sale-would-be-a-step-up apartment. It was actually worse than the screen saver! It was how I pictured the digs of a serial killer.

I had always viewed Lurch as painfully straight, dim as a burned-out bulb, and often smelling like a zoo animal that attempted to cover his skanky tracks with cheap cologne. I thought that he hated me so vehemently because of his tilting the scale to the straight side of the gay/straight balance.

He had a big shoebox full of mail in his lap. Responses to my ad! And all of them had been opened.

"I've got something for you, bitch," he said. *Oh, shit,* I thought, *no wonder he has carpeting that looks like pizza sauce—it hides blood-stains better!*

I took a step closer and said, "Are those letters mine?"

"Is your name Faggot?" he barked.

"You know," I said, "tampering with another person's mail is a federal offense; you could go to jail for this."

"Been there, done that," he said in a soberingly flat voice. "You and your Chelsea buddies are into sissy sharing, right? So why don't we do some sharing right now, and you can get to know me better. Judging from these here letters, I've already got a pretty good idea of who you are, Nancy Drew. So sit down and I'll read you a few, Milk Boy."

Since Lurch was about 6 foot 6 and easily weighed 300 pounds, and was known to punch holes in the wall periodically to deal with his mood swings, I reluctantly brushed a few crumpled beer cans out of the way. I pushed another half-consumed six-pack (the big kind that resemble cans of motor oil) to the side of his recliner and sat down Indian-style at his feet. "I particularly like this one," he said, pulling a letter from the box. He started to read in a painfully slow, obviously condescending tone:

Dear Porkchop:

I like a good bitch that knows how to take it like a man. I am a fat, hairy piece of perversity into really rank powerplays with little bearcubs like you. I am a biker, a Hell's Angel apprentice. That means I'm going through my initiation right now, and once I pass it I can get my revenge out on the next up-and-coming waterboy piss-drinker like you.

But for right now, I have to get fucked up the ass by the ugliest dude in the clan in front of the entire gang. It was either that or eat a plate of fresh cow shit with pork-n-beans. It's not my bag, boy. So this is where you come in. After I get fucked, I'm gonna' spread my big greasy gorilla ass over your scum-sucking, ass-kissing faggot lips and fart my bud's just-deposited load into your trashy little mouth. Sound good? You still wanna be a biker's bitch? Call me, faggot! I've got what you need.

Butch (212)963-2848 (that's 212-YO-EAT-IT)

Lurch leered at me with what I read as complete disgust and contempt, and said, "I didn't know you were such a perv under those button-down shirts and that pansy-ass soft leather jacket of yours. I knew you was a dirty faggot and all, but I wouldn't have guessed you as such a filthy pighole."

The idea of him calling me filthy really stung! Yet in a way, I liked how it sounded in that deepened deadpan tone.

"Now it's your turn—why don't you reach in the box and pull out one and read it to me."

Half stunned that Lurch could even read, scared and thoroughly humiliated, I leaned forward onto my knees and reached into the box. I felt something that resembled a beer can made of chamois. It couldn't be, I thought. This is the kind of prank that high school guys pull on their dates with buckets of popcorn at the movies. Maybe this was a movie, because I couldn't believe it was really happening. I tried to ignore the appendage I had just touched, and snatched a letter from the box. "Read, boy," he said. I gulped slightly, and started:

Dear Porkchop:

I like to have my girlfriend watch while I demonstrate 101 ways to properly use a faggot like you. Up for it? I'm a bearded biker just like you like, and I got a real hairy, smelly ass that my girlfriend refuses to eat. She's a pretty good cocksucker though, but ain't into tossin' the salad. She knows I'm writing this letter now. She'd like to watch a faggot eat out my ass.

I'm a middle-aged, Mediterranean, Vietnam vet, with dark, curly ass cheek hair, long enough that my gal combs it sometimes. She's a hairdresser by trade. She's a real hot bitch and our sex is real good, but she knows I get real hot with a tongue up my pink hole. In Nam, me and some of my buds would do it to each other in the foxholes. When you think you're about to die, you might as well go out with a smile on your face. Really passes the time.

I kinda picture our "scene" like this: After a long ride, we meet up at a neutral place, a rest stop or something, and I'll strip outta my jeans and jockstrap. Wring out the sweat of my strap into your hungry mouth. You lay back flat on the asphalt, face up, naked as the day you were born. Then I spread my ass cheeks and sit down on your face while my girlfriend feeds me her pussy.

If you're as good as you say you are, I'll pop off a load on your belly that'll look like someone just dumped a quart of yogurt on ya'. My lady and me will scoop it up and feed it to you. If you're real good, I'll spit some of her pussy juice in your mouth too, after she comes. Sound good, Boy?

Answer box #7448

Stag

P.S. You ever been pissed on by a woman, Fag Boy? We'd both like to golden shower you and then hop on my bike and leave your piss-drenched, sorry ass behind.

I sighed in complete embarrassment and looked at the floor, my body flushed hot with shame. The yellow-red-orange carpeting was making me nauseated. I looked up to see the clump of hair pouring out from the gray ribbed neck of Lurch's dirty sweatshirt with no clear separation between his chest and chin. Just a frosting of hair growing upward from my "kneeling before swine" point of view. Further up, his eyes seemed to almost snap, and appeared to be watering a little bit. For a split second, he looked almost vulnerable, like an animal out of its customary domain. "Read me another," he commanded.

Great, I thought, my humiliation's providing a story hour for a seriously dangerous psychopath with the mind of a 12-year-old on steroids. "Please, not another," I begged, "you've made your point." By this time, my head was replaying news footage of the Matthew Shepherd tragedy. I was rapidly planning my own funeral.

"Get in the box," he said, "unless there's another box you'd like to get into. It's pretty sloppy, though; I just took a shit before you came. Had Mexican last night too."

With that thought, I reached into the box and again felt his prick, now stiff and throbbing. Ever see a lion or bear play with its still-alive food before stripping it to the bone on one of those nature programs? That's I how I felt at that moment. Obviously Lurch was enjoying this game of mind-fucking more than I was. A lot more.

His big, hairy paws grabbed the nape of my neck and pushed my face into the box. I struggled like a hamster attempting to get out of a box of paper shavings. I tried to pull back, but Lurch held my head like a cantaloupe he could crush on a whim. I could barely breathe. I literally saw stars, like when Bluto would have Popeye in a pre-spinach choke hold. Lurch's dick smelled unwashed and cheesy. Between the smell of his foreskin's ripe head cheese and the steady perfume of envelope sealers, I was getting faint. "Show me some of that stamina, Fag Boy," he growled. "You'll suck until I say stop, you fuckin' slaghole."

His cock felt as thick as a Pennzoil can surrounded by a spilled box of Brillo. Déjà vu! It was just like Brian Ramos coming at me!

I could feel the sides of my dry mouth split, tearing slightly as he forced me onto his dick. He jerked my head up and down like a rag doll, and for him, he was only remotely applying pressure. His meat rammed at the back of my throat repeatedly, and I'd swear that if anyone were watching, they'd see his cock poking and plunging out the back of my neck like a fist in a nylon stocking.

"This is what you want, isn't it, Porkchop," he said snidely. At that point my eyes were tearing, partly from the act, partly from the smell. His bush was thick and scratchy and smelled rank and musty, with at least a week's worth of dried cum caked to each follicle. When he began to really break a serious sweat, his pubes let off the scent of High Karate or some other cheap cologne. It took me back to that locker room shower when I was 16. Brian's face came back to me like neon flashing before my face as Lurch pushed me down on his monster meat against that rancid, ripe bush. It seemed almost exactly like the same thick King Kong killer bush whose memory I had savored for so many years!

I slurped and chewed like a puppy on a corn dog. My body gave over to some kind of Neanderthal desire I had only imagined might live inside me. I growled in an almost primitive tone in a register practically lower than Lurch's. My body combusted with spontaneous heat! I devoured his fat dick like a beast after a kill.

"That's right, Porkchop, eat me up, you little faggot fuckhole. *Now* you're getting into it." Lurch's head snapped back like a bowling ball. The sheer weight and thrust of his head dropping behind forced the chair into recline mode. I was flipped one third into the box and lost total control of my body.

Lurch pushed my head up and down with a volatility I had seen him use on a plunger in my apartment. Finally, he gasped like a man who had just been shot, and it was as if hot cement were pouring down my throat from a dump truck chute. His body convulsed as if the La-Z-Boy were an electric chair. He flailed like a just-caught trout.

Just when I thought the last of his sharp, hot cum had whooshed into my throat, he convulsed again, and I felt something equally warm but not as thick or salty filling my mouth like a tidal wave. He let go of a bitter, almost rancid piss that pushed his cum into my belly with a veracity that stopped my breathing. He was so deeply lodged in my throat that I couldn't even gag, but choked and swallowed, and with my uncontrollable quivering and all his movement, all that jerking and spasming, I shot in my own pants without even touching my dick.

It was a pure tribute to his bravado. To his pheromones. To his adrenaline. To his ultimate power over me. Lurch forced his chair upright like a temperamental stewardess with PMS at the end of a flight from hell. I fell to the floor like a stuffed toy, the letters spilling over me like trash. "Get outta here, you scum-eatin' faggot," he barked.

Lurch kicked me out into the hall and tossed out the box after me. I scurried around collecting the letters in the hallway for fear that the neighbors might find one with my address on it. I rushed into the elevator and held my floor's button, praying that this would keep it from stopping. That started the elevator alarm ringing like a giant alarm clock, so I removed my finger and the door opened right into the lobby. Brad from 8G got on; I didn't know him much beyond an occasional hello at the local gym. Thank God he was gay too! He didn't say a word, but I knew I was just minutes away from becoming Internet chat room gossip.

I reeked of cum, piss, sweat, beer slobber, and unbathed stink, and my face looked like a red balloon. Soon Brad and a hundred of his dearest buffed and bitchy friends would all be creating juicy scenarios to support "the trash" he had just found in the elevator. Yet, shockingly, a part of me didn't care. Hell, maybe the gossip would actually give me a reputation and possibly give my dating life a jolt, helping me overcome the dry spell that had induced the whole embarrassing situation anyway.

When I got inside my apartment, I collapsed on the living room floor. I pulled down my sticky, wet pants, lifted them to my face, and breathed their wet, potent stench like poppers. The fresh ammonia-like fumes smelled like Lurch's crotch. I fingered the cum on my matted pubes and tasted it. I hadn't come ropes like this in years. I rolled over onto the thick faux polar bear rug on my floor. I wallowed upon its white fur like Ann-Margret in that living room scene in the movie *Tommy,* with the pork 'n' beans spewing from the TV set. The rug felt like Lurch's bush against my face. My body flushed with heat.

I went to the kitchen and grabbed a fresh can of Crisco from the cabinet and dug three fingers into it. I returned to the living room rug, feeling its tuft against my body, its mane against my buttocks, and I started stroking my dick with the Crisco. The more I stroked, the hotter it got. I fingered my asshole with a big glob of it. First one finger, then another, until I practically had my entire fist inside me. I tasted my shitty fingers. Lurch had released the pig boy inside me!

I fantasized about Brain Ramos's King Kong dick in my mouth, his almost flowering bush brushing my face as his balls banged against my chin. Then I imagined what it would be like to have Lurch's massive Pennzoil-can meat in my ass, his Brillo bush bristling against my ass cheeks. I imagined him getting off a Harley, all hot and sweaty, looking like some kind of giant mythical man-goat, smearing a little motor oil from his bike onto his dick as lube. When he'd fuck me, it would heat up and get hotter and hotter, burning my stretched hole more than my warped passion.

I exploded again like Mount Vesuvius. As I lay on my living room floor, peering up at its chic postmodern whiteness, the exact opposite of Lurch's pad—I'd thought I was the exact opposite of Lurch, but now I knew better—it dawned on me that Lurch did-n't hate me for being gay. It was my buttoned-up, snot-nosed, better-than-thou, Chelsea-boy attitude he couldn't stand.

I let go a scorching piss that arched right into my wanting mouth. I closed my eyes and imagined it to be his urine, and I passionately swallowed every savory drop!

The next day, I'd call in sick to the office, and wait for Lurch to finally come and fix my leaky faucet and to plunge my tight hole.

A Bear in August

Eric Karnowski

The bar where I met him was called August, which was meant to allude to the "autumnal" years of life. The owner wanted it to be a bar for older men, and I did notice that there weren't many guys my age there—but that was fine with me. Guys my age were still boys, and I was ready to be bedded by a man.

After getting a beer, for which I was carded, I moved to a spot along the wall just past the main bar. There was a little more light there, which was good for me. Several men had looked my way when I settled into my spot and upended my bottle, taking my first swigs of brew. A few walked by me, their eyes appraising what they saw: a body refined by years of training with my baseball teams, first at high school and now at college. A tight T-shirt showed my pecs and arms to good advantage. I doubt any of those men even noticed my face, cublike with a short Vandyke outlining my mouth, as they obviously undressed me, imagining what they would find under my clothes. I kept my face neutral, and they continued past.

When I saw *him*, though, I almost choked on the last swallow of my beer. A little taller than me, with broad shoulders and a short beard that had a little gray in it. As he moved, his unzipped leather jacket exposed a hairy chest and a perfectly round belly, similarly covered with dark fur. I tried to keep eye contact when he looked over at me, but a slight scowl crossed his face and I looked down at the floor, embarrassed.

Before I could gather my nerve to look up at him again, a pair of boots walked into my vision. I raised my eyes but not my head, hardly daring to hope, and my heart skipped a beat when I saw it was him.

"How much?" he asked.

"What?" Confused, I raised my head to look him in the eye.

He reached out a gloved hand and placed it on back of my head, pushing me back to the position I had before, gazing at the floor. "I asked how much you're charging, boy. Don't act innocent."

Charging? "No, sir, you've got me wrong. I'm not a hustler."

"Why are you at the wall then, boy?"

"The wall?" *Shit,* I thought. *How the hell was I supposed to know? Or is he just joking with me?* "My mistake, sir. I didn't realize."

He held my head and stood there silently for a moment. "Let me buy you a beer, boy, and you can tell me about yourself."

I smiled and started to look up at him, but a slight pressure on my head told me he wouldn't approve. His control turned me on. "Thank you, sir, I would enjoy that."

The gloved hand moved down to the small of my back, and he guided me back to the bar. As I walked in front, he let his hand slip down a little further, and he lightly squeezed my buttocks. Once I was sitting at a bar stool, he leaned forward and whispered into my ear: "Firm ass, boy. I like firm asses."

What am I getting into? It didn't matter, I realized—at the moment, anyway. He was hot, and he was interested in me. I had time to find out exactly what he wanted, beyond the obvious.

"Hey, Mack, how's it going?" the bartender asked him.

"Pretty good, Curt," the man—Mack—replied. "Regular for me, and another beer for the boy."

Mack turned to me. "Look up at me, boy, it's all right." I complied, nearly gasping when I saw his magnificent face up close. His mouth was set in a stern expression within his full beard. He kept his cheeks smooth, but the dark hair from his sideburns to his chin easily commanded attention from any observer. A sprinkling of gray, especially in the temple and jaw areas, gave a distinguished air to his quiet presence. My eyes moved up, from his beard and mouth, to his strong Roman nose, and on to his steel-blue eyes. The corners wrinkled ever so slightly, and I felt as if I could die in his gaze without a whimper. "Tell me," he said, "what do you see?"

"Woof," I said lamely, but he smiled—and I wanted so much to make that smile permanent. "You have a beautiful smile," I said, and instantly it was gone. *What did I do?*

"First, you were doing well before when you called me 'sir,' " he told me. "Show the proper respect to your elders."

"Yes, sir," I answered, and he smiled again.

"Good boy." He took off his gloves, showing more dark hair on the back of his hands, and even on every knuckle. He grasped my chin and turned my head, first left and then right. "Kiss me," he said. "And use that kiss to tell me how much you want me to take you home tonight."

I hesitated. The bartender knew him, which was a good sign, but I still didn't know what he would try. Clearly, he liked to dominate, which was fine with me—but it meant I would have to put a good amount of trust in him.

He nodded. "Just give me a friendly kiss then, no obligation."

Gladly. I smiled and leaned forward, tilting my head to approach his from slightly below. His lips gave a little as they pressed against mine, and he grabbed my upper lip between them as I pulled back from the kiss. I smiled coyly at him, then lowered my head and looked at the bar. "Thank you, sir," I said.

He put a bottle in my hand. Carefully, I put it to my lips. I could practically feel his eyes on me. I kissed the mouth of the bottle, then slid it past my lips, slowly moving it further and further into my waiting mouth. The gag reflex started, but I relaxed and suppressed it. I took a breath and pushed the bottle even further in, feeling the glass hit the back of my throat.

Then I let the bottle move back out, stopping it at a comfortable position to take a gulp. Curiosity was burning my eyes, but I kept my head down and didn't look at the man.

"What else do you do, boy?"

I shrugged. "What would you like me to do, sir?"

He grunted in response. "Eventually," he answered in a low, gruff voice, "I'm going to fuck your ass so hard you'll cry for Daddy to make it stop. But before we get to that, I'm going to enjoy you stripping naked for me and kneeling at my feet." Wide-eyed, scared, and excited beyond belief, I could feel my erect cock straining at my jeans. A drop of precum leaked into my underwear.

"You need Daddy to tell you how to please him, is that it, boy?"

I considered the question for a moment. "Yes, sir. Will you be my Daddy tonight, sir?"

"You bet I will, son," he replied, and my stomach leapt into my throat. "Come here and sit on my lap, son."

I moved off my stool and half climbed into his lap, half standing between his open legs. His hard manhood pressed against my leg, and I smiled. "Daddy, you're big!"

He grinned and hugged me to him, grinding his crotch even harder into me. "But I bet my boy can handle it, can't he? What do you think, boy, are you ready to serve your Daddy?"

Leaning forward, I put my head against his chest and my hand on his hairy belly. "Yes, sir, but what will you need me to do? If I'm not ready for what you like—"

"Hush, son. I understand, don't worry. You'll make Daddy feel good, and Daddy will make you feel good." He ran his furry hand up my leg, to my crotch, and he held my package firmly in his paw. His lips touched my neck, and I practically melted into his arms. "On your knees, son, and kiss my boots before I'll take you home."

As I lowered myself to kneel on the dirty bar floor, he stood and planted both feet firmly in front of me. I put my hands behind my back and bowed over his feet. Wondering who might be watching, and getting harder at the thought of it, I kissed first one boot, darting my tongue out and licking the leather hard, and then the other. "Good, boy, I felt that," Daddy said. As I sat up again, he grabbed my head and shoved my face into his crotch. I opened my mouth and found his pole through his jeans, trying to suck him through the cloth.

"Enough, slutboy," he told me. "Get up. I can't wait to have that ass naked and begging to be filled."

As we left the bar, Curt handed Daddy a handful of condoms. "I hope this will be enough," he chuckled.

Daddy's home was a modest townhouse. The first floor had a living room–dining room with a kitchen off it. A door on one side led to a small bathroom, and there were stairs leading up.

"Strip, boy. You won't need your clothes again until I'm ready to take you back to your home."

I quickly removed my clothes as Daddy watched. I've never been anywhere near as hairy as the men I'm attracted to, but I have a nice diamond-shaped patch in the center of my chest, two corners reaching out to a bit of hair circling my tits, and the bottom corner trailing down to my pubes. Once I stood in front of him, completely nude and exposed, he nodded. "Turn around, boy. Show me your ass."

I turned to face the front door. "Nice," he said. I heard him, felt him move to stand behind me. His paws moved over my ass, kneading the muscles, then slid to my chest, the fingers running through the patch of hair. "You smell like an ashtray, boy, and I bet I do too. The shower's upstairs. Go up and find it, and get started cleaning yourself. I'll join you in a minute."

"Yes, sir."

The bathroom was easy to find. I resisted the temptation to take a look at his bedroom. I had washed my hair and soaped my body up when Daddy moved the curtain and stepped in, fully nude, showing off his sexy Daddy-bear body. The hair on his chest was turning gray, like the jaw of his beard. The rest of his fur, which covered his arms, legs, back, and ass—even his cock had hair on it—was jet-black. I wanted to touch him so much that it hurt, but he turned me around and reached down, spreading my ass cheeks. I bent over to give him better access.

He lathered up his hands and slid the suds into my crack, rubbing at my hole. He pulled his finger out and stood up. "Wash my cock, boy," Daddy told me. I worked up some suds with the soap, and gently grasped his cock, rubbing the suds on his skin. I moved on to his hairy ball sac and gingerly washed it as well.

"Good boy; now the rest of me." I rubbed the soap bar directly on his chest. As the suds grew, he lifted his arms and I moved to his armpits, and then to his arms themselves. Before long, I'd washed his entire body. The only part not covered with hair was his palms, his soles, and between his fingers and toes.

He put his arms in front of him and leaned forward, exposing his furry ass to me. "Clean me well back there, boy."

His ass was incredibly muscular, and it felt great to slide my soapy hand between those hot cheeks. "Get on the hole, son," he said. "It's OK, Daddy's had fingers in his hole before."

I grinned, wasting no time doing as he commanded.

After he'd rinsed the suds off himself—and I'd rinsed my hands too—he turned off the water. He leaned forward on his hands again. "On your knees, boy, and get that tongue working."

This was something I'd never done before, and I wasn't sure I could do it. I moved to my knees and put my hands on his hairy ass, pulling the cheeks apart. The hole was ringed in hair as well, but that didn't prevent me from seeing the muscle twitch, inviting me toward it. I moved forward and put my tongue out, but couldn't bring myself to touch him. "Come on, boy," he encouraged me, "I don't want to be here all day. Lick Daddy's ass, son. For me, boy."

"Yes, sir," I said, and put my tongue out again. I touched his cheek, a couple of inches to the side, then moved in. A second later, Daddy moaned his pleasure.

He was clean, of course, and tasted of soap. I lapped all around the rim, circling his hole carefully. The hair gave his skin a rough texture, but it felt so good to share this with Daddy, to please him in this special way. It felt more intimate than anything else I had done to anyone. He allowed me into his most private area. I was honored to be licking his asshole.

He only let me continue for a few moments, though. When he told me to stop, I moved out to kiss his ass, one cheek and then the other. I let the globes move back to their usual position, and his hole disappeared from my view.

Daddy stood and turned, me still on my knees, so his cock was at eye level for me. He reached down and grabbed my shoulders, lifting me up to my feet. That beautiful smile made his face glow. "Thank you, son. Now get us some towels," he commanded as he pulled the shower curtain back. I nodded and stepped out onto the bath mat, quickly bringing a towel to him, taking one for myself.

After I dried myself, he handed his towel back to me and lifted his arms. I took the clue and carefully dried him off as well. Once he was dry, he smiled and said, "Don't move." He went into the bedroom, then returned a minute later. "Bend over."

I bent, and I felt his fingers spreading my butt cheeks. He smeared something cold and slick in my crack, greasing my hole. *Surely he's not going to fuck me this soon,* I thought. A cold object pressed against me, either a dildo or a butt plug. With a little effort on both our parts, he slid it into my opening; my ass muscles closed around the sex toy and pulled it inside me. I liked the feeling of my hole being filled, the tightness and the tension as I worked to relax and not expel the plug, but Daddy's command over my body and my hole thrilled me even more. "I want your hole relaxed and ready for something more substantial when I'm ready to give you my dick—don't want to have to loosen you up when I'm ready to fuck you."

"No, sir, of course not," I replied weakly. Despite being so horny, second thoughts crept into my mind; I wasn't so sure I could handle what this man wanted to give—or take.

"Stand up and face me, son." His voice was a little softer, and as I turned to him in obeisance, he pulled me close and hugged me tightly. His hand drifted down to my ass, and he tugged gently on the plug. The movement helped my ass adjust and seated the plug in my hole a little better. "Just a short while, boy. Just long enough for me to see the weather forecast, then we'll have some more fun."

"Thank you, sir." I'm sure my voice showed my relief. I wasn't used to butt plugs, and I wasn't sure how long I could take it.

He released me, then gestured with his head at the steps. "Go downstairs and turn the TV on for me."

As I found the power switch for the television, Daddy settled into his chair. "Come sit in my lap, son," he told me. With my naked, plugged ass nestled between his legs and my head cradled on his shoulder, he fumbled with the remote until a news station came on to the screen. He put the remote down, then began to pat my leg gently with his left hand, in a slow rhythm. My cock was hard, oozing slowly onto his stomach. I reached my own hand out and gingerly touched his hot chest, running my fingers through the sexy mass of hair. He rested his left hand on my thigh and squeezed, signaling his pleasure.

Within minutes, I was relaxed and content. Sitting in the lap of such a hot man, I almost forgot the discomfort in my ass, until the weather came on. Daddy began patting my leg again, and when the weather report was over, he took the remote and turned the TV off.

"OK, boy." He didn't speak loudly, which was good—I was relaxed, and his voice was almost soothing. His hands pushed me off his lap. "Get on your knees on the floor, facing me," he ordered. "Between my legs." I moved to obey.

In the bar, I had the idea that he enjoyed it when I didn't look him in the eye, so I kept my eyes downcast—straight at his crotch. "You look great on your knees, boy." As I stared, his cock grew hard. It was beautiful—just under seven inches long, but very thick. The head poked out of the foreskin, and he rolled the skin back to reveal a large knob, pink with a slight purplish tint. "Come closer."

I inched closer, and he grabbed the back of my head with one hand and pulled me forward. I eagerly opened my mouth to take his cock, but he stopped me. "I didn't tell you to suck me yet, did I? Lick my balls first."

His nuts seemed a little small for such a thick cock, but I didn't care. Daddy told me to lick them, so I buried my nose in the crevice between his thigh and his package, and began to lap at his balls. They were loose in their sack, and I chased them around with my tongue, enjoying the game, the feel of his hairy skin, the taste of his sweat.

"The shaft. Lick it."

I moved to his hairy cock, worshiping it gratefully with my tongue. I moved up to the head, but the temptation to just swallow it whole was almost too much. Quickly, I moved back down to the fur-lined root of his dick and continued the tongue bath.

"Good boy," he crooned to me. "What a marvelous tongue. Yes, Daddy's boy knows what he's doing. Daddy's boy's made many men happy, hasn't he?"

Luckily, he clearly didn't really want a response, or I would have had to admit that I hadn't, actually. I'd only had a few boyfriends, and even fewer one-night stands. But I'd learned well, I guess, because Daddy was moaning like he was in heaven.

"Suck it, boy!" he demanded, and instantly I dove onto his prick, sucking and slurping. "Oh, yeah, son, make Daddy proud!"

I sucked, I bobbed, I tickled his glans with my tongue. I blew, I teased, I rubbed his cock head against my closed eyelid before slipping it back into my hungry mouth. "Back off!" he suddenly commanded, pushing me off his crotch with one hand and grabbing his cock with the other. He wrapped his fingers around his thick pole and pumped hard, once, twice, and then with the third a thick rope of cum shot out of his slit and hit me on the forehead. The next hit my nose. "Yeah," he said, his cock continuing to spurt, less forcefully.

The cum on my nose rolled onto my lip, but I didn't wipe it away. I didn't want to. I didn't even want to move. The last of his orgasm deposited a few dribbles onto his fingers, and he leaned back in his chair, breathing heavily. After a few deep breaths, he opened his eyes and looked at me. Daddy reached out with his cum-covered fingers and wiped them in my hair.

"Good boy!" he said emphatically. "Didn't fuck you, did I?" I shook my head, and he sighed. "Ah, but that was a great blow job, son. And a very nice rimming."

"Thank you, sir."

"You made me proud," he added. "Stand up and turn around."

I became aware again of the plug in my ass as I presented my backside to him. His hand settled on the small of my back and he pushed gently. "Bend over, let's get that plug out."

Gently, he pulled on the toy. "Push, boy, but not too hard." I did as he said, and as my muscles responded, the plug slowly began to come out. Another inch, and it finally was expelled in a rush. My hole contracted quickly, but not completely, and I felt empty, loosened by the plug just as Daddy had wanted. I was surprised that I wanted to be filled again, and I imagined his cock replacing the plug. I sighed.

"Clean this in the bathroom. You can use the towel from your shower to wipe yourself off too, boy."

As I was finishing, Daddy stood in the door of the bathroom. "Time to go to sleep, boy."

He isn't going to get me off? "Yes, sir," I answered, although I felt more than a little annoyed. It must have showed.

"Boy, you have a few things to learn," Daddy told me. "Many Daddies do enjoy watching their boys squirt. Not all of them, but I'm one of those that do. Now, that doesn't mean that a boy needs to come every time Daddy does, understand? I'm a man, son—and like a lot of men, after I come, especially after a good blow job like that one, I'm ready to fall asleep!" He grinned at me for a moment, then opened his arms. "Come here, boy."

I walked into his arms, laying my head against his shoulder again. He spoke softly into my ear. "You're a good boy, but you've got to learn a little patience. You'll get to come, but not until the morning, do you understand me? Don't even think about sneaking away to jack off in the middle of the night, boy. You'd wake me, I guarantee it, and I would *not* be happy. You don't want to disappoint me, do you?"

"No, sir," I replied. *But would I have the willpower?*

Daddy turned me around and slapped my ass, grabbing my right buttock and using it to guide me to the bedroom. He directed me to get in bed on the left side as he crawled in on the right. "Move onto your side, facing away from me," he commanded. Even the tone of his deep voice made me hard.

With me in position, he snuggled close and put his arm around me, our bodies spooning close together. He nibbled my ear and slapped my ass a few times, before finally whispering, "Good night, sweet son." He turned out the light; I heard his breathing change as he fell asleep in seconds.

The warmth of his body felt right to me. His cock lay limp against my leg, while mine stuck straight out from my pubic bush, swollen and aching. I concentrated on relaxing, starting with my toes and moving slowly up my body: calves, thighs, stomach. I spent a good 30 seconds, or more, on each body part. Moving to my arms: fingers, forearms, biceps. Chest. Shoulders. I don't recall getting to my neck.

The morning sun lit the room faintly through the shades when I emerged from my dreams, a warm hand massaging wet coolness between my cheeks again, teasing my ass. Suddenly, a hard rod pressed at the hole. Within seconds, before I was even awake enough to say anything, he was forcing his cock inside me. My ass opened up and he slid in, all the way, his balls resting against my ass and on his own leg.

"Good boy," he crooned, and he pressed his body tightly against mine, trying to push his hard-on even further up my intestines. I could feel it inside me, filling me more than the plug had the night before.

"Yes," he hissed happily as he pulled his body away, retracting his cock from the new home it had found. Before it was completely out, though, he pushed back in, slowly. He found his rhythm, giving a little moan of pleasure each time he was completely inside me, his body pressed so tightly against mine that I felt every inch of it, just before he began another retreat.

I could feel his cock head sliding in and out, pressing against the walls of my intestinal tubing, but there was nothing I could do, even had I wanted to. I was being filled with his manhood, his masculinity, his sexuality. But the true pleasure came from the lubricated slide of his hard cock against my hole, massaging the muscles, and the insistent pressure deep inside me at the end of each thrust.

He used my body as the sex toy I undoubtedly was at that moment. He fucked me ruthlessly, holding my head against the pillow so I couldn't move it. His hips slapped against my buttocks, his ample stomach so sexy against my lower back. His furry pecs rubbed against my shoulder blades as he pushed his face into my hair, his beard tickling my neck.

He began to thrust harder, his rhythm picking up speed. He shifted position, more on top of me than beside me, and suddenly his pumping cock pushed me from pleasure to ecstasy. I moaned from the sensation as my own hard cock jumped against my stomach, and I imagined this man might be able to make me come just by fucking me. I clenched my ass muscles tightly against his manhood when he thrust in, releasing with his outward movements.

"Oh, yeah!" Daddy dug his fingers into my hair as he thrust his body hard against me, his thick rod so far inside me it hurt in the most exquisite way. He held it inside and shook as the orgasm overcame him; a couple of times, the tremors became additional thrusts. He squeezed my hip affectionately as he continued to come.

After a few moments, the thrusts and shakes slowed. My cock was aching, stimulated, and desirous of release, while his remained nestled inside me. He slipped his right arm under me and held me close to him.

"Mmm," he purred. "Nothing like a good fuck in the morning." He reached up with his left hand and played with my tit.

"Not a single protest, boy—you did well."

"Thank you, sir, but how could I have protested?"

He patted me gently on my hip. "It was too early, you were too sleepy..."

"No, sir," I said. "I mean, you were already inside me before I realized it."

"Then do you have problems with me raping you?"

I blinked at his words. *Is he testing me?* I wondered. He was certainly taking a chance, putting his actions in those terms. "That wasn't rape, sir. I didn't have a chance to retract my consent, but I wouldn't have anyway. You wanted to fuck me, and I do want to please you, sir."

He was so still for a moment, I thought he had fallen asleep, with his cock softening inside me. "You're a good boy," he finally said. "Hold on, I'm pulling out."

I could feel the condom slip a little as he pulled his cock out of my ass, but he reached down and pulled it out with him. His cock popped out, then the tip of the condom slid from my stretched hole. My own cock began to soften as Daddy grabbed a paper towel and wiped the lubricant from my ass.

He turned me onto my back, grabbed my hand, and then spit in my palm. "All right, boy. You can get yourself off now."

Yes, I was a little disappointed that he was going to make me do it myself. But then again, I had enjoyed sucking his cock last night, and I had enjoyed the morning fuck—I had even enjoyed the feeling of being used like a blow-up doll. So I made no protest, and I slowly rubbed his saliva onto my shaft.

Daddy reached up to play with my nipples again—or so I thought. An intense pain spiked at my tit, and I stopped stroking and looked down. He had clamped it with a clothespin. He laughed lightly. "Keep going, boy. The faster you get off, the sooner I'll take the clothespin off."

"Yes, sir," I rasped, and I began to stroke my cock more determinedly. He moved around to my other side and a second clothespin clamped onto my other tit.

"Many boys would find a couple of clothespins fairly tame," he told me. "You need a little more work done on your tits."

"Yes, sir," I agreed absently, concentrating on making my boner sing over the scream coming from my aching nipples.

He reached up and flicked one of the clothespins, then the other. Strangely, the sensation made my cock jump—and then I was there. "Oh, I'm going to come, sir!"

"Let it go, son!" His muscular right arm held me tighter and his hairy left hand closed over mine. I began breathing harder, all of the muscles in my cock and ass preparing for the release. The intensity grew, as it always did, but it had never built for so long. I heard a growl, not realizing it was coming from myself. I pulled my head off the bed as the first wave hit me. The growl became a roar as I shot, a spurt of cum flying out of my cock, and my entire body shook with the force and effort.

"Good boy!" Daddy pumped our hands, and another spurt was ejected, then another, and another. Every inch of my flesh pulsated in time with my cock. Daddy continued to whisper encouragement as my orgasm settled into a few dribbles and finally stopped. I lay back, exhausted.

Daddy lifted his hand and wiped the last of the cum from my cock head, then rubbed it over my face as he kissed my ear. A new pain shook through me as he removed the clothespins and rubbed my sore tits gently. His expression was full of warmth when he grabbed my chin and made me look at him. "You did good, boy."

I smiled, contented. "Thank you, sir."

He gave me a strong bear hug. Without a word, he got out of bed and walked around to my side. Easily picking me up over his shoulder, he carefully carried me down the stairs and into the living room. Settling himself in his chair, he shifted me smoothly onto his lap. I nuzzled his neck as he watched the morning news, and one of his fingers played with my still gaping asshole. He pushed it all the way in and left it there, and I fell asleep again.

I don't know how long I slept, but my dozing was filled with dreams of Daddy—his chest, his belly, his arms, his cock.

"You be a good boy," he told me in my dreams, "and maybe one day you can be a full-time boy for some lucky Daddy."

I opened my eyes and looked at his beard, his lips, the steel-blue of his gaze. *Fool,* I told myself, *you don't know anything about the man.* But even through the roughness of the last several hours, there was a loving tenderness behind his actions. Just what I wanted. What I needed.

"I'd like to be yours," I said.

Bubbacious
JOJO

I still feel like I'm walking stiff-legged from all the exertion, but I'm at least warm all over. But I'm jumping ahead of myself.

I was out in east Texas a few weeks back to pick up some stone for some stuff outdoors I was building, and coming home my truck was making funny sounds—maybe a cracked bearing, and in any case, it was time to stop. There I was, in the middle of flat, hot nowhere, and I came alongside a wrecking yard. I pulled off the road in a cloud of dirt, and went on in.

The guy behind the counter was a real tasty number—6 foot 5, big ole head, shoulders wide enough for a couch, muscles even on his fingers. He hadn't shaved in a few months, and the dirt and heat covered him with a fine sheen. He looked up with big brown cow eyes and asked if he could help me out. I thought about how, then asked if someone could take a look at my truck.

He turned away from the counter and yelled out back, and I saw how monstrous his legs and butt were, his big shitkickin' boots, and how his arms flexed under a thick layer of fur. Well, more like carpet—he even had a ring of hair poking out around his cutoff T-shirt sleeves, and at the back of his head was another ruff poking out.

Two more Bubbas came out, one bald as a cue ball with a pointy head, very short, and even wider than his buddy, and another more my size, but with nasty, curly red hair he just couldn't get control of. "My size," that is about 5 foot 10, 250 pounds, can squat 400 and bench 300—muscles on muscles, if you know what I mean. The three took a look at me, also all sweaty and in a tank top, my blond hair and beard all over the place. They looked, but it wasn't just curiosity.

I kicked back in a chair while they checked out my truck, and talked a bit to Bubba. They had a gym out back they had made out of old wrecks, he said, and it was just about time for a workout. He said that with a sleazy grin, gaps in his white teeth, and a big tongue that hung out just a little bit. He leaned out the door and yelled at the other guys again, and when they came back in, grins on their faces, I was still reeling from the sight of him out from behind the counter.

Now, there are different kinds of big guys. Some are plain old overweight, some are big-boned but not much meat, and some are lots of pretty muscles but look breakable. Some, just a few—what I call "Bubbas" out in Texas—are big bone, big meat, and big weight. When this guy leaned out the door, a big, firm, hairy belly poked out from under his shirt, and I could see his huge, slablike pecs squeeze through the armholes on his shirt. He was big, big fat, fat muscle—I could almost hear the muscles and flesh moving under his skin. A true Bubba.

"Come on back!" he yelled, and the four of us headed back, while short Bub (his name, I found out later, was "House") locked the door. Out back, there was an enormous warehouse with layers of old bags for a roof, and under the warehouse were axles, tires, chains, and welded frames that gave the place the look of a gym, without all the pretty paint and mirrors. Old car seats strapped to frames and poles served as deluxe leatherette couches and benches. "We got some rules for the workout, friend," Bubba said. "You'll just have to find them out."

I jumped as the three of them started stripping. Well, down to their Y-fronts. My first Bubba, "Stack," was just magnificent, a gigantic muscular bear completely covered in that fur front and back, shoulders connecting to his half-shaved head just under his ears, lats like wide rolling hills, hard six-pack belly that hung over the edge of his Y-fronts, huge ass that rolled like bowling balls in the white shorts, and fat legs almost as big around as my waist. The front of the Y-fronts seemed to be packed with some sort of Chihuahua, the hugeness of which moved and rolled around. House stripped down and was even hairier than Stack, but it was all blond and two knuckles thick. His height—about 5 foot 4— combined with how wide he was, same big hard belly, and even bigger pecs than Stack, if that's possible, and big legs made him look otherworldly. He also had something big in his shorts, but as he sort of waddled around with his big legs, it didn't so much hang to a side as it poked down; I could even see it swinging from the back. "Loop," the third guy, was very square-shaped—big coconut-looking shoulders with that red hair, squared-off hairy chest, belly, a dick that seemed to keep trying to poke out over the top of his shorts, and massive, square legs. I can't describe how, but Loop just looked like he was cut out of a square block of freckled marble, and then painted with thick fur.

House lay back in a reclining seat, with an axle over him resting in looped chains, while Stack and Loop started putting on wheels for plates. House started benching like it wasn't anything, then we alternated with Stack and Loop and me. I asked how much the weight was. Everyone stared at me, then at each other. "Dunno" was the answer. These guys did it for the fun, not the sport. House was back, pressing what looked like 10 tires now, his chest squeezing together, with tight, hairy fans on either side of the center, while he arched his back a bit. He put his feet up on the chair, and his surprisingly downy balls flopped to either side of his underwear while he continued the presses. He yowled for a second when one got caught, and he yelled "Fuck this shit" and pulled off his shorts, which were already soaked in sweat.

His cock, which was already pretty thick, lay like a massive brown, almost black log against his leg, almost to his knee. His height, thickness, and cock size made it look like he really did have a third leg. It disappeared into a mound of blond hair so thick the bush sprang out almost up to his belly and spread between his legs. Really animalistic. Stack was pressing at this point 14 tires, belly heaving and legs flexing like he was going to shoot a load. He got up and stripped off his shorts too, revealing not as long a cock but one as thick as my forearm. Well, come to think of it, it *was* pretty long, but he was so tall in comparison to House, it only seemed short. His pubes were as short as the hair on the rest of his body, and he had the same perfect cover all over his ass. Loop grinned and pulled off his shorts. He had a long thin cock with a fistlike purple head, which, since he was uncut, looked like a baseball shoved in a snake's mouth. His ass was very smooth, but with thick, wiry red hair in the crack, I could practically taste and feel it just looking. I played the game and slipped my skivvies off also, and the three looked on appreciatively. Curved down, normal blond hair, thick, and long. Suddenly I felt like Goldilocks and "Just Right." Eight inches is, in my book.

We began the last press, and when House put his feet up on the chair, to my surprise Stack squatted down and shoved his tongue up his ass just when House was at the peak of the movement. House yelled, but continued the press and squeeze, and almost doubled his output. I was impressed. Loop began, out of turn, and I just had to. I put his legs over my head, and at the peak of his press, I sucked on his asshole for all my might. His muscles were too hard, and all my tongue could reach was that thick, funky ass hair. "Hep him, boys," he grunted, and House and Stack pulled his legs wide apart. I was able to get my tongue in his asshole and ream it out like crazy while I felt him squeeze down on every rep. Tasty. We all kept at this for a few minutes, until the chair seat was soaked, and we were all starting to get hard.

It's a funny thing, working out. When you're pressing like crazy, you have a hell of a time getting or keeping a hard-on. Otherwise our little party would have gotten out of hand immediately, I believe. We took a break for a drink. "That's a rim press, boy, and you see some of the rules," Stack grunted, slapping me on the back.

We walked over to another rack, clearly for squats. Loading up the axle with tires again, Stack started this time, and grunted and strained as he squatted, keeping his back properly tensed, legs and thighs flexing, massive calves like cantaloupes with veiny hands grabbing them. His cock scraped the floor and he yowled while the others laughed, and we all kept on taking turns. I was waiting to see what would happen. Sure enough, House lay down on the floor mat, muscular ass cheeks flexed, feet against the frame, then taking his cock with both hands, held it straight up (it had to be almost a foot!) while Stack squatted, thighs bulging, neck strained, and ass cheeks flexing. He paused, then the head popped in and he almost sat against House's belly. He repeated this several more times, hairy legs straining, more rapidly, and this time with his big ole log sticking straight out of his brown bush, eyes bulging and tongue protruding as he grunted and gasped with the weight and the fucking. He yelled and threw the bar back on the rack while I almost fell over from the surprise. He stomped away, shaky from the exercise, slapping his legs, which were cramping with each step, and then cramming a couple of fingers in a can of cream and smearing it in and around his asshole.

"Fucksquat," he yelled, and beat on his chest like a gorilla while Loop started the exercise. Loop looked back at House with big blue eyes, and there was a sort of silent agreement going on. Loop first fucksquatted a while, beautifully controlled leg muscles getting warmed up with low weights, pausing at the bottom while House really booted up into him. Then he put on another couple of tires, and House moved around. Stack motioned to me, and we began spotting, and House quickly got up, smeared more creamy grease all over his hands, and then rolled back into place. Loop squatted, very slowly, legs flexing like crazy, then to my surprise, House held up a fist, and Loop lowered exactly down onto it. Up it went, until I was certain it would come out his mouth. His asshole and cheeks were visibly munching on that hand and fist, the red hair like a bracelet on House's arm, while his ass sucked in as much as it could get. Loop whooped and yelled like a demon, then stood back up. Sweat was pouring down his back and legs, all through his chest hair and beard, and he looked back at me,

"Thank God there's a spot!" He repeated the squat, this time faster, and I gulped as I saw House's entire arm just slide in while Loop yelled and screamed with abandon, sweat flying off his beard, his cock furiously dripping long, creamy streams of precum out the deep-purple slit. His ass got fisted for the next 10 minutes, while the muscles on his legs started spasming from all the exertion until he too threw off the bar. House fucksquatted Stack for a while, and I don't know what was worse—Loop getting fisted on House's arm or House getting plugged by Stack's firepole. In any case, my turn was coming up.

I started the squat, with Loop below me. I felt the lemon-size head pressing against my asshole, and with all the weight pushing me down in the half-squat, I wasn't sure what to do. I straightened up, and then Stack and Loop put chains around the bar to spot me. Stack and House creamed up my asshole roughly then started pulling me toward Loop's fistlike head again. I paused, with all that weight, then felt House positioning the head against my ass. I squatted further, then in one moment of intense pain, I felt the head pop in. I continued to squat, waiting to feel his furry crotch against my asshole, then I understood what *really* long is, as 14 inches slid up my slick rectum. I felt it pop my second sphincter, and continued to squat, almost not feeling the weight until I hit bottom. A warm sensation poured over my body, the weights almost disappearing from my mind, and then I began to straighten up. I couldn't wait to repeat, and this time it was a tiny bit easier to fucksquat down, and my own cock began also to stream precum as my prostate was mercilessly ground by that huge purple fist.

Then I had an inspiration. The next time I squatted, I squeezed as hard as I could on his shaft and straightened up. I knew my ass was strong, but when the three yelled, and I felt the extra weight, I knew I was actually pulling Loop up off the ground by his cock head, then I heard the pop. House got some blue rags and wiped off my ass excitedly, Stack doing the same for Loop's cock, and then I tried again. This time I was actually able to pull him a foot off the floor, and then I squatted again, banging his ass against the floor and his shaft back in my ass. Loop started playing with my ass, and after one moment again, he spoke out, "Go easy—you got my balls this time too." He had crammed his balls in my ass, and as I stood with the weight on my shoulders, I could hardly stand straight up, as there was practically a double fistful of balls and cock head in my ass!

We broke off again and, after some water, walked over to another set of chairs. These were set up like old football linebacker pads, and then we got into shoulder fun. House bent over, stuck his furry blond ass in the air, and wrapped his arms around the pad with his shoulder braced against it. Loop came over and, after plugging his cock carefully in House's wiggling ass, grabbed his huge thighs and lifted his legs, sliding his hands back to the knees. House was like a wheelbarrow against the frame, and Loop proceeded to begin some shrugs while House grunted in appreciation at every raise and lower. Stack pulled me over and positioned me behind Loop. First, I shoved my cock in Loop's ass, which, although having been fisted already, was still tight as he squeezed me. I actually only got my head in between the cheeks, but Stack helped out again, pulling them apart until I got all my equipment in. Loop then bent over House, wrapped his arm around House's belly, resting his bearded head on the broad, sweaty back, and I had to lift his legs up. Heavy—shit! But I got them up and began the shrugs also. Finally came Mr. Monster, Stack. I didn't know what would happen, but I began feeling his log against my asshole, his thick thumbs probing to stretch it open. A velvet rock started pressing against it, and as relaxed as I could get fucking and shrugging, he managed to work more in. I was stretched to the limit, and a red-hot poker felt like it was working in, then again I felt a relax as my asshole stopped spasming and all of it finally slid in. I was so full—fulfilled—that I thought my belly was going to pop out from that monster, warm electric waves going all over me, and the shrug tugged almost weightless. I leaned over Loop and rested my head on his back, licking and sniffing while Stack pulled my legs up. He must have been shrugging 500 pounds by then.

Then the fun began. Stack began fucking me, not gently but with big, hard Bubba thrusts as I yelled out, holding my thighs up and apart while House continued grunting, being pummeled against the football pad by all three of us. The whole menage was creaking while Stack shrugged and fucked like a wild animal, yelling out anything he could think of, singing "My Bonnie Fucks Over the Ocean" and then "Red Rose of Texas" in complete craziness. "Feel that big meat pole, boy!" he yelled.

The pounding continued while my ass was burning, and I felt more and more of the squeezing and kneading of Loop's ass against my cock, and I knew I wouldn't last for long. "This babe's gonna blow," Stack yelled, "I can feel his 'tate getting hard." House and Loop were yelling now on every thrust, and finally as Stack took the last shrugs, jamming my asshole down on his cock like he was capping an oil well, he started gushing a fountain of sperm all over my insides. I felt it rush through and then burst out my asshole, dripping between my legs. I couldn't hold back from this hose monster, and began the same in Loop, who did in House. Poor House, his long cock just jerking and dripping out just off the floor while everyone else was heaving and hawing, spewing and creaming like there was no tomorrow. Stack backed off, dropping my legs unceremoniously, and then I untangled from Loop, and from House, who turned around with a monster cock dripping and waiting for service. Stack grabbed me and, shoving four fingers up my tired ass, scooped out some cum and drubbed it on his belly, grinning and licking his lips. Loop did the same with House; "Mmm! Smells *good!*" he grinned, offering his ass to me. I wiped my hand along it, then suddenly he opened up and I got my fist in—and came out with a wad of my own cum, to rub on my belly. "Fertilizer, baby," Stack groaned, "for that belly. Get ready."

Stack lay down on a mat, his cum-slick belly sticking up, arms behind his head, then on one side Loop began licking the hairy pits and arms, chewing on the nipples, and I felt obliged to do the same. House squatted over Stack, his cock sticking out like a yardstick. Stack then did a sit-up, with House resting against his knees and House's cock popping in Stack's mouth. But he didn't relax. He did little crunches, sucking in House's monster cock head, his tongue lapping up all over, while Loop and I continued to chew those pits and nips, our own cocks getting fully hard again. Stack had a hard time getting all that cock in his mouth—not from the size, but his big belly, when it was flexed under all that fur, was holding him back. He clenched and flexed and leaned, getting more and more of House's cock in his mouth until it was pretty much fully in, then he lifted his knees in the last part of the crunch and got all the rest up to his pubes. His eyes bulged, and snot ran all over the place, then he relaxed. And started over, while House jacked off his yardarm, then came the crunch again. After 25 of these, House was about ready to blow. First came the first drops, then suddenly exploding wads of white-hot cum all over Stack's beard as he licked and finished his crunch as hard as he could. My own cock didn't need much help, nor did Loop's, and when Stack suddenly wrapped his arms around our asses, jamming his greasy fingers deep in to grind our 'tates, we both exploded over his beard as his greedy tongue lapped it all up. He collapsed, wiping the beard cum again into his chest.

Jeezus. We went on and on that day, the four of us with complicated arm exercises, things for necks I ain't never seen, and just these big fat musclebear Bubbas going at it like apes. My muscles, cock, and ass were so used up, and pumped, that I felt half again as big as when I began, and very dried out. I still feel like I'm walking stiff-legged from all the exertion, but that's where I began this story, isn't it?

Guts

Simon Sheppard

Even before he joined the gym, his body wasn't bad. Tall, lean, 25, Rand looked sort of like a skateboy, only more clean-cut, less hip. But whenever he saw those pictures in the fag magazines, pics of boys with perfect biceps and chiseled chests, he felt some-how...inadequate.

Working downtown as he did, Rand decided against the glossy gay gyms of the Castro district and joined the nearby Central YMCA instead. The Y was big, funky, convenient; he figured he could squeeze in a quick workout during a long lunch. The place was filled with an amazing collection of folks: men and women, young and old, buff and not-so. But, this being San Francisco, there were a lot of other gay guys, including, thank God, other guys like Rand—young, cute, lean, some of them downright skin-ny. So he didn't feel out of place, even when he stripped down in the locker room and surreptitiously compared himself to the demigods of the place, pumped-up men with bulging calves and washboard abs. Someday, he said to himself, with enough work, I'll have a body like that—he left unvoiced the rest of the thought—and then someone will love me.

Three times a week—well, sometimes maybe two—he'd force himself to change into shorts and a tank top and surrender to the gruesome mercies of the Cybex machines. He stopped working out at lunchtime as soon as he realized he was getting back to his office starving, exhausted, and glum. Instead, he slotted in the gym between the end of the workday and dinner. In place of the elderly, saggy Russians who jammed the sauna every noontime, the 5:30 crowd had a high proportion of queer young professionals. The showers were packed with guys giving each other the eye, some discreetly, others brazenly soaping half-hard dicks for unconscionable periods of time.

And then there was the steam room, its misty precincts dripping with overheated lust. Mostly the cruising was semi-discreet, but every so often Rand was witness to an unapologetic blow job or even a jacked-off spurt of cum.

He began to recognize the regulars. The muscular black guy with the dazzling smile. The middle-aged queen with too much jewelry who never took his towel off, never took a shower, and never, ever worked out. The matched set of maybe-18-year-old maybe-brothers who slowly, deliciously showered their impeccable bodies and long, uncut schlongs; they chattered in Croatian or Italian or something, oblivious, while the trolls just stared and stared. And then there were the ones whom Rand had crushes on, the boys with perfect V-shaped bodies and flawless faces, the ones he never quite worked up the courage to speak to.

But, he'd remind himself, I'm not at the Y to get laid. I'm here to get hunky so I can get laid. Some other time. Elsewhere.

"Hello."

Rand had been toweling himself off; the insistent attentions of a Steamroom Troll had persuaded him to cut short his post-workout lounging. He turned, letting his towel drape over his crotch. A cute guy, cute enough, about his age, but...big. Not fat, exactly, but stocky. Really stocky.

"Hi, I'm Chris. I've seen you around." Chris was naked, not even a towel.

"Yeah, I've seen you around a lot too." A lie: The guy didn't look anything more than vaguely possibly familiar. Nice smile, though. Pretty green eyes, light brown hair that would probably be curly if it grew out. Trim mustache, a close-cropped beard that was hardly more than stubble.

"And you are?"

"Oh, sorry. Rand." His gaze slid down Chris's body. Too big for him. At least 200 pounds, more. Broad shoulders. Fleshy chest matted with hair. Tits you could grab hold of, nipples you could suck. Down lower, a round belly where washboard abs should have been. At least a 37-inch waist, at a guess. Nope, too big for him. So why, Rand wondered, was his dick getting...

"Thirty-eight-inch waist, six-inch dick. You like?" Rand looked up, meeting Chris's broad smile, then down again, down lower. An average-size dick, maybe, but plump, nestled between big, meaty thighs.

"Yeah," said Rand, "I like."

What struck Rand about Chris, once they'd been to bed, was...well, the phrase that kept coming to mind was "his generosity of flesh." In place of the tense hardness of the muscleboys, Chris offered a body you could grip onto, sink into, surrender to. Surrender not to the power of muscle, though Chris was plenty strong, but to something else, something Rand couldn't quite name.

Meanwhile, back at the Y, Rand's efforts were paying off. He'd often sneak a glance at himself in the full-wall mirror, semi-amazed at his swelling chest and shoulders, the bulge that arose when he'd flex a bicep. Watching his reflection using the overhead-press machine, he was gratified to note that his torso looked damn near V-shaped at full extension.

"Hey there." It was Chris. Rand had three more reps to go. Two. One. He let the handles return to shoulder level.

"Chris! How's it goin'?" He still hadn't figured out how to play things at the gym. Though he'd fucked with Chris four times in the last month, and even gone out with him to see some overrated queer movie at the Lumière, he didn't want the guys at the Y to know the two of them were having, well, maybe not an affair, but a something. Because Rand didn't want to get a reputation as a cub chaser, which would give the wrong idea to the buff boys who were, he had to face it, still his ultimate quarry.

"How's it going, Rand?" A quizzical smile.

"Fine. Listen, I've still got a lot of workout to do. If I talk with you now and lose concentration, I'll never be able to finish."

"Yeah, sure." The smile faded.

"See you down in the locker room."

"Uh-huh." Chris turned to go. Turned back. "Maybe we should talk sometime." And then he was gone.

Yeah, maybe they should talk. About why he, Rand, thought this good-looking, funny, attentive, yes, sexy man was somehow...

Might as well say it. Not good enough for him. Because he was big. Goddamn it. Big.

Rand had just finished stripping down when Chris walked over, naked too.

"Talk now, Rand?"

"Here?" A few lockers down, a guy was zipping up his fly. "Sure, Chris. Why not?"

"You mad at me?"

"Mad? No. It's just...I need time." Or something. Jesus!

"We both know what it is, right? If I looked like them..." Chris gestured with his head across the locker room, toward the Italian-or-Croatian-or-whatever brothers, looking yummy in their little matching Speedos.

"I just...I just want to be, I don't know, pumped up. Buffed. Hunky." Rand could feel himself starting to blush.

"It's important to your, as we say in California, self-esteem, right?"

"Yeah, and you—"

"Don't fit in?"

"No, you do. I mean I think you're really great, but...I don't know what I'm saying." Rand's face was hot. He hoped no one could overhear. "Listen, we're both standing here naked. Don't you think that—"

"No, you listen. You can like me and sleep with me and that won't change what you look like. Not a damn bit. What you want to be and what you want to fuck don't have to be the same. I mean, look at heterosexuals. Look at Arnold Schwarzenegger and Maria Shriver."

"I'd rather not."

"Well," Chris grinned, "you get the point. You like yourself skinny? I like you skinny. Be skinny."

"Skinny?"

"OK, lean, slim, whatever. There's this myth that all bears go for other bears. Some of us do. I don't. Big fucking deal. And, believe it or not, some gym-body guys might actually lust after me. You, for instance. I thought sex was supposed to be where you could want whoever the hell turned you on, with no apologies. But for fuck's sake, as Mom would say, be happy being who you are, whether that's a Tenderloin drag queen or the president."

"I want to be whichever one's sleazier."

"Honey, it's a toss-up," Chris said.

And they stood there naked in the YMCA and grinned at each other, just grinned. Then Chris grabbed Rand in his big, strong arms and held him to his belly and his chest and his dick. And as soon as their dicks touched, Rand felt himself getting hard. The rest of his body tensed, but then relaxed; he realized he didn't care who saw.

As the next few weeks went by, Rand underwent a shift in his tastes. The young lean boys started looking distinctly undernourished. The muscle guys seemed armored and contrived. It was the big men who started catching his eye. At first it was just the stocky guys, boys like Chris, the ones whom he used to maybe glance at then ignore.

Not anymore. Whenever he walked into the steam room, he'd survey the naked guys and pick a nice thick thigh to sit beside. A thigh he could inch toward with his own lean leg, till contact was made and cocks got hard, stiffies in the mist. Sometimes, if they were the only two men in there, there was time for a grope. But while the big guy was playing with Rand's hard-on, Rand would slide his hand upward from the man's dick to his belly and slide his palm over convex flesh slick with sweat, stroking and stroking until they heard the door inevitably open and they jerked their hands away.

Rand cut back on his weight training and spent more time on the aerobics machines. It was where the guys who were trying to lose weight hung out. It was where he could, while climbing to nowhere on a StairMaster, gaze across the room at men whose bellies hung over their gym shorts. There they sat on the stationary bikes, their big, naked legs pumping away in circles, and some of them, when they noticed Rand's stare, stared back in a friendly way.

Then Rand moved on from the stocky to the really overweight. Before, he'd focused on big young guys with largish dicks. But now he cruised them all as they stripped down or lathered up, all the extra-large ones, young or older, hairy or smooth, well-hung or with little dicks that half disappeared beneath their bellies. The frankly fat. Anything but the truly obese or old men with big guts and spindly legs—he still had some standards. *Oh, my God! What's happened to me?* he thought. But his dick kept getting hard. And, as Chris had said to him one Sunday afternoon in bed, "Hard dicks don't lie."

Still, except for Chris, whom he continued to fuck once or twice a week, Rand never got together with any of the big guys outside the Y. Things never went beyond a grope in the steam or maybe letting somebody give him head for a few seconds when nobody else was around.

Until one evening in the spring. He went into the sauna and sat on a lower bench. Facing him on the other side, but sitting on the upper bench so his crotch was at Rand's eye level, was a guy who was, frankly, huge. Not sloppy obese, but easily in the high 200s.

"Hey," said the fat guy, "how you doing?"

"Fine," said Rand. "Never seen you here before."

"Just joined." He spread his legs a little wider. Rand stared at his dick, which was medium-size, uncut, and shorn of hair, like a baby's. The fat man smiled and played with his cock in the half-hearted way that guys in saunas do.

"Can I touch it?"

"My prick?" the big guy said.

"Your...your belly," Rand replied.

The big guy nodded, and Rand sprang to his feet. Watching sidelong through the glass door for approaching intruders, he laid both hands on the man's belly and stroked all that flesh, all that flesh. The guy leaned over, grabbed Rand's head, and pushed it down toward his crotch. *But I'm a top, damn it,* Rand thought, *and besides, this is risky as hell.* Nevertheless, he took the guy's hardening dick in his mouth and sucked, furtively, for all of five seconds until, of course, the sauna door creaked open. Rand jerked upward, hard-on jiggling in the hot, dry air.

It was the black guy with the great smile. "I'll just pretend I didn't see that," he said, and his smile grew brighter still.

"Bob!" said the fat guy, unruffled. "How ya doing?"

"Oh, fine, Vince. Just fine."

Rand uneasily left the sauna and went to take a pee, but Vince followed him to the urinal and smiled. "Want to come home with me, guy?" And Rand did.

Rand had begun to feel like some damn ABC Afterschool Special about the pitfalls of prejudice—"Size Doesn't Matter" or

"The Bigger They Come." He'd become an equal-opportunity lecher.

The thing with Vince had been kind of weird. Rand had let Vince fuck him, only the third guy who ever had, and the sight and feeling of all that weight above him bearing down and into him really got Rand off. But afterward it turned out that Vince really wasn't happy with the way he looked, with all that weight.

"Yeah, you wanted me to fuck you, sure. But most guys...most guys look at me like I'm some kind of freak."

And Rand realized he sort of did too. He was attracted to Vince not despite his size, not regardless of his size, but because of his size. To him, Vince was just a big belly with a man attached. As if this guy, who had certainly suffered because he was so fat, were one of those weird-looking goldfish the Japanese prize for their physical grotesqueness. Rand had, in a way, become what he'd never been before: a size queen.

And things with Chris had become kind of strange too.

"Jesus, Rand. I didn't mind being objectified because of my weight," Chris said one day. "After all, every guy wants to feel like a sex object, whatever the hell he might say out loud. But this obsession of yours—well, I feel like an aging wife whose husband goes chasing after younger and younger girls. Only you're chasing after fatter and fatter. And short of binge eating..." he went into his best Bette Davis imitation, "I don't know how to compete, my darling, I just don't." Chris was smiling, but clearly something serious was there. And what could Rand say: "I don't love you only for your fat"?

One afternoon at the gym, Rand remembered the way things used to be, before. He noticed a slim Latino guy on the back extension machine. The guy was wearing Spandex bicycle shorts, and every time he leaned back into resistance the outline of his basket was clearly visible through the stretchy black fabric.

Rand had just finished his biceps curls, but he decided to skip his triceps and stand beside the back extension machine as though he were waiting to work in. Each time the Latino leaned back, his crotch jutted upward and his lean torso flexed beneath his thin tank top. And each time he sat upward, his eyes met Rand's. After his final rep, he removed his Walkman's headphones and smiled at Rand, a dazzling grin.

"You waiting to work in?"

"Yeah."

Rand adjusted the footpad and began to strap himself in. The Latino was still standing there. "Or are you waiting for something else?" he asked.

Miguel ("Call me Mike") had damn near 0% body fat. A nice uncut dick. And hardly any attitude, for such a gorgeous guy. Three days after they met at the gym, they had dinner at a place on upper Market Street, Mike leaving over half of his curried tofu and sun dried tomato wrap. Then they went back to Mike's apartment, which was, like its owner, spare, tasteful, and carefully arranged.

The sex wasn't bad. Where Chris's belly had been soft and yielding, Mike's six-pack abs were hard as a rock, his pretty brown butt taut as a drum. Rand knew he wasn't on a par with him, but he guessed he must be in the same league. After all, he was in bed with him, right? So all those hours in the weight room, all those squats and curls and presses, hadn't been a total waste of time after all.

Each had assumed he was going to top the other, so they never did get around to fucking. But they sucked each other's dicks and came and wiped up. And while they were lying there, Miguel on his stomach, Rand softly stroking those perfectly developed lats, the firm Latino said, "I like you. Let's see each other again, huh? Sometime."

Rand had made it: He'd had sex with one of the hunkiest Y guys, and now they were talking about a second time. So Rand said what gay men often say in similar situations: "Yeah, sounds great.

But I'm real, real busy with work for the next week or two. So why don't I call you?"

Mike's folded-up number went into his wallet, then to his bedside table, but Rand didn't use it. Instead, day after day, he found himself thinking about Chris: his yielding flesh, relaxed smile, the way his big old ass moved when he walked.

"Chris," he said, finally, over the phone, "you're more than just 'some bear cub' to me."

"I know I am, Rand. But you had to realize it as well."

Aww, thought Rand, *just like in the movies.* But within 90 minutes, they were together, naked, in Chris's king-size bed.

"I thought you were going to call me," Miguel said the next time that Rand saw him at the gym.

"Well, I...yeah, but I've sorta gotten involved with someone." *I must be crazy,* Rand thought. "So thanks anyway, but..."

And indeed, Rand and Chris had become an item. Rand introduced the big guy to his friends, who tended to use the words "cute" and "sweet" rather than "big" when they talked about him afterward.

And within six months, Rand actually did it, moving out of his overpriced studio apartment and into Chris's overpriced one-bedroom instead. They'd decided, early on, it was going to be an open relationship, so when Chris wasn't around, Rand would take other guys back to the king-size bed, some of them big men, others lean. But the intensity with which he sought out the heaviest of the heavyweights was a thing of the past. Skinny, fat, or in-between, buff or flabby, Rand either wanted to play with a guy or not. But most of all he wanted to crawl into bed each night and find Chris there and throw his arm around his boyfriend's reassuring bulk, the two of them sleeping spoons all through the night.

He even thought seriously about letting his gym membership lapse and just forgetting about ever pumping iron again. Just let his body do whatever it was going to do. But Oh, fuck it! he decided. And so he continued to work out at the Y, sweating and straining and grunting, and, as a matter of absolute fact, can be found working out there still.

The Bearwych Project
Bob Condron

In the summer of 1999, three men went into Bearwych Woods, Alaska, for a long weekend of hiking and fishing. They were never to be seen again. One year later, one guy's personal journal was found...

Thursday, August 19th

Hope I can read my handwriting after the event. The way the pad and pen are bouncing off my knee, I doubt it. Seb is in the driver's seat, Russ is in the passenger seat alongside him, and I'm in the back of the Range Rover. I'm sure Seb is deliberately heading for every pothole on this old dirt road. I tell him to slow down. He just throws back his head and laughs. Tells me not to be such a wuss. And the trees fly by in a blur of green and brown.

Whose crazy idea was this anyway? Dumb question. It was mine. Seemed like a good idea at the time. Miles from civilization. Getting back to nature. Raw. Down and dirty. So much for the well-laid plans of mice and men.

Call me a creature of impulse, but I couldn't help myself. Couldn't help but suggest this weekend in the woods. Just as I can never resist the urge to flirt with Russ.

Would even flirt at the drop of a hat...

He dropped his baseball cap. I picked it up, handed it to him. "Admit it, Russ," I said with a wink. "You just wanted to see me bend over, didn't you?"

He smiled—one of his killer grins. Even, white teeth thrown into stark relief by his thick black goatee. He shook the dust from his cap, slapped it against his thigh, then settled it in place once more over a close-cropped head of hair.

And the words spilled out of my mouth before I could stop them. "You are so handsome when you smile, Russ. Does anyone ever tell you how handsome you are when you smile?"

He turned to walk away. "Yeah, Melanie tells me all the time." He turned his head to look back over his shoulder. Another grin. "Anyhow, you're just saying that 'cause you just want to keep me sweet."

"No." I shook my head. "No, Russ. I said it 'cause it's true."

Russ continued a step or two further, then spun around and retraced those few steps. "You know, if I wasn't 100% committed to Melanie, I do believe you would be an interesting guy to get to know better."

I was speechless. Literally speechless.

"What's the problem? Cat got your tongue?"

"You're so handsome!"

"You said that already."

"Let me know when you're only 99% committed?"

"Sure thing, big guy."

Then we were back to the task at hand—erecting the pipeline. Just couldn't get his words out of my mind. And after considerable thought—and, that evening, not a few beers—it struck me that it was likely simply a question of the right time, the right place. And if it wasn't going to present itself, then I'd have to make it happen.

Russ's enthusiasm when I suggested this weekend away did surprise me, though. Delighted me. Especially when he suggested that we could stay in his friend's log cabin deep in the heart of Bearwych Woods. Delighted me, that is, until it became clear that said friend, Seb, would also be along for the ride. Did Seb know I was a big, hairy gay man? Russ asked if he should tell him. "Why the fuck not, it's not something I apologize for," I said. Then again, maybe the question said more about Russ than about me.

What's the story? Did Russ really feel he needed a bodyguard? If he did, then Seb is certainly up for the job. Standing over six feet, he's a hunk with a full head of thick red hair trimmed short, bull neck, goatee. Red hair betraying his Scottish origins. A big muscle man in a checked shirt and faded blue jeans, the bulge in the front of his buttoned fly threatening to explode. All man. Wouldn't want to get on the wrong side of him.

Still, Seb seems wary of me. Polite but not yet friendly. Let's see how things evolve.

Decided to keep a journal of developments. Hence these scribblings.

Friday, August 20th

I was awakened this morning by a wet flannel slapped across my face. Seb and Russ, already up and dressed, were doubled over with laughter by my rude awakening. Not enough sleep, I had to pry my eyes open. I felt like shit. The guys left me in no doubt that I also looked like it! Breakfast eaten, pots washed, I've got a window of opportunity to write before we head on out. We're off to explore!

Looking around me now, in the cold light of day, I can see that the cabin looks comfortable enough and well-equipped, if some-what basic. Hidden from view up a long and winding dirt road. Inside, it's just one big room and with a second room half the size. The smaller houses bunk beds, while the larger houses a well-worn sofa and chairs and a big stone fireplace. The john is a hut outside. But at least there is one! There's something fossilized about the place. Maybe it's the old-fashioned decor; it seems like a remnant from a bygone era, somehow frozen in time. Antique mirrors line the walls. They give a sense of space but at the same time...all those eyes staring back.

We arrived yesterday evening around 7 o'clock and, having parked half a mile away, we had to lug our provisions up the dirt track for the last stretch. Once we'd arrived, Seb set to work, warming up a stew on the portable stove. Russ lit a small fire in the grate and I got to lay the table, a job that took all of about two minutes. I set out the enamel bowls and spoons and opened three beers—the first of many to be drunk that night. Seb slopped what turned out to be a delicious concoction into our dishes and we all sat down and broke bread.

Stuffed full, we retired to the sofa and chairs. More beers. Flames licking over the logs. Shadows flickering on the walls as the sun went to bed. Talking about our plans for the morning. Seb, sitting in the chair opposite me, threw one leg over the arm of the chair, the glow from the crackling fire spread across his thighs, warming his bulging basket. Me staring it at, mesmerized. Looking away, looking back, looking away. Finally, looking up to Seb's face from the corner of my eye. Apparently oblivious, he was sucking on the neck of his beer bottle.

Up to this point I had been fairly quiet, but it was time for a much-needed distraction. I asked how long Seb had had the cabin. He told me it has been in his family for generations, although it was effectively abandoned until he got his hands on it and renovated the place over the past two summers. Russ encouraged him to tell me the "whole story" with a mischievous gleam in his eye. And the story unfolded.

Seb's great-uncle Ewan built the place. A "confirmed bachelor," he spent most weekends in the woods with one or two of his best buddies. Until, that is, the fateful Thanksgiving weekend when the massacre occurred. Uncle Ewan and his friends failed to return to town, and the search party found their bodies bound and gagged and very much dead in this very cabin. If you looked closely, Seb told me, you could still see the blood splatters on the walls.

"And the culprits were never caught?" I asked, somewhat perturbed.

"Never," came the answer. "The crime remains unsolved to this very day."

Needless to say, sleep didn't come easy. A situation that was exacerbated by the sounds of Seb beating his meat under cover of his sleeping bag. Apparently, the guy has no shame. As Russ snored, Seb thwacked his hammer like his life depended on it. And when he came, it was with grunts and growls. Mopped up, I heard him yawn and smack his lips. Within seconds, he too was snoring. I could only envy them both. I lay awake for hours and listened to the wind outside, straining to hear beyond the rustling of the trees.

Friday Afternoon

It's 3 in the afternoon. I'm sitting on a boulder, bare-ass naked, baking in the sun. Seb and Russ are splashing around in the lake like a pair of kids. I can hear their laughter as I write and look up from time to time. Man, this is a beautiful vision. Back to nature. The world outside forgotten, if only for a moment. This is the life.

Up to this point, the hike had been fairly uneventful though enjoyable. The hours flying by in amiable conversation, punctuated by my yawns. Seb led the way—a chance to get to know each other better. Underneath his gruff exterior, Seb appears to be almost childlike, in the way that kids can be charming—honest, guileless, amusing. And I begin to really warm toward him. The scenery around here sure is beautiful, but Russ had assured me that Seb was saving the best till last. He wasn't exaggerating.

As we climbed the final ridge I was ill-prepared for what lay on the other side, and it almost took my breath away. "Bearwych Lake," Seb announced, and, without waiting for me to catch my breath, he was hop-skip-jumping down the hill path. Agile as a boy, he sprang down the incline. Russ slid after him, with me bringing up the rear.

No sooner had we arrived at the water's edge than Seb shrugged off his rucksack and began peeling off the shirt from his damp back, revealing a carpet of bronze fur in the process. Fur that began as a ring around his neck before spreading out across his shoulders, back, and chest. "What d'ya say we take a dip," he said matter-of-factly. Russ tugged his shirttails free of his belt, clearly game. And me? Suddenly, I felt wide awake! Within minutes we were naked and racing into the water. Water that is clear as crystal. Nothing hidden. Everything exposed to my hungry eyes. Seb's pale, chunky ass cheeks displayed as he kicked his legs and swam past. Russ's thick, long cock bobbing in the water. My erection? If they noticed, the guys didn't seem at all perturbed by it.

Now here I sit having had the pleasure and the privilege of seeing my friends both naked and abandoned. Russ the Musclebear, who doesn't know he's a musclebear, and Seb the Caveman. And it strikes me as something of a crime that two such big, hunky, hairy bodies should have to hibernate beneath the confines of their clothes for the best part of the year. Both are hung, both covered in fur, both with bodies to die for. And I feel the all too familiar ache in my nuts. Natural for me. True to my nature.

The guys are calling me back. Enough writing. I answer the call.

Saturday, August 21st—Late morning
Last night was some night!

Russ made his excuses and took himself off to bed, once Seb had produced the bottle of Scottish malt whisky. "I'm off. Scotch always makes Seb maudlin. G'night," Russ said as he stumbled off toward the bunkroom.

With the door closed, Seb and I sat side by side on the sofa and stretched out before the fire. Coconspirators. The glow of beer flushing our faces as he poured each of us a shot, then another, and another and... What do I remember? Asking all the right questions. He said his childhood ambition had been to be a career soldier—when questioned further he admitted this was largely for the brotherhood aspect. Did he believe in friendship? His best (only) friend from high school was a queer (his word) who ended up committing suicide because of the intolerance of those around him. Seb's parents? They are physicians. And their love and approval seemed to be sadly lacking. Seb has a fraught relationship with his dad—absent-father syndrome—and he loves his brother but...

I asked about his birth sign and he was mildly annoyed. Was that when I realized he'd been infected by church morality? Sure enough, he had been "ministered to" by the born-again brigade—with all the septic baggage that entails.

"Yes, Seb, I know what the Bible says about homosexuality. I also know what it says about eating shellfish. Everything is relative, only the condemnation is the same."

Then the sudden realization that we were sitting on the sofa alongside each other, my hand was on his chest, absentmindedly stimulating his nipple through his plaid shirt. How long had I been doing it? How long had he been letting me? He never flinched, only to screw up his face with the pain of repressed desire. So much pain. So much energy invested in bolstering his crumbling defenses.

The guy is literally dying for it. His body language was a dead giveaway. Hugging me, bringing his face up so close to mine that our lips were a hairsbreadth from touching. Touching my face in a way that was far too intimate for a heterosexual man. How long had I had my arms around him? How long had he had his arm around me? I remembered earlier, how he drew close, shoulder-to-shoulder, leaning into me. And then the finality with which he ultimately pushed me away. He was letting his family down, he said. He pushed me away physically and emotionally. Intimacy was just too painful. Fucked up, big time.

Off to bed, and I climbed into my bunk with the certain belief that sleep would come, no problem. It did. But I was awakened with a start around 3:00 a.m. A loud clatter, then something moving beyond the outer walls. Scraping against the walls. And then silence. Another virtually sleepless night followed. I'm feeling bushed now. Exhausted.

Seb, in contrast, is as bright as a button and full of smiles despite the weather—which has taken a severe turn for the worse. As the rain battered the roof, he'd already challenged Russ to a bout of arm wrestling over a lit candle and slammed him into the flame—best out of three—on a number of occasions. Demonstrating his unquestionable masculinity? Russ is putting salve on his wounds even as I write.

Saturday Afternoon

No letup in the weather. Worse, if anything, and any plans to go fishing today had to be abandoned. In their place, an endless round of card games until Seb bowed out and took himself off for an afternoon nap in the armchair over by the crackling fire.

Spent the next couple of hours playing "Agony Uncle" to Russ, who was bemoaning his relationship with Melanie. Complaining that their sex life had gone off the boil after 3½ years together, how he needed to come at least once a day and how she just wasn't up to the job. What did he expect me to say: "Slap it on the table, big fella"? I wish!

Wrong of me, I know, but I couldn't resist teasing him. I asked if she gave good head and he clearly found it difficult to respond in the affirmative. So I went into raptures about how I felt sorry for straight men, that it was a shame they would never know the ball-bursting pleasure of having their dick sucked by an expert— an expert being another man—one who knew all the right buttons to push and did it willingly and with enthusiasm. Poor bastard kept looking at Seb asleep in the chair. I felt sure that if he could have wished him out of sight, he would have!

Sunday, August 22nd—The early hours
What the fuck?

When Seb produced his second stash of scotch this evening, Russ performed his disappearing act on cue. This time Seb and I ended up on the rug before the blazing fire. More probing questions. His tongue and his inhibitions loosened by liquor once again, we snuggled up close, as he confessed to his strong, if unwelcome, attraction to Bearish men. It was a short step from that admission to having his cock down my throat.

I can still taste the flavor of his precum on my tongue, can still feel the fullness of his dick bruising my gullet with its width. Filling my throat to capacity as he plunged ever deeper. Thrusting his hips, bucking his hairy thighs to meet my ravenous mouth. And when he came, pressing my head down, holding fast, pumping a deluge of thick, creamy man juice into the back of my throat. Blasting a path to the center of my universe. Groaning and grunting. On and on. Squirting cum in copious doses. Draining his big, big balls.

I lay down, resting my head against his furry belly as he stroked my head. And then came the unmistakable sensation that we were being watched. Slowly lifting my head, I turned, fully expecting to see Russ in the doorway to the bunkroom. No show. The door was closed tight. And then the laughter, bubbling low, building until it echoed throughout the room. Maniacal laughter. Seb sat bolt upright, grabbed my shoulder. "It's coming from outside," he said, scrabbling for his jeans.

No sooner had he yanked open the door to outside than the laughter stopped. The rain still lashing down, we strained our eyes to see through the torrent.

"There. Over there!" he said, pointing.

Shapes? Shadows? A reflection of the moon dancing between the trees?

He spun around and reached for his windbreaker and the shotgun propped up in the corner. "You stay here. Lock the door."

"Don't go out there!" I begged, but he was not to be dissuaded.

"I'll be a minute. Just a minute. Some fucker's out there."

An hour has passed. He still hasn't returned.

7:30 a.m.

I didn't so much fall asleep as pass out. Passed out on the chair beside the fire. Seb still hasn't returned. What am I going to tell Russ?

11:00 a.m.

Russ is in shock. So am I.

He never heard a thing last night. Not a thing. When I told him what had happened he thought I was winding him up. If only! When I finally managed to convince him, he suggested we have a look around, at least head down toward where the Range Rover is parked.

There had been a welcome break in the storm, and though the ground was muddy underfoot, the sky was clear and the forest didn't seem half so scary in the cold light of day. Not scary until we got to the Range Rover, that is. A Range Rover with no engine under the hood is not a laughing matter. And still no sign of Seb.

Then the sky turned black in an instant and we had to dash back to the cabin. Drenched by the time we got there, we both began to peel off our sodden clothes before we caught a chill. Buck naked, Russ swaggered to the bunkroom to get a change of clothes and his mobile phone to ring for help while I dried off before the fire. Moments later, he stood in the doorway as pale as a ghost and trembling. With fear? With rage?

"What have you done with it?"

"Eh?"

"What have you done with the fucking phone?"

"It's not there?"

"You know it's not there. You fucking took it!"

"Me?"

"You. What's your game? What are you two fuckers playing at?"

"Playing at? Nothing! You mean it's not there? But it must be."

Balls swinging, I crossed the room and tried to push past him but he blocked me, launched himself at me like a wild man, slamming my back up against the cabin wall. The rough bark scraped my skin as I fought to throw him off.

We wrestled each other onto the floor, a grappling mass of fur and muscle. Does fear make a man horny? The harder we fought, the harder we got. Russ's stiff dick pressing up against mine. Rolling over onto my belly in an act of submission. Parting my buttocks, exposing my vulnerability. A vulnerability he didn't hesitate to take advantage of. His cock, slathered with spit, penetrated me to the very core with the first powerful thrust. No mercy. Jabbing into me with a vengeance. Pumping his hips as I pushed back to willingly receive the punishment. And then came the howl of triumph as he shot his seed into the depths of me. Firing on both cylinders. Hitting bull's-eye with his very first attempt.

All anger dissipated along with the sexual tension. He collapsed on top of me and nuzzled my ear with nose and lips and beard. Stayed inside me until he was soft. Rolled off me then cuddled up like a big old Teddy Bear. We fell asleep on the rug before the fire. A deep, untroubled, but all too brief sleep. Time out. A blessed release from the real issue at hand: What the fuck are we to do about Seb?

Late Afternoon

Over a pot of strong coffee we discussed our limited options. (1) Sit tight and wait to see if Seb returns. Not a good idea if he was out there somewhere injured. (2) Hike down to the main road and get help. Also not a good idea given that it would be dark by then, with little to no chance of passing traffic. Or (3) Go look for him. We decided on the third option. But together. We would stick together. Safety in numbers.

In any event, it was a fruitless search. Russ insisted (wisely) that we mustn't venture too far from base. Hampered by the unremitting downpour, we could barely see a hand in front of our faces and still we searched. No stone unturned. And, ultimately, all for nothing. As darkness fell, we returned to the cabin empty-handed, soaked, and chilled to the bone.

Russ had been mostly silent throughout. Me too. Back in the cabin we decided on yet another change of clothes, then food and bed. Tomorrow morning we plan to hike back to civilization. There's nothing more to do.

Now our damp clothes hang by the fire, steam rising. The smell of canned chili simmers on the stove and reminds me of just how hungry I am. Famished. Exhausted. Roll on tomorrow.

Monday, August 23rd, early hours

All will become clear—or maybe not.

Russ climbed into bed with me last night. Naked. Fur covered from head to toe. Cuddled close. It was a matter of seconds before we were hard at it. Me sucking on his gorgeous, huge hunk of an uncut cock. My tongue playing with the thick, heavy foreskin. Driving a path underneath it. Suckling on it before swallowing his big dick whole. Using it as a pacifier? Fuck knows. It seemed an age before he came, and I enjoyed every long, l-o-o-o-n-g minute of it. Finally, he released a gush of semen so pungent it threatened to overwhelm my senses. I struggled to contain it all and this time won the battle. And all the time he was yelping and whimpering in the throes of an extended orgasm. His whole body shuddered with each pulse from his full, ripe plums.

His hand resting on my hairy belly, his face nuzzled against my furry back, Russ fell asleep in no time. But me? I lay awake in the darkness, listening to the rain beat on the roof, listening to him snuffle and snore. Eventually, I slept, albeit fitfully. But around 2 o'clock I gave up a losing battle, got up, and went into the main room, carefully closing the door behind me so as not to wake him. Having brewed some coffee, it was only when I wrapped the blanket around myself and settled down by the fire that I heard the subtle but unmistakable sound of scuffling against the outer wall. A sound like claws, scratching. An animal looking for shelter? Or was I simply hallucinating through lack of sleep? That wouldn't have surprised me either. But then the scratching began to grow gradually louder. Not one set of claws but a second, a third, and finally a multitude, tearing at the walls. Ripping sounds, wood splintering sounds, and growling, building inexorably. And then a bang from next door and...silence.

I leapt from my chair and ran to the bunkroom but it was empty. No Russ. The windows were thrown wide open. The wind and the rain were beating back the shutters. I rushed to slam them shut, fasten them tight. My heart was pounding, fit to burst. And now I'm alone. Completely alone. The storm continues to build outside, the thunder crashes, and the lightning flashes. Fuck! Fuck! Fuck!

Later

I lit a candle and checked out the bunkroom. Blood on the pillow. Signs of a struggle. I've barricaded both doors now—outer and inner. Got to hold tight. Keep it together. Wait until morning and then get the hell out of here.

And I am haunted by memories from my childhood.

Memories of how I would sleep with the light on in case *they* came to get me—the Bogey Man, Count Dracula, whoever. In the darkness of my bedroom it was always easier to believe that something was out there in the night. Something evil. Something out to get me. But I'm a big boy now. A big boy and scared shitless. This is no irrational childhood fear. This is happening. It's really happening. And I wish I was home in my own bed with the light on.

Later still

No rest. None. How long since the voices began? Unremitting. Droning on and on. Squalling. Crying.

This has to rank as the longest night of my life! Will the sun never come up?

Now laughter is ringing. Ringing all around me. And the sound of Seb's voice is joined by the sound of Russ's voice begging me to open the door, pleading with me to join them. But I will not. *I fucking will not!* They can hammer on the walls. They can claw at the roof above my head. But I will not let them in. They will have to break the damn door down, tear it from its hinges. They will have to rip off the fucking roof and drag me out. But I will not give in to the voices. I will not. I will—

Jack and the Bus Bears

BOB HAY

Jack has this idea that bus drivers are the best bears. Quite often, when there's a long weekend or he has nothing better to do, he buys a pass and spends hours taking one bus after another, perving on the driver rather than going anywhere in particular.

Of course, most of the time, his luck's out and he ends up being taken for a ride to the Back of Beyond by some bald-faced youth or a woman at the helm. His nemesis, he says, is a tall, thin dyke who always wears a leather hat and who, it seems, invariably turns up driving the bus that he has decided just has to be the last. Over the past few months he's spent hours and hours of his spare time taking one ride after another. He's seen suburbs no other bear even knows exist and has become an expert in routes, numbers, sections, Sunday timetables, and termini, but so far for Jack, as for most fishermen, the biggest and best have all got away.

Jack's taste is rather specialized. He likes older men. A good bushy beard is a must. He doesn't mind if a man is bald from the eyebrows up, but he likes his men hairy from the cheeks down. But what Jack likes above all else is big, hairy forearms, thick thighs, and a good-size gut above the belt line. There are drivers like that around—we've all seen them—but despite his best efforts, until very recently, not once has Jack found a driver to his taste with a welcome on his fly.

That was until one wet Sunday night after an Ozbears meeting last winter. As usual, Jack was almost the last to leave, dusting off the knees of his jeans and wiping the smile from his face as he said good night to his brother bears who were busy locking up and putting the rubbish out. He had had fun, but overall, the night had been a bit of a disappointment: While he enjoyed renewing old friendships—or, more accurately, sucking a few familiar dicks—a new guest or two to greet with his famous one-handed Ozbears Hug (one arm around the neck to do the hugging while the other hand gropes the basket) would have brightened up the rather limp, damp night.

And so he trudged up the road and hailed the first bus that came into sight. The night was so cold that the windows were all fogged up, and it was not until he was actually on board that he realized he was the only passenger. He shoved his ticket into the green machine and, while waiting for it to pop back up again, glanced at the driver. And glanced again: Thick gray curls topped a big, broad brow beneath which an equally thick, curly gray beard grew in luxurious profusion. Tufts of hair showed above the white T-shirt he wore beneath his open-necked Transport Authority uniform. Clearly not one to be intimidated by winter, this driver wore short sleeves and shorts. His forearms, as Jack quickly noted, were thick and very, very, hairy while heavy thighs bulged from beneath his shorts. All he needed for perfection was to be a bit fatter, but Jack was not one to look a gift horse in the mouth: Here, after months of bus hopping, was the treasure at the end of his rainbow.

"Bugger of a night, eh?" said the driver as he closed the doors and pulled out from the stop.

"You can say that again," said Jack. "Just the night to have the car in dock."

"Well, look at it this way," said the driver, grinning, "you've got me and the whole bus to yourself. How's that for service?"

Jack didn't quite know how to take that, so he sat on the nearest seat and looked longingly at the driver's hairy forearms.

Suddenly there was an ominous silence. "Fucking hell!" said the driver as he coasted the dead bus to the curb and pulled the brakes on. "It's the second time tonight the bloody thing's conked out on me. Just as well we're not full of pooped partygoers dying to get home, eh?"

"What's the matter?" asked Jack, a little nonplussed but more interested in watching as the driver heaved himself out of his seat, opened the little door, and squeezed out into the passageway. Those thick hairy legs went all the way down to his boot tops and all the way up to a broad, well-cushioned arse packed tightly into the shiny blue shorts.

"Dunno," replied the driver as he bent over (Jack got an even better view of his arse as he did so), punched on the emergency signals, and then picked up his microphone. "I'll give them a call at the depot and they can send out the breakdown bloke. Just as well he's a mate of mine or he'd really love me for calling him out on a night like this."

The driver did whatever he had to, replaced the microphone of his emergency radio back on its hook, and took some swaggering steps down the aisle. "Christ, it's good to stand up," he said, stretching his thick-set, hairy arms up to the skylight and chinning an imaginary bar. "Worst thing is, sittin' like that for hours makes your nuts feel as though they're about to drop off. Poor squashed-up little buggers need exercise..." As he spoke he wriggled his arse and then cupped his hand under his ample basket and heaved it up and around a couple of times. Jack could feel his eyes jutting from his head and his cock hardening in his jeans.

"You like that, eh?" asked the driver, openly rubbing his crotch as he spoke.

"You're a real bear," said Jack, croaking a bit with nervousness as his voice strangled in his throat.

"You like thick, hairy cocks then, man?" asked the driver, still rubbing what was an obviously growing bulge.

"Best of all," said Jack, confident this time that his prayers had been answered. He stood, the swelling in his own jeans making it clear that he spoke the truth.

"We've got awhile before Tony gets here, then," said the driver. "I guess the windows are too fogged to see in, but I'll switch most of the lights off just to be on the safe side and then, if you like, you can have a swing on this!"

He moved over to the dashboard and with one hand switched off the overhead lights, while with the other he unzipped his shorts and swung out a heavy, thick, cut cock that quickly took advantage of its freedom and stiffened fully in his hand. He turned back to Jack, who immediately dropped to his knees and in one fell swoop swallowed the driver's meat to the full.

"Christ, you know how to suck cock," said the driver. "Mouth like a vacuum cleaner..."

Without breaking his up-and-down rhythm, Jack reached up and with one hand began to undo the driver's belt.

"Here, let me, matey," said the driver, reaching down and gently removing Jack's mouth from his cock. "Let's get a bit more comfortable." And so saying, he moved over to where the two seats faced each other in the front of the bus. He undid his belt, dropped his shorts around his ankles, and lay back on the seat, spreading his knees and allowing Jack full view of his hairy belly and, for the first time, his egg-size furry balls. Jack dropped his jeans too and once again knelt, cupping his fingers beneath the driver's nuts, weighing them and squeezing them before again going down on the thick, stiff cock before him.

A few minutes of this and Jack had to come up for air. While he gulped in oxygen, the driver heaved himself further onto the seat, straddled Jack's head and, placing one foot on the opposite seat and the other on the small rail at the side, once again invited Jack to go down on him. Jack did not hesitate. This time he ran his tongue around the big balls, up the shaft, and around the flaring, red head, and then for a moment he poked the tip of his tongue into the driver's piss slit, wriggling it around and making the big bear squirm beneath him. At last, one hand on his own cock, he bent once again and swallowed the iron-hard weapon to the hilt.

The driver's change of posture had forced Jack too to change position, this time standing bent over, his arse up in the air as he leaned forward once again to swallow the driver's cock. *I hope he's right and no one can see in,* Jack thought as he felt the cold air on his arsehole and the back of his balls. Still, he didn't waste too much time worrying, just went to town working on the best and beariest cock he had had the pleasure to meet in a long while.

Just as the driver was beginning to breathe very heavily and Jack too could feel his own load beginning to swell up at the base of his balls, there was a click, the doors opened, and a cheery voice said, "Wonderful night for a breakdown, Andy."

Jack sprang up and tried to pull his pants up but only succeeded in tangling himself in the driver's legs and falling backward onto the opposite seat.

"Don't let me spoil the fun," said the newcomer as he closed the doors and walked up the steps. He loomed huge in the cramped quarters of the bus: If the driver was a desirable bear by Jack's standards, the guy who had just entered was Jack's dream of Heaven.

"Shit, you bastard, Tony," said the driver, making no effort to move. "You might have at least knocked."

"And miss seeing you in your favorite position? Worse still," he said, his luminous dark eyes shifting from Jack's exposed cock to his trim-bearded face, "miss seeing that lovely furry arsehole winking at me? Reckon you were getting pretty close to coming there, mate," said the mechanic to Jack. "Just as well I got here in time, don't you think?" And as he spoke he shucked off his overalls and stood stark naked in the middle of the bus, his hand wrapped around one of the biggest cocks Jack had ever seen. Already hard, its head protruded yet a handbreadth and plenty more above his fist. A drop of precum glistened like a diamond in the weak light of the bus's interior.

"Don't let me stop you, mate," said the mechanic again, and with his free hand he gently directed Jack's head back down toward the driver's cock. And, as Jack shifted back into position, the mechanic's other hand caressed Jack's hairy arse, his thumb massaging Jack's ring. Before Jack had time to realize what was happening, the mechanic's thumb had slipped all the way in.

"Great arse, mate," said the mechanic in his soft, deep voice at Jack's ear. "But don't you guys come just yet, I need to get some lube and a johnny on."

Jack slowed his rhythm slightly and let the driver relax a little beneath him. He felt the mechanic's thumb withdraw and, a few moments later, his fingers return with their slippery load. He shifted his position a little and arched his arse higher as the mechanic positioned himself behind him, the head of his huge cock nudging impatiently at Jack's arsehole. Letting go of the driver's meat for a moment, Jack lowered himself onto the mechanic's cock, stopping only when he felt the man's balls hard against the hair on his bum. He gave a few practice strokes, just to make sure the big dick was well-positioned and moving freely before bending forward again and once more swallowing the driver's thick cock as far as it would go.

They say it's not the size of the tool but how well it's used that counts—but you can't argue against the fact that a big cock backed up by an expert really takes the cake. Whatever the reason, it didn't take any of them long to come. Tony the mechanic pounded so hard and so fast at Jack's arse that within a couple of minutes the big man had fucked the cum out of him. Just as Jack felt his cock spurting, he tasted the driver's load in his mouth. "Shit, oh God!" said the mechanic, pounding faster and faster, each stroke so hard the bus rocked in time to his battering: "God, here it comes," he almost screamed. Then for a moment, all was still.

Jack slowly eased himself off the big cock that was still throbbing within him. Andy, the driver, stood and carefully wiped the mixture of Jack's spit and his own cum off his cock before pulling his uniform shorts back up over his thick, hairy thighs. "Bloody noise queen, this one," he said to Jack, nodding at Tony.

The big mechanic took no notice but concentrated on carefully peeling the condom off his deflating cock. When he had it off he tied a knot in the end to stop the big white load escaping and, with a mock bow, handed the little rubber parcel to Jack.

"Plenty more of that if you feel like doing it again sometime, mate," he said, his eyes expressing a request.

Jack was so breathless and his knees still so weak that he could only eagerly nod his agreement. He pulled his jeans back up and, even before he zipped back up again, took out his wallet, from which he took two cards and handed one to each of the men. "Anytime, you guys," he said. "And I mean *any* time."

He was about to say more, but right then, two bright headlights appeared at the back of the bus and lit up the interior.

"Shit, it's the next bus. I forgot there'd be one about now," said the driver. Hurriedly the three men finished straightening their clothing. Because he was the nearest to them, the mechanic went to the doors and opened them.

"You might as well catch it, mate," said Andy to Jack. "We'll be awhile getting this one back on the road. And thanks for a great night."

"You too," said Jack. "See you soon?"

"You bet," said the driver. "Tony and me live together, so you can have us both any time you want. By the way," he added, grinning from ear to ear, "best you don't try givin' such great head to the driver of the bus behind us."

Jack grinned back at Andy but didn't get the point of his joke until he boarded the other bus. As he popped his ticket in the green machine he glanced sideways at the driver. But his luck for the evening—like his load—was all spent. Sure as eggs, the driver of the new bus was the skinny dyke with the leather hat.

Bear Trap

Eric Mulder

Jim stopped with one foot off the sidewalk to watch a muscle-laden hustler march off down the hill. The river shimmered in the moonlight down below past a shadowy strip of marsh. Jim's gut urged him to chase the hustler down, but who, down there in the bushes, would ever notice his fresh haircut or the tight curve of his ass? The bushes would dirty his boots and scratch his leather vest. Jim didn't need the marshes anymore.

The Spike was Jim's bar, and it was alive with men. Noise and smoke billowed out of the door as Jim waited for his eyes to adjust. In the dim red haze the men were just shadows lining the walls. Pressing by them, he recognized a solid young blond from the week before, and the crusty bald daddy that had introduced them. Jim barely gave them a nod as he passed, eager to squeeze something new. Find a new mouth to fill, a new ass to tease. All the way to the back bar, where a husky Italian was playing pool. Jim glanced at every youthful face that lined the wall. He had done none of them before, yet he knew them all. At the bar an overeager waif of a boy ran a finger along Jim's exposed biceps. Jim glared down at the counter until the kid left, only to be jostled out of his space by a broad, firm belly.

"Sorry," the man said, patting his belly. "Sometimes it gets ahead of me."

The man was tall and broad, but the roll of his stomach wouldn't bump anyone unless he wanted it to. He wore a baseball cap and looked down on Jim with a goofy grin curling his beard. It gave him an innocent appeal strong enough for Jim to run his eyes down the man's tight shorts and along his fur-covered calves. But Jim wasn't in the mood for innocent tonight. He took his beer from the barkeep and headed for an open spot along the wall. The man turned to watch Jim until a wiry, silver-haired gentleman slipped himself under the man's arm.

"Markus!" Jim heard the newcomer say. He turned away to let the couple get acquainted and looked back to the dark corner. The bar had a deep alcove on this end, dark enough that the barkeep claimed he couldn't see the clusters of men gathered there. Jim could catch glimpses, as the men shifted, of a bright white face thrusting in time with the blaring music. He took a step to the left for a better view, but the crowd shifted and all he could see were tight-fitting jeans and leather chaps. Markus brushed by, tipping his cap to Jim, but Jim ignored him. The scene in the corner was far too enticing, even if he could only catch glimpses. Markus took a long look at the groping going on and chuckled. It didn't hold his interest though, and he took a spot by the pool table to watch the Italian bend over.

There was no one for Jim to pursue that night. None of the young studs gave Jim the pull in the groin he was looking for. Thin waifs and pockmarked old men—the entire scene made his stomach churn. After his second beer, Jim was pushed toward the dark corner. There was nowhere else to stand, except by the wall where men lined up for a run through the gauntlet. Tonight, Jim wanted something new. He'd looked down the bar for a boy that looked fresh, and couldn't find even one worth a closer look. That left the shadowy corner, where you couldn't see a face until you were close enough to brush whiskers. Jim recognized more people in this hot and sweaty crowd, rubbing hands across familiar asses as he slipped deeper into the corner.

A kid, with bleached spiky hair and oversize leather jacket, worked his way toward Jim. The boy was an expert at what he did, maneuvering himself so that every shift of the crowd pressed him into Jim's crotch. The kid wasn't Jim's type, but despite himself Jim was growing hard with the attention. With every pass the boy would pause longer to explore the bulges in Jim's pants until he finally took a firm grip on the base of Jim's rod and slowly worked his way down the pants leg, squeezing every centimeter Jim had to offer, feeling it stiffen even more in his hand. With a swipe of his hand, the boy released Jim's mighty cock and sank to his knees with a smirk. Experienced beyond his years, the boy went at it with such vigor that Jim stumbled back into the man behind him. A beard tickled the back of Jim's neck, making him shiver with unexpected pleasure. When he looked up, it was into the eyes and goofy grin of the man that had bumped him earlier. He stood there, steady as a brick wall while the boy went at it. Jim tried to move away, but the man held him back with great gentle hands on either hip.

"Lean against me," he said, resting his great jaw on Jim's shoulder. Jim was in no position to say yes or no.

As the boy worked him down, the man licked and tickled the back of Jim's neck. He was firm, and strong, and his tongue rough against Jim's earlobe.

A gap opened in the crowd. Across from him Jim could see a pockmarked old man leaning against the wall while an underage boy blew him off. He licked his lips at Jim, the dim light catching the few strands of hair on his wrinkled head. As he zipped up to leave, he stopped to pat Jim's boy on the head. "He's a good one, ain't he," the old man said with a wink before leaving. They were dressed just alike, Jim and the old man. Same leather vest and white T-shirt. They were identical, down to who would get them off. Jim went soft inside the boy's mouth. He pushed the kid away and struggled out of the corner. He was out the door before even finishing zipping his pants up.

Outside the air was cold and clear, and Jim couldn't pull enough of it into his smoke-filled lungs. He leaned against the boarded-up window, waiting for his head to stop spinning. Something was wrong tonight. Bars had always been full of potential. He'd walk in with a hard-on and leave with one even after shooting his load three times around the bar. He'd never gone soft before at all, especially while a man was blowing him. The old thrills didn't thrill him anymore. Jim wanted to believe he was just growing up, but it felt like growing old.

Markus emerged, smiling down on Jim with his goofy grin. A callous hand stroked Jim's back ever so gently, rubbing the tightness out of Jim's back with one hard thumb.

"You doing OK?" he asked.

"I'm fine, just couldn't breathe in there," Jim replied.

"It was getting kinda stuffy."

Markus continued to rub Jim's back with one hand, the other a warm presence on Jim's thigh. The gentle touch cleared Jim's head. He let out a soft moan as the man worked deeper into the tense muscles. Markus reached over Jim's shoulders to massage his chest, but Jim stepped away. He didn't want it to go further, didn't want to lead the man on. This guy was the type who would want to go home and cuddle until dawn, and Jim was dead set against that.

"Where's your boyfriend?" Jim asked.

"Don't have one. He dumped me, told me to find someone younger who could keep up."

"You don't want me, then," Jim laughed. "I think I'm slowing down."

"You going to be all right? Can I give you a lift anywhere?"

"My car's just a couple blocks away."

"Well then, have a good night." The man smiled and tipped his cap. Without another word he stepped past Jim and continued down the street. Jim sighed in relief, but was just a touch disappointed. Even if he was going to reject the guy, it would have been nice to be chased for a little while longer. The man seemed pleasant enough, and Jim was sure if he ran after the guy, the man would be agreeable. It reeked of a mercy fuck, however, and Jim would never lower himself to that point. At least not yet.

With the smoke clearing from his head, Jim was feeling lusty again. He did not, however, want to pick through whatever trash was left desperately waiting outside the door. He left for his car, which meant following the goofy man. Jim's eyes rested on Markus's powerful hips as they walked. He preferred his tricks toned and much shorter than himself, the opposite of Markus. There was, however, a charm in the gentle, amused way the man carried himself. At Park Street the man turned to his right without hesitation and trotted down the hill. The move left Jim with his jaw gaping, then he chided himself for ever thinking of the man as the innocent type. Jim didn't want sex in the park, and he wasn't about to go lurking through the bushes, but he was curious as to what type of stranger a tall, meaty man with a goofy grin would pick up. Markus was already past the streetlights when Jim started down the hill, but Jim knew where to start looking. It took only a minute to pass the streetlights himself.

Trees lined the road, their leaves rustling in the wind. Several paths led down to the water, and Jim chose the trail most worn, open to the moonlight. Jim's last little escapade here was years ago, but he could still find his way blindfolded and handcuffed if necessary. The moon hung like pure silver in the sky, but down by the water all Jim could see were the fiery ends of cigarettes bobbing like will-o'-the-wisps along the trail. Jim leaned against a tall oak tree, waiting for his eyes to adjust. A dozen men were down there, walking alone or pairing off.

Markus stood in clear view, hands on his hips as he pissed into the river. The moonlight made the arc sparkle. Another man approached while Markus shook himself off, and they talked for a while. Deep, low laughter rolled up the park to where Jim stood. The stranger moved off, alone. Markus watched him go, then turned directly toward Jim.

"This isn't the safest place to be, you know," Jim called out. "Some college kids have been coming down here causing trouble."

"Then I'm glad you're here to watch my back."

Markus broke a grin as Jim approached, wrapping one heavy arm around Jim's shoulders. Heat rolled off the man, taking the edge off the evening's chill. Jim leaned into him, finding refuge in the warmth of the man's touch as Markus massaged him again. Such a gentle, unusual way to attract a man. Jim smiled, despite himself, as his shoulders relaxed. The first deep breath of the evening filled his lungs with cold, crisp night air.

"You spend a lot of time here?" Jim asked.

"Not at all. I was just feeling—"

"Horny."

"Yeah, it's been awhile. I'm glad you came down tonight." The man took Jim's hand and pulled him gently down the trail.

"Look, I don't really want to do anything."

"I just don't want to stand in the open. Let's find someplace to talk."

Talking was the last thing that would happen, of this Jim was certain. Even so, Jim put up little resistance. They wandered through high weeds and bushes where the ground was damp and soft, until they came to where a giant maple had fallen on its side. Weather had stripped away the bark to leave it a pale and naked bench sitting beside the river. A cool breeze blew in from the river, making Jim shiver. He crossed his arms and rubbed them hard for warmth as the man sat up on the log.

"Aren't you cold?" Jim asked.

"Naw, I got a fur coat to keep me warm, see?" The tank top stretched tight across rippled abs as the man pulled it over his head. All Jim could see was the faint glitter of sweat left from the bar hanging in the dense hair. The man took Jim's hands, burying the fingers deep into the silky chest hair.

"Nice and warm. Let me keep you warm."

Strong arms wrapped around Jim, pulling him into an embrace. Jim pushed away, but they held firm. The man pressed no further, just held Jim to him while stroking Jim's back. He whispered, "Shhh...let me just keep you warm, just keep you warm." Jim stopped struggling as the chill of the night fell away with a simple swipe of those fur-covered arms. Chest hair, thick and curled, rolled up Markus's belly and around his pecs. The fur began again on the back of his neck, descending in silky waves all the way to his ass. It was soft to pet, and so tempting to follow the pattern down into his shorts and take a grip on the firm butt cheeks. The man tickled Jim's neck again with the bristled edged of his mustache and beard. Warm, gentle, slow, when their mustaches locked, Jim almost didn't realize they were kissing. With a jerk, Jim ripped himself away to the freedom of the cold, dark night.

"You seduce men for a living?" he asked.

The man smiled. "Nope. Just for sport."

The answer didn't sit well with Jim, who was looking left and right for a quick escape. The man looked at the ground, kicking his heels against the splintered bark of the tree.

"Isn't it what you went to the bar for?" he asked.

"Not exactly," Jim answered.

"I saw what you were looking for."

The man hopped off the log, approaching Jim with that innocent country boy swagger. Without turning his sparkling eyes from Jim's, he reached down and unzipped Jim's pants, pulling the soft flesh into the evening air. The man sank down and slurped up Jim's hardening manhood. He flailed it with his tongue, rolling it from side to side in his mouth until it was too stiff to bend. He worked the rod, slowly at first, slapping the tip of its head with the tip of his tongue. All at once he buried the shaft deep into his throat, tongue lashing against Jim's scrotum. Jim leaned heavily on the man's granite frame, feeling the hair beneath his fingers grow moist and slick with sweat. The rough tongue scoured his cock, swiping over every inch of it in quickening waves. Jim's knees began to shiver; a warmth was building up in him, becoming a fiery pressure demanding release. The man kept going, working up and down the rod until it was only a flaming spark ready to explode. He held tight to Jim's hips to keep Jim from backing away. Then, when the pressure of the expanding cock was just enough to explode, he bit down just hard enough to keep all the tension in. Jim sobbed as the throb reversed itself, rocking through his body without the freedom of release. He crumpled over the man, holding the heavy head and strong jaws tight to him until the threat of coming had subsided.

Markus pulled back, chuckling low, to pick up his fallen cap. He remained squatting, bright eyes gleaming in the darkness, while Jim's cock beat against his face with each throb.

"That what you were looking for?"

"Almost."

The man stood and took Jim's cock in his great hands and pulled Jim close. The intended kiss landed on the stubble of Jim's cheek, but the man kept moving along, licking the tender underside of Jim's jaw until reaching behind his earlobe. He worked one hand around inside Jim's vest and down his pants to cup one of Jim's buttocks in his massive hand. The man was warm, like a furnace. At once the leather vest was too warm to wear, and it fell to the damp earth. Still too warm, Jim let the man pull Jim's shirt up to his throat, trapping Jim's hands above his head, before Jim pushed him away.

"Stop. This isn't what I wanted for tonight."

"What did you want?"

"Just a quick fuck, then go home."

"Oh? Get your rocks off and leave the guy panting?"

"I'd be fair about it. I just don't want romance."

"Is that so?"

Markus lifted Jim's shirt again, running his thumb along the trail of hair that climbed up his chest. As slowly as possible, he leaned over the ripe nipple, tickling it first with the point of his beard, then with a flash of his tongue. Both hands worked the denim on Jim's ass until they exposed the pale skin to the air. One hand disappeared, leaving a cold impression on Jim's right cheek. Something crinkled far below, and the hand was back, in a fist, sliding deep along the muscles up Jim's back. The man pulled him tight, biting on his nipple with such violent intensity that lightning ricocheted along Jim's skin. The pleasure was too strong to stand, but the man kept Jim on his feet as he slid down again to the waiting, pulsating cock. Both the guy's hands fell away to work on something that crinkled in the darkness as the man nibbled up and down Jim's long cock. The condom was placed on the head with casual ease, but the man unrolled it down the long shaft with only his lips and tongue. It took a torturous amount of time, all the while with Jim leaning hard with one hand on the man's back to steady himself. For a moment he was certain he'd lose himself, but the man knew just when to back away. Spitting into his hand, he gripped around Jim's shaft and pulled him toward the naked maple.

"Come on, big guy, fuck me."

The man's shorts fell away as if blown off. His body was covered in swaths of auburn hair that darkened his pale skin. Sweat glittered in the hair on his chest like stars Jim could run his hands through. One hand found a nipple, a heavy pointed knob buried in the fur; the other fell down along the trail of hair to the man's own thick cock. It was a handful, large enough to be exciting without getting in the way. Jim found his lips falling toward the round nipple, exploring its hard, rough ridges with his tongue as his hands explored the smooth, wide dick. The man pulled Jim close, pressing Jim's face into his huge furry chest, letting Jim's cock slide between his legs. He backed onto the log, lying down along its smooth surface to open himself to Jim. Licking more spit into his hand, he greased himself, then took hold of Jim to guide him in. Jim's dick didn't need any guidance. It pressed its way into the hot opening, only getting the tip in before meeting resistance.

"Gently, gently..."

The resistance fell away, and Jim's entire shaft slid into the hot, wet furnace. Both men cried into the night, the man clutching tight to Jim's ass. As both began to breathe again, the man let Jim back himself out only to ram in again deeper than before. The man cried out again but left Jim free to move about on his own now. It was so hot inside the man, fiery hot. A rough hand twisted Jim's nipple, adding to the intensity. A tongue crawled along his jawline and into his mouth, and Jim found himself lost. He kissed the man with savage intensity, and the man kissed back, grunting a little with each thrust that seemed to reach deep into his chest. They were locked together, tongues warring, hands gripping and clawing at each other. Their bodies throbbed together at a quickening tempo. Heat and energy flowed from the man into Jim with each thrust. It was too much for Jim. He felt his entire body expanding, hardening. The man fell away as Jim straightened himself, unable to focus on anything but the furnace he probed and the pressure growing within him. He pumped the white-hot hole, oblivious to everything as all the fire in his body condensed into the tip of his prick and exploded, shooting back into the man in waves of volcanic ecstasy.

Jim's body continued to convulse, out of reflex, as he crumpled on top of the man. Violent shivers took control, but the man helped stroke them away. Thick, rough hands worked their way from Jim's ass to his shoulder, gently keeping Jim's head resting on the man's firm pec until the convulsions subsided. Jim could breathe again, but barely. He withdrew himself from the man, giving a faint cry with every inch of meat that was exposed to the air. Standing there, shivering and weak, he had to let the man peel the condom off. He threw it over his shoulder and into the river, showering an arc of sperm onto the water. A single drop fell on the man's red shorts, where they hung on a nearby bush. He took a handkerchief from the back pocket and wiped it off, then turned to clean Jim. Jim's cock was still stiff and throbbing, and sensitive to the touch. He had to breathe deep while Markus cleaned him. After patting the cock dry, Markus went down on Jim one last time. A farewell kiss. Jim stepped back, struggling to pull his pants up and fit inside them again. The man sat with a smile.

"You're not going to run off now, are you?" he asked, chuckling. Jim turned red, all the way to his emerging bald spot, and left himself hanging out.

"No, I'll get you off," he said. Grabbing the man's heavy balls,

Jim rubbed up beside Markus, his still-hard cock against the man's thigh. He licked some spit into his palm to slather over Markus's stout rod. The stiff appendage, now slick, stood out from the man like a pole. Jim worked it slow, taking the time to nibble on one of the great nipples. The man only laughed, and reached into Jim's pants to grab his ass again.

"Won't work out here," he said, messing Jim's hair around to kiss the thinned patch. "Too nervous, can't ever get off in a park."

"Then what do you want to do?"

"Go back to my place, start all over."

Moonlight shimmered in the thick hair of the man's beard as it twisted into the goofy grin. The man stroked Jim's mustache with one finger, straightening the hairs, before leaning down for a kiss. Jim let it happen, long and hard, without daring to breathe before it was over. The stranger's tongue descended deep into him, brushing aside all resistance. Arms with knotted muscles wrapped around him like the jaws of a bear trap.

"Come home with me. I'll cook you breakfast."

Jim gave a dry laugh. He buried his face in the man's chest, enjoying the hair as it tickled his nose.

"You live far?"

"Just a couple minutes. We could walk if you wanted."

Jim slid away, but Markus caught his hand before he could run off. They held hands, like old friends finding each other in the pale moonlight. Jim turned away shyly as Markus slipped his shorts back on. He threw his tank top over his shoulder and they walked together, hand in hand, back toward the glittering streetlights. Jim bowed his head as they passed people, feeling like he was taking his dog for a walk. He withdrew his hand after the third stranger.

Markus lived only a block down the road, much to Jim's relief. If things turned sour, it was a short walk to his car. Even as Markus led him up the driveway Jim planned his route home. The earlier passion was fading, and when Markus stopped him at the door Jim nearly took off.

"I want you to know, I still live with him. My ex, Don. We still get along, we just don't sleep together anymore."

"Is this going to be a problem?" Jim asked. Here was a smooth way out, though he wasn't quite ready to take it.

"Not at all, I just didn't want to surprise you."

Whatever more to the story there was, the man hid behind his goofy grin and a quick peck on the cheek. He took Jim's hand, holding it firm, and it was the gentleness of the touch as much as the insistence that pulled Jim inside.

"Can I get you something? Coffee, tea, anything?"

"Nothing." Jim pulled Markus down to lock their mouths together, pushing his tongue past the other to lick the roof of the man's mouth. He didn't want to think anymore about where this night might lead. Markus pushed back, gently, and eventually suc- ceeded in dipping Jim so low they nearly collapsed onto the living room carpet. The man righted them, withdrawing his tongue to nuzzle Jim's neck. For a minute they just stood there, swaying slowly. Jim sagged against the man, growing drowsy with his warmth.

"Will you stay the night?"

"No."

"Why not?"

"Because...I need to get up early."

The man let the lie pass unchallenged. Instead, he took a firm grip on Jim's backside and lifted him up, forcing Jim to wrap his legs around the man's massive waist. Jim felt like a toy doll in the man's steady grip, kissing more passionately than before and wrap- ping himself tighter around the man. Down a short hallway behind them a dog scratched at a door. Jim barely had time to rec- ognize what the scratching was before the door opened and a great white dog, almost glowing in the dim light, came bounding down the hall. Completely unafraid, the dog walked right under Jim to sniff his hanging ass.

"Markus?" A voice as deep as rolling thunder called down the hall. "You home?"

A light flicked on, flooding the hallway and blinding Jim. For a moment he saw a naked man standing in the hall, covered from head to toe with a thick mat of gray fur, before he had to close his eyes against the light. Blinking, the man vanished, but his gravelly voice was laughing.

"I'm sorry, boys," he said, emerging from his room while tying a white robe around his waist. "Didn't mean to disturb you, just wanted to tell Mark that his mother called. Nothing important."

Jim disengaged himself from the man, stepping apart. The dog took this opportunity to bury his snout in Jim's crotch, nearly knocking him down.

"I'm sorry," Jim said. "Are you lovers?"

"Hell no," the older man assured him. "We haven't been that for years. Just roommates now. Get back to what you were doing, I'll go back to bed."

The older man didn't move, but stood in the hall with a fatherly grin on his face as if hoping to watch his boys at play. Jim took another step back, with the dog still pressing against him so that the two fell. Flat out on his back with the dog on top of him, Jim couldn't avoid getting a savage licking of his face.

"Foo Foo!" the man barked, quickly moving to pull his dog back. "He's harmless, really, but I'll take him to my room," the older man said, taking Foo Foo by the collar. Markus helped Jim up from the floor.

"We were going to have some tea, do you want some?" Markus asked.

"Oh no, I don't want to bother you two."

Tufts of curly gray hair crept out of the V where his robe came together. Jim couldn't take his eyes from it, or the way his pecs and paunch pressed firm against the thin white fabric. He forced his eyes to the floor, running them over the older man's thick calves and heavy feet where hair grew on the knuckles of his toes. Without another word Don pulled the dog back into his room and shut the door, light still shining on the carpet from under the door.

"This is OK, isn't it?" Jim asked, falling back into Markus's arms. "Will he be mad? Are you two really broken up?"

"We're just good friends now, he won't mind." Markus said, but did not smile as deeply as normal.

Markus entwined his fingers with Jim's and pulled Jim down the hall. They turned a corner to a room where moonlight shone on the narrow bed. The man made the first move again by pushing off Jim's vest and pulling his shirt over his head, but he did not remove the shirt entirely, so that Jim's arms were trapped above within the fabric. Markus left him there, bending down to nibble on Jim's nipple, then work his rough tongue over to Jim's exposed flank. While Jim gasped and squirmed, the man rubbed his beard against the shivering skin. He tickled Jim with his tongue all the way from Jim's hips to his armpit, pressing Jim against the wall to hold him still. Jim struggled in the man's grip, breathing only in controlled gasps to keep the electric shudders rocking his body from exploding into laughter that wouldn't stop. Lack of air was making him dizzy, letting the tingles reach down into his bowels, where a night's worth of beer was waiting to be released. "Stop," he managed to gasp as he sank down the wall. The man did not stop until Jim was laid out on the hardwood floor, shivering with withheld laughter. He pushed against the firm, unmoving body on top of him until Markus moved up to nuzzle his neck. Any touch now made his skin tingle with a spiderweb of electricity. Jim found himself chuckling in the man's firm grasp, holding tight to the hard body until he could breathe again.

"Get off me," he said, rolling the two of them over and throwing off his shirt.

The man rolled off without resistance, looking a bit concerned and startled. Jim could only smile in response and run his fingers through Markus's thick beard. He explored the ridge of the man's impressive pecs, following the pattern of hair that swirled around the red nipple, before swooping down for a kiss.

"I'll be right back," he told the man and pushed himself to his feet. Markus rolled on his side to watch as Jim left the room.

Jim found the bathroom across from the older man's room,

unbuttoning his pants as he walked, hoping his hard-on would go down enough for him to piss. He clanked the toilet lid against the tank, trying to angle his stiff prick toward the bowl, when the scratching started again. Just as Jim relaxed enough to release his bladder in a satisfying stream, the bedroom door creaked open. Foo Foo pushed through and headed straight for Jim, with his head down and tongue lolling. Jim grabbed the dog's collar and tried to hold him back, but the dog fought to sniff the bowl with canine persistence.

"Foo Foo, come here," the older man barked from the bedroom door. Jim caught a flash of the man, naked except for the mat of peppery fur covering his body. The broad pink head of Don's cock peeked out from the thicket of pubic hair for only a moment before Don pulled his robe on tight.

"I'm awfully sorry about this," he said, entering the bathroom to pull the dog away. "Foo Foo, bad dog. Bad dog!" He squatted down to shake his finger at the dog's face, but the dog was too busy straining to sniff Jim while he was zipping back up. When Don yanked the dog back by the collar the dog retaliated by licking his thick beard.

"I'd better take him outside," Don said. The dog became aggressively affectionate, leaping up to knock the older man on his ass. For a moment Don lay sprawled out, legs spread wide open, in front of Jim. Jim took a moment to admire Don's stout cock and heavy balls before helping him with the dog.

"Come on, pup," Jim said, and pulled the dog away by his collar. "I can't imagine which one of you he takes after."

"What's going on out there?" Markus asked, standing in his doorway.

"Just putting the dog out," Jim assured him.

Jim was already in the living room, dragging Foo Foo behind him. The dog was happy enough to be with Jim until he saw the sliding glass door they were heading for. All through the small living room and into the dining room the dog dug in his claws and did his best to resist. The linoleum in the dining room offered nothing to hold on to, and the startled dog found himself sliding right out of the house. Jim closed the door quickly and stood on the other side as the dog scratched and whined at the glass.

"He'll be fine," the older man assured Jim, coming up behind him. For a moment they stood there together to watch the dog. Jim stood close to the glass door so he could see the man's reflection. He liked how the man's nipples made small knobs in the robe.

"You going to fuck my boy tonight?" The older man asked. Jim laughed in response.

"Already have," he said.

"So it's his turn to fuck you?"

"No, I don't do that. I don't let anyone—"

"Why not?"

"I don't know. It feels safer being on top."

"With the right man, being a bottom can be wonderful." The older man said, putting a warm hand on Jim's shoulder.

"And that would be you, wouldn't it?"

The older man chuckled and turned away, blushing. "I've taught a few boys how to take it. But Markus knows what he's doing. He'll be good for you, gentle."

The older man's dark eyes caught Jim. There was a strength there, a self-assurance that didn't care if he got laid or not. It felt safe to let Don wrap one strong arm around Jim's waist while the other explored the light covering of dark hair on Jim's chest. There was none of the urgent need in Don's touch, like Jim found in each and every person he had fucked in the bar.

Markus clomped down the hall and into the living room, making enough noise to be heard long before he reached them. Jim pulled himself away from the older man to hide in the darkness of the kitchen, for once embarrassed, though he couldn't say why.

"Now, Don," Markus said, "I might share, but I'm not giving him up without a fight." He put both arms around the older man to hold the man still and look deep into his eyes. Don looked away, struggling to leave Markus's grip.

"No. I wasn't...I was just putting the dog out."

"Sure you were," Markus pulled him into a bear hug, lifting the man off the floor. "You should have come out with me, we could have had a party."

"Yeah," Jim chipped in. "There was a cute boy there who could use a man like you to teach him a few things."

"No," Don said. "I'm just a dirty old man now. Nobody wants to touch me unless I trick them into it."

"Nonsense," Markus insisted.

Don struggled to free himself from Markus's tight embrace. It almost worked, but as Don pushed Markus's thick arms apart, Jim came up from behind to hold him still again. The man was trapped between them, unable to move or resist at all.

"Plenty of men must want to play with you," Jim said.

"If Markus hadn't brought you home, you wouldn't have even talked to me," Don said, leaning into Markus with an amused grin.

Jim wouldn't deny it. He looked over the man's shoulder into Markus's dark eyes, trying to read the concerned expression he saw there. Markus's thick eyebrows were curled into each other and his goofy smile darkened into a frown. It was clear how well the two fit together, and it made them irresistible. That Don might think himself unappealing to Markus made Jim want to laugh, or cry. He slipped a hand inside Don's robe to let his fingers wander through the forest of hair on the man's chest. It took the slightest nudge to slip the robe to the floor, leaving the man naked and vulnerable between Jim and Markus. Don covered himself, blushing deeply while casting an amused grin at Jim.

"What are you doing?" Don asked.

"Just letting the dog out." Jim set a quick kiss on the man's lips and moved the arms aside. He ran his tongue along Don's chin, through the curled peppery hair on his chest, and over the firm bulge of his belly. The man grew rigid with expectation as Jim's nose brushed his belly. A shudder passed through the man's body as Jim licked his inner thigh, sending a wave of satisfaction through Jim. He burrowed in deeper with his tongue and tickling mustache until the man released a soft gasp, then moved up to suck the man's pulsing cock deep into his throat. The man stifled a laugh and pushed Jim away hard by his shoulders.

"It's not nice to tease an old man," he said.

"Who's teasing?" Jim said. He stood up again to press Don into Markus and keep him still. "Is this all right with you?" he asked Markus. Markus responded by leaning over the older man's shoulder to lock lips with Jim in a hungry kiss. He shoved his thick tongue down Jim's throat as the two rubbed and probed each other through Don. Caught between them, with a hairy hulk on one side and a dashing stranger on the other, it was all Don could do to breathe. Jim pulled his lips away from Markus's to relish the rough touch of Don's beard against his chin. For a moment their lips met, and the older man's tongue flashed out to lick the roof of Jim's mouth before Jim moved down to suckle on the older man's stout nipple. Don's rock-hard prick pressed against Jim's abdomen, and Jim rubbed it with his belly while sliding his hands around the curve of Don's ass to free Markus of his shorts. His hot, thick cock hooked the elastic of his shorts; Don pulled it free and let it rub against the crack of his ass.

"Let's use my bed," Don said. He took Markus by the hand and led the man, still kicking his shorts off, back through the living room to his bedroom. Jim expected them to close the door behind them, but instead Don was waiting at the doorway. He hooked his fingers into Jim's belt loop and guided Jim to the bed. While he unbuttoned Jim's pants, Markus moved behind Jim to lick the back of his neck. He squatted down slightly to press his cock between Jim's legs, dry-fucking Jim while the older man nibbled on Jim's dick. The pleasure set Jim's body tingling far too fast. He pushed Don onto the bed and crawled on top of him. While they kissed and groped each other, Markus pulled off Jim's boots and pants. Jim sucked Don's nipple hard while rubbing his cock through the fur on Don's belly, not noticing what Markus was doing until he felt a hand, warm and wet, slide between his butt cheeks. Markus slathered lube on Jim's ass, massaging Jim's tight hole with a callused finger. Pleasure bordering on pain flooded Jim with such intensity that he jumped off of Don and spun to the edge of the bed. Don, panting a little, started to laugh.

"He's a little shy about that," he assured Markus. Taking a gentle grip on Jim's arm, Don pulled them both to the center of the bed, where Markus was waiting. Their arms surrounded Jim, lips caressing him from both sides. When Jim closed his eyes, he could not tell if he was making love to two men or one. Strong arms held Jim still against the bed. The rough tickle of a beard descended slowly from his nipple down his exposed flank until a nose was pressing against his scrotum. Another beard tickled his neck, behind his ear. One callused hand squeezed his nipple, stabbing him through with pleasure while another thumb pressed, a solid irresistible weight, against his ass. Jim at once grew rigid, breathing in gasps. Markus showered his cheeks in kisses and whispered, "Relax." Down below, Jim could see the length of his manhood disappearing into Don's gray beard. Warm, wet pleasure washed over him. Jim could only groan, arching his back to open himself to the older man. Then, like the intake of a breath, Don's thumb fell into him. Jim couldn't breathe at all, the sensation was so intense. Markus held him firm while Don prodded Jim's prostate with his thumb. With each prod Jim let out a cry, squirming, wanting Don to go deeper and terrified at how good that might feel. Markus pulled himself down Jim's body to lock beards with Don. They kissed, and fought over Jim's cock with their tongues.

Don withdrew his thumb, sending tremors throughout Jim's shuddering frame. More lube, cold and soothing, was applied to his steaming ass. One leg, then another, was thrown over Don's shoulders so when he sat up he lifted Jim's ass off the bed.

"May I fuck you?" he asked. Jim was insensible—he could only reply by pulling Don down on him for a rough kiss. Don pulled himself away, grinning from ear to ear, to reach for a condom. Markus rolled on top of Jim, his balls pressing against Jim's nose. Jim buried his head again in Markus's crotch, breathing in the dark scents of manhood before taking Markus once more deep into his throat. The hot tip of Don's prick pressed against him, sending waves of pain mixed with absolute pleasure through his body. Jim took hold of the great tight buttocks hanging above him to hold himself steady as Don pressed into him. Jim writhed with ecstasy. He tried to crawl on back and away from the overpowering explosions of sensation that accompanied each of Don's thrusts, but Markus was there to hold him still. Markus bent down so that each thrust Don gave would push Jim's dick into Markus's waiting mouth. The heat washing over Jim made him dizzy and faint; he had to free himself of Markus's dick just to breathe.

Don, working slowly at first, reached deep inside of Jim. He did not let up but pumped harder with each thrust, reaching ever deeper into Jim's virgin ass. Markus, his cock like a slab of granite slapping against Jim's chest, sat up to beat himself while Jim buried his tongue between the open cheeks. He could no longer tell who was inside who, who was crying in pleasure and who was causing the cries. The fiery pressure in his crotch was about to explode when warm, wet waves of Markus's cum splashed across his chest. Jim released a cry that shook the house. Jim couldn't even catch his breath when Markus backed off Jim's face and brought Don into view. Every tendon in Don's face and neck bulged to their limits; his mouth hung wide open, holding back the impending scream as he beat his meat only inches above Jim's balls. The great purple head exploded in a stream of cum reaching all the way to Jim's chin. Each burst shot more of the warm, sticky fluid that dripped between the hairs on Jim's chest and rolled down the sides of his body.

They collapsed on top of each other, holding each other tight as their heartbeats slowly returned to normal. Don nuzzled Jim's neck until a spasm would return to make him gasp for air. The spasm would move from body to body like aftershocks.

When they could all breathe again, Markus got up from the bed. Jim could hear the faucet go on in the bathroom while Don ran his hands through the mess of Jim's hair.

"You could stay here tonight," Don said.

Jim shook his head. "No," he said. "I can't."

"But you can if you want," Don replied.

Markus returned with warm, moist hand towels. He wiped off Jim's body while Don wiped splatters of cum from Jim's chin and brow. When they were done with Jim and each other, Markus crawled back in bed with them. He cuddled up beside Jim, resting his face against Jim's chest and throwing a long leg over Jim's waist. The older man watched over them both, running his hands along Markus's shoulder blades while rubbing his bearded chin against Jim's small bald spot. *I'll leave soon,* Jim promised himself. Don settled in, the curve of his belly filling in against the small of Jim's back. A bristly kiss brushed Jim's shoulder, his neck. The room grew dark, until all that was left was warmth and peace.

Jefferson Head
Karl von Uhl

"Nolan?"

I looked up from the store shelf. All I wanted was groceries. Groceries and relaxation.

"Nolan Urquhart. You're George and Dorothy's boy, right?" said Mr. Hanson, affable as ever, walking over from the cash register. "I haven't seen you since—"

"Since high school," I said, trying not to turn pale at yet another recognition. I had come to the family vacation house, my vacation house since my folks died, for a month's leave. And Indianola, while friendly, hardly granted me the anonymity I had hoped for. It's conveniently located, though—a little over an hour's drive from Seattle if you include the ferry ride across Puget Sound, so it's easy enough to treat a bout of cabin fever.

"Good to see you back," he said. I tossed a few more items into the handbasket. "You're Navy, right?" he asked.

"Yes, sir. Lieutenant commander," I said, walking toward the register. "Been a good career for me."

He started ringing me up. "Yeah, you Navy boys could wear beards," he commented. *He hasn't seen me for 20-odd years and the only thing he can think of is, Garsh, he has a beard,* I thought. "We couldn't do that in the Marines," he said. *And some of us Navy boys think the only reason they put Marines on aircraft carriers is because sheep would be too obvious, Mr. Hanson.*

"Yeah," I said, paying him.

"You know, I should tell my Tommy you're here. He's up from

California. You boys could catch up on old times."

"That'd be all right," I said, walking for the door. "See you later, Mr. Hanson."

Walking back to the house, the crotch of my sweats began rubbing the top of my cock head, reminding me just how heavy my cock was hanging and how many opportunities I'd missed. Maybe it was time to take the ferry across the sound for a little release.

Subic Bay. Now there was a place for release. Plenty of whores in Subic, all of them monotonously eager to help American sailors break the tropical tedium. Buddying up made it easier; Mike Canady and me used to hang out at Johnny Limo's Pearl Club, and made a sport of rebuffing their advances: "I can't because your pussy's too tight" or "My thing's too small." They never believed us, but the opportunities for entertainment in Olongapo were slim enough to warrant any indulgence.

One night, after just such entertainment, we started back to our weekend hotel room with a bottle. I noticed Mike was walking a little funny, taking two steps, then a third sort of half step, and so on. On a tall man like him, the effect was exaggerated.

"Some jarhead finally cop yer cherry, Mike?" I asked.

"Fuck no," he said. "I gotta piss."

"So piss."

He stopped and glared at me. "Well, I would, Captain Obvious, but do you see a head here in the street?" he said in his north Texas twang.

"I'll cover you."

"Cover me? I'll just fuckin' wait."

We started walking again. "You know, Mike, sometimes I get to thinking."

"Yeah?" he said, trying to minimize the awkwardness of his gait.

"Thinking about the rolling ocean, the vast expanse of water. How it's fed by a multitude of streams and tributaries, rivers cascading recklessly through—"

"All right, all right!" he said. "Goddammit." He trotted a few feet ahead of me and turned into what looked like an abandoned doorway, the lintel scarred and pitted. He fumbled with his fly. "Fuck."

"Need some help there?"

"Fuck you."

"There isn't anybody coming," I said. Snatches of an Abba song played in the distance, the melody plaintive and sweet in the night air. I watched him take his cock out of his pants, watched as his stream began to flow.

"Fuck," he said.

"What?"

"I hate it when it fuckin' hurts to piss." His cock was drained of color in the harsh streetlight.

"Maybe you got clap."

"Not a chance."

"Why're you so sure?"

He looked me straight in the eye. "Because I haven't done anything to get it."

"You're a virgin?"

"No, I'm not a virgin," he said, squeezing out the last drops of piss from his cock before he stuffed it back in his pants. "I just haven't done anything."

"Not lately."

"Yeah. Not lately."

"How come?"

"No reason to."

"No reason to get laid?" I asked. "Don't you get horny?"

"Fuck yeah," he said. "Just not for these skanky whores."

We walked the rest of the way to our hotel discussing the merits of sport fucking versus having an actual girlfriend to lend an occasional assist. As soon as we got in the room, Mike started undressing. I kicked off my shoes, dropped my trousers, and walked to the meager bathroom, where I pissed in the sink.

"That," said Mike, "is a disgusting habit." He lay on the bed, scratching his nuts through his skivvies.

"What?" I asked from where I stood.

"Using the sink. Christ, man, I shave in there."

"I wash out good, ensign," I said, imitating the nasal, clipped intonation of the whores. "I wash out good, you me get it on." Mike laughed. "You pretty ensign, you sexy, you fuck good."

I brought two glasses with me from the sink, poured whiskey in them, and offered one to Mike. "To simple pleasures."

"Simple pleasures," he said.

The whiskey burned its way down my throat. Mike laid his head down and said, "I don't think I shoulda had that one."

"Too late," I said. "You gonna be sick?"

"Nah," he said. "Just drunk." He turned his head toward me, deep in thought. I sat on the edge of my bed. A few drops of piss made a small translucent window in my skivvies. "You're a real good buddy," he said.

"Yeah, you're drunk," I said.

"You horny?"

"Mike, I'd expect that question from a fucking jarhead, not from you."

"You horny?"

I grabbed my glass and licked the last few drops of whiskey from it. I didn't care if Mike was drunk. "Yeah."

"All right then." Mike rose toward me. He was easily a head taller than me, and moved with an obviously hard-earned grace. He knelt beside my bed and put his face in my crotch.

A barking dog brought me out of my daydream. I got to thinking about Tommy Hanson, the shop owner's son; we were pretty good buddies three months out of the year way back when. We went to different high schools but occasionally saw each other at football games and wrestling meets during the school year. Summer was all ours: water skiing on Puget Sound, salmon fishing, and sneaking beer were our summer rituals, along with the occasional circle jerk with a couple other guys.

Once home, I put my groceries away, grabbed a beer and the

latest Patrick O'Brian novel, and walked out to the deck my father called the flying bridge. The yard gave way to a bramble-covered cliff, the beach, and the sound below; the pier to the right, Big Rock almost dead ahead, and Jefferson Head far to the left. In the distance across the sound was the Seattle skyline, dwarfed by Mount Rainier.

A knock at the door interrupted my reading. At first I thought I was hearing things, but the knock repeated. I put my book down and ambled to the front of the house. It was Tommy Hanson, no longer a teenager, but certainly recognizable. His beard was full, though not especially bushy, and rose high on his face, almost above his cheekbones, but still it couldn't completely dull the harsh angles of his face. His boxer's nose sat askew of his mustache. What was visible of his face was a little windburned. His cutoffs and baggy blue T-shirt covered what appeared to be a still appealingly stocky frame. As I remembered him from summers past, he was barefoot.

"So you remember me?" he asked, smiling.

"Tommy," I said, mock-scolding him. "Come in."

"I brought some beer," he said, offering a six-pack of Olympia.

"Ah, the taste of postpubescence," I said, taking two and offering him one. "It's even cold. Thanks."

We walked out to the deck. I was happy to see him, but unsure what to talk about.

"It's odd being back here," I said, leaning on the rail.

"Well, Nolan," said Tommy, imitating his father's voice, "you really ought to have dinner with us some time soon. Muriel'd love to see you, and you know Heidi? Had puppies not two weeks ago."

I laughed. "It's just you look so different. The beard and all," I said.

"Yeah, I'm no longer the barefaced boy with feets of, er, something," he said, taking a swig of his beer. "It's practical. Protects the face. Hides a fair amount of ugly." We watched the tide come in, the scent of ozone light on the air.

"So where did you go after high school?" he asked.

"Annapolis," I said. "You?"

He paused a moment and said, "After much turmoil, our hero found himself at the esteemed Scripps Institute."

"No shit?"

"As good a reason as any to keep myself on a beach," said Tommy, sitting in a deck chair. "They gave me a doctorate, now I work for 'em. Talk about owing your soul to the company store." He smiled. "So you made Annapolis. You always did like boats."

"One of these days they're even gonna give me my own. Hoo-boy."

Tommy gave me a questioning look.

"OK, so the commander needs a little more enthusiasm," I added.

He took a pull on his beer. "There's gonna be a good low tide tomorrow. Wanna go geoducking?"

"Sure," I said. We looked at each other, then to the sound, then back to each other.

"You got any girlfriends?" he asked.

"Nah," I said.

"Ah," he said. "Um...is it true that the Navy is the friendliest force?"

I looked at him, puzzled. He squirmed a little in his chair.

"A lot's happened, buddy," he said, taking a long pull and finishing his beer.

"A lot of what?" I asked, my nuts already buzzing.

He put his hand on his crotch, saying, "It ain't the beer, Nolan. I just have a hunch about you."

Shit, the boy's quick, I thought, feeling my cock getting heavy in my skivvies.

Next thing I knew, Tommy was out of his chair, his tongue was in my mouth, wrestling thickly with mine, his beard was flowing everywhere mine didn't, and his hand was on my stiffening cock. He wrapped one of his arms around my neck and opened his jaw wider, driving his tongue through my mouth. I slapped his butt with both my hands and kissed back as hard as I could.

"Shit," he said, breaking off. "Someone taught you how to kiss." He took a slug off my beer and pressed his mouth to mine. The liquid dripped down our beards, wetting our shirts. I felt his hand squeezing my cock, softly, insistently, instinctively knowing how much pressure brought a small rush of intense feeling.

He shucked his cutoffs and got on his knees, put his face in my crotch, and mouthed my cock through my sweatpants. It'd been a long time since someone had worked my cock this way, and I wanted it to last. I held his head to me, feeling him tonguing the material, feeling the heat from his mouth.

I looked down at Tommy's cock: same length as I remembered, maybe seven inches, but it had fattened a little in the intervening years. It stuck out straight from his dark pubes and bobbed against the wood deck.

I felt Tommy's hand working my sweats open. "Tighty whiteys," he said. "It's easy to tell the officers from the enlisted."

He put his mouth on my nuts, using his breath to heat them. They sank in their sac, and he took to licking them through the cotton, pushing one up, then the other. My cock stood out in relief. Tommy starting licking the length of my cock, soaking my skivvies with his spit, licking at the underside through the material.

"You gonna suck it?" I asked.

"I've thought about this for a while," he said. "I'm gonna do what I'm gonna do." With that, he pulled at the waistband until my cock was freed and my skivvies were around my knees; immediately he took the head of my cock into his mouth, covering it with spit and his hot tongue. He worked his tongue slowly around the underside, circling the edge of the head with the tip of his tongue. Slowly, he started taking my cock further into his mouth, taking his time getting the shaft wet. When his beard finally reached my pubes, he held still for a moment, then started swallowing, massaging my cock with his throat.

My nuts were hanging low against his beard, getting pleasantly scratched. I started an easy pistoning motion, moving slowly out and in. Tommy squeezed his lips against my cock, working his tongue from side to side as I fucked his face, spit dripping from his lips onto the deck.

I felt a breeze against my bare ass and pulled my cock out of Tommy's mouth. He looked at me and stood up, our cocks touching. He took off his T-shirt, revealing an expanse of hair that ran from armpit to armpit and neck to crotch. He grabbed both our cocks and began stroking.

"This remind you of anything, buddy?" he asked.

"Fuck," I said, feeling his callused hand.

"Feeling good?"

"Fuck yeah."

He spit in his hand and continued stroking, making my cock drool on his. I bent my head forward and kissed him, lightly flicking my tongue on his lips. He responded by licking my face and beard, all the while stroking our cocks.

I pulled back a moment and took off my T-shirt. "Fuck," he said, and he started licking on my chest, following the trail of hair from my belly to my chest and back again. He raised my left arm and put his face into my pit and began licking. With my sweatpants around my ankles, I lost my balance and hit the deck hard.

"You OK?" he asked.

"Oh yeah," I said. I kicked off my sweatpants.

"That's better," said Tommy, lying between my legs. He opened his mouth and started working on my cock again. I felt the hot ring of his lips rise and fall on my shaft, his tongue occasionally sticking out, licking my nuts. I felt his throat muscles contract on my cock as he swallowed; my cock throbbed involuntarily in his throat in response. He played with my nuts, pulling on them every time he had my cock buried in his throat and releasing them when he pulled his head back.

I felt him start massaging my taint, slipping a few fingers into my ass crack while he sucked. I grunted. He started poking directly at my hole, working his fingers against the pucker, plying the muscle. My cock flinched in his mouth, his tongue licking the head, catching all the fluid leaking out. He continued working my hole, spit dripping from his mouth, down my cock, onto his fingers. The spit was all my hole needed for encouragement; two of Tommy's fingers slid in.

He let his fingers rest while he sucked my cock, working his tongue in a circular motion around the head. I felt my ass relax as he began slowly to move his fingers. The motion was slight, barely perceptible, and made my nuts buzz. I grabbed his head and pumped, fucking his face, driving my cock in and out of his mouth, his mustache grazing the shaft. I sunk my cock deep in his throat; he held still while I let my cock throb.

He took his mouth off my cock. "Can you stand up?" he asked, holding his hand toward me.

I bent my knees and rolled forward from my shoulders, trying to keep his fingers in my ass. Tommy had the same idea and wiggled his fingers for encouragement, making my cock jump. Holding on to his arm, I pulled myself into a squatting position, feeling Tommy push at my hole with a third finger. As I stood, sweat dripped down my neck and chest. Tommy slid his third finger in, and a big drop of dick spit oozed from my cock onto the deck. Tommy stood, his fingers still in my ass, his cock pointing at mine.

He began stroking his cock, pulling the skin along his shaft, squeezing out dick spit and smearing it on my spit-slick cock. He started working my hole with his fingers, sliding them in and out. I grabbed my cock and likewise began stroking.

I ground my ass against Tommy's fingers, feeling them right behind my cock, sliding on the smooth muscle. I wanted them deeper in my hole, fucking me wide. Tommy opened his mouth, spit into his hand, and returned to jacking his cock. I squeezed my hole tight on Tommy's fingers, released, and felt his fingers slide easily further up my ass.

We jacked off, cock head to cock head, my nuts bouncing against Tommy's arm. I reached up and started pinching one of his nipples; he grunted and squeezed his cock hard. "What's the matter?" I asked, teasingly.

"I really like that."

I leaned forward and put my mouth where my hand had been. I licked his nipple, tasting sweat and skin and hair. I closed my teeth on it, Tommy's breath hot on my head. He grunted and began working my hole harder now, fucking it in rhythm with the stroking on his cock. "Shoot it, buddy," I said through my teeth.

He stroked hard on his cock, aiming right at mine. I watched his balls as they drew up, his stroking more insistent. His breathing grew deep and fast as his load oozed slowly out of his cock onto mine, dripping down my balls and onto the deck.

My hole wide open now, he stroked in and out with ease, paying special attention to the area right behind my cock. Whenever he pulled out, he would spread his fingers, stretching my hole, then slide them back in fast, expanding my rectum. I felt flushed and pushed my ass back against his hand, and I jacked hard and steady, feeling my load building.

"Gonna shoot for me, buddy?" he asked. I grunted and he pulled my hand off my cock so he could jack it. "C'mon, buddy to buddy now."

His fingers stroked nonstop up my ass, and with him in control of my cock, I lost it. I felt my load come on, starting in my ass. At first nothing came, then a large glob of jizz shot out, hitting Tommy's leg. I pushed back hard on his fingers and clamped my hole. My cock kept shooting, my load dripping from his fingers onto his feet. His fingers slowly slid out of my ass.

We stood close for a while, catching our breath and sharing a beer. I turned to him and said, "Want to stay for supper? We're having spaghetti."

Tommy grinned and said, "Yeah, but I gotta tell my mom."

Golden Boy and the Bear

ADAM GAWRON

I met Rodney online one evening in an M4M chat room after a hard day at work. I was on the fast track at my company and under a lot of pressure to produce. The week before, I had given the airhead who had been occupying the role of boyfriend his walking papers. All in all, I wasn't in a very picky mood. Anyone who was prepared to give me what I wanted and whose picture didn't crack the monitor, I thought would do.

Rodney's screen name left no doubt about his desires. Since these matched what I was looking for, we started chatting. He was agreeably straightforward, asking for my stats and HIV status, and suggesting we trade pics. "I'll be up front with you, Chuck," he said in one message, after I had sent mine. "You can see I'm just an average guy, not a looker like you. But I give great head. I've had guys come back lots of times because of the way I serviced them. If we hook up, I promise you won't be disappointed."

I looked at the smiling, bearded face on my computer screen.

"Well, you said I don't have to do anything, right?" I typed back.

"No, all you have to do is kick back, relax, and let me do my job."

I stopped by his house the next day, following the directions he had given. In person, both Rodney's age and girth were greater than his picture had suggested. He really wasn't my type at all. But he was very friendly and obviously was glad to see me. Not wanting to be rude, I entered when he invited me in.

"Chuck, you're even better-looking in person," he said, shaking my hand. He had green eyes that glinted when he smiled. He reached out and playfully groped my crotch. "Looks like you could use some service, buddy."

I found to my surprise that my cock was responding. Rodney's frank pleasure, no, *lust* at the sight of me was having an effect. Heck, this might be fun. "I guess so, Rodney."

"Well, come on in the bedroom and make yourself comfortable."

Well, to make a not very long story even shorter, Rodney turned out to be everything he had promised and more. His mouth was hot and slippery, his tongue agile. It was only a few minutes after I had dropped my shorts and sat on his bed that I shot my load down his throat, gasping and moaning. Rodney swallowed every bit and even lapped up a stray drop that leaked out after he had released my softening dick.

I lay back on the bed with one arm over my head and let out a long sigh. "Damn, you're good. Sorry I came so fast."

Rodney chuckled. "Don't apologize, Chuck, that's my job. I was trying to get you off nice and quick; I could tell you needed it."

"I did, but I still wish it could have lasted longer. Getting there is as fun as getting off."

Rodney looked at me thoughtfully. "Well," he said, "I have ways of making it last. Sometime maybe you'll come back and let me show you. I love giving head for a long time. That's when I have the most fun. My record so far is two hours."

"Really, how'd you do that?"

He grinned again. "Come back and find out. Of course, I like quickies too, like today. My aim is to please, Chuck. Drop by anytime. I work out of my house, so I'm pretty flexible."

At the time I didn't say anything, not wanting to commit myself. But I did end up going back to Rodney's place, more than once. At first, it was a pretty one-sided relationship. His talented mouth would draw my load from me, we would chat a bit, then I would be on my way. Eventually Rodney asked me to get naked, and I obliged. I'm not an obsessive muscle queen, but I have a good body, and his admiration turned me on.

About the third or fourth visit, as he started to kneel before me, on an impulse I said to him, "Why don't you get comfortable too?"

He looked at me, surprised. "You sure, Chuck?"

I shrugged. "Why not? It's your house."

Rodney said diffidently, "Well, Chuck, to be honest, I wasn't sure you'd want to look at me. I mean, you've got a great body. I know I'm not exactly your type."

"Rodney, don't be silly. You look just fine." For some reason, I was curious to see exactly what he looked like.

It took some more persuasion before he stripped. He was a big guy, all right—not a gym body by any means. He had broad shoulders; thick, powerful arms; and a barrel chest covered with dark hair lightly peppered with gray. One nipple was pierced with a gold ring. His stomach was round but solid, somewhat dwarfing his cut, good-size dick, which curved downward, half erect, as he looked uncertainly at me.

"Very nice," I said, my mouth unexpectedly dry. Seeing the brute power and strength of Rodney's body was causing strange new feelings inside me. He might have seen something of this in my eyes, for his face relaxed into a smile and he fell eagerly to his task. That particular session was the hottest one yet, leaving me drained and spent.

I caught myself wondering more and more often what it would be like for him to do me for a really long time. One day, I took the afternoon off and called him after lunch.

"You're early today," Rodney said on the phone.

"Yeah, I got the afternoon off," I replied. "Are you free?"

"Always free for you, Chuck. Come on over."

He greeted me at the door in his usual friendly fashion, and we went into the bedroom. I stripped quickly and stretched out on my back on Rodney's bed, spreading my legs so he could lie between them. I watched Rodney pull off his own clothes as I stroked my cock.

As he mounted the bed, I voiced what had been in my mind for days leading up to this meeting. "You know, I've been thinking," I said.

"What about?"

"About your two-hour blow job."

Rodney grinned. "You're serious?"

"I was just wondering how you would make it last that long."

"Hard for you to imagine, isn't it, Chuck?" Rodney said. "So far, you haven't lasted very long at all with me."

I snorted. "It's 'cause you're so good, Rodney. So just how good are you at not letting a guy come?"

Rodney's eyes glinted with an excitement that intrigued me. "I'm the best, Chuck. You really want to try it?"

I looked back at him, and after a moment, I said, "Yeah."

"To do it right, Chuck, I need to be the one in charge, no questions asked. Think you can let that happen?"

I held his gaze. "I do," I said. It was true. I liked Rodney, not only because of his untiring mouth but because he wasn't into playing games. What you saw was what you got.

"OK then," Rodney said. "Now, the first thing I'm going to do is restrain you. Let me get the cuffs."

I felt a momentary flicker of unease. I had never been handcuffed before. "Why?"

Rodney smiled. "Chuck, trust me. If your hands are free, you're going to try and stop me. You might even try and hurt me." He took a hold of my dick, almost painfully erect now, and licked his lips. "Do you trust me, Chuck?"

My breathing quickened. "Yes. Do what you have to do, guy."

Rodney said, "You won't regret it."

He reached over to the nightstand on my left side and began to rummage around in it. "Think they were here the last time I looked—let's see—oh yeah, here they are." He brought out first one, then two, pairs of shiny steel cuffs. "One for each arm," he said, grinning at me. He placed them on the bed and reached back into the drawer, coming up with two keys. "Always a good idea to test the keys before we put them on." He suited the action to the words, making sure the cuffs opened when he turned the key in each lock.

Watching him manipulate the restraints made me even more excited. I was nervous, yet unbelievably horny.

Rodney saw me looking at him and smiled. "Spread your arms out," he said. I obeyed, and he snapped each cuff around one of my wrists, then fastened the other cuff in each set to the headboard. For the first time I realized why holes had been drilled in each end of the solid wood piece. I was now locked in place, my arms unable to protect my body. Rodney looked at me, and when he spoke his voice was thick with lust. "Damn, you look so hot like that. Sure wish I had my camera."

He bent down and took one of my nipples in his mouth. I moaned softly as I felt his soft tongue on the sensitive flesh, his beard raking across my skin. Then I gasped as his teeth nipped just hard enough to hurt. Rodney looked up at me and grinned. He reached out and into the drawer again, and brought out something that, after a moment, I recognized as a pair of tit clamps, connected by a short steel chain.

"Hey," I protested, "you didn't say anything about those."

Rodney's voice was soft but unyielding. "Remember, Chuck, I'm in control now. You said you trusted me. Don't worry, I know you haven't tried these before, so I'll go easy on you. They're screw clamps, so I can adjust how tight they are. They won't hurt you...too bad." He laughed softly.

He tongued my right nipple again until it stood stiffly out from my chest. Then he took one of the clamps in his hand and adjusted the jaws around the tit. Slowly, he turned the screw, until I felt the small teeth begin to grab my flesh. "Stop," I said, but Rodney continued to turn until pain began to stab through me. I cried out and he said, "Got to make sure it stays on, Chuckie. Now for the other one."

He repeated the procedure with the other nipple. When he finished I was gasping and writhing against the cuffs. Rodney watched with a slight smile. "If you can't stand it, I'll loosen them."

Through gritted teeth, I whispered, "I can take it, man. Leave them."

Rodney nodded, satisfied. "Good boy. This is going to be fun."

His preparations finished, he moved down my body. As always, instead of taking my cock right away, he took my balls into his mouth—first one, then the other, rolling them around just enough to cause me to jump without really hurting them. Fear that he might bite down on my nuts and I'd be helpless to stop him mingled with my arousal. I was relieved when he let go of my ball sac and began to tongue the area underneath.

Despite my urgent pleas of "Eat that asshole, man," Rodney took his time, lifting my legs in the air and moving slowly down, licking my cheeks, circling closer and closer to his prize until, at last, he found my hole. He gave me the full treatment, from the lightest flickings against the sensitive flesh to all-out tongue fucking, grinding his mouth against my butt as he thrust inward as far as he could go. Then, as I whimpered and thrashed, he reached up with one arm and shook the chain that imprisoned my nipples. My moans turned into an anguished yell.

Rodney paused in his labors, looked up at me, and grinned. "How're you doing?" he asked.

"How do you think?" I replied, dizzy with all the sensations coursing through me.

"You sound like you're enjoying this, all right."

"I don't know if *enjoying* is the right word."

"Well, do you want to stop? Say the word and I'll let you go, Chuck."

I looked into his eyes. After a long pause, I shook my head no.

"Good man," Rodney said. He took my cock, which had softened just a bit, in his hand, and looked at it with a smile. "I'm gonna make this baby feel *real* good."

He opened his mouth and his tongue darted out, just barely contacting the head. He began to move delicately around the flesh, wetting it little by little. My cock quickly became hard and engorged again, precum beginning to ooze. Rodney lapped it up, then flicked his tongue gently along the sides of my piss hole and across the sensitive area just below it, until I saw stars.

"Come on," I urged him. "Take it all the way down your throat. Take it."

But Rodney was not to be hurried. With exquisite slowness, he let his lips surround the head, letting them make contact just below where it joined the veined shaft. Gradually I began to feel his hot breath on my cock. His lips squeezed until I was firmly sealed in his mouth. Then he descended in one tight, quick stroke, taking me down to the root. "Oh, God!" I shouted.

Then, slowly, he began to ascend, keeping his lips tight and using plenty of spit. As he tongued my cock head again, I was in an agony of anticipation awaiting the next downstroke, which eventually came, causing another shock of pleasure. After a few repetitions of this cycle, I began to buck and thrust with my hips to get some friction. He released my cock, and I groaned in frustration.

"Every time you do that, Chuck, I'll slow down even more," he said. "Is that what you want, buddy?"

"Oh, God no, please no. I'll be good, Rod, I promise," I pleaded.

"That's right. And remember, I can pull this any time too," he said, suiting the action to the words.

"OK!" I shouted. "Not that again!"

As my head was spinning from that latest jolt of pain, he suddenly grasped my cock hard and gave me a few rapid strokes with his mouth. I gasped again. Being kept off balance, not knowing whether I was going to feel pleasure or pain, when or how, was driving me close to insanity. I was mesmerized, totally in this big man's power.

I lost track of the number of times Rodney repeated this cycle, his mouth and tongue slowly stimulating my eager cock, alternating with bursts of ecstasy as he suddenly deep-throated me. At last he let go and said, "I need a break."

I laughed with a hint of hysteria. "You and me both, man."

Rodney hitched his massive body up on the bed until his bearded face was next to mine, and I could feel his warm breath. In a low voice he said, "Chuck, you are so hot."

He took my face with his hand and pressed his lips to mine. A part of me wanted to protest. This wasn't supposed to happen. But my resistance had been broken and Rodney knew it. His tongue darted into my mouth, and we exchanged a long, passionate kiss.

We broke apart, gasping. "How long has it been?" I asked.

Rodney grinned. "How long do you think?"

"God, it's got to be almost over, right?"

"Wrong," he said, "there's a clock above the bed here. If you twist your head around, you can see what time it is."

I looked upward and saw that it was 2:10. I had come to Rodney's at 1 o'clock. I groaned. "Jesus, are you really going to hold me to this two-hour thing?"

"Sure I am," Rodney said. "And if you don't behave yourself, I might extend it. I don't have anything to do for the rest of the afternoon. Besides, we haven't gotten to the best part yet."

"What do you mean?"

In response, Rodney lifted his hand and crooked two of his fingers at me. "My favorite sex toy. Get ready for a little ass play, Chuck."

He reached into the nightstand again and took out a tube of lubricant. He squeezed some out onto his right hand, then pushed at my knees, compelling me to spread my legs. He applied the cold, thick substance to my ass crack, paying special attention to the soft flesh of my asshole. After teasing it from the outside, he began to push in. My sphincter muscles resisted only for a moment, then I sighed as first one, then two, fingers penetrated the entrance.

Rodney was watching my face intently. "Feels good, doesn't it?" Suddenly I grunted. "Yep, you can feel that, can't you? That's your prostate." He pressed his fingers upward several more times. My breathing began to deepen and my cock unwillingly began to rise once again. The sensation was unlike anything I had experienced—I had been fucked before, but it hadn't been this peculiar, irresistible mix of discomfort and pleasure. "I like doing this. Gives me a bigger load to eat when you shoot, which," he leered, "won't be for a while yet."

I knew what was coming but was helpless to stop it. Rodney resumed his slow, methodical oral stimulation—only now, his downstrokes, when they came, were accompanied by a further jolt as his fingers poked the sensitive gland inside. Occasionally he would stop and simply massage my prostate, looking into my face as I tried unsuccessfully to will myself to come. Then, every once in a while, when I least expected it, would come a few sharp strokes with his mouth, with his fingers fucking my ass in tandem with his oral play. Again, he would stop just as I was about to reach the point of no return, then grin at my moans of frustration.

My entire body became covered with a sheen of sweat, although the air conditioning blew cold in the bedroom. My eyes focused only on my tormentor. I could not think of anything except wanting release from this pleasure that had turned into torture.

"Please, Rodney."

"Please what, Chuck?"

"Please, let me come."

"Not yet, Chuck."

"Please!" I shouted, a sob in my voice. I was playing it up because I knew he liked it, but the frustration was real.

"No," he said, softly, implacably.

"Please," I begged again. Ignoring me, Rodney ceased all movement until my organ began to deflate slightly, then took me again in his mouth.

Handcuffed to Rodney's bed that afternoon, I became a different person. I'd been blessed with a good face, body, and cock, and I had gotten stuck on myself. Sex had become something that

I engaged in solely for my own pleasure. I'd thought of Rodney as just a service provider, a guy lucky to have me. But now he was totally in control, causing me to groan with ecstasy or scream with pain, taking me to the brink of release and then pulling me back, again and again, manipulating me like a puppet. Even while pleading for him to stop, I realized that I wanted to be and welcomed being in his power. I knew that when I was finally released, I would beg him to make me his again.

The moments melted together. I lost track of time and the number of times I shouted, sobbed, and pleaded, only to hear his soft *no*. At last, tears running down my cheeks, I lay back on the bed exhausted, my chest heaving. After a pause, I heard him say, "It's time."

Before I could utter more than a disbelieving "Wha—" he engulfed my cock and began to slide up and down with long, wet strokes, his fingers pressing hard against my prostate. It took only a few seconds for the orgasm that had been building up all afternoon to explode in my loins. My whole body seized up in spasm as I let out a full-throated shriek of agony and delight, delivering blast after blast of hot cum into Rodney's waiting mouth and throat.

Rodney's cheeks bulged as they filled with my load. Dimly I saw his eyes looking at me with that familiar glint. He let go of my cock and bent over me, cum running out one corner of his mouth and into his beard. I realized what he was going to do and opened my mouth just as he opened his. The sharp pollen odor filled my nostrils as he released the load, dumping it into me before joining his lips to mine. Our mouths ground together as we passed the thick, salty liquid back and forth, letting it spill out and cover our faces. He broke free at last, and rose to a kneeling position over my chest, jacking himself off with quick, fierce strokes. I closed my eyes in anticipation, opened my mouth, and thrust my tongue outward. A few moments later, he grunted loudly. I felt his load hit my face in hot spurts and trickle into my mouth.

Rodney reached down and quickly unscrewed the tit clamps.

I shrieked again from the flaring pain caused by the blood rushing back into the tender flesh, but my cry was cut off as his mouth descended again onto mine, his full weight crushing me as we swapped sperm for a second time.

It took us long moments to lick each other's face clean and swallow the last of the cum. When we were finished, he released me from the cuffs. My arms, free at last, caressed his big body tenderly. We stayed on the bed for a long while, drained and exhausted. At last, he looked at me and asked, "So how did you like your two-hour blow job?"

I said, "Rodney, I hate you." His eyes widened in astonishment. I smiled and said, "I'll never enjoy any other kind." He grinned back and squeezed my tender cock.

"So you'd do it again, golden boy?" he asked.

In answer, I gave him one more cum-flavored kiss. "What other stuff can you teach me? Sir."

He laughed, delighted. "Chuck, I'll teach you whatever you want to learn."

After that, things changed between us. I guess you could say Rodney and I became buddies. We did stuff together and even hit his favorite bars a few times. Most of Rodney's friends were his age and physical type. He and I got a kick out of seeing them eating their hearts out, unable to figure out for the life of them how their compadre had managed to snare himself a boyfriend like me.

I wasn't running around with Rodney out of mercy. He was sociable, smart, and great fun to be with. I like to think I broadened his horizons a bit too. He said to me once, "I used to hate guys who looked like you. I knew I could never have anyone like that."

"Well, you were wrong, weren't you?" I said.

He smiled, his eyes sparkling. "Was I ever."

There was also the power Rodney had over me that only the two of us knew about. I've never told anyone about a lot of the things we did. In the dark of a lonely night, the memories still come back to haunt me.

I'm naked, my hands tied behind my back with a rawhide cord, struggling to crawl on my stomach toward Rodney's bedroom. He's ordered me to keep close to the floor and my head down, but I raise my eyes furtively as I wriggle across the threshold. I catch a glimpse of him looking impassively down at me, his arms crossed. He is naked, except for the black leather boots I will soon be forced to lick. In one hand he holds the cat-o'-nine-tails that will be my scourge.

Rodney is standing in front of me, gently holding my face. The entire back of my body, legs, back, and butt is burning from the welts he has raised with his lash. He kisses me softly, licking away the tears of pain trickling from my eyes. I'm helpless to wipe them away myself because my arms are over my head, secured by leather cuffs to chains dangling from his basement ceiling.

I'm handcuffed to the bed again, my legs suspended in the air by loops of rope dangling from ceiling hooks. Rodney is staring intently at me. One of his hands grasps a string that dangles out of my asshole, the other grips my dick. I groan helplessly as he slowly pulls the string of hard rubber balls out of my rectum, one by one, as his other hand draws the third orgasm of the afternoon out of my exhausted, unwilling body.

He opened up worlds for me that I never knew existed. I don't know how far we would have gone had it not all suddenly come to an end a few short months later.

My hard work had paid off. I was being promoted by the company—and transferred to another city.

We had never thought of ourselves as lovers, but when I saw the tears start from Rodney's eyes as I gave him the bad news, I knew just how close we had become. I was having a hard time not crying myself.

We met one last time just before I left town. There was a particular fire, mixed with sadness, in Rodney's eyes that night. My cock stayed aching and hard throughout the evening, though, of course, he wouldn't let me come or even touch myself. I can still feel the pain in my knees as I crawled after him on all fours, him pulling the lead attached to the collar around my neck, swatting me sharply on my bare butt with a rawhide quirt when I faltered.

He then tied my hands behind my back, ordered me to kneel in front of him and thrust his cock down my throat, fucking my face until I choked and my eyes watered. Then it was down to his cellar. As I screamed into the gag every time the whip cracked against my body, I sensed the additional passion in his strokes that night, as if he were determined to mark not only my body but my memory.

Finally he claimed his ultimate prize as I lay cuffed to his bed on my back, bent double with my ankles bound to my wrists. He drove into me so hard that the bed shook with every thrust. As he approached his climax, he pushed his body forward so that my lower back rose off the bed. He grabbed my cock and at last began to stroke it. We both grunted in unison as we rushed toward completion. "I'm coming," I finally gasped, and he aimed my cock directly at my face. I opened my mouth in a tortured groan as cum rained onto my face and tongue. Rodney's face contorted and he slammed his cock in up to the hilt as he dumped his own load into me. As his orgasm passed, his body began to shake, and I realized he was silently weeping. Sadness overwhelmed me and I began to cry as well, my tears mixing with the splashes of cum on my face.

In the early hours of the morning we hugged each other tightly one last time at his door. I'll never forget his warmth surrounding me, soothing my aching body, as he whispered in my ear how much he would miss me. I backed slowly out of his driveway as he waved, his big frame silhouetted in the doorway.

I've never seen Rodney again.

Ten years and many miles separate us now. My career has taken off, and my material success, together with, if I do say so myself, my physical charms have kept my love life going. But I've never found anyone else like Rodney. Even now, when I've quarreled with my current buffed, elegantly dressed soul mate or my schedule gets too hectic, the responsibilities too stressful, I long for his hulking presence. I want to see his kind face, his sparkling green eyes, the gray in his beard. I want to feel the strength of his arm as it brings the whip down on my quivering flesh. I want him to bind me and use my body any way he pleases, with his hands, mouth, dick, and any of his seemingly hundreds of toys. Most of all, I want him to take me to the edge of coming and keep me there until I'm begging him for release, then make my drained, milked body come when I'm begging him to let me rest.

I want to feel safe again.

Really Hairy Jesus
R.E. Neu

I moved to Santa Monica when I was 18, and though I'd renounced the Catholicism I'd been raised with, I didn't want to give up religion entirely. After some searching I finally found a congregation that seemed a good fit: I mean, I went there two years before I ever heard God's name mentioned. This congregation prided itself on being liberal. The priest tried so desperately to attract younger parishioners that his sermons sounded more like *Cosmopolitan* than Catholicism. Sometimes he'd talk about dating tips, sometimes about fashionable apparel, and once even spent 19 confusing minutes discussing something he called "Hope Implants for the Female Soul."

I'd never been to a church before that so rarely brought up religion. But this group prided themselves on being inclusive, trying to focus on the positive side of religion while ignoring the negative. Theirs wasn't the kind of god who'd ask you to kill your son: Their god would detail your Saturn, alphabetize your CDs, or whip you up a double-foamy cappuccino. Unfortunately, believing in a loving, supportive god meant you couldn't mention most of the Bible, so, for example, a sermon based on the crucifixion might turn into more of a discussion of woodworking.

While I appreciated how well I'd been accepted, their clumsy attempts at "inclusion" made me long for the day when the word "gay" wouldn't appear shortly after the name "Steve" in their conversations.

So it didn't strike me as odd when I was unanimously selected in absentia to be director for their first Christmas pageant. I was the congregation's only out gay man, and since gay people were obviously so good at putting on shows, I had to be drafted in some capacity. No matter that I could wield a circular saw like Michelangelo used a paintbrush or that I once constructed a working amplification system out of a hair dryer, a sponge, and two jars of pickles. No, I'm gay, so I had to do something gay. With clenched teeth and a fake smile I said, "Director? Sure."

Right then I decided: If they wanted inclusion, they'd get it. They were going to see a pageant of freaks P.T. Barnum would trade his grandmother for.

Nobody was around when I cast the supporting roles, so it went pretty easily. I auditioned hundreds of women before finally spotting a gray, oddly shaped woman who chain-smoked Virginia Slims in a long silver holder. After a bit of thought, I realized that she looked just like a flounder: Her eyes were small, circular, and right next to each other, and somehow I got the uneasy impression that if she ever would lie on sand too long, one eye would venture across her nose to unite with the other on the far side of her face.

She also swore like a sailor. In our short conversation, I found that she'd never been on the fucking stage before, that she hadn't done anything like this shit before, and that though some of her fellow parishioners were all right, all the rest was bastids.

She would be "Mary."

Next I convinced the parish priest to portray Joseph. He protested at first, joking that with his prominent ears, low forehead, overbite, and hunchback he'd be better cast as a camel. Mentally I agreed. I decided to dress him in something brown and furry to accentuate the resemblance.

The woman I appointed "Mary Magdalene" also thought I couldn't be serious until I impressed upon her the importance of her mental image, that of a robust young woman in her 30s, over that of her physical image, that of a wizened prune of 84.

I cast the three wise men with the unspoken intent that they look as much like the Three Stooges as possible. "I'm sure Fred will make a fine wise man," Fred's wife chirped, "but don't you think his bug eyes and bowl haircut will detract from the play?" Why, of course they will.

When the day came to cast Jesus, though, the auditorium was packed to the rafters, and there were 20 gorgeous men on stage. No ugly men bothered to audition—realizing, perhaps, that an ugly man will play Jesus around the time Pat Boone appears in *Naked Boys Singing!* Oddly, though, while most of the men auditioning would have had to gain weight to appear in a Calvin Klein ad, there was one blue-collar applicant who weighed 250 if he weighed an ounce. I'm surprised I didn't spot him earlier: While the other auditioners had shown up in caftans, taking costuming tips from either *Godspell* or *International Male,* he was dressed in old 501s, a dirty white T-shirt, and well-worn brown steel-toed boots. This man was stockiness personified: If the other audition-ers were forks or spoons, this man would be a side-by-side refrig-erator. He was the hunkiest thing I'd seen in years, and I fre-quently accidentally tape professional wrestling on TV. I was absorbing all the details that divide conventionally attractive men like me from blue-collar breathtaking—his wrists slightly larger than his hands, his waist slightly larger than his hips, his neck slightly larger than his head—when, finally abandoning myself to his animal magnetism, I muttered aloud "Jesus!" and realized that was that.

I instantly knew he looked familiar, but it took me a couple minutes to place him. I've never been attracted to conventional beauty. I realized this when I was 13: All my friends were jerking off to *Josie and the Pussycats,* me to *The Flintstones.*

The first time I fell in love was in history class. The teacher pulled out an evolutionary chart—you know, that series of pic-tures that's got like a monkey on the left side, a guy in a suit on the right, and the various stages of evolution in between—and I fell head over heels for one of the guys in the middle. He wasn't over-ly monkeyish—when we went out he wouldn't be like "Eek eek

eek!" all over the place—but he was definitely more primitive than the "This is not nonfat milk in my latte" types on the right. Third-from-the-left was more like "Trog like Steve. Steve like Trog?"

Right here, on this stage, was Third-from-the-left.

When I told the men to take off their shirts, the whir of video cameras switching on sounded like helicopters evacuating Saigon. I kept my eye on Third, and as he unbuttoned his shirt, hair pushed its way to freedom like music lovers at a Christina Aguilera concert. Most of the other eyes were focused on the more conventionally attractive men, so it took some time for the audience to notice him, but when they did you could hear it: There were so many sharp gulps of breath that it sounded like Katharine Hepburn with the hiccups.

The audience seemed to be split between two favorites. One had a swimmer's build, warm brown eyes, and curly golden locks worn David Cassidy–style. The other, too muscular for Jesus, considering Jerusalem had a startling shortage of Gold's Gyms, had the soulful eyes of a Saint Bernard and an air of humility that hung on him like a muumuu on Kathie Lee Gifford. Either of these two men would have been absolutely terrific, so with a quick "I'll call your people" I waved them both out. I dismissed all the others with a heartfelt "You're not quite what we're looking for, thank you," because I'd already found exactly what I'd been looking for.

By the time the audience realized who it was, they'd formed a mob looking not unlike the torch-bearing villagers who went after Frankenstein. Protests rang out, ranging from the angry to the furious.

"I'm confused," a tight-faced woman in brightly colored separates snarled. "I didn't know we were casting Crucifixion on the Planet of the Apes. Jesus did not look like he was wearing a brown warm-up suit."

I tried to reason with her. "Nobody knows what Jesus looked like," I said.

"Oh, come on!" she spat. "If Jesus had looked anything like that, the shroud of Turin would just be another sheet covered with hair."

The parish priest intervened, taking the side of the parishioners. "She could be right. There aren't any pictures of Jesus, but there is some evidence that he wasn't hairy." He paused to think, scratching his hump. Nothing came but the feeble "When Mary Magdalene washed his feet, for instance, did she need shampoo?"

I mustered up the best "I'm disappointed in you!" look that I could remember from adolescent viewings of *Leave It to Beaver* and shot it across the audience. As I slowly raised myself to my feet, a hush fell over the angry crowd.

"I'd just like to say one thing: I am truly embarrassed by what I've seen here today. We aren't auditioning replacements for the Backstreet Boys. We aren't casting a new Aaron Spelling pilot. We're putting on a Christmas pageant where, contrary to public opinion, Jesus will be chosen based on what's inside the man, not outside. So I regret to inform you, my Jesus will not be a hunky David Cassidy look-alike with warm brown puppy-dog eyes or playful golden-brown ringlets."

A murmur of disappointment scattered across the hall, but disapproving shushes overwhelmed it. I went on talking about peace and love and blah-blah-blah, and by the time I finally used the word "inclusion," there was no longer any dissent.

Jesus would be played by a 33-year-old Italian plumber from New Jersey named Sal.

This was no Cecil B. DeMille production. We had exactly $400 budgeted, $300 of which went to photocopying the scripts, with the other $100 going to Walter Bogle, who'd volunteered to construct the sets. Walter was a retired Dow chemist whose incompetence with power tools had exponentially increased after 30 years spent inhaling experimental oven cleaners. Oh, and if he somehow got the impression that I wanted the set to look like Edvard Munch's version of Smurfville, that would be puzzling, but easily understood.

One of the secretaries at the church was also an accomplished seamstress, so I'd had her run up a loincloth for Sal. Her first version was completely unsatisfactory, being slightly larger than my Sony projection television. She happily altered it, then again, then once more, finally starting to grumble when it reached the size of a Kleenex. I went to her home to try to persuade her.

Edna brought out lemonade and quickly put her foot down: It would be indecent to make the costume any smaller. I set my drink on a small linen coaster and impressed upon her the need for Jesus to be able to move unhindered. She refused to budge.

"Fine," I snarled. "If you'll just give it to me, I'll have someone else finish it."

"I gave it to you 10 minutes ago," she spat. "It's under your drink."

We also had just one day of rehearsal. I decided that, since the role of Jesus was so integral to the play's success, maybe Sal and I should do a little work one-on-one.

He showed up at my apartment straight from work on Friday, bearing a six-pack of Schlitz and smelling intoxicatingly of plumber's putty. He was so solidly built that I began to wonder if this might present a problem: I mean, getting this guy up on a cross would make building the pyramids look like slicing bundt cake. There was no way I could get him off the ground without an intricate system of pulleys and a crane. I began to think that casting twin asthmatics as the Roman soldiers might have been a mistake.

I'd already seen Sal shirtless, but this was at a distance, so it hadn't prepared me for him in the flesh. I suspected he had a ruggedly attractive face, but he had the sleeves of his shirt pushed up to his elbows and, try as I might, I couldn't budge my eyes from his paws—er, hands. The backs of his hands were completely covered with thick fur, which continued up his arms, ebbing and swirling like an old-growth forest before Reagan sold the Earth to National Lumber. As mentioned earlier, I was raised Catholic—so I have some experience at being duplicitous—but even I strained under the task of trying to look interested in what he was saying while suppressing an urge to lick him head to toe, starting from somewhere slightly below the middle.

I'm a pretty hairy guy myself, but standing next to him, I began to wonder if I had in fact gone through puberty. Aside from the hair, his voice was so low that it rattled my windows, and he had 5 o'clock shadow you could clean lasagna pans with. And he could open his mouth and form words. All in all, this just about covered everything I wanted in a man.

I asked Sal to put his costume on and pulled it out of my shirt pocket. He seemed a little shocked, but seeing my determination, his protests dwindled while I led him to the bedroom to change. About five minutes later I heard the bedroom door open and, holding my breath, watched as he slowly lumbered back into the living room. I figured that we'd bonded enough, so I gave up the effort of looking at his face and instead began to focus on the sea of fur that was his body.

It was incredible. You couldn't see skin anywhere. If Proust had liked hairy men, there wouldn't have been enough writing paper in 19th-century France. Hair caressed and cascaded across his body in waves, every inch covered except for his palms and the soles of his feet. It started from a circle shaved at the base of his neck and ran like wheat fields across his shoulders, where small peaks formed, gently giving way to a curly whirlpool that swam down his biceps. His chest looked like thick black velvet, covered in coarse swirls of black wire with a velvety sheen that reflected light but exposed no skin. The horizontal chest hair slid diagonally just below his pectorals and turned vertical down his stomach, where it veered in whorls around his belly button before plunging straight down to his hips. Then in thin spirals like steel wool the tumbleweeds of leg hair started, looping and whorling to his ankles, ending in a thick carpet atop his feet that looked to me like nothing other than two black mats beckoning WELCOME.

We stood silently in the center of the room, where I noticed that my $60-a-yard shag carpeting was looking a little thin. He stared down at his costume, embarrassed.

"Dis is kinda small, ya dink?" I figured he had to be straight, because although some people might have mistaken this costume for a coaster, most gay men were accustomed to wearing smaller suits than this at the beach.

I could not have been more emphatic that the costume was the proper size, though Sal was definitely well-endowed. From what I could tell out of the corner of my eye, it looked like somebody had put a doily on a dolphin.

"Maybe I'm just, ya know, sensa-diff. 'Bout bein' so hairy."

"Oh?" I tried to make a quick, unfeeling appraisal of his body, abandoning to the futility of this task somewhere south of his ankles. "Hey, I guess you are, aren't you? I wouldn't give it a second thought."

He looked relieved. We polished off two beers each before he spilled the entire story. After high school he was so embarrassed by his body hair that he'd immersed himself in his work. Finally, after a couple more beers, he admitted that even his ex-wife had never seen him naked, since he'd always switched off the lights before taking off his clothes. Nobody had ever seen him as naked as he was now, he said. And he was really grateful that he didn't scare me and that I accepted him like he was, like the other parishioners had.

I felt we were bonding, so I thought I'd give him a warm hug, but when I touched his shoulder, my hand disappeared. Though I knew it had to be still attached to my wrist, my first instinct was to send out a search party. So I grabbed the other shoulder with the other hand.

To my surprise, he seemed to appreciate the affection, and the more I held him, the more he returned it. Parts of him were soft and warm, other parts thick and coarse, and I reveled in discovering what was where. Gradually the brotherly hug turned into kissing, which rapidly led to sex, and he became somehow simultaneously affectionate and domineering, leading our movements with a strong word and a firm hand. Now I knew what the Chicago

Bears must have felt like under Mike Ditka, and I mean "under" in several different senses of the word. He'd forced various parts of him into various parts of me with such animal grace and athletic prowess that by the time we collapsed in mutual exhaustion I was completely happy, limp as a dishrag, and covered head to toe in rug burns. I also had a pillow of his hair the size of a Brillo pad taking up most of the space in my mouth.

Sal and I spent every moment together until the pageant began the next night. I told him that I loved his body but didn't want to share all of it, so for his costume I slit open an old pillowcase and tied it on him with rope.

The pageant went about as I'd predicted. Every time a character debuted onstage, gasps echoed through the crowd, coupled with a few nyuk nyuk's when the wise men appeared. The pastor prompted the loudest audience outcry: Playing Joseph in the furry brown robe I'd had made for him, he couldn't have looked more like a camel if bedouins were perched on his head. Helping the likeness, an allergy to hay had made his lips double in size and his nose plug up, so the thoughtful, heartfelt lines he himself had written sounded more like the inflamed snorts of an irritated animal. Seeing the shocked looks on the parishioners' faces, he quickly gave up all attempts at speech and just stood on the sidelines, occasionally kicking away hay.

Sure, we could have worked a little more on Sal's accent: I mean, everyone pretty much laughed when he said, "And den when da cock crows for da toid time one'a youse'll betray me." But there were fewer chuckles by the time he got to "Take dis and drinka it, 'cause—hey!—dis is my body!" And by the time he whispered, "Fadda, fadda, why have youse forsaken me?" everybody was reaching for tissues.

The stagehands prepared to lower the curtains as Mary approached Jesus's body for one final look. Since the production time was so short, Carol hadn't met Sal prior to this, and in fact hadn't seen him before, since her earlier scenes had all been with the infant Jesus. So when she saw this refrigerator of a man, covered in fur, and realized she somehow had to cradle him in her arms, she completely blanked on her lines.

"Jesus!" she gasped, nearly dropping the cigarette holder from her lips. "What the..."

Earlier we'd agreed on a compromise: She could smoke, but not swear. Unfortunately, I hadn't realized that she'd be ad-libbing her part, and that about six seconds into it she'd run out of words.

Instead of speaking she cleared a spot on the ground next to him and plopped down. She tried to drag his prone body into her lap but after eight fruitless attempts succeeded only in getting the dead Jesus to finally slap at her hand. The exertion made her puff harder on her cigarette, and by now there was more smoke pouring off the stage than during a Broadway production of *Cats*. She sat fussing at Jesus, making bizarre, jerky hand gestures, like Liza Minnelli fighting off locusts. She glanced at the ground around her, trying to look forlorn but instead giving the impression she'd misplaced her gin and tonic. Finally she fixed her gaze at Sal and, overacting like Bette Davis on Benzedrine, she yanked frantically at the hair on his arms and chest and spat out her final comment:

"They killed ya, the bastids. And they din't even take off your fuckin' sweater."

The curtain could not fall fast enough.

Well, the good news is, nobody in the crowd slugged me. But I was trapped in their midst, and as they screamed and gesticulated at me I began to have serious concerns about my safety. It was an outrage, sacrilege, blasphemous, people yelled. A wiry little man heaped abuse on me with a French accent and poked at my stomach until I realized that this is what sex between the Marquis de Sade and the Pillsbury Doughboy would be like. Finally, a bespectacled woman with a cane who had to be 90 pushed her way through and, while I waited to see where she'd punch me, she gave me a frail hug.

"That was bee-yoo-teeful, just bee-yoo-teeful!" she declared in a thick Brooklyn accent. The mob looked puzzled, and as they began to mutter among themselves I took the woman's arm and tried to push our way out. "Jesus looked just like my first husband, God rest his soul," she announced.

Though they still looked like they wanted to inflict serious bodily harm on me, the crowd began to dissipate. I'd follow this woman to safety, I figured, and begin breathing again. As we reached the crowd's outer perimeter I thanked her and started to say goodbye, but she grabbed my arm and pulled me to a stop.

"There's one thing I wanna know, though," she said, perking up everyone's ears. "How'd ya get that fuckin' camel to stand so still?"

Everything went black.

When I opened my eyes I was in my bed. The light on my answering machine was blinking frantically, so I hit the button to play the messages. Of 47 messages, only one was positive: Oddly, that was from the pastor. He didn't mind that the pageant was so controversial, he said, because it made people think. Plus he'd already sold 300 tickets for the Easter pageant.

I heard the shower shut off, and saw Sal's face poke around the bathroom door. In a scene that would have sent Oregon backpackers scrambling for their video cameras, he came running naked straight for me.

Journey
DALE CHASE

Halfway to hell and gone, for no good reason. Waking up when I've never been asleep, when miles are the only reason and an open throttle the means. A rising sun tells me where I am, and only then do I allow any thought as to why.

The Mojave Desert goes by in a blur—right or left, doesn't matter—while straight ahead everything stands still, as if I'm rushing toward a photograph. It's a gritty plain dotted with gray-green scrub and cactus, desolate two-lane miles that begin to seem appropriate. Maybe there was method to my madness. Hop on the bike and go, find a place where there are no jobs to have or to lose. My fingers ache against the throttle. I haven't loosened my grip for hours.

The cool of the night quickly gives way. Nothing lasts on the desert floor in June, and I wonder how long until I have to stop and get down to shirtsleeves. Soon, and then I'll take that long look around, a meaningless 360 like some bug on a windshield. I'd rather sweat.

For a while I push everything aside and just listen: to the engine below, to the steady rush of wind streaming by. In a daring move that could net me a bug, I open my mouth and draw in pure, unadulterated air.

I don't look at the speedometer—numbers don't matter out here—and then another motorcycle is suddenly beside me, a big honking thing come up out of nowhere sporting a rider equally large. Man-mountain himself. He glances over and we exchange the nod customary between enthusiasts, then ride along as a pair. Part of me hates the intrusion; part of me welcomes it.

It's a Honda Gold Wing, dressed out with every possible extra, a rig that looks more half-car than motorcycle and dwarfs my Yamaha 750. The rider is massive though not particularly fat. He has on worn jeans, scarred brown boots, a battered leather jacket, and half-shell helmet. Trim red-brown beard, hair clipped short at the neck. His eyes are shielded behind dark glasses set in wire frames, but I imagine them blue and, as we speed north through the desolation, I begin to realize just what I might have here—and also to consider the parts of him I can't see.

That's the trouble with open highway: You can lose yourself with very little effort. I venture down between thick thighs to envision hair engulfing a cock appropriate to this biker bear. My own prick, already buzzed from the long ride, begins to fill, taken not only with the idea of what might be inside those jeans but also where it could go. I begin to squirm on my seat, squeezing my ass muscle as if a tongue was tickling my rim, and all the while this guy rides along oblivious to screaming potential beside him.

We roar up the highway, and I start thinking I'm gonna come, mind alone conjuring a load. I picture myself shooting inside my jeans, then wonder if my friend might be doing the same. I look over. So calm, so sure. Quit dreaming, I tell myself, but I can't resist the idea of this big thing getting on me and in me, and I find, within this little bit of self-torture, a promise as persistent as my prick.

The sun is high, and I am sweating like a pig when a tiny burg approaches. I glance over at my buddy, and he points toward a coffee shop. I nod and follow him into the parking lot.

"You were going like a bat out of hell," he says as he pulls off his helmet to reveal closely cut auburn hair. "You rob a bank or something?"

"Not yet," I tell him. "Got laid off work yesterday and was so pissed I just took off."

"Gonna outrun it?"

"Yeah," I say, as if I actually can. He grins and offers to buy me breakfast. When he takes off his shades, I see that his eyes aren't blue but I can't tell the exact color. Hazel maybe, or green. Only as we start into the diner do I realize how tired I am.

The place is old and worn, something out of the '50s with checkered vinyl floor and lumpy black booths, but it smells good. The waitress is friendly, which surprises me. I can't imagine living out here, much less waiting tables.

My friend orders steak and eggs, biscuits and gravy, coffee black, while I simply have the number 3 breakfast: ham, eggs and toast. My plate looks half of his.

"So where are you from?" he asks.

"Fullerton. You?"

"Long Beach. This is the first day of a week's vacation."

"Must be nice."

He concentrates on his steak for a minute, and I know he's not going to indulge my situation, and maybe that's best. "I'm Brody McCall," he says, offering his hand and a look that throws me off guard for a second. I stammer, then laugh. "Alan Traylor," I finally manage as I savor his grip, big fingers, rough palm. My cock starts in again, and I think if I don't go jerk off in the men's room, I'm not going to survive. A chuckle born of pure frustration escapes me.

"What?" Brody asks, and for a second I don't know how to answer.

"Uh...that's a great name," I tell him. "Irish?"

"You bet. Grandad Seamus came over from Dublin in 1912. My dad was born in San Francisco. He's Killian, and my brothers are Paddy and Colin."

"I haven't heard of Brody before."

"Means 'ditch.' "

I laugh. "Did they know that when they named you?"

"No, Pa just liked the sound of it. I was the one who looked up the meaning. Looked them all up. Killian means 'little' and 'warlike,' which gave us all a hoot because there's not anybody in the family little. We're all over 6 feet, including Ma, even though she's not Irish. Good German stock, though. She's a Hartung, but Pa forgives her. It was him who did all the naming. Colin means 'child,' which is funny because he's the oldest and the most serious, a college professor. And Paddy means 'nobleman,' which is even funnier because he's a total fuckup."

"What about Seamus?"

"Irish for 'James,' which is English for 'Jacob,' which is biblical."

I sit back, wanting to ask more, but am unable to think of anything beyond fucking. I need to keep him talking because I like the sound of him, so warm and inviting, and also because he calms me down even as he stirs me up. My dick pokes at my jeans, and I hope to God his does too.

"So you're vacationing alone?" I ask.

"Yep. Had a buddy lined up to come along, but he backed out at the last minute. Family crisis. So, I'm on my own."

"Where are you headed?"

"Yosemite, up across Tioga Pass, then west until I hit San Francisco. From there, down the coast back to L.A."

"Sounds great."

"It is. I did it a few years ago, one of the best rides I've ever taken because you get everything California has to offer: desert, mountains—there's usually snow at Tioga Pass, even in June—then those dry yellow hills to the west, and then the ocean, the cliffs, sea lions down below, fog, you name it."

I take it all in and feel a pang of envy. We're both free but not in the same way. I can't begin to imagine the trip he's describing, and then he cuts in. "Want to come along?"

It takes everything in me not to climb onto the table, pull my pants down, and offer him my ass in gratitude. I look into this mountain man's face as sunlight streams through the window and lights him like a movie star. I see that his eyes are green, and even though I know the sunlight is doing it, I decide the sparkle is his alone. He watches me watch him and takes note as I drop down into that V where hair fills his shirt. "Well?" he prods. "You said you got laid off, so I figure maybe you don't have to get back. Unless..."

I hesitate. "No, there's nothing," I finally manage. "God, I hate the sound of that."

"Then we won't dwell on it," Brody says. "That's way back down the road, and we're headed an entirely new direction. One hell of a ride comin' up."

"I don't have any gear with me, just what I'm wearing."

"We can pick up what you need along the way. It's not complete wilderness."

I think he'll ask more about me, but he doesn't. We get to talking bikes instead and keep on until it's time to hit the road again. Fine with me, and it adds a little mystery, although I'd like to know how old he is. Mid 30s is my guess, which makes him the oldest guy I've ever been with, but then I'm anticipating where maybe he isn't. I can't read him and, worse, can't figure out why. As we stow our jackets and roll up our sleeves, I wonder how it would be with someone who counts years instead of bodies. I glance over at Brody, whose arms are covered in more of that reddish fur, and I hope to God this is headed farther than just up the road.

By early evening I've nearly worn myself out. Heat, sweat, frustration, and the fact that I haven't slept are adding up. My body feels like it's slowly melting, but my cock stays rigid. It's the longest hard-on I've ever had.

When we arrive in Bishop, having finally left the Mojave behind and begun the long climb toward the mountains of the Sierra Nevada, Brody nods toward a rustic motel and I follow. At this point I'm willing to forgo fucking; exhaustion has me, everything limp, including the once-persistent dick. "I stayed here before," Brody says as he takes off his helmet. "Rooms are good and it's a decent price." He pauses as I shake myself out. "How about we get a double? Be a lot cheaper."

"Fine," I tell him as I stagger around, trying to regain my equilibrium. It feels like I'm still on the bike, engine buzzing my legs.

"You OK?" Brody asks.

"Yeah, just beat. I didn't sleep last night."

"Well then, it's good we stopped now. I'll go take care of things, you relax."

I lean against the bike and feel an ache so deep it's scary, then allow that maybe this is real after all, maybe it's gonna happen.

All I can think of is getting reamed and coming buckets. I need the edge taken off in the worst way. Brody comes out of the motel office and walks toward me with a grin on his face, and I realize at the very least I'll get to see him naked. As he reaches me I'm planning a long jerk-off in the shower.

"Sixteen," he says. "Over there."

It's nearly dark as we roll the bikes to the front. Brody unlocks the door and I step in. I try not to anticipate, but my cock has other ideas, and as Brody brings in gear from his saddlebags, I pull off my shirt. "I need a shower," I say, and he eyes me so briefly I can't tell anything. Can't fucking tell.

"You go ahead," he says. "I'm gonna settle in a bit, get outta these boots."

I purposely leave the bathroom door open and drag my swollen meat into the shower. My balls are tight, aching for release, and as I soap my aching sausage, I envision Brody in the next room, clothes in a pile, horse-cock dangling over furry balls. I picture hair inside his crack, smothering his hole, and I want to get down there and snort around in it. I can see my nose probing like some anteater, feel my tongue poking into his steamy pucker, and then the shower curtain sweeps aside and there he is, everything I've imagined: massive shoulders and a chest so broad it's like two of me, hair so thick I can barely see his nipples, fur that funnels down across his stomach and onto his thighs. And down between his legs is what I want most, and I squeeze my soapy dick and nearly cry with relief as he steps in with me. He says nothing. His prick is primed and ready, shiny in its latex sheath. Its size is something more appropriate for bull than man. He lets me take in the sight, and as I do he draws his hand down my front, lingering briefly on my smooth chest. He slides his palm down my stomach and plays around with my cock, then he turns me around and pushes a soapy finger up my ass. I grab my prick and hold on as juice squirts out of me. My squeal echoes off the tile.

I pump out what seems a gallon of jism, Brody prodding all the while, and as I slowly settle, he adds a second finger. I squirm back into him, let him know I'm ready. He moans softly, withdraws, and I feel his cock head brush my crack.

I take a wider stance now, bent forward and braced against the tile. He spreads my cheeks but takes his time, and I begin to whine and beg, to wiggle in his grasp. And then he does it: starts in and just keeps going. He's well-lathered; his smooth, fat prick snakes past my gaping sphincter and slides so deep into my rectum that it stirs my cock again. When he's fully inside, he grips me at the waist, then begins a slow thrust and I am gone, stepped off into a world inhabited solely by big furry creatures rutting without reason, animals on the loose, organs perpetually hard. As Brody rides me, I swear his dick is up in my gut, and I love the feel. I want to be filled, occupied, owned.

He is not quick, and I lose myself to him. We are together now, embarked on what feels like the ultimate fuck, the one that will solve everything. He drives into me powerfully, steadily, and I reach a hand back to his thigh, feel the muscle. I slide a finger up to his crotch, get it between us. I've never done this before but can't resist. I close finger and thumb around his prick, my palm at his bush. I want to feel him outside me as well as in. He hesitates as he draws back in his stroke, lets me play with him, then pushes in, trapping my fingers.

The water gradually turns cold and Brody stops, reaches past me, and turns it off. Then he resumes, but he's picking up speed, and what couldn't possibly get any better does. His fingers dig into my hips, and grunts escape him with each thrust. I can feel his climax building, and imagine its volume, imagine not the drops I produce but torrents, gushers. I picture the condom full, his massive balls taking ages to empty.

He lets me know when he's there, and I love it. "I am there, baby, I'm gonna blow, I am gonna send a load up your fucking ass..." Words fail him when it hits. Long growls accompany each pulse, each massive squirt, and he slaps into me so hard my entire body jerks forward. The force of him is intoxicating. I reel from the idea as much as the feel and listen to the sound of us, that distinctive squishy slap that runs through me and sets everything tingling.

When Brody is finally done, he slumps forward, wrapping those big arms around my chest. He pulls me to him and nuzzles my neck. "One sweet ass," he tells me. I want to respond in kind but can't begin to put it into words. I pull my arms around his, clutch him to me. He gets the idea.

Out of the shower, he discards the condom when I really would have liked a look at what he did. He takes a towel and dries me. It's the first time we've really looked at each other up close, and I note a light smattering of freckles across his nose and the square cut of his jaw. I also decide he's about 6 foot 2 and, since I'm just under 6 feet, it's a good fit. As for his cock, it's an absolute wonder: long and thick with a big flared head, impressive even at rest.

We say nothing during this interlude, and once I am dry, once he has turned me around and gently patted my ass, letting his finger slide up my crack, he turns me again and finishes up with my prick, tossing aside the towel finally to play with me. As he diddles my cock head, I think about the trip ahead, about fucking our way along. When I twitch my prong, he chuckles.

In the bedroom I find he has pulled back the covers, readied things for us. I slide between cool sheets, feeling as if I could sleep for a week, but Brody reminds me we haven't eaten since breakfast. "I'll go get us something. You nap." I think maybe he'll kiss me, but he doesn't. I watch him dress—jeans, plaid shirt—and head out the door. I lie there thinking this must be a mistake because my life never goes this well. I worry that the famed higher power has made a mistake, gotten the wrong guy. Just before I fall asleep I hope with all my might He doesn't notice.

When Brody nudges me awake, he's already naked. I smile at the sight of him standing there with bags of food in hand. The familiar smell of hamburgers gives him a homey appeal. I look him up and down, linger on his big cock. "Dinner first," he says. "Then dessert."

We lie back atop the covers, legs outstretched. The food energizes me, makes me think how much I spent in anger. When the burgers and fries are gone, Brody says, "So tell me about getting laid off," and I do. It feels good to have someone finally listening. I'd said it all when the ax fell—made a scene, actually—but knew all the time nobody really cared. They tolerated me. Let him run down, then he'll leave. It had been like dying, in a way. Once I was gone, the space I'd occupied just closed up.

Brody understands all this and is tactful enough not to offer platitudes or assure me that things happen for the best. He takes it all in and halfway through slides an arm around me and pulls me to him. His sole comment when I've finished the lament is "Fuck 'em." Then he kisses me. As his tongue explores, I think about getting his cock into my mouth. There is so much ahead.

I count the journey as beginning at this moment because, as tired as I am, I start waking up to things. And it isn't what Brody says as much as that presence of his, as if he's got answers when the rest of us don't even know the questions. He's also the first person I've ever met who doesn't go on about himself, and I find it refreshing. I learn only that he has a landscaping business and is 37. I volunteer that I'm 22.

Bellies full, we ease into our "dessert." Sprawled across the bed, we play for hours, exploring each other in a long rise that ultimately takes me beyond anything I've ever imagined. I come twice, the first time as I crawl around on him like a kitten climbing its mama, licking his fur until he is damp in places. I'm almost purring when he takes hold of my cock and pulls a climax out of me. The next time he's pulled me over on top of him and trapped our dicks between us. I can't get over the full-body feel of him, like I'm riding some bear. He grabs my ass and gets me to humping against him, and we both come, me, then him, filling our crevice until cream is running down his sides. And still we keep on. There's one point where we're just nosing around each other and I get down to his balls, get one into my mouth and suck gently, all the while looking down at his furry crack. Part of me wants to run a finger down there and find his hole, get something of mine into him, but I hold back, wondering if he's ever had anything in there. I can't imagine one of these big guys getting done yet find the idea excites me. As I let go of one ball and suck in the other, I knead Brody's thighs. His muscles tighten, and I swear his asshole beckons.

We don't get back on the bikes the next day. By the time we awaken it's half gone; by the time we fuck and dress and eat, it's late afternoon. We go back to the room and get on each other again. "You're playing hell with my schedule," Brody says as I suck his dick.

When we finally do resume our trip, I tell him I want to do it up on Tioga Pass. "You'll freeze your nuts," he says, but we manage. He takes me standing in a small grove of pines, baring just the essentials. I suck in frigid air and pine forest smells and it drives me wild. I imagine bears and wolves and mountain lions fucking along with us, everything in a powerful heat, never mind snow nearby. Brody is pure animal now and, as much as I like him in bed, I know this is where he belongs, that he's part of the wilderness. I think of warmer climes to the west, of us rutting in another forest at a lower and more hospitable elevation.

There are sights along the way, of course, but they lose their grandeur in the face of what is happening to me. I gaze at brilliant vistas and sun-drenched peaks, nodding as Brody goes on about their beauty, but all I can think of is running naked in the woods, the bear mounting me after a spirited chase.

As we descend from Yosemite and head west, we trade cool green for warm yellow, winding along a two-lane ribbon of road that curls so tightly it makes speed impossible. Heat comes as well, and we ride along in shirtsleeves, hot wind stoking the fire even as it dries the sweat. When Brody has us stop in Groveland, famous for its gold rush garrotings, we share a meal but not much talk. He knows I need more than food, that I can't get enough of him, and after we gas up at a tiny filling station, he gets me into the minuscule bathroom, pulls off my pants, braces me against a wall, and fucks me. Seconds later I'm spewing jism across a dirty tile floor, but Brody doesn't take note. He's doing me in his own time, knowing how badly I need to be ridden. I listen to him grunt with his thrusts, feel his big balls slapping forward, and reach a hand back to blindly pet his fur. All I can think of is a bear in the woods, never mind it's a fucking bathroom. And then he's coming and he starts that growl and slams into me so hard I almost lose my footing. He pumps and pumps, always good for a massive load. When he finally relents and slides out, I turn. "Lemme see," I say like some anxious kid. He holds the amply filled rubber aloft. "Geez," I add, and he tosses it away without comment.

He doesn't immediately close up shop. Instead he pins me to the wall, drives his tongue into me, then pulls back and says, "You never get enough, do you. Goddamn, I love it." I'm totally spent yet I'd go another round if he so much as hinted at it. "But..." he adds, "we'd best get back on the road. I want to get to San Francisco by nightfall."

From Groveland to San Francisco, monotony is the word. Golden hills that seem to crank up the heat are endless, stretching, rolling, baking. Highway soon turns to freeway, traffic thickens, and finally, east of Oakland, I smell salt sea air. It's worked its way back through the hills to announce San Francisco Bay long before it appears. We're in the real world now, cars and chaos, paying attention, changing lanes, dodging drivers. We ride with a sense of purpose, sun slipping toward the horizon like it's a race.

It's cool once we hit the bay, and the seven miles across the bridge wake me from my heat-driven stupor. The view is spectacular, San Francisco up ahead, and once there Brody guides us down onto the streets like he knows them well. We stop at Fisherman's

Wharf and feast on fresh crab and sourdough bread. His appetite is twice mine.

Afterward we wander among the tourists, and I experience the thrill of us as a couple in public, a silly kind of validation because I know people are probably oblivious. We stop to watch sea lions that have claimed part of the marina, and Brody barks back at them. We pick out the largest, make a game of his antics, then turn to watch a brilliant sunset. After that it's a motel on Van Ness Avenue.

Relaxed from dinner, mellowed at the end of a perfect day, we descend into our own world. Brody undresses me slowly, and when I am naked, pulls me into bed and begins to fondle my prick. He gets me into his mouth and cradles me with his tongue, gradually closing to begin a languid suck. I whimper and moan because he's a goddamned wonder, and he periodically pulls off to play with my knob and glance up at me. I'm ramrod stiff and oozing precum, and he slides up next to me, nuzzles a bit, then rolls over onto his stomach and raises his rump. I am stunned into momentary paralysis, awed at the sight and the offer. Was it always there and I was just blind? He wriggles his ass and that does it. I wet a finger and push it into him. "Sweet Jesus, yes!" he cries, squirming with delight. I add a second finger and probe and prod, then withdraw and get my face down into his crack.

It's an absolute forest down there, and I lick my way to the center, him moaning the whole time. And then I hit paradise and begin to poke, and he, in turn, begins to squeeze, as if he can suck my tongue into him.

"Get in there, baby," he says, and I play a bit more, then go in, savoring the familiar bittersweet taste. He has a hand on his cock now, and I can feel him working, and love the idea that I can make him come this way. My own dick is stiff, swimming with promise. I pull back, hesitate, and Brody makes the call. "Do it, for chrissakes. Fuck me."

I suit up, grease my meat, then take aim, savoring what I am about to do. It has to be the ultimate. The idea of riding a big, hairy ass juices me beyond belief. "Come on," Brody demands, and I do what he wants, jam my swollen prick into him and bury myself to the root. I look down at the fur engulfing me and can't help but think I'm fucking some animal that could turn on me and kill me and eat me. The idea takes me even higher. Brody, meanwhile, starts squeezing his muscle, and that sets me pumping. He responds with a wonderful growl.

I thrust into this big furry creature long after Brody announces himself and unleashes a load into the sheets. "Oh, shit, man," he says as he lets go. I murmur encouragement but keep on fucking. "Do it, baby," he says as he regains his breath, and I feel him settle into the action, pushing back as if he can get even more of me into him.

Twice I pull out to add more lube; twice he moans as I go back in. Sweat runs off me, drips down onto his pelt, but I keep on, and then the climb begins, that stir that tingles my spine, tenses my thighs, that draws my balls up and sends a sweet delivery up the chute. I squeal as I come, fingers digging into Brody's hips as I ride wave after wave. My body reels, everything in me unleashed, and then I am empty and possibly more done than ever before. I pull out and collapse—lying so still, Brody grows concerned. "You OK?'"

"I am so done," I manage. I don't even attend the condom, and Brody says "Allow me" and removes it. Nobody's ever done that; I had no idea anybody would.

I drift off to sleep in Brody's arms, listening to his plans for the rest of our trip. A couple days here in the city, then on down the coast. "There's a nice grove of redwoods I want you to see," he tells me, and I picture us deep within it, returned to nature. I see it so clearly that my cock stirs against Brody's leg. "Sweet dreams," he murmurs. It sounds like he's drifting off as well.

My last blissful thoughts are of his ass thrust up at me. I recall how my cock felt pushing through the forest, how it feels to fuck a big bear of a man. As I begin to ride his furry thigh, he strokes my back, petting me, emitting a low rumble.

Fuzzy Butt
Doug Harrison

Bare! I'm all bare! From head to toe. That's the way my master wants me—completely naked. Well, I do wear a locked collar all the time, but I guess that doesn't count. And sometimes it has a leash or a chain attached to it, but that's OK. I feel sexy being naked and secure wearing the collar. I'm actually free because Master makes all the decisions.

I have broad shoulders and a terrific chest. Occasionally I have to swallow a smirk when I catch Master admiring me from the corner of his eye, even if I do stand a little straighter and subtly flex my muscles.

Master is very considerate: He keeps the house warm so that I don't get cold. And he has a wool blanket on the floor next to his bed. I curl up there and fall asleep with a contented smile on my face when he hooks my leash to one of the eyebolts in the bed frame. I like it most, though, when he lets me sleep in his bed. I cuddle up next to him to keep warm.

I try my best to keep his house clean. Sometimes I'm not very good at it and Master punishes me. I must confess, I really do enjoy being punished, but that's another story.

Master is very handsome. He's a tall leather daddy and looks so spiffy in his black leather cap, vest, chaps, jock, and boots. And when he carries that crop of his—ooh, my dick gets hard just looking at him!

In fact, I'm told we make a very good-looking couple. I get so excited when we go out together and he shows me off. Like when we went to the Folsom Street Fair last September. He led me around on my leash and we got lots of compliments. I stuck my chest way out, I was so proud to be with him.

And I got to look at all the boys being led around by their masters. Most of them were like me and didn't have much on. Some wore jocks, and a few wore harnesses. Like me, they all had bare butts. I looked quickly from one to the other, disappointed I couldn't take them all in at once and afraid I might miss one. God, I think I had a hard-on the whole time we paraded down that street.

And such bubble butts! Some were smooth, some were covered with a light golden down like wheat in a field, and some were disguised by thick, dark, curly hair. But, if there were a fuzzy butt contest, I'd be the one to win! In fact, that's my nickname: Fuzzy Butt. Sometimes I think it's cute, and sometimes I'm just plain embarrassed.

I really wanted to lick these boys all over—in particular, their butts. But I couldn't. When we go out, I have to wear my muzzle. Damn! That's the condition under which Master was able to buy me from the defunct circus.

Oh, well, it sure beats being sent to the bear cage at the zoo. I get to have a nice home, go out with my master, and look at all those yummy boys. Maybe, just maybe, we can bring one of them home for a three-way sometime.

About the Contributors and Editor

David Bergman is the author or editor of more than a dozen books, including *Gaiety Transfigured*. He is a three-time Lambda Prize finalist, and winner of the award for co-editing *Men on Men 2000*. His most recent book of poetry is *Heroic Measures*. With Joan Larkin he edits the book series *Living Out: Gay & Lesbian Autobiography* for the University of Wisconsin Press. "Honey" is David's first published piece of fiction.

Skip Brushaber resides in Portland, Maine, where he works for the Maine College of Art. He holds a master's in American Studies in Film/GLBT Studies. His writing is included in the Painted Leaf Press anthology *Mama's Boy: Gay Men Write About Their Mothers*. Skip's a bear lover from way back.

Trevor J. Callahan, Jr.'s writing has appeared in numerous publications, including the magazines *Men, Freshmen, Unzipped, Beau, In Touch, Indulge, American Bear,* and *Cruisin',* and the anthologies *Slow Grind, Men for All Seasons, Twink,* and *Cybersex*. He currently resides in southern New England.

Dale Chase has been writing erotic fiction for several years and has been published in *Men, Freshmen, In Touch,* and *Indulge* as well as the *Friction 2, Friction 3,* and *Friction 4* anthologies. One of his stories has been acquired by an independent filmmaker and will soon reach the screen.

Bob Condron is the author of two published novels, *Easy Money* and the bear-focused *Sweating It Out*. His short stories have appeared in numerous anthologies, including *Bar Stories* and *Slow Grind*. His work as a writer-director for fringe and community theater has been performed in the United Kingdom and United

States with notable success. He works and lives with his Irish hus-bear, Tommy, in Germany.

Jess Davis is the pen name of a deviant beardyke who is fre-quently known to scandalize her contemporaries. Her work has appeared in *The Second Coming* and *Hustler* magazine, and she's the perpetrator of www.doesitquack.com. Davis (or whatever her name is) dedicates this to her beautiful, brilliant, and completely twisted wife.

Ben Ensyde is the pen name of a poet whose writing has appeared in over 60 periodicals, including *Chelsea, Many Mountains Moving,* and *Barrow Street.* He has also penned a humor manu-script titled *Bitch Rants at the Crossroads of a New Millennium: A Pseudo ~~Hysterical~~ HIS-Storical Memoir.*

Lance Gap is the nom de plume of an Oregon poet, angler, and pornographer who was a hospice volunteer for four years.

Adam Gawron grew up in the Northeast but is a longtime res-ident of Texas, where he pursues a career in the arts. Although he has written professionally, this is his first published piece of fic-tion.

Doug Harrison's writing appears in *Black Sheets* and *Body Play* as well as the anthologies *Men Seeking Men, Still Doing It, Best Bisexual Erotica,* and *Best Gay Erotica 2001.* Doug appears in S/M videos as Brad Chapman and is a San Francisco switch who can be reached at puma@dnai.com.

Bob Hay is an antique gay activist and paleo-bear, long-term secretary of Ozbears Australia, founder of Bears Down Under and BearsCanberra, honorary life member of Bears Perth and author of the "Down Under" chapter in *The Bear Book;* currently obsessed with gay sculpture, digital photography, and video chat.

Daniel M. Jaffe's short stories and essays have appeared in dozens of literary journals and anthologies. His novel, *The Limits of Pleasure,* was published in 2001 by Harrington Park Press under their Southern Tier Editions imprint.

Jojo, 38, has spent a quarter of his life in Europe, with time in Asian jungles and on West Coast beaches. Since childhood, he has been a musclebear fan due to undue influence from Steve Reeves in *Hercules.* He can be seen extensively undraped in Edward Lucie-Smith's book *Flesh & Stone.*

Eric Karnowski makes his living developing materials for mathematics education. His short story "Traffic Signs" is expected in a forthcoming issue of *Harrington Gay Men's Fiction Quarterly.* A longtime admirer of bears, he lives in Boston with his thin but furry partner.

Jeffrey Lockett is the pen name of a journalist working mainly for daily newspapers and magazines in England, although his articles have been sold into publications all over the world. His specialty is interviewing celebrities about their love lives, marriages, and the contents of their fridges.

Gareth MacKenzie grew up in rural southern Maryland. He now resides in the mountains of southern Arizona. His erotic fiction has appeared in *Bear, First Hand, American Bear, American Grizzly,* and *Bunkhouse.* He is a bear lover but considers himself more of a wolf.

Jim Mason lives with his partner of 20-plus years in San Francisco, where he spends his time lying naked in the sun at Baker Beach and drinking beer with the Saturday afternoon crowd at the Lone Star Saloon. He also is a member of Bears of San Francisco.

John McFarland lives in Seattle. His work has appeared everywhere from *Cricket* magazine to *The Badboy Book of Erotic Poetry.*

Born and raised in the backwoods of Oregon, Eric Mulder grew up chasing animals through the woods. Now living in the city, he's moved on to larger game.

By day, a rocket scientist; by night, a bear pornographer. Jay Neal has always been attracted to husky, hairy men; he's been writing about it since 1998. Several of his stories have appeared in *American Bear* and *American Grizzly* magazines. He lives with his partner in suburban Washington, D.C.

R. E. Neu's writing has appeared in many publications, including *The New York Times Book Review, Los Angeles* magazine, and the *Los Angeles Times* as well as numerous fiction anthologies, including Alyson's *The Ghost of Carmen Miranda* and *Wilma Loves Betty.* He was also a contributing writer for *Spy* magazine, back when it was funny.

Simon Sheppard is author of *Hotter Than Hell and Other Stories* and coeditor of *Rough Stuff: Tales of Gay Men, Sex, and Power.* His work has appeared in over 50 anthologies, including the *Best American Erotica* and *Best Gay Erotica* series. He lives, hairily but slimly, in San Francisco.

Fred Towers growls in the Midwest with his teddy bear, Mel. Even though he has a master's degree, he loves his hardworking, blue-collar man. In June 2001, they celebrated five years together and are new to the leather scene. He loves to watch his teddy bear transform into Big Daddy.

Karl von Uhl's smut has appeared in *Bear* and *Powerplay* magazines, *Best Gay Erotica 2000, Best Gay Erotica 2001,* and *Rough Stuff.* For 3½ years he wrote the column "Vox Clamavis" for *Bear* magazine. He is an occasional correspondent for *The Life We Lead* on cable access. He shaves. Ha-ha, made you cringe.

Thom Wolf was born in 1973 and has been writing erotica since he was 18 years old. His work has appeared in *In Touch, Indulge, Men,* and *Overload* magazines, and the anthology *Friction 3.* His first novel, *Words Made Flesh,* is published by Idol. He lives and works in northeast England.

Ron Suresha has been involved with bear communities since the late '80s, when he lived in San Francisco with one of the creators of *Bear* magazine and created signs, graphics, and promotions for the bear bar Lone Star Saloon. Since leaving the San Francisco Bay area, he has been a member of the Chesapeake Bay Bears, New England Bears, Rhode Island Grizzlies, and Motor City Bears. He acted as a judge for the International Mr. Bear 2000 contest in San Francisco.

His interview column for *American Bear* magazine has featured discussions with comedian Bruce Vilanch, "Survivor" Rich Hatch, former New Hampshire state senator Rick Trombly, artist Tim Barela, and authors Eric Rofes, David Bergman, and Michael Bronski. He has also written for *Gay & Lesbian Review, White Crane Journal, Art & Understanding, Southern Voice, Lambda Book Report, Gay Community News, Transgender Tapestry,* and *Visionary,* and the anthologies *The Bear Book; The Bear Book II; My First Time, Volume 2; Quickies 2; Bar Stories; Tales from the Bear Cult;* and *Dads and Donors.*

Ron's groundbreaking collection of Bear-themed interviews and discussions, *Bears on Bears,* is published by Alyson Publications.

Ron lives by the verdant Emerald Necklace in Boston.